"An extraordinary literary novel driven by incredible characters, *First Sons and Last Daughters* by Samar Reine intimately explores the intricacies of family relationships and marriage."

—*Readers' Favorite*

"Libraries seeking a novel that exemplifies family dynamics at their best and worst will find *First Sons and Last Daughters* a powerful addition to their collections. It's highly recommended for its astute, poetic descriptions of personal demons that can even arrive in the guise and promise of family connections."

—*Midwest Book Review*, Diane Donovan

"Reine again showcases an ability to touchingly weave sorrow, grief, humor, and love with complex and resonant blended family dynamics and an eye for environments, especially physical landscapes."

—*Publishers' Weekly BookLife*

"Reine charts the characters' lives with remarkable skill, drawing them together through their family ties. Peyton's internal struggles, which are deepened by her difficult relationship with Gideon and her struggling marriage, are skillfully unveiled. The breathtaking landscapes of New Mexico and California are described in lush detail that left me feeling as if I had traveled to these places. The novel brims with romance, conflict, joy, friendship, and love, deftly blending the lives of its characters and creating a cohesive and memorable story. Set against stunning backgrounds and told through a rich set of characters, *First Sons and Last Daughters* by Samar Reine is a splendid novel that will remain in readers' minds and hearts long after reading it."

—*Readers' Favorite*

"Fearlessly untangling the complexities of relationships, loss, and perseverance, this is a novel that is both hopeful and relatable... The magical realism, respectful interest in Navajo and Ute cultures, and deep spirituality contribute in bringing captivating depth to every character."

—Publishers' Weekly BookLife

"Reine's ability to capture the flavors, sights, and psychology of her characters lends a compelling feel to this story of dangerous attractions, relationships, and family dynamics that wind from past to present, leading Peyton into new and dangerous territory in romance and family ties."

—Midwest Book Review, Diane Donovan

"Be prepared to get enthralled by incredible, vivid imagery of scenic beauty, detailed and lively descriptions of characters… relish the writing and not get entangled in the mystery alone."

— Reedsy Discovery

"It was a page-turner, and the suspense kept me on the edge of my seat. The descriptions of New Mexico were so vivid that I could visualize them. The characters were intriguing and dynamic. I could relate to them, and they could be anyone I know. My favorite character was Peyton. I could relate to her struggle with her demons."

—Readers' Favorite

"I enjoyed the developing romance between Peyton and Blake. Relationships, self-discovery, and struggles were woven into the plot. The story was vivid and beautifully written, and it is a lovely story about family and love."

—Readers' Favorite

"Reine's painterly prose evokes her characters' creative endeavors as well as the gorgeous New Mexican landscape."

—Kirkus Reviews

First Sons
and
Last Daughters

THE PIONEER RANCH SAGA

Book Two

SAMAR REINE

Published by

Carmel-by-the-Sea Publishers

Gilbert, Arizona

Cover Design by Tim Barber, dissectdesigns.com

Interior Design by Danielle H. Acee, authorsassistant.com

Library of Congress Cataloguing-in Publication

Reine, S.

First Sons and Last Daughters / Samar Reine

p. cm.

Library of Congress Control Number: 2023917527

Paperback ISBN: 979-8-9884110-6-2

First Edition

First Sons
and
Last Daughters

By The Same Author

She Died Then Showed Me
Book 1 of The Pioneer Ranch Saga
(5-Star Reader's Favorite Badge Winner)

The Three Layers of a Moment
Book 3 of The Pioneer Ranch Saga (Coming Soon)

Dedications

List of Characters

– Alphabetized by First Name

Ashton Grant: Peyton's first, big love interest.

Blake Adler: A cowboy turned Navy SEAL.

Bryce Adler: Peyton's biological daughter.

Father Gabriel: Franciscan monk. Peyton's personal priest.

Geraint: Peyton's Welsh friend and art gallery owner.

Gideon Adler: Peyton's youngest son.

Koda Hoarnhorse: Layli's much younger brother, and Peyton's surrogate brother.

Kelcy Loving: Texan mogul, who treats Peyton like a daughter.

Harlow Peyton Chase: Peyton's mother.

Layli Hoarnhorse: Puebloan estate manager, whom Peyton regards as a sister.

Lexi: Peyton's maternal half-sister.

Margot: Peyton's niece; Lexi's daughter.

Mason Elliott: Rebecca's husband.

Mikey (Honovi): Peyton's oldest adopted son.

Peyton Chase: Protagonist. Daughter of Sorensen and Harlow Chase.

Rebecca Elliott: Scarborough's love interest.

Ricky (Awanata): Peyton's middle adopted son.

Royce Kent: Peyton's godmother and closest friend.

Scarborough: Buckaroo boss cowboy of Pioneer Ranch.

Sorensen Chase: Peyton's father.

Tansy: Help at the Big House.

Vegas Rose: Trainer with orange hair.

William Charles Kelcy Loving: Kelcy's grandson; integral part of the family.

Willie BearClaw: Adler's Native close friend from their military days.

one

Abiquiú, New Mexico

Peyton gazed at the raw beauty of Abiquiú through the wide windows of her studio. The early hour of crushed peaches and raspberries had passed, leaving behind an aqua desert sky. Eagles swooping over herds of oryx and ibex mirrored her life, and she considered what hunted her and what she chased. The people of Pioneer Ranch—those who had consecrated its grounds, and those who had sprung from it—were her solace. Her father's words resonated, reminding her that life tried her, and she wondered why she still deserved to be tested. He'd say, "Hardship foils or is foiled, prevails or is prevailed on." Her memory banks flooded with the booms and busts of her life until an incoming video call whirled her from her trance.

Her oldest son's face appeared on the screen. "Honovi? Dearheart, you almost never call."

"I had to, Mom." He stood barefoot outside a sweat lodge in the red dirt of Monument Valley, wearing only a breechclout, an ancestral loincloth.

Peyton's heart palpitated. Honovi had been embedded in her fiber since she adopted him. When she met him at the age of nine, he'd told her what would forever alter the course of her life. "I know this face and voice. Just dish it as is, honey."

"Death is not far, Mom."

She respected his visions, which had proved accurate. "For me?"

At thirty years old, Honovi was a successful artist and spiritual leader. He focused his eagle eyes on his mother and spoke in a baritone voice. "No, but you'll be pained to the degree of a serious life pivot." His lower lip quivered and his nostrils flared. "When Death comes for you, he'll come riding. Death is near, but this time, he walks."

She knew he could feel the questions skipping in her mind. Honovi was selective in what he shared, and she never probed.

"Mom, my vision was compelling and for you alone. I had to tell you right away."

"Thank you, honey." Peyton bent her head, a sense of foreboding rushing through her veins. "Those who fear death, fear life. I'll prepare, but I know I won't be ready."

"Those who face their truths are already prepared."

She brimmed with love for this man, who had brewed in her psyche. "The day you came to live with us was our luckiest. Our lives would've been poorer without you."

"You took my brother and me not just into your home, but into your very soul. You didn't just show us, you involved us. Because of you, we understand this world better."

"You and Ricky expand my spirit. See you soon, dearheart."

"I'll see you at Bryce's celebration dinner. And I'm sending her blessings for her upcoming showjumping competitions."

Layli barged into the studio. "Mikey is coming also?" She drummed her feet on the floor, and twirled her hips, hooking her hands over a substantial leather belt, studded silver and turquoise. "We haven't had all the children together since Mikey opened his gallery in Sedona." Layli had been the household manager of Pioneer Ranch since she was in her early twenties. She'd been living in a log cabin on the ranch, becoming Peyton's surrogate sister and dear friend.

Peyton turned back to her easel and dipped her brushes in solvent, quitting for the day. "*Honovi,* you mean. He doesn't go by Mikey anymore, but you know that."

"I don't care what he uses. Who does he think he is, Cher? He only goes by one name now. And I blame you for this Honovi stuff."

When their grandmother's passing orphaned them, Mikey and his younger brother, Ricky, came to Pioneer Ranch. Thanks to Layli Hoarnhorse's Puebloan heritage, the state allowed the brothers to remain until Peyton and her husband, Blake Adler, could adopt them. Under their care, Honovi and Ricky earned their advanced degrees and launched substantial careers.

Peyton aimed a fan at her latest painting to speed up the drying process. "He's Honovi to the marrow, and don't forget, his grandmother gave him that name." She snickered, remembering little Mikey before he'd become a muscular man with hair that reached past his shoulder blades. "He was all skin and bones, with the energy of coffee, in love with his blue mohawk. I'm sure he'll remind us why he's Honovi when we see him. He always does."

Layli chuckled, her cacao eyes as spry as ever. She was past her prime, but a retired racehorse can still outrun a colt. "He'll always be Mikey to me."

"And yet thousands follow him for spiritual and artistic inspiration. It works for him. You're just mad you can't boss him around anymore."

Layli played with the belt she always wore. "It works for his ego, more like it, but I'm proud of him. Few Puebloans are respected by the White world, even when they're this successful."

Peyton went to the sink and lathered her hands with lavender soap. "I can't wait to have all the kids at the same table."

"Gideon too?"

She tucked her chin down and bit her cheek, resisting tears. "The shortest distance between two points is always a squiggle for that stupid boy."

"Only he's wicked smart," Layli said.

"Because he's only nineteen and almost done with his nuclear engineering degree? He's lacking in so many other areas."

Layli placed a hand on Peyton's back. "Gideon is nothing like you or Adler, but he has tremendous potential."

"It's a horrible thing to say, but I wish he wasn't coming. Gideon only deducts." Sadness caked her voice, then she chuckled. "I wish Adler had given him the wrong date."

"I'm sorry. I hate that I made you cry."

"Gideon makes me cry, not you. He's coming between Adler and me more and more. It gnaws at me."

Layli craned her neck to force Peyton to look up. "Maybe he'll change in time."

"Change? He's been a pain since he took his first steps." For years, she'd longed to become a mother. Part of what had drawn her to Adler was that he wanted children as well. Never did she think their firstborn would grow up to be Loki. Peyton realized she was spitting every syllable and changed her tone. "Poor Father Gabriel almost wrote to the Vatican to ask for an exorcist."

"We all think Gideon might be possessed." Layli giggled. "How's your latest painting coming along?"

"Not at all. It's just not clicking. I've been stifled lately… don't know…" Peyton opened the fridge she kept in her studio and fished out two bottles of sparkling water. Like her mother before her, she'd become a successful, well-known painter, but she continued to explore and push her medium. "I'm looking forward to everyone coming. I miss William so much, and so does Kelcy, of course." For twenty years, Kelcy had spent half the year in the adobe casita on the ranch, built before the Declaration of Independence was signed.

Layli was on the cusp of her winter years. A streak of white framed her face, yet the rest of her hair remained as raven as ever. "You'd think William was Kelcy's only grandchild. How he adores that boy."

"Kelcy really raised him, took him everywhere he went." Peyton led the way out of the studio into the fresh air. In May, the perfume of jasmine and hummingbird mint mingled with the smells of horses, dogs, and burning wood fires. "William is twenty-five years old, hardly a boy, and we all love him."

"Especially Bryce—even more so this past year."

Peyton stopped in her tracks. "You know?"

"What am I, hard of seeing?"

Peyton's daughter had had a crush on William for as long as she'd had breasts. "Let's watch Bryce practice. This new trainer rubs me the wrong way. I've disliked him since I heard his prickly voice on the phone." She ran her hand through her long, wavy chestnut hair. "Do you think anyone else knows how Bryce feels about William?"

"I hope not. She tries hard to hide it." Layli sighed. "I don't blame her. William has Kelcy's brain and integrity, and his mother's looks to boot. Ooh la la! That boy is on fire."

"I wonder if Ricky would've blossomed the way he has if William had never entered his life."

"William has the heart of a lion. Ricky was never fierce like his fore-fathers or like Mikey."

"*Honovi!*"

"Fine." Layli stuck out her tongue and snickered. "I'll take the ATV and get us some coffee. Meet you at the arena."

Peyton's eyes strayed to the aqua sky and the mounds of clouds with glossy, stiff peaks found only in the desert. Finn, her American Foxhound, attempted to rub against her. "A bath, first. Which swamp did you fall into, anyway?" His fur was encrusted with mud and slime. She pointed to the stables. "Go to John for a bath."

Finn panted a smile and arrowed to the stables.

The Chase family had been rooted on Pioneer Ranch since the con-quistadors introduced horses to New Mexico. Timber and stones alone had not built Pioneer Ranch. History made up its skeletal structure, hard work its musculature, and ritual its skin. The potion the Chases had brewed continued to age into the magic of modern-day Pioneer Ranch.

After her father's death, twenty years earlier, Peyton Chase had inherited the massive estate, and pulled it out of debt. She'd added a lap pool, a manège for her daughter's showjumping ambitions, indigenous gardens, and a studio. She'd become known for her Southwestern and Coastal paintings, depicting active and expressive figures, and she'd grown her talent. But her greatest investment had been in her family and friends, loved ones like Kelcy Loving, better known as loving Kelcy, who was waiting outside the equestrian arena with her godmother, Royce Kent.

Royce never left her house without a wig and a scarf. Today she'd coordinated her emerald-green dress with a red wig and a Chanel scarf that spilled over one shoulder. "Glad you're here," she said. "Kelcy is driving me crazy again."

"She started it," Kelcy said, combing his white chevron mustache.

Royce's nails were as shiny as ever, and her lipstick was just as bright. She'd become a fragment of her stout younger self but was still towering. "Did you bring me a drink?" she asked, flitting her false eyelashes.

Peyton raised her hand, chuckling. "I thought you already had your breakfast."

Kelcy was the image of Teddy Roosevelt: portly with blue eyes behind round spectacles, his remaining hair a single tuft of white on top of his head. "Will you need my cane, Royce?"

"Only if I can trip you with it," she replied, cutting her pruned eyes at him.

Peyton heard the trainer's sharp voice and rushed into the ring.

The man was pointing a long stick in Bryce's direction, shouting instructions. "What part of yank his head higher, don't you understand?"

Bryce was riding Big Red, a pure-bred Hanoverian the color of rust. She lifted high over her saddle, bracing and balancing, a thick braid bobbing on her back. She'd become successful at showjumping by carrying her horse as much as he carried her.

Royce caught up and leaned on the pony wall. "Is that a man or a banshee?"

The trainer had a wild look: orange hair, a wide nose, pencil arms and legs, and a bulbous gut.

Bryce's golden eyes widened into coins. "It's cruel. I can't." She was a striking portrait with upturned eyes, high cheekbones, full lips, and hair the color of raisins.

"You'll have to noose him if you want him to obey!" the trainer yelled. "Why am I here if you know better?"

Kelcy raised his voice enough for the trainer to hear him. "Yeah, why is he here?"

"That troll better tone it down," Royce said, "or I'll hang him on my rearview mirror."

Kelcy chuckled. "Subtle, as always, Royce."

"I shouldn't say such things, but I really mean them!"

Peyton laughed, but another shriek from the trainer made her steam with anger.

Bryce said, "I won't abuse Big Red."

The trainer waved his stick at her as if etching the mark of Zorro. "You wouldn't have to if you'd keep your head down and your fat ass in the air."

Kelcy growled. "Did he just tell that hummingbird she has a fat ass? Her waist is smaller than my wrist."

Peyton bulleted to the center of the arena, gesturing for the trainer to cede. "Don't you dare speak to my child that way, you tedious little man!"

"This is not kindergarten," he said. "This is a serious competition. And she's not good enough."

"*You're* not good enough!" Peyton shouted. "Get your stuff and get out!"

"Mom, no!"

Peyton lanced her with livid eyes. "Don't you ever let anyone speak to you in that manner ever again. Do you understand me?" She threw a straight arm at the trainer. "You trample him before you allow him to denigrate you."

He spread his short, spindly legs. "I'm Vegas Rose! How dare you?"

Kelcy gave a belly laugh. "Vegas Rose? Does he work at the Love Ranch in Nevada?"

"And I am Peyton Chase. Now get the hell off my property, you sorry buffoon. You're fired!"

Bryce thudded to the ground with tears in her eyes. "Mom, but—"

"—but nothing. No win is ever worth someone demeaning you, Bryce!"

"You're so mad."

"As you should be, allowing this arrogant lowlife to talk down to you." Her daughter's anguish calmed her down, and she splayed her arms. "Come here. You deserve much better."

Bryce came into her mother's embrace, apologizing.

"Be strong and always advocate for yourself."

"The next two competitions are the hardest," Bryce said.

Peyton took her daughter by the shoulders. "You know all there is to know about jumping, and I know all about horses. The next two races are about Big Red, not you. You got him this far. Let him take you the rest of the way."

Vegas Rose gawked at them. "I won't leave without cash or a transfer."

"Scram, dufus!" Royce said.

"Or what, you'll kick my ass, you hag?" He crossed his arms over his spilling belly. "I'll stay right here till you give me my money."

Before Peyton could reach for her phone, Kelcy held up his. "No matter. I already sent for the cavalry."

"What's that supposed to mean?" The trainer roamed his enlarged eyes on them as they exchanged knowing looks. "I'm warning you. If you set dogs on me, I'll sue."

"We'd never dream of setting dogs on you," Kelcy said. "But don't leave. Stay where you are."

He shifted from leg to leg and pulled his shirt over his shorts. "What're you up to?"

Layli came in hot, driving the ATV. She didn't cut the engine before dashing with her bow and arrow aimed at the trainer. "You're a very wide target. If I were you, I'd bolt to my car on the double."

He danced in his spot and tried to bully her with his scowl and threats of a lawsuit.

"Okay, then." Layli let fly the first arrow, and it landed between his feet. He jumped as if firecrackers had gone off at his ankles. "The next one will be about three feet higher at what I suspect is a tiny target, but I'm dead accurate." Layli reached into her quiver for a second arrow and pulled her bow. "One, two…"

He careened to his car, shouting, "Crazy bitch!"

Layli laughed. "Should I put one in his butt, or his tires, at least?"

"I'd like to see that," Kelcy said.

Peyton pointed at the trainer, grinning. "He can use a part in his hair."

She released her arrow. It grazed the trainer's bouffant do, snipping a tuft of his hair as he wailed and cursed. She fired off an ululation. "I'm Stands-with-a-Bow for a reason!"

Royce shook her head, watching the shrieking orange-haired man cannonball out. "He's the offspring of a banshee and a troll."

"And a donut," Peyton said. How satisfying it was to expand her wings again. Arguments and setbacks had molted some of her feathers, but she promised herself she'd grow them again. And she knew that without an enormous leap, she wouldn't.

"Layli, that was sick as hell!" Bryce said.

"Now be like Layli next time you're confronted by a bully," her mother told her. "That sure made me happy."

High on adrenaline, Layli locked her eyes on Bryce. "This is your battle. Do a war cry with me like I taught you."

They released a primitive, raw ululation, and Peyton joined, her fists in the air. She found more release in a war cry than a prayer. "Man, did that feel good, or what?"

Kelcy's grin was puckish, his speech a genteel Texan drawl. "Bryce honey, you don't need that clown. You're ready."

She kissed Big Red as she did after every practice, removed her helmet and hugged her horse, who bowed and rested his head on her shoulder, flicking his ears forward, ready for what she always told him. "Hold me up, and I'll never let you down." Her dainty features were borrowed from her mother and her coloring from her father.

Kelcy brought his watch close to his eyes, straining to see. "It's lunchtime. Let's go eat something, okay, doll?"

Royce said, "You need a full-sized clock on that wrist, you're so blind."

"I'm getting you back on that one, but it's good."

"I'm not hungry." Bryce undid her braid, fluffed her waterfall hair, and faced her cheerleaders. "And I have to attend to Big Red first."

Peyton frowned. "Eat a proper meal for once."

"I only have to watch it this much for two more weeks, Mom."

"Are you telling me you're ready to retire after the next two competitions?"

"I guess, yes."

"Hallelujah!" Peyton said. "Thank you, Mother of God!"

"You didn't tell me you wanted me to be done," Bryce said, stretching her hamstrings.

"I wanted you to make that decision yourself."

Kelcy elbowed Peyton. "Bryce is like a ballerina. She takes after her mama in grace."

"Thank you, Kelcy, but she takes after you in spunk. You taught her how to pull herself up by her bootstraps."

"She fell on her behind enough times. Someone had to tell her she had legs." He used his cane to adjust his position. "Where's your Adler?"

"Still up in the Jemez Mountains. Mr. Hunter can't stay away from the wilderness for long these days." She thought of her husband's strength and intensity, lamenting that he used them to push against her lately.

"Adler lives in the mountains nowadays, seems to me." Kelcy unholstered a cigar and plunked it between his teeth.

"Don't you light that cigar, old man," Layli said. "You're eighty, not eighteen."

Through clenched teeth, he replied, "Do I ever listen to you?" He carved a grin worthy of the Cheshire cat. "Doll, what have I always taught you?"

Bryce indulged him. He was the closest she had to a grandfather. "Get up, look up, show up, and never give up."

"That's my girl!" He raised an index finger. "Now, promise you'll remember that when I'm gone."

Honovi's warning knelled in Peyton's chest. Death was a friend in the end—if he didn't arrive early.

"Don't say that!" Bryce replied. "I'll meet up with you at the house."

Peyton drove them to the Big House and parked the ATV by the kitchen garden.

Kelcy used his cane to step out. "William asked me what to buy Bryce for a present now she's going to college. I said to get her something shiny and weighty."

Peyton played with the emerald ring that had been her mother's. "Knowing William, he'll get her something soulful."

"What did *you* get her?" Layli asked.

"Hell, my presence should be enough for all of you. What's for lunch? Roast, I hope."

Layli opened the door at the back of the house and waited for Kelcy and Royce to catch up. "Your doctor said no salt, no sugar, no fat, and no cigars."

"My doctor prescribed no food and no life. I prescribed myself no doctor." Kelcy could always make them happy and grateful. Most of all, he motivated them. He stared at the kitchen garden before entering the mudroom. "I remember when this garden was barren. Twenty years later, it feeds all of us. Never seen fatter organic produce or honeysuckle in my life."

"It's all that composting from everything green you refuse to eat." Peyton had resurrected the garden with her own hands. "I wish I could find that same energy now."

"I wish I can find some lunch," Kelcy said. "And not salad… again."

Layli said, "Okay, not salad. Roasted vegetables."

"Say, what? Why not gruel?"

Layli entered the mudroom, shed her boots, and slipped on her indoor sandals. The heavy door, as old as pieces of eight, swung noiselessly, letting them into the kitchen.

"Ah, the aroma of coffee." Peyton crossed the lustrous Azul Macaubas quartzite floor. She'd been born at the ranch and had raised her own family on it, but its rare properties still delighted her. "Wait, who made coffee? Tansy already left for the day."

"I did," William said, entering the kitchen.

"Christ, am I happy to see you, Tiger!" Kelcy said. "You're a day early."

William walked into his grandfather's embrace. He was a foot taller than Kelcy, with shoulders sculpted by years of tennis and a smile that melted hearts. He smirked, made his straight eyebrows dance, then hunched over, so his grandfather could hold him in a long hug. "I got you steaks, Grandpa."

"William Charles Kelcy Loving the Third, I've never been happier that you carry my name than I am now."

"Over steak?" Layli asked.

"Over freedom. This boy liberates me from your vegetarian oppression."

Peyton hugged William. He'd begun visiting the ranch on holidays and summer vacations when he was in kindergarten and slept at her house so often he had his own room. He'd lost his mother when he was four years old and considered Peyton a surrogate.

"How come you're here early?" Kelcy asked.

William's chocolate eyes smiled. "I have a special gift for Bryce. It couldn't wait."

Peyton examined the aged steaks he'd brought. "Enough for ten people. Thank you, honey. Throw these beauties on the grill while I manage a nice side dish?"

"Not salad!" Kelcy blurted.

Peyton raised her fingers in surrender. "I prepared the most artery-clogging side dish I could think of."

"Something bacon and cheese topped with more bacon?"

Royce rolled her eyes. "I bet dating apps would match you up with bacon."

William chuckled. "Where's Bryce?"

"She'll come up soon," Peyton replied. "Just finished her practice."

William had become all man and was even more handsome when he smiled. Peyton cupped his face and pulled him down to kiss his forehead. "You make me proud." He reminded her of her husband in a way Gideon never did—a constant bittersweetness in every chamber of her heart.

"Well, I am what all of you helped me become. All those hours you read to me and Ricky and the times you sang me to sleep didn't go to waste." He washed his hands at the sink, careful to avoid wetting the platinum and sapphire bracelet Bryce had given him on his twenty-first birthday. She'd bought it with prize money she'd earned with sweat and determination.

"Give me plates and utensils. The steaks are pre-seasoned." He headed to the gas grill on the patio abutting the vegetable garden.

"I know Bryce isn't eighteen yet, but that girl is mature and bright," Kelcy whispered. "I wish William would just ask her out. She's real sweet on him."

Layli expanded her eyes. "You know?"

"Last time he was here, I caught her watching him while he napped on the sofa." He brought a palm to his chest. "She even covered him with a blanket."

"Kelcy!" Layli shrieked. "You spied on Bryce?"

"Hell, I spy on all of you."

Peyton said, "One Christmas when Bryce was twelve years old, she had an acute case of the flu but insisted she'd get better because William was coming, and he needed her. She was feverish, so I thought it was delirium. Five years later, she looks for him and to him as intensely as ever."

"William told me how Bryce is his soothing, peaceful place," Kelcy said. "And that boy is like me. He does best when a strong, loving woman is in the foreground."

Peyton pulled a jug of iced tea with floating lemon slices from the fridge. "Bryce is barely a woman. They're both precocious, focused, and tenacious, but too young still."

"Now that I have a foot in the grave, I think waiting is stupid. Either it is or it isn't."

Layli gathered the plates. "My Arapaho grandmother used to say waiting is half the gift."

"Your grandmother must have gotten only half gifts then," said Royce. "And where's my whiskey?"

Kelcy rose and said, "I got you covered."

About to defend her grandmother, Layli raised a finger, but Bryce's jubilant shout interrupted her.

"What was that thing you said about Bryce hiding it well, Layli?" Peyton asked. "Everyone in New Mexico knows." She retrieved two dishes she'd prepared earlier. "Look, Kelcy, a Hawaiian salad, which is really a dessert, and spicy macaroni with bacon. Some vegetarian oppression, huh?"

William and Bryce returned to the kitchen with the steaks. "Still talking tough, Grandpa?"

"Put the platter on the terrace, honey," Peyton said. "We'll eat gazing over Cerro Pedernal, where my husband is prowling. William, message Ricky. We're about to eat, and he should've been here already. He's driving from Boulder, not Helena."

As if magically summoned, Ricky entered the kitchen, his dark hair spiked and stylized, still wearing the same polymer turtle necklace Peyton bought for him when he was seven years old. He hugged William first, who had been his shadow for as long as he'd worn the polymer turtle. He was sweet then, sweeter now. At twenty-seven, he was as plump as he'd been as a boy, with glistening short hair and a unfailing, tender smile. "I didn't know you were already here, buddy."

"It's a surprise," William replied.

Peyton cuddled her son, cupped his cheeks, and pecked kisses on his face. "You brighten up every space you enter, honey."

One-by-one, Ricky hugged the others, leaving Bryce for last. "You look amazing, little sis, like you've exploded this past year." He adjusted his silver belt buckle and straightened his collar. Precise with his appearance, as if he aimed for the best sequence of musical notes, Ricky's clothes were ironed and perfumed, and his smile, like his heart, was genuine and generous.

"Everyone, grab something and let's go set up and eat," Layli said. "Still enjoying teaching music?"

"Not as much as I like performing it," Ricky replied. "Thank God for Boulder's lively music scene… Mom, got any chocolate chip cookies?"

Peyton snickered at his sweet tooth. "Do I ever? It's not like I prepare a batch to bake fresh every time you come home or anything."

He grabbed his mother from behind and squeezed. "You're the best ever!"

On the terrace, sphinx moths with fast beating wings, mimicking hummingbirds, hovered over red petunias, blue thistles, and lush honeysuckle. The breeze was delicate, and the fog had cleared, leaving shafts of light over mesas and saddlebacks.

William pulled out a chair and sat Bryce at the table, then ran his fingers over the side of her neck. She held her breath and colored.

Peyton's memories whirled back to Adler of long ago. At his merest touch, she'd dissolve yet feel bigger and sturdier. He'd made her feel the way William made their daughter feel. Only one other man had fanned her fires that way—Ashton Grant—whom she'd once not only loved, but lived. She brought herself back to the present, put a cut of meat on her daughter's plate and gave her insisting eyes. "Eat it."

William shifted his chair to within inches of Bryce's. "I won't make your next competition, but I'll be there for your last."

Peyton realized that he already knew Bryce had decided to retire from showjumping. Their intimacy must be deeper than she understood.

Bryce cut her steak in half, split it between William and Ricky, and played with the platinum and sapphire bracelet she wore, which matched the one she'd given William. "Thank you, Mom. I love it when it's just us. And thank you for the lunch you're giving me tomorrow."

"I wish you'd wanted a big graduation party like your brother had."

"Why, so he could embarrass me in front of my friends again?"

Peyton steeled her nerves. "Honey, Gideon is arriving today."

"Why so early?" Bryce struck a fist on her thigh. "It's bad enough I have to see *Damien* all next month!"

She used her firm mama voice. "Don't call him that!"

"I don't want Gideon here before my big competition. He'll ruin it like he ruins everything." Bryce had every right to dread her brother. "Dad invited him, didn't he? It's so unfair!" She tore into the house, her hair spraying behind her.

"I'll talk to her, Mom," Ricky said. "Don't worry."

"Sorry," William said, then he and Ricky went after her.

Peyton was still bouncing a knee when she heard skidding wheels, crunching metal, and shattering porcelain.

The dreaded Gideon had arrived.

She ran to the loggia and stared down at her youngest son, who sat in his car, blaring rap music, distracted on his phone, unfazed, though he'd crashed into his mother's large ceramic flowerpot.

two

Gideon spilled out of his Camaro, laughing. "Why is there a pot here?" He was the height of a quarterback, but spindly, with narrow feet and probing pale blue eyes.

"That pot is older than you. It's an Anduze!" Peyton's neck tensed, and she clenched her jaw. "Why did you park here instead of in the garage like I always ask?"

He gawked, his eyes devoid of affection. "It's just a pot, Mom. What if it's French?"

"Look at the front of your car!"

"Oops, but it's just the light and bumper. Broken glass, mangled metal, no big deal." He started up the wide granite steps. "You're loaded enough. Buy me another one."

Her son embittered her days. "You forgot to get your bag out of the car."

He shrugged and tried to hand his mother his keys. "Tell Tansy to bring it up."

Peyton gave him the stern look he never minded. "Park your car in the garage, clean up the mess you made, and never ask Tansy to fetch anything for you."

"She's the servant here, isn't she? I'm the owner, right?"

"*I am* the owner, actually." Peyton resisted the urge to scream. "How many times must I tell you? Don't call those who help us here servants. It's demeaning and disrespectful. It's what you called Scarborough last time you were here. The man who has seen *me*, not just you, grow up on this ranch. When will you learn?"

"It's the truth. Maids are servants. Horse handlers, wranglers, gardeners, and all the other rubes you hire are also servants. Only you think of them as family. None of my friends have servants for family, just me. You should see how this guy I met lives—a butler, a garage with nine cars, a private plane and helicopter, and a table at any restaurant he wants, any time he wants it."

Peyton choked back tears. "Where are the values I taught you? Kindness, hard work, generosity of soul, humility. And love binds people, Gideon. Love!"

"Love?" he scoffed. "Respect and power matter, not love. And where's your kindness to me?"

"And respect means what? Money and that's it?" To her relief, Adler's Jeep peeked around the bend. It was easier dealing with their son as a team, though lately events crashed into each other like a multi-vehicle wreck. Blake, whom everyone else called by his last name, Adler, calmly parked parallel to the stairs and jutted out of his Jeep. He was past his prime, but still teemed with vitality and strength, never having shed the aura of a cowboy and Navy SEAL captain.

Peyton scuttled down the stairs to greet him.

Adler stared at his son, assessing him with a patient smile. "Why don't you follow me in your car? We'll park in the garage, all right?"

Gideon stiffened his spine. He was as tall as his father, with the same straight nose. "The driveway is the size of a piazza, can fit a dozen cars. Why can't I park here?"

"Because your mother likes order and neatness. I think you know that."

"If it were Bryce's car, she wouldn't have said anything." Gideon ran down the stairs, got in his car, and pulled out too fast, screeching his tires.

"I can't stand the way he envies his sister every little thing," Peyton said.

"Let it slide." Adler wrapped his long limbs around her and kissed her mouth with the fondness of absence.

"The house is empty without you, Blake. Ten days away is too long." She touched his beard, which she associated with his absences. "Shave this."

"I've been thinking the same. Two, three nights should suffice. I missed you something deep, sweet Pey."

"You smell of pine."

"My wife requires cleanliness, and you smell of home. Give me ten, and I'll meet you inside."

"Please, speak to Gideon. He can't ruin things for Bryce."

"I spoke to him when I invited him to come."

She bit her lower lip, wishing he didn't insist on forcing the kids together when neither of them liked it. "Why did you do that, though? You only messaged me this morning with little warning. Why did you decide to include him without talking to me first? He's unpredictable."

"Because they're both my children. Gideon needs to be part of this family as much as Bryce does. And I don't need permission to include you or any of my four kids in anything."

"What if he acts up?" She took a step back on the paved driveway.

"He won't." Adler ran a hand through his silver hair. "He takes after my father, who never listened either. Maybe I cursed him by giving him my father's name."

"We named him Sorensen Gideon after both of our fathers. Yet he's nothing like my dad. We didn't make Gideon into anything. He is what he is."

Adler reached for her hand and pressed it. "We enabled him, Peyton. You know we did. And you not wanting him here on special days makes it worse."

She yanked her hand away, scowling. "I want him here on Thanksgiving, Christmas, or any general holiday. I only dread his presence on occasions earmarked for Bryce, which end up being about Gideon instead. On her last birthday, he fed her cake to the dogs. I don't want him ruining this sendoff for her too. And she's depriving herself of a graduation party just to avoid him spoiling it."

Adler ran his tongue over his teeth. "He didn't spoil her sixteenth birthday. Gideon *can* have good stretches."

"Yes, but the current stretch isn't so good." She wanted Adler's first evening back to be pleasant and resented that their son came between them. "See you upstairs." Peyton climbed the steps that led to the foyer, fighting tears. Bryce was her fortune, Gideon, her scourge. Then again, sometimes, life took more than it gave.

In the past, Peyton would've joined Adler in the shower for bonding time. She loved scrubbing his back and rubbing her soapy body against his. But not for a while now. She gathered his laundry, left him to bathe, and bumped into Bryce in the wide hallway decorated with antique furniture and rich textiles.

"Gideon is in your studio," Bryce said. "If I were you, I'd check on my paintings."

Peyton's anxiety soared, but she hid it behind a calm smile. "He won't hurt what would cut into his riches."

William came out of his bedroom, cradling Bryce's surprise gift. "I've been planning it for months. Congratulations, Bryce, for graduating with honors and for having been accepted into a tough pre-veterinary program at Berkeley."

"A fennec fox?" Bryce cradled the long-eared, furry white pup, identical to the fox they'd grown up with. "My God! I can't believe it."

"Remember how much we loved Solace?" William asked. "Of course you do. I thought maybe you'd like your own fox."

She kissed the furry bundle. "How do you always know what's perfect for me? What's her name?"

"You get to name her, sweetheart."

Peyton had never heard William call her daughter that. "Honey, this is such a thoughtful gift for Bryce." Her memory flung back to the first time she saw him, a five-year-old with ketchup on his nose. She loved his intelligent eyes and the way he often swept his fine, brown hair away from them, only to have it fall in his eyes again. But she hadn't expected Bryce to reach up and brush his hair away for him.

William swallowed and took a step back. "Solace was with us for twelve years. I hope this little one can be with us even longer."

Bryce said, "Remember how Ricky used to say Solace was half dog and half cat? He called her the 'Dat'."

William played with the platinum and sapphire bracelet she'd gotten him. "Do you really like her?"

"Are you kidding? She's precious."

Peyton led them to the terrace so they could show the pup to the rest of the family. "I remember when your dad got me Solace. I loved her so much, I couldn't bear to get another after she passed, but now I think perhaps I should've. How I missed having a fennec around."

"I told you." Kelcy puffed on his cigar. "Waiting is a waste of time. Either it is or it isn't."

"What should I name her?" Bryce asked.

"Name her exactly what she represents to you." Peyton had named her fennec Solace because that was how Adler felt to her back then. It pained her that he was less so today. Was she also less to him in some ways?

"Myriad," Bryce said. "I'll call her Myriad."

William leaned against the sliding doors in the sunlight, staring at Bryce. "Myriad is something so great it's beyond counting, isn't it?"

Bryce colored and buried her face in Myriad's softness. "That's about right."

William stared at her and swallowed.

Adler stepped onto the terrace. He was clean-shaven, wearing a green T-shirt and shorts that exposed his muscled thighs and legs. "Another fennec?" He hugged his daughter and kissed her forehead. "Seems impossible I got your mother Solace over two decades ago."

William said, "Ricky and I are skedaddling with Bryce to Santa Fe. Sorry to stick you with Myriad so soon, but is that okay?"

"More than okay, honey. Have fun." Peyton watched them leave and nestled the fox on her lap, reels of sweet memories playing in her head.

Adler said, "Must be from William with a name like Myriad. Do you think he understands what this gesture means to Bryce?"

"Sometimes I think he understands everything," Peyton said. "At other times, he seems like he's just his generous, thoughtful self."

Layli said, "If youth isn't stupid, it's confused."

Nostalgia tugged at Peyton's chest as she thought of her favorite golden Labrador, long gone. "How I miss Cooper, the human dog."

The cloudless dawn was spotlit by a full moon. Peyton and Adler lay side-by-side in bed, listening to the great horned owls screech and the coyotes howl as they watched the liberal skies through the enormous windows.

"They say the full moon brings on resolutions," Peyton said.

He spoke with the morning voice she loved. "I believe life does that regardless of the moon cycle."

"I'm happy Bryce is retiring from showjumping. She barely eats. It's affecting her circadian rhythm."

"She's like you that way," he said. "If she thinks she can see something through, by God, she'll try, even if no one else sees it."

"There's something else I want to run by you. How do you feel about allowing the public onto a portion of our property? Would that bother you?"

"Hmm, sounds radical."

"You know me, after suffering the scare of losing the estate, I'm always thinking of the next thing to preserve its future. With the additional funds, we could create a museum for my mother and Mikey."

"You mean Honovi?"

"Yes, Honovi." She giggled, remembering the first time her son let her hold him in Monument Valley, after his first sweat lodge. From their earliest moments, they'd helped each other grieve, heal, and grow.

Adler raised himself on one elbow and played with her hair. "It would be a lot of construction followed by crowds. I don't want people here."

"We'd restrict them to the lower end of the property." Peyton lay on her side, facing him, and kissed his heart. "It'll pay off in the long run."

"But the estate is doing great, and your paintings are well into the six figures. What's there to be scared about that requires ruckus and crowds? I want peace."

"We're young still, Adler. We can handle excitement and change, can't we?" When he didn't speak, she plopped a kiss on his lips. "It's good for me too. I already keep some of my works to sell as giclées like Honovi does. It would be good to display the originals at a museum on our property… If not bound by blood, this family is bound by paint. The museum would be a confirmation of that."

"You want to buy back some of your mother's paintings? You don't even know who owns most of them."

"I'll have to figure it out. I love that Harlow and Honovi have the ranch in common. Both paint with a focus on Native culture. Harlow was the past of Pioneer Ranch. Honovi is its future, and their styles are contrasts, which makes for a beautiful comparison." She grinned. "It has the potential to generate passive income and promote us anew. Why not sell giclées of Mom's work as well?"

In the moonlight, Adler's eyes glimmered like copper. "How much money is enough?" he asked, sitting up.

"It's not about money. It's about preserving a legacy and ensuring the future for the kids. Passive income and diversification are wise." Peyton needed more ammunition to convince him. "Harlow and Honovi under one roof. One a Mormon, the descendant of early settlers, and the other a Native Puebloan. They even share the same initial."

"Does this mean you'll spend more time on the ranch in the future? Seems to me you prefer to be in California these days."

Peyton straightened up and pressed her back against the headboard. "Must everything be conditional?"

He looked at her with fading patience. "It's a simple yes or no, Peyton."

"I'm here more often than not. Do you even miss me anymore?"

"Always."

She leaned closer and traced the wrinkles around his eyes and the laugh lines near his mouth as if reading the map of his life. "You don't ask me about my work, or my schedule. You haven't popped into my studio in months. And you almost never want to be with me at Carmel-by-the-sea."

"I've had to center myself more lately, but I always rush back to you." He nuzzled her neck. "I miss you enough to want to glue you to me."

That surprised her; their sex life had become sporadic. "And you're up for it?"

He laughed and ran his hands under the straps of her tank top. "I have some mileage on me now, sweet Pey. I'm not as good as I once was, but *once* I can be as good as ever." He had a way of cuffing her neck and pressing his weight on top of her that made her feel consumed yet preserved.

Peyton was setting up in the dining room for Bryce's celebratory lunch. The oval room was decorated with Navajo textiles, scalloped edges and zigzag designs. She lit tall beeswax candles Bryce loved. As she lit the last one, she caught the smell of snuffed wicks and turned to see Gideon blowing them out. "Don't do that. The idea is to perfume the air, not stink it up."

"I hate this smell. It reminds me of Mass."

His skinny arms and round, dark eyes reminded her of a spider. "Then leave. Don't extinguish my candles."

"I live here too, okay?"

Peyton started relighting the candles, wishing she'd agreed to send him to boot camp after he set a squirrel's tail on fire.

He stood between her and the next candelabra. "I saw the placement cards. I don't want to sit next to that Franciscan monk. Last time he was here, he flicked me with holy water, ruining my suede jacket."

"You're not wearing suede now, are you?"

"He looks at me as if I were a tarantula from hell. I hate him!"

Peyton took a step back, wishing she had holy water to flick on him herself. "Father Gabriel is a blessing to this family. He's wise, kind, and has always been patient and generous with his time. He officiated at my wedding, baptized you and your sister, and blesses this estate."

"I don't care, and I don't want to be seated next to him, Mother!"

Peyton raised her long lighter. "Only those who hate their moms call them 'mother.'"

"Is that right, *Mother*?"

She knew he sought to see pain in her eyes, fed off it. All his life, she'd been the giver. Why stop now? "Fine. You won't have to sit next to Father Gabriel."

Tansy rushed in, flashing a toothy smile, and announced that Honovi had arrived. "He has guests with him, Ms. Chase, and his hair is different. He has blue in his hair again." She made exuberant gestures with her thick arms. "Gorgeous though, stunning."

Gideon rolled his eyes, hemmed and hawed. "You don't have to gush over him as if he's some celebrity. He's just an orphan who paints fantasy crap stupid tourists pay too much for."

"Honovi can't be an orphan if he shares your parents." Peyton turned on her heels. She hadn't seen her oldest son since she'd last dropped in on him in Sedona. She scuttled to the foyer, her red chiffon dress swishing, heels clicking on the rare rose Numidian marble floor. Honovi was in reverie, standing before a Remington sculpture with a couple she'd never seen.

The strangers, tall and slender, resonant of art déco statues, surveyed the foyer, which was ribbed with pale granite and crowned by exposed beams and a substantial chandelier.

A thick blue streak framed Honovi's aquiline nose, high cheekbones, and dark eyes. As a child, he emoted a little. At thirty, he emoted less, yet he exuded radiance. He extended his hands to her and leaned down, wafting the scent of eucalyptus. "Mason and Rebecca Elliott," he whispered. "I brought them just for you, but they don't know that."

Peyton touched the bracelet he wore, silver with turquoise and mother-of-pearl mosaic inlay in a feather motif. "I remember when that bracelet was so awkward and loose, you'd push it all the way past your elbow. Now, it barely fits around your wrist." It was a bracelet that once belonged to a Navajo Medicine Man whose daughter gave it to Honovi on his tenth birthday.

"Time to cast your spell." He turned to the Elliotts and raised his voice. "Mason and Rebecca bought my painting of Koda taming horses. When I told them he was real, they wanted to meet him."

"But learning that you're Honovi's mother brought us here," Rebecca said. "What an honor. We had no idea you were connected." She shook hands with Peyton, and craned her neck, riveted by the historic character of the Big House. "They don't make them like this anymore."

Peyton welcomed the guests with New Mexico flavor, assuring them she was pleased to have them. Honovi did nothing without purpose. She trusted his reasons for bringing the Elliotts all the way to Abiquiú.

"Mason and Rebecca are art and history lovers," Honovi said. "They have many questions about Pioneer Ranch."

Peyton assessed the flamboyant couple, dressed in white and gold. "Champagne? We have a full bar today, but maybe you prefer something else."

"We'll take what you're having," Rebecca said.

"Cosmopolitans?"

"That would be ideal."

Honovi, who never drank alcohol, had to only look at Tansy, who was lurking around the corner. "One yerba maté tea coming up," she said. "Extra sweet."

He balled a fist to his heart and pitched his chin. "Thank you, Tansy."

"Can I make one for myself?" She wrinkled her forehead. "Maybe if you look hard, you can find me a husband in those leaves."

"I don't need tea dregs to tell you to stay close to your porch. The winter will not pass without a pleasant surprise for you."

"Oh my God, for real?"

"It's your time," he said, then looked at Peyton. "I'll be in the billiard room, Mom. I need some quiet and solitude."

Peyton stood at the Kiva fireplace of her great room under a thirty-foot tall ceiling, explaining the history of the *Peyton at Nine* painting hanging above the mantle. The portrait Harlow had done of her had never been photographed. *Peyton at Nine* was crocheted in her psyche and development as an artist—a painting she considered a lifesaver. "I'm happy Honovi brought you here to see Harlow's home."

"And yours," Mason said. "Is this really the only one of your mother's paintings you own? We have two of yours and three of hers."

So, that's why Honovi had brought them.

"We have the one of the three girls husking corn; *Three Girls*, it's called," said Mason. "*The Medicine Man Treating the Sick*, and *The Crown Dancers V* with elongated shadows. We know there's a similar one with shorter shadows."

"Yes, different hour, different light." Peyton thought of her father's affinity for time and how its symbolism had permeated her mother's artistic interpretations. "How I love that last one. I've only seen it in pictures."

Rebecca said, "Come see it whenever you're in Lake Tahoe. We're there full time in summer. We'd love to show you our house and all our paintings. Funny thing, we bought a tiny Mary Cassatt with some damage. Maybe you'll take a look? We realize you're quite a reputable art restorer, but selective."

Mason said, "We read the interview you gave in *Art in America.*"

"In their Christmas edition?"

Rebecca smoothed her straight blonde hair. "You gave an interview that recently? We didn't realize."

"Might you look at our Mary Cassatt?" Mason asked.

Peyton pressed her lips together, excited at the thought of seeing her mother's paintings, which she hoped to buy back. "It'll be my pleasure. I'm serious when I say I can come soon."

"We're serious when we say please do," Rebecca replied.

Bronze bells pealed, reminiscent of historic cathedrals. Peyton said, "That means Scarborough is here. Perhaps you noticed the pierced belfries on your way in? We ring those bells on special occasions. Today we're celebrating our daughter's upcoming equestrian competitions and her graduation."

"Who's Scarborough?" Rebecca said.

"He taught me all I know about horses and dogs and that we're all borrowers in the end, owners only of what we cultivate within ourselves."

"I like him already."

"He's not the Scarborough of his thirties, but as soon as you lay eyes on him, you'll understand why we think he should've been a movie star."

Scarborough came into the great room, holding his ten-gallon hat against his chest. He still had the body of a cowboy in the saddle, but his hair and beard were the color of winter, accentuating his bright blue eyes. "Ma'am, a cowboy is never early, and he's never late. He shows up precisely when it's time for ringing the bells."

"I always know when it's you. No one else gets the bells to ring like that. Will you ever call me Peyton?"

"I will, ma'am."

"Scarborough is retired now, but he managed Pioneer Ranch for as long as I can remember. He taught me that good decisions come from experience and experience comes from a lot of bad decisions."

Rebecca licked her lips and introduced herself. "I see what you mean about a movie star." She shook his hand, grinning at his vice-like grip. "Tall and strong as well. Are you in any of Honovi's paintings?"

Scarborough chuckled. "Every one of us is, Mrs. Elliott."

"Please, call me Rebecca."

"Mighty fine idea, Rebecca." He stretched his spine and spread his long legs, then studied her husband who had been quiet.

"Scarborough," Rebecca said, "will you show me around the ranch?"

"I'd be honored. Walking this ranch prevents a man from forgetting his daydreams."

Peyton grinned and pressed her palms together. "I'll leave you to get better acquainted." She made a circular gesture. "Scarborough, meet us in the dining room in an hour. I'll go see where Gideon is. He's too quiet."

He flicked his gloves on his wrist. "Saw Mrs. Kent and her granddaughter on my way in. The kids hijacked them, but Mrs. Kent said to join them if you can."

"But you didn't see Gideon?"

"No, ma'am."

three

Music ensnared Peyton, and she followed it. In a solarium she considered her music room, Ricky was playing the violin accompanied by Royce, who was an accomplished pianist and his musical mentor.

Claire waved. She was a brunette, much shorter than her grandmother. "I saw Bryce heading to the stables. She's stunning. Why isn't she modeling?"

"It's nothing she aspires to. Did Royce show you the three magazine covers she's been on? *Horse & Style* asked her to pose for their fall cover again this year."

"Will she do it?"

"She doesn't crave the limelight, but she sure enjoys it." Peyton winked and struck a vogue pose. "A Chase always does."

"You see her as a Chase, not an Adler?"

"I see her as Bryce, with many of her father's exquisite qualities, but she's more my side of the family."

"I saw the cover they shot when she was fifteen. Grandma says she's famous in showjumping circles today."

"Which is partly why she feels so much pressure to be perfect." Peyton played with her gold earring. "I don't like it for her."

Royce and Ricky finished the sonata. "Are you laughing because I'm old or because Ricky is an unknown conductor?" Royce loved teasing him. "You know, a guy with a starched collar and a flailing stick."

Ricky said, "A composer, not a conductor, and it's called a baton!"

Royce raised her microbladed eyebrows and spoke with a high-pitched voice. "And the difference is?"

"A composer prays to God he gets it right. A conductor thinks he's God." He laughed and kissed Royce on the cheek. "Composing is stressful. That's why I get headaches. Don't you?"

"Darling, I am like Moses. When I get headaches, God sends me tablets."

"Have any of you seen Gideon?" Peyton asked.

Claire replied, "I saw him heading to the stables."

Heat flared through Peyton's body as a scene from the past played on the screen of her mind. Scarborough banned Gideon from the stables after he set snakes loose at the feet of penned horses, who panicked and were injured. "Uh-oh, where you also saw Bryce?"

They heard shouts in the distance. Someone was wrangling with someone else.

"Goodness me." Peyton sprinted toward the noise, Claire and Ricky at her back.

She dashed down the path, her delicate dress raised mid-thigh. What she feared was already transpiring.

Gideon was holding a riding crop above his head. Peyton shouted for him to stop, but he swung it at his sister. William stepped between them, pushing Bryce out of the way, but the crop clipped his face. The sting forced him back a step. Fueled by rage, he lunged and punched Gideon, knocking him to the ground. He kicked the riding crop out of Gideon's hand and was about to kneel and punch him again, but Peyton's shouting halted him. "I swear to God," he yelled, "if you ever lay a hand on Bryce again, I'll kill you!"

Down in the dirt, Gideon wiped his bloody nose while Bryce examined William's face, horrified at the welt on his left cheek and ear.

"It's going to mark and get worse." Bryce looked at her mother through a cataract of tears. "Gideon meant to strike me, Mom! Ask that cruel, violent, conniving monster to leave!"

"Are you all right, William?" Peyton examined his face. "It might swell up your eye."

"I'll put an ice pack on it. Don't worry."

Gideon was still down. He tested his nose and kicked dirt with his heels. "I'm the one who's bleeding, and your heart is breaking for fucking William!"

"How're you this out of hand? You're violent with your sister again?"

Gideon spit and rose to his feet like a seaworm rising out of the sand. "Your precious William broke my nose! He's the violent one. You should ask *him* to leave!"

"Your nose doesn't appear broken, but you need an ice pack," Peyton said. "Come, let's get you cleaned up."

"I'm your son, not William, but you always loved him more!"

"Will you stop comparing? It's possible to love others without loving you any less, isn't it?"

"No!" He pinched his nose and stormed off, cursing and spitting.

"I'm sorry, William," Peyton said, her hand on his cheek. "Thank you for protecting my daughter."

Ricky hugged Bryce. "You're going away for college soon, sis. You'll see less of Gideon in the future."

"Gideon is dangerous. He shouldn't be here."

"He's my son, Bryce, and though I don't like him, I love him very much, as I love all of you."

"He soiled my dress on purpose. He didn't just try to hit me, he threw manure at me first." Bryce's new blue dress was now filthy, her hair was mangled, and her mascara smudged. "Worst of all, I feel unsafe in my own home. Unlike you, I can't stand him. None of us can."

Peyton didn't encourage lies or obfuscations under her roof and wouldn't deny what had become the reality of their family. "It's a delicate situation, honey."

"He can go back to his condo in L.A. No one wants him here, and it's where he prefers to be." Bryce's face grew a deeper shade of scarlet. "Send him away until I leave for my last competitions."

"I'll speak to your father. Maybe we can seduce him with a trip, though that would be rewarding him for his destructive behavior, which makes me very conflicted."

Ricky said, "We'll take Bryce up to the house. Sorry, Mom, this is excruciating for you, and we can't help."

"I'm sorry too," Bryce said. "I'm being difficult."

"No, honey, you're just speaking your mind and I want you to. Eat a little something to raise your blood sugar and shake it off. It's your day, after all."

"So sorry," Claire said in a small voice.

"I don't know what to do with that boy, hell-bent on causing mayhem." Peyton couldn't stop her tears as she slogged up the path toward Royce.

"Is Gideon unwell? He even made Grandma cry once."

"We took him to every kind of doctor we could think of, sent him to elite private schools, and hired top professionals. No one found anything seriously wrong with him, but they all quit when nothing worked. Maybe he's just wired funny. He was never diagnosed with dangerous neurological or psychological disorders, if that's what you mean. Some told us he's a genius and a narcissist. But how do we correct that?" One psychiatrist labeled Gideon a dark personality—the evil trifecta of narcissism, psychopathy, and Machiavellianism. But Adler refused to accept it.

"Sorry, I didn't mean to upset you with my nosiness."

"You're not the one upsetting me." Gideon seized every opportunity to hurt them with premeditated malice. She could repair it for one child, but only at the expense of the other. For Bryce to feel protected, Gideon had to be ostracized. And for Gideon to feel loved, Bryce had to be rejected. She wasn't sure even her intellectual, logical father, had he been alive, would've known what was best to do.

Royce was waiting for them at the top of the path. She tottered, as if she were on stilts. "What happened? When I asked the kids, Bryce pointed to William's bruised up face and Ricky said, 'Gideon did it.'"

"Gideon always does it! That's the problem." Peyton bent over and welded her palms to her knees. "He'll be the death of me."

Royce said, "It's time now, Peyton. Gideon can't be allowed to devastate the family. If you want to pay for the last bit of his education, fine. But I don't see why you continue to allow him under your roof. If Sorensen had been alive, he would've crucified him by now."

Peyton thought how resolute her father had been under pressure. Sorensen believed in Occam's razor: the most obvious explanation was the most likely one.

Claire gave Royce big eyes. "Don't hold back, Grandma."

"This *is* me holding back. Want the full version? He's an aberration, a cancer. I really don't know what you're waiting for, Peyton, for him to kill one of you?"

"Grandma, that's harsh!"

"That's the truth!"

"He's my son." Peyton burst into tears. "I've thought of forbidding him to come back to the ranch, but I'm afraid he'll harm himself."

"Pish-posh, he's too selfish and arrogant for that. Enough worrying about Gideon. Worry about the people he hurts." Royce was wobbling and gave each of them one of her hands. "I should hire four buff men to carry me around on a palanquin, and make them wear nothing but loincloths, even in winter."

Peyton tittered. "I needed that image. Thank you, Royce."

"Darling, it was no image. Where's my phone? Who would I call to order them?"

Claire laughed. "If anyone would, it would be you, Grandma."

"Why don't you freshen up before lunch, Peyton?" Royce asked. "Take a shot of something… or three."

"I need to check on William and my idiot son."

"*Evil* is the word," Royce said. "He's brilliant, able to push everyone's buttons just right. Name his behavior for what it is, and I'm sorry, Peyton. I'm beyond saying Gideon behaves in evil ways. His core is malevolent."

Peyton wrapped an arm around her, supporting her.

"The only person remotely like him was your grandmother, Chase. Supposedly, she was ruthless, but even she didn't hurt animals. I still think Gideon was the one who poisoned Colossal."

"That pig was old, Grandma."

"And that's an excuse? She was a pet."

Peyton's mother suffered from bipolar disorder, which led to her suicide. Peyton worried that the disease had worsened in her son. "Sit in the dining room. I'll send drinks and appetizers."

"Send two old-fashioned cocktails," Royce said, leaning on Claire.

"Thank you for sharing, Grandma."

"What? Darling, send a pitcher."

As Peyton sat at her toilette, swabbing her face and reapplying her makeup, Adler came in and put a hand on her shoulder.

"I tried speaking to Bryce, but she wasn't up to it," he said. "All I ever wanted was to resolve everything for you." He pulled her to her feet and fenced her to his chest. "My pride in myself is complete only when I take burdens from you."

She thought of what had brought them together. He'd helped her surmount her inferiority complex and emerge from the shadow of her mother's giant success. "This is not your burden alone." She kissed him with open lips. "Gideon is an adult. He has to help himself now."

"How are we doing this wrong?"

"You can't lay Gideon's maliciousness on either of us."

He held his wife away from his body. "Gideon is not malicious. He's pressured and feels misunderstood."

Peyton stared at him. "Bryce genuinely fears him. He would've injured her again if William hadn't been there."

"What do you mean?"

"Something should be done, Adler."

He ran a tongue over his teeth. "Whatever it is, it can't hurt Gideon."

"No one wants to hurt Gideon. What a ridiculous thing to say." She studied him. He wasn't open to further discussion, but she needed to protect her daughter. "I have a sense of foreboding."

Stock-still, he said, "I need to pray deeply on this one."

"Bryce is not the only one who fears him. He worries me more than ever. I wish he wasn't here."

He shook her and squeezed her arms. "No, you don't, and I can't hear such things from you! You just want him to stop!"

"Remember the psychiatrist who diagnosed Gideon with a dark personality disorder? If she was right, he's capable of anything."

Adler took a big step back. "No, he just lacks discipline and control, but that's correctable. I can teach him that."

Peyton knew when her husband was pliable and when he turned into iron. "Did you show Father Gabriel to the dining room?"

"Yes, Royce was already there to keep everyone going. I told them to start without us." He watched her dab at her smudged eyeliner. "God has never abandoned us, Peyton. He won't now."

"My problem is not with God."

The beeswax candles had melted, and the dining room smelled sweet, but after the fiasco with Bryce and Gideon, the atmosphere was taciturn and edgy. The table was decorated with fresh flowers and candied fruits. Cold mint cantaloupe soup had been ladled into shallow bowls, and peach wine glistened in chilled glasses, yet no one ate.

William's eye had swelled and the welt on his face was turning purple, but he smiled, sitting beside Bryce, his arm stretched over the back of her chair. Bryce's hair was brushed, her makeup shimmery, and she wore a pretty yellow dress, but her sorrow seeped from under the veneer of celebration.

Peyton cradled her glass, her eyes on the daughter she'd raised to hold herself accountable. "To Bryce, who graduates with honors, be it at school or in life. *Da'ohdlą́!*"

The table rumbled, joining in the Navajo cheer. "Da'ohdlą́!"

Adler raised his glass aloft. "To the apple of my eye, who is a gift everywhere she's present."

Scarborough spoke in the parlance of dusty trails and gestured for the others at the table to join in. "May your belly never grumble, may your heart never ache, may your horse never stumble, may your cinch never break!"

The table roared with joy until Gideon's entrance muted the room. He yelled out his own idea of a toast, though the acoustics in the room were excellent: "To Bryce, my anorexic sister sitting at a feast. If irony had a name…" He took his seat beside his father. "What, no one wants to raise a glass?"

"I'm not anorexic, you oaf. I'm a competitive athlete."

"What you've got is an expensive hobby paid for by my future inheritance."

Kelcy said, "You know, son, if you have honor, nothing else matters, and if you *don't* have honor, nothing else matters."

Gideon slurped soup as loudly as he could. His nose was swollen. Bruises underscored his pale blue eyes, but he acted as if he were enjoying himself. "Doesn't honor mean privilege? Bryce is privileged, all right."

Royce plunked her spoon. "Listen, kid, your mother may not be ready to ship you to Timbuktu, but I am."

He chuckled, avoiding her glare. "Aren't you a hundred or something?

You'll probably be shipped to a home before I finish eating this soup."

"Gideon!" Adler shouted. "I don't want to hear another word from you."

"I'll shut up if you buy me a new car. Mine's all bashed in the front, and I prefer a Corvette."

"Your Camaro is still new," his mother said. "We'll get it repaired."

He spoke through a mouthful. "I heard the friar needs a car. He can have mine, and I can have a Corvette."

Father Gabriel, dressed as always in a long gray tunic belted with a hemp rope, pasted a hand over his tonsure. "Egoism is not living as one wishes to live. It's expecting others to live that way. You should've attended Sunday school as your parents wanted you to."

"Sunday school is for morons. And don't lecture me on egoism when you're a Catholic priest. Besides, don't you have a child to go molest or something?"

Peyton pushed her chair back hard enough to make it skid. "Apologize to Father Gabriel and to Royce this instant!"

"Forgive me, Father, for I have sinned. But wait… Is the truth a sin?"

"Stop!" Adler said.

In a controlled voice, Peyton said, "I'll send a tray to your room. Go."

"Or what? You'll send me for another psychiatric evaluation? I'm an adult now, Mother. One day I'll have a say over your life, so watch out!"

Peyton gripped the edge of the table. "I want you to excuse yourself."

Gideon pointed his finger at several people in succession, as if shooting them one by one with a handgun. "Mikey, Ricky, William, and some strangers in matching costumes can stay, but me, the heir, must vacate the table?" He clasped the seat of his chair and twined his ankles around its legs. "Well, I won't!"

Honovi stood up, plucking the Elliotts out of their chairs. He spoke to his mother as if they were alone. "All will be well if you follow your heart." He waved and left, taking his guests with him.

Gideon was all but foaming at the mouth, shouting, his dagger eyes trained on Honovi as he withdrew with grace. "Mikey says the wind and the trees talk to him, but that's okay. You call him gifted. He speaks with the dead, but that means he's psychic. I threw some nasty kittens in the river, and you wanted to have me committed. Dad and Kelcy shoot animals, but they're just hunters. I'm a fucking psycho. Everyone else gets a pass, but I never do!"

William said, "Shame on you for speaking disrespectfully to those who tried so hard all your life to help you."

"Ah, Prince Charming saves the day again. This is not your family. It's mine! Maybe your mom died because you don't deserve one." Gideon tucked his chin into his chest and eyed Bryce with sinister eyes. "You're just a toy to him, but you're too stupid to know that."

William stood up, his neck veins bulging. "Bryce is a million times the person you are. How dare you?"

Adler darted out of his chair and clamped down on Gideon's shoulders with a Navy SEAL's determination. "I've never laid a hand on you before, but so help me God, I'll hog-tie you and carry you out if you don't go to your room right now."

Gideon placed his feet on the floor and raised his hands.

"But first, apologize to everyone."

"Okay, okay… sorry."

His father released him, but hovered over him until he stood up. "Go!"

Tansy brought in the second course. On his way out, Gideon tipped the tray out of her hands, toppling filet mignon with a red wine reduction on his mother's Persian rug.

"So sorry," said Tansy. "I'll clean it right up."

"It's not your fault," Peyton replied, her hand on her throat. "We owe *you* an apology."

"We owe apologies to all of you," Adler said, still standing with his hands on his hips. "We've made you uncomfortable. Please find your appetites and eat something. It's over now."

Royce tapped her glass for a refill. "There's nothing to apologize for."

"It's over?" Bryce teared up and stiffened her back. "Can't you see, Dad? It'll never be over!"

Layli went to Bryce and placed a palm on her shoulder. "You're moving to Berkeley for college. Lots will change on its own."

Scarborough drained his glass of beer and smoothed his beard. "Listen, jumping bean, you've got more guts than you can hang on a fence. In this life, that's all you need, apart from a beer or two."

"You're all trying to cheer me up, and I'm grateful, but Gideon is venomous, and it's getting worse."

"Bryce, that's enough!" Adler said. "Your brother isn't a demon."

Father Gabriel led the group in prayer, giving everyone a chance to breathe. "Dear girl, God is watching."

Peyton's rage threatened to strangle her. "Sometimes, Father, I fear the devil is watching too."

Adler cut disapproving eyes at his wife. "Gideon is often nothing like this. I'm not excusing him, but let's not make him out to be Lucifer."

Bryce angled for her mother and hunched over her, generous with hugs and kisses. She looked at her father with swollen eyelids. "Sorry, I don't mean to be unforgiving."

"Folks, may I give you a piece of advice?" Kelcy said. "You get to decide how much Gideon gets to change you." He unsheathed a half-smoked cigar. "A recipe is improved by what's *not* in it. As an excellent cook yourself, little lady, you know this already."

Adler, who hadn't eaten a single morsel, turned toward the door. "I'm taking Gideon up to our house in Chama for some fishing, just the two of us."

Peyton tossed her serviette on the table. "Another interesting unilateral decision."

"Gideon may be too much for us. But we're also too much for him."

"A man's soul never tires of fishing," Scarborough said. "The Chama River and a couple of rods sound mighty fine to me."

"That's right, Scarborough," Layli replied, flashing a wicked grin. "I saw you hooking Rebecca Elliott this afternoon, just as fine an angler as you describe."

Peyton was grateful for the change of topic and gave Layli a nod.

"Don't interfere with a man's prospects."

Kelcy chewed on his cigar. "That's right. It's bad luck."

Scarborough straightened his spine. "Mason and Rebecca are what you call an open couple."

Peyton snickered. "Do you mean they have an open marriage?"

"Well, ma'am, something is clearly open for me there, but Layli can't help herself. Now she has no children to boss around, she tries to manage her elders."

Kelcy flashed his mischievious grin. "Just ask me about Layli and her elders."

She furrowed, turning her straight, thin brows into swords and curled her lip. "Don't you dare, Kelcy, you who listens to no one, not even your doctor."

He twirled the whiskey at the bottom of his glass. "My doctor said to take care of myself—I am."

Adler said, "I'll check on Gideon."

Royce struggled to stand up but refused help. "I'll check on the bartender."

"I'll help you there, Royce," Kelcy said and drained the last of his whiskey. "The bartender always needs at least two checking on him."

Scarborough smoothed his hair, ready to don his hat. "I have a certain lady to catch up with. Will be seein' ya."

William said, "I think we should have dessert and forget all this. Today is Bryce's day, right?"

"It slaps!" said Ricky, toasting with sparkling water.

Tansy came into the room and told William a young lady was asking for him. "Her name is Carina. She's waiting in the front salon."

"Who's that?" asked Kelcy.

With all eyes on him, William cracked a sheepish smile. "My girl-friend. I didn't realize she'd come here, though."

Peyton watched in horror as her daughter followed him out. "No, Bryce. Stay here." Bryce kept walking. She groaned and went after her.

four

Peyton watched her daughter scrutinize William as he kissed a young woman who had the potential to rival a super model. She grabbed her by the shoulders, whispering, "Come now, honey. Don't stare at them anymore."

Bryce's cheeks hued cranberry, her chest heaved, but she didn't budge.

"Come on," her mother said and guided her out.

Her nostrils twitched, and her lips trembled. She tucked her chin in and let her mother hold her up as they sparked away. "I suspected, but I didn't think she'd be a model."

Peyton led her to the study, which was just as her father had left it—masculine and bright, brimming with books, early Americana artifacts, and automatons. Peyton had replaced the textiles in the room using the same fabrics Sorensen had chosen. It looked identical to the original photographs, down to his American mahogany banjo clock still hanging in its original spot.

The moment the door was closed, Bryce burst into sobs. "Mom, I've lost him now. I hate this awful day from hell!"

"You always had eyes for William, but it was probably never meant to be."

"I can't help how I feel about him." Bryce collapsed to her knees and stamped her forehead on the marble floor, wailing like her mother had never seen her do.

"I know you're grieving, my dear girl. I'm sorry."

She clasped her belly. "William called me 'sweetheart.' He shouldn't have done that."

Peyton lifted her from the floor and placed her onto the sofa. "You didn't tell me you suspected William was seeing someone."

"He's conflicted. One moment he treats me like a younger sister, the next like I'm under his skin." She bawled and pinched her thighs. "Now that I see how beautiful she is and how different from me, I think this is it."

"Different how?"

Bryce looked down at her chest. "She's buxom, more womanly."

Peyton sat close and rocked her. "You probably don't want to hear this now, but honestly, if you'd just eat enough, you'd grow hips and plump breasts. Harlow's daughters and granddaughters have got it going on… when we're not trying to survive on boiled eggs and carrots. You've seen your cousin, Margot. At your age, she was a swizzle stick, not the lush beauty she is now."

"Maybe this is temporary," Bryce said, blowing her nose. "Maybe she'll go away in time. Then William—"

"—no, don't give yourself reasons to stay stuck on William forever, please."

Bryce balled her fists. "Like the Pharaohs loved their pyramids, the Romans their aqueducts, and the Persians their hanging gardens, I love William. Do you understand what I mean, Mom? No bird ever loved his feathers or fish their fins like I love William."

The drama of youth doused Peyton, who shook her head. "Honey, choose your pain or life will choose it for you."

"Give up William?"

"I'm telling you to give up suffering." Peyton felt she, too, needed to give up suffering, but she carried it in her DNA.

"Can I go to Auntie Royce's tonight? I need to avoid them."

"Royce wouldn't mind at all."

Bryce rubbed her puffy eyes. "Is Dad mad at me?"

"He's mad at me, not you."

"But why?"

"I let the others denounce your brother and didn't protest when they said we'd be better off without him. I suspect your father feels I didn't stick up for him when I should've."

"But how could you? Gideon was impossible, mean, and overbearing."

"That's beyond the point for your dad. I believe he faults me for not protecting Gideon more."

"That's really unfair!"

"The problem with truth is it comes with perspective." Peyton sighed and slumped back against the down pillows. "There's so much to resolve these days. I don't know where to start."

Bryce's tears returned. "This is the worst day of my life. Yesterday was the happiest, but today…"

Peyton gathered her daughter to her, recalling how she'd had to smash into walls, not just climb over them. "What does a Chase do?" she asked the question her father used to ask her. "To get through, go through. Sometimes, that's the best way."

"William must know how much I love him."

"I'm sure it's complicated for him like it is for you."

"My age is a problem for him, I think." After a grounding, deep breath, Bryce looked at her mother with wounded hopes. "Who was your first love? Real, big love?"

"Ashton." For the first time that day, Peyton smiled from deep within. "Breathtaking, charming Ashton." She sighed, recalling how she'd loved watching him move as much as she'd loved watching him sleep. "There was a time when I loved him madly." Peyton didn't tell her daughter she had seen him recently. "So much, I thought I'd never love another. It was a passionate, frenzied love, but—"

"—but you loved again after meeting Dad."

"Absolutely. It came years later. I was better prepared by then. And I love your dad even more. It's possible to fall crazy in love with more than one person in this life."

Bryce kissed her mother's cheek. "My head understands, but my heart says I won't ever love anyone but William." Peyton couldn't hide her agony, so Bryce said, "I scare myself with that thought as well."

"Just stay open to possibilities, okay?"

Bryce nodded, then she burst into another round of tears.

"I'll go hold the fort for you. Freshen up in your room. Come down only when you're done looking miserable."

"Then I'll never come down," Bryce replied, laughing through tears.

"Go up Bryce the Wounded, return Bryce the Champ. It's a choice. Healing is a choice, my girl."

She piled one foot over the other and cupped her jaw. "I'm scared."

Peyton scanned the walls of books surrounding them. What had they taught her? "Listen, honey, unless you're part coward, we can't call you brave. You launch on a horse like a missile. Have as much moral courage as you already have physical courage, okay?"

"I'll try, but Dad is so disappointed in me these days."

"Not in you, honey." Peyton kissed her and tucked her hair behind her ears. "He's disappointed in me, and it's mutual."

Bryce trudged to her room while Peyton circumvented the house to the stables, where she suspected she'd find Adler.

Her husband was brushing his favorite horse, Lightning, an Appaloosa, blind in one eye. He no longer rode him but refused to put him down. The stables were airy and clean, smelled of hay and oats.

Peyton stood outside Lightning's pen, her dress hiked up to her knees. "Your horse is an unwell living soul you can fix. Do you feel better?"

Adler looked at her with unnerving intensity. "Hard to know what that is lately."

"Don't be hard on me."

"Don't be hard on Gideon."

Her heart raced, pulsing through her limbs, urging her to give up on a lost battle. "Bryce asked where you were."

"Bryce has everyone. Gideon has no one."

"He has us. Why do you say unfair, extreme things? He's always had both of us. Do you think I wouldn't be there if he needed me?"

He put down the brush and patted his horse, who was jostling at the edge in Peyton's voice. "You're agitating me, not just Lightning."

"What's happening here? Will you keep withdrawing from me forever?"

"Gideon feels isolated and caged. He grows angrier. And on top of that, you're egging on the situation against him."

Peyton went from feeling that she let him down to the reverse. "You see me as an inciter?"

He yelled, "You didn't temper the attacks against him! Gideon is fragile! If he acts like a porcupine, it's because he feels vulnerable and besieged!"

"Is that how *you* feel? Is that why lately you keep going on trips?"

"I'm not projecting, Peyton." He closed the gate on Lightning and vigorously scrubbed his hands at the stable's sink. "Gideon is not a hopeless case." He shook his hands dry and started out.

She followed him. "I'm not done talking."

Adler dialed, stared at her, and aimed a finger. "I need *you* to listen to me now."

A rebellion in her bones wanted to mute him. "Listening."

"You and I have often disagreed on how to handle Gideon. It's too late now, except for you to stop calling him on every little thing. Let him be for a while. And don't encourage others to criticize him."

Peyton plopped down her dress and glowered at him with enlarged eyes. "I'm the villain here? Is that what you're saying to me?"

"I'm saying be his mother!"

The perfidy cut so deep, it quaked her core. "You, of all people, say this to me? You couldn't have said anything worse." Harlow had abused her, and she'd sworn she'd never do that to her own children. "I am a *good*, devoted mother!" She pressed her lips together, refusing to cry. "Don't follow me!" She flounced off. The buttresses that held the roof over her marriage were cracking around her.

"I'm sorry… Wait." Adler caught up, grabbed her by the wrist, and spun her to him. "I know you're a good mother, Peyton. Of course I do, but we're losing him."

"Did we ever have him? The first time he got kicked out of school, he was a toddler who bit the other kids." She tried to wrestle away from his grip, but he was too strong. "I don't believe you, Adler. You mean what you say. In your eyes, I'm the opposite of what I tried hard to be. Now let go."

"I didn't mean to hurt your feelings."

"Let go. I want to be alone."

He released her and spoke gently. "We don't walk away from each other. We sort things out, right?"

"Said the hermit in the woods! I'm walking away from how hard I always try, only to have you tell me it's not good enough."

"You're trying so hard, you're ramming it in!"

She inched closer, aggressive in a manner she rarely displayed. "You want less, you got it!"

"Are you threatening me?"

"We should all be careful what we wish for." Peyton could always count on her husband to read her well. She knew Adler understood the fissure that had started years before was growing wider. "Why do I feel you're about to tell me something I'm loathe to hear?"

"I'm not coming down to Texas for Bryce's next competition."

They'd never stood on opposite sides before. "It used to be the two of us, no matter what. What changed?"

He returned her hurt look with one of his own. "You want me to keep Gideon away? Well, I will."

"You're punishing Bryce for Gideon's bad behavior. Can't you see?"

Anger pitted his voice. "I'll go pack for those few days up in Chama with him. And actually, I'm doing what Bryce wants."

"But you're basically confirming to Gideon that he's victimized when he isn't. And you only came back last evening from a ten-day solo trip."

"I've never turned my back on you!"

Peyton watched him move away from her in long, angry strides. "You just did," she mumbled.

Royce was on a terrace bordered by lavender bushes and tall orange poppies. She took one look at Peyton and asked, "Gideon again?"

Peyton grabbed the tumbler of whiskey on the table and downed it.

"But you hate whiskey, darling."

"I don't care." She leaned both elbows on the table, defeated. "Can Bryce spend the night at your house?"

"Is it the girlfriend?"

"Oh Royce, she's devastated. I don't know what curse was unleashed on us today, but everyone is pained and livid."

"Why didn't William say anything about this Katrina?"

Peyton pressed her temples. "Carina, not Katrina. Anyway, I don't think William knew how to explain to Bryce he'd decided on a course that excludes her."

"Feels cruel to me."

"William is young. He probably didn't know how to bring it up."

"What then? He shows her the guts, but not the glory?" Royce eyed her empty tumbler. "I don't know why the young complicate everything… and you drank the rest of my whiskey."

"The old complicate everything too," she replied with Adler on her mind.

"Is everyone a masochist or just us Abiquiú women?"

"How're you a masochist?"

"At my age, a good time is a tall drink and a very thin book."

"You want to go home, and Bryce needs to hide. If William is around, ask her out loud to take you home."

Royce raised her eyebrows so high they touched the bangs of her red wig. "You want people to blame me, not her?"

"Exactly."

"When you put it that way, darling, how can I resist?"

Peyton messaged Bryce with the plan she'd concocted with Royce.

Kelcy came out on the terrace, scowling, and slowly lowered himself into a chair, his joints cracking. "What's William doing?"

"Carina is a beautiful woman," Royce said. "You know men's hearts are in their pants."

"Trust me," Kelcy said, "William's heart is nowhere near that girl. I know when he sees and when he's merely looking."

"Please, don't tell Bryce that," Peyton said. "The sooner she lets him go, the better."

"There's no way you want her without William in this life. I don't care how young they are."

"It's true that for me, William is ideal in every way, but it's foolish to hope against all hope. It's not the course he's chosen, and they're very young."

Kelcy topped his cane with his hands. "In time, William will smarten up. Unlike what Ms. Wig here thinks, William's family jewels are his heart and brain."

"Who're you calling Ms. Wig, Mr. Monopoly Man?"

Kelcy laughed till he was red in the face. "I am that rich, aren't I?"

"You're that old, you hick." The ring on Royce's snarly finger was so loose, it swiveled. "Not giving you a get out of jail free card."

Bryce showed up with too much powder on her nose. "Let's go, Auntie Royce. I already stowed an overnight bag and Myriad in my car." She gave her mother a kiss and steadied Royce.

Kelcy asked, "Who'll rescue me?"

"I'll see you to the casita with a large whiskey and a chunk of cake."

"You know me too well, Peyton dear. I don't know when a snooze in front of the TV became such a joy."

The casita was much older than the Big House, but its original design and most of the furniture were unchanged. A baker's hutch painted pale country green and a butcher's block counter lent the kitchenette a homey character. Stone floors in natural tones contrasted with cobalt blue and yellow Mexican tiles. Textiles collected over many years were strewn about, and a classic Kachina doll collection had only grown under Peyton's care. Even the hardware was original, very much like the family.

"Will you sit a minute with me?" Kelcy fiddled with the remote, found one of his beloved vintage westerns on the Turner Classic Channel, but set the television to mute. "I almost never find myself alone with you. Know that?"

Peyton sat on a chair overlooking vermillion vistas, islands of pink and lilac clouds, and the humps and flat backs of mountains framing the occasional osprey. "You only have to ask."

"I think of mortality an awful lot lately. It's natural at my age." He waited to be sure he hadn't worried her. "I find myself concerned for you and Adler. Do you mind my asking why you don't ride or take long walks together much anymore?"

Peyton clasped her face and rested an elbow on the arm of her chair. "I've been asking myself the same question."

He dipped his fork into the chocolate cake. "And?"

"Something between us is different." Her heart felt like a boulder. "He's been off with me ever since I told him I was passing Pioneer Ranch to Bryce alone. She knows horses, values this land and its historic buildings, and is vested in nurturing it. The older kids don't want the responsibility, and Gideon would turn his back, sell it to the highest bidder, and buy swanky property in L.A. He's not a guardian, but Bryce is—"

"—a preserver, like you." Kelcy chewed more cake, staring at her with the eyes of a patriarch. "And Gideon gets what, nothing?"

"He gets money he can spend, like Honovi and Ricky. I have a trust fund for each kid. And we'll also leave the vast property up in Chama for the boys to enjoy, though I suspect only Ricky would ever spend time there."

She took Kelcy's empty plate and handed him his drink on a napkin. "He'll get his fair share, but not the ranch."

"Want me to break down what Adler feels as a man?"

Peyton nodded. Kelcy would understand the situation in a way she couldn't.

"Adler is a proud man—in the best sense—and you're telling him, in as many words, that your wealth will go to your daughter and his wealth will go to his son." He wiped the corners of his mouth. "Without meaning to, you created a girls versus boys battle."

Peyton rested a palm on top of her head. "Not what I want to do."

"I know, but Adler doesn't." He punched the pillow behind him until it molded to his lower back, then pressed his index finger to his nose. "You see Gideon as an Adler, and Bryce as a Chase." He raised his hand to keep her from arguing. "Rejecting Gideon is rejecting his father. I think your man is awfully hurt."

"I don't reject Gideon!"

"Well, no, in all fairness you don't, but you reject the part of him that troubles you. The snag is all of him is troublesome." Kelcy sighed. "I'm not judging you, hon. If Gideon had been my son, I would've fed him to the coyotes by now. No offense. But Adler has a different take. I saw his reaction at lunch, as I have before. He isn't happy with any of us, so he takes off to his lonesome."

Peyton rubbed the back of her neck. "What am I to do, Kelcy? Because I won't have my son tear down in an instant what twelve generations have built over centuries with toil and sacrifice."

"You're doing it, darlin', but you make sure Adler isn't hurt."

Peyton watched the mountains bump their heads on a deck of clouds and earned a headache. "How do I do that?"

"Hell, damned if I know, but I'm not an enticing, irresistible woman."

She tittered. "Long gone are those days. I don't ride bareback anymore."

"Little lady, Adler loves you something deep. You have the power to make it right."

Getting to her feet took effort. "He believes Gideon can still change. I don't."

Kelcy took off his round glasses and used his shirt to polish them. "What do you do when you can't change a situation?"

Peyton remembered what her father had said to her after her mother died. "If you can't change a situation, change yourself."

"Uh-huh, and will Adler change himself?"

"He sure is changing us." She leaned on one hip. "*We're* changing us. I don't mean to put it all on him."

"Then change it back, or change it sideways, but don't let Gideon cost you Adler."

Her eyes misted, and her nose burned. She knew it wasn't up to her. "And what if he already has?"

"Listen to Mr. Monopoly now. Change is a rule in life none of us can escape. Change is a damn commandment, but you're the ruler, Peyton… *you're* the ruler. Find a way."

"All I do is find ways."

"Then you're already good at it." Kelcy raised the volume on his show. "I trust you to do the right thing, like I trust my William."

"The day we met you and William at that rodeo was a blessing. You changed my fate."

"For us, more so, and we didn't change your fate. We merely confirmed it."

"Do I seem to love Bryce more than Gideon?"

"You and your easy questions." He chuckled and pointed to his cedar humidor. "Pass me one of those bazookas, and I'll answer you."

Peyton scooped up the fattest cigar she could find and handed it to Kelcy, who sniffed it with relish.

"I have several grandchildren. Do I love them all very much? You can bet the farm on it. Do I love them equally? It would be a lie if I said I do and a sin if I did." He lifted a green marble lighter from the table and lit his cigar. "None of my other grandchildren comes close to William. None are as caring, sharp, or compassionate. Hell, I don't even like them half the time. How am I to love them the same?"

"I wish Gideon believed I love him."

Kelcy rocked and toked. "He knows you love him. That's not what he protests."

"It's that I'm not proud of him." Peyton cast her gaze to the horizon. The sky felt like a river of dreams, and she longed to flyfish wishes.

"Adler isn't proud of him, either, but he makes Gideon think he can still believe in him."

"Do you believe Gideon can grow?"

"To keep an even keel, we must adjust as we do to the seasons." Kelcy's eyes dimmed. "I remember how cold Gideon would get, playing outside in winter, and I'd tell him to wear a coat. Know what he'd reply? He'd say, I don't wear one in summer."

"Thank you, Kelcy."

"For bashing your hopes?"

"For being like a father to me and a grandfather to my children."

He relit his cigar and toked harder. "Only to Bryce and the older boys. Gideon wanted no coat and no old goat, either."

Peyton snickered, though she was sad enough to feel cold.

"Thank you for giving me a daughter in you and for giving William a mother. He loves you something fierce. It confuses him regarding his feelings for Bryce."

"What do you mean?"

He made well-practiced smoke rings. "Now, this is my guess. Not something William has said, all right? He wonders if his feelings for Bryce are to stay in your orbit, or if they stand alone because of who she is, regardless of her relationship to you."

"It's confusing to us all, not just him."

"All her life, Bryce put her nose in her books and her riding. Nothing needs to change just yet. William is going around the track is all. My gut says he'll circle back to her. I hope Bryce knows it."

Peyton strolled to the front door and opened it. "She can't know that, Kelcy."

"Well, I do," he said, stretching the last word as he blew more cigar smoke.

With one foot out the door and another in the land of apprehension, she said, "I'll find Adler and get him to be less mad at me."

"Great idea." He twisted in his seat and groaned. "Send William to me. Maybe I can get him to be less mad at *me*." He smoothed the one white tuft of hair he had left on his head. "I wasn't very nice to his girlfriend, Carolina."

"Carina, not Carolina."

"Whatever, just send him in."

As she climbed the stairs to the second floor of the Big House, Peyton was processing what she'd say to Adler. She found him in their bedroom, packing. "Can you forgive me, if only a sliver?" she asked the man who struggled with forgiveness. "I don't want you to leave."

"Forgive you for what?"

She'd loved him for over two decades. "I haven't given up on you or on our marriage."

Time had been kind to him. Age hadn't worn him down. It buffed his edges into a patina of distinction and fortitude. Intelligent, golden eyes gazed at her with longing and nostalgia. "You sound like you miss me again."

"I've been missing you as you stand before me. There's a gap between us, even when we lie in the same bed. I want to return to when we felt like one."

He stepped closer and took her hands in his, strong but uneasy. "Me too."

"I owe you an apology. Maybe I didn't make it clear enough. In my book, Bryce is you in all the ways that make her special."

"Is Gideon also me?" he asked, underlining just how shrewd Kelcy had been in his assessment.

"Gideon is himself, be it in his highs or lows. I don't blame his conduct on you, and I don't want you to think for a second that I don't embrace you. I mean, you know that, right?"

"Do you embrace Gideon in the same way?"

"Can we please not make every conversation about Gideon? I want to talk about us—you and me, of our bond, our history, and our future."

"We're also the children, Peyton."

She took a step back, no longer smiling. "Once, 'us' meant you and me. Soon, with both of them elsewhere, there'll only be us again. Are we still lovers and friends, or are we just parents?"

"You're raising your voice." Adler tossed items into his duffle bag, flinging them in a way that made her feel pelted. "We should discuss this later."

He hadn't heard her soul crying. Worse, he hadn't heard the warning shots, though he was a Navy SEAL at heart. Peyton pressed a hand to her forehead, hiding her face. "Okay, Adler, I'll do what you want."

Though his voice was even, it felt like a shout. "Don't kid yourself. Not much happening here is what I want."

"What do you want?" Peyton looked at a man she knew well, yet not at all. "Why am I screwing up so much in your eyes?"

"We'll talk more when I get back."

"Sorry, but I'm trying my best. Please, let me."

He locked her to his chest with a hug that was part love, part anger. "I'll go find Gideon. He disappeared."

"He's not a baby," she said. "Please, let him be and focus on us."

"He's not a man either. He should be at his age, but he isn't."

"He's not the man we want, but he's an adult." Peyton stared at him, her eyes warning that the gap between them was about to become a gorge. "Stay with me. It's one of those days today. I need you with me." In a voice that emphasized they stood at a pivotal moment, she said, "Stay."

He kissed her forehead. "Gideon is not replying to my messages. It worries me. I won't be long. Abiquiú is a small town. There are few places he can be. I just want to be sure he's okay."

As he walked away, dressed in black, Peyton felt she'd dissolve into darkness. She kicked off her shoes, curled up on her bed, balled herself, and wept. The smaller she made herself, the bigger her problems felt. She needed time to herself, a place where she waited for no one.

five

Peyton was sitting on her father's desk chair, deep in thought when Tansy knocked on the closed door.

"Ms. Chase? This just arrived for you." She held a golden Labrador puppy. "There's also a big basket of dog stuff in the kitchen."

"Oh my! You're kidding." Peyton jumped up with newfound energy and took the puppy, already in love with it. She read his tag and cooed. "Your name is Apollo?" He was the image of Cooper, full of exuberance, pawing her face and nuzzling her neck. A silk rose and a note were attached to his collar. "Did Adler bring him?"

"He was a special delivery."

Peyton returned to the chair and nestled Apollo in her lap. Excitement bubbled around her, buoying her mood. She undid the silk rose and unfurled the note. Once she read it, she was puzzled. The note wasn't signed.

The words of Mercury are harsh after the songs of Apollo.
This I feared; this I suffered.
For when Apollo plays, even the caged nightingale sings.

Only one person she knew could've been behind this gesture. But she couldn't believe it. So many years had passed. Though the style was unlike her husband's, he was still the likely candidate. It ought to have been him. Adler wasn't home yet, but she was too excited. On a large tablet propped up like a mirror, she video called him, hiding Apollo on her lap. "Did you send me something special?" she asked, hoping he had.

"It's not our anniversary," Adler said. "Did I miss an occasion?"

"You don't need an occasion," she said, though he wasn't the type to woo her with presents.

"What did you get?"

She raised Apollo and showed him. "He reminds me so much of Cooper. I thought maybe he was from you since you once got me a fox, and you also know how much I've been missing Cooper."

"I wouldn't be that thoughtless."

"Thoughtless? Apollo is cute."

"You're going on the road and you already have Myriad. Why would I stick you with a puppy?"

She fidgeted, frowning. "Not at all how I see it. I'm deeply touched. I love bonding with such an adorable angel. The fennec is Bryce's, but this treasure is mine."

He crossed his arms over his chest. "Well, who's sending my wife puppies?"

Peyton knew exactly who. "Still looking for Gideon?"

"Did you get anything else?"

She wanted to look away, but forced herself not to. "He came with food and toys."

"An extravagant gift." He clenched his jaw, squinting. "Why did you think it was from me? Wasn't there a note?"

"The note must've fallen off somewhere." How could she tell him how thrilling it was to get a mysterious note or how Apollo should've been from him? "Besides, you understood how much Cooper meant to me. It's no coincidence Apollo is a golden Labrador. My mind jumped to you."

"Hmm, weird."

The puppy yawned, which made Peyton pet him more. "Maybe you should leave Gideon to blow off some steam and come home."

"I'll track him. Won't be long."

Peyton hung up and sandwiched her phone in her palms, braving herself to make a call she feared might change more than she intended.

"The caged nightingale must sing before you finally call me?" Ashton asked.

She heard him ask someone to leave and close the door behind them. "Apollo is gorgeous. Thank you."

"I'm glad you knew he was from me."

How could she not have known? Ashton had been her first love. His immeasurable support had expanded her career and secured her future many years ago. "I'm sorry. I said I would call after we saw each other in Los Angeles last month, but I had my reasons."

"I loved seeing you so much, and there's something I need to tell you in person. When can I do that?"

Seeing him once had been overwhelming and dangerous, but to see him twice? "Tell me now."

"It's important, and I have to do it in person. I can meet you anywhere."

Peyton reflected, biting the fleshy part of her index finger. "I'm in Fort Worth next week for my daughter's showjumping competition. We can meet for coffee." The minute she suggested it, her intestines knotted, but the excitement uplifted her.

His chuckle said he'd agree to what she wanted but would do what he preferred. "Text me your hotel info."

"Coffee, I said."

"Hotels have coffee, Peyton."

She could hear his excitement and felt she was back in her twenties.

"I'm instructing my assistant to arrange a plane for next week. Send me the details right now, okay?"

She hung up, did as he asked, and murmured to Apollo. "Let's get you delicious food and play some more."

Koda snuck up on her. "With that prescription, you can send me to my room any time."

"How happy I am you made it!" She jumped to her feet and hugged him. She'd loved him since Layli brought her three-year-old brother to Pioneer Ranch to raise. "Let me take a good look at you," she said, clasping his shoulders. "Still a stallion. Happier than you were last time I saw you."

"Layli says I'm now a mule." He was thirty-nine years old now, as cheerful as ever, fit and strong, with long hair. High cheek bones and a prominent nose balanced the sweetness in his eyes, and his vulnerability was so charming, it was hard to overlook him. As always, an eagle's talon on a deerskin string hung around his neck. "Peyton with a golden Labrador! It's like I never left."

"When I told you to go and explore, I didn't think you'd only come back every other year. I'm not saying that to make you feel bad. It's my way of expressing how much I've missed you. Though if you hadn't left, you wouldn't have become the amazing equine veterinarian you are today."

"I put my stuff in my old room on the third floor. Is that okay?"

"That room was too small for you at nineteen. I think you should take one of the bigger ones with a king-sized bed and an en-suite, don't you?"

He squeezed her hand. "I listened to you last time, but I love that room. It's the right size for me." He flashed his bright gummy smile. "It's where I'm most at home." Koda squatted and played with the puppy. "I haven't seen everyone together since Layli's sixtieth birthday. Where's Adler?"

"He's out looking for Gideon."

Apollo nipped at the plump part of his palm. "Scarborough is sitting with some blonde."

"I wouldn't be surprised if he leaves early for the first time in his life."

Scarborough had been Koda's boss at the ranch, but he'd treated him like a son. "He puts me to shame. I don't have a woman on my arm, but he does."

She squatted beside him. "You want one?"

"I'm getting up there in age. Sometimes I get ideas." He sat in a lotus position, his eyes the color of walnuts. "Is everyone okay today? I sense something is way off."

"Of course, something is off. Gideon is here, isn't he?"

"Is that what's wrong with William's face? That's some mean wheal."

"He makes me sad in my marrow. At Gideon's age, you were sweet, kind, helpful, and dependable."

"Don't forget gullible."

His meaning wasn't lost on her. "Falling crazy in love in your youth is mandatory, and Margot was a stunning firecracker," she said of her niece.

"Gideon hasn't improved any?"

"If he's no worse, he's no better."

Koda tucked his long, silken hair behind his ears. "Honovi asked us to a sunset ceremony. You're invited as well."

"I won't intrude. Maybe time alone with Adler and Gideon will help matters."

"Intrude? That's ridiculous." As agile as ever, Koda rose to his feet faster than Peyton could come to hers.

Honovi walked into the study, frothing with high energy. "I heard what you said, Mom, and you're coming to the ceremony. No later than seven-thirty. BearClaw will lead. Homage to the Western Skies softens the Great Spirit's heart. We can all use Grandfather Sky today." He brought his hair forward, framing his angular jaw. "You can use it more than the rest of us."

"BearClaw is coming? Your dad didn't say."

"BearClaw didn't say he's coming," Honovi said. "But I see him here at sunset."

Peyton assessed her son, who had the spirit and eyes of an eagle. "Are your visions strengthening with age?"

"They're becoming more frequent, but not because I turned thirty. I filter better now."

"Will the ceremony be on the ridge?"

"We'll take the ATVs. There's room for everyone. I'd invite Dad, too, but I don't see him there."

Peyton said, "I'll take Bourbon. I need to engage my core and feel real muscles."

Honovi winked. "You always had a big horse."

"I have to tell you, honey, I just don't feel it."

He touched her arm, smiling down on her with eyes as sage as they were dark. "We're all trying to arrive at the same place. Gideon too."

"And will he?"

He pointed to the sky and closed his eyes. "The Great Spirit says live to love, don't love to live, for only one is eternal."

Peyton needed to stop focusing on Gideon. "It's bittersweet you're all grown up." She smoothed the blue streak in his hair and fastened it against his geometric jaw. "You've been warning me for days."

"I'm sorry, Mom, but something big is coming."

"We'll leave you," Koda said, as the banjo clock tolled. "See you at sunset."

It occurred to Peyton that the antique clock was due for the monthly winding that kept it alive. What did *she* need to feel alive? She'd been feeling untethered, her routines no longer weighing her down. Her father's extensive library beckoned her to spin her wheel of fortune. She shut her eyes and ran her fingers over the spines of beloved books. She knew her restlessness was a combination of disappointment and resentment. A tickle at her ankles snapped her out of her stupor. As she stooped to pet Apollo, she heard footsteps.

"Another gift from William?" Gideon asked. "Don't worry. I won't set him on fire or anything. He's not a squirrel."

"Honey, I dread your unpredictable behavior, but I don't expect the worst from you at all times."

"Don't you, Mom?"

When Gideon was his softer self, he reminded her a smidgeon of her bloodline. He was the only other person who had read a sizeable chunk of her father's books. It was her favorite part of him. "I know you can appall, but you can also delight. I'm your mother. I wiped your every tear and bandaged your every scrape. You didn't have nannies or babysitters. You had me."

He fixed his blue eyes on her. "Why do you love Bryce more than me?"

She collapsed in a brown leather chair. "I don't love her more, but she gives me less grief. I quarrel less with her."

He took the chair next to hers and fiddled with a bronze statue on the end table between them. "And that's my fault?"

"I'm not interested in assigning fault… What would help you be less angry with me?"

"Not having anyone else here is a good start. And I don't understand why you're giving my inheritance away to Honovi and Ricky."

She scanned the portraits she'd painted of each family member, including Kelcy and William. Vibrant and textured, as complex and layered as their subjects. "We're one family here, even if not tied by blood. Honovi and Ricky are also my children. Others, like Layli and Koda, are used to treating this house as their own. What do you suggest?"

"Tell them they can't do that anymore and disinherit Honovi and Ricky."

The puppy jumped onto her lap and curled into a donut, putting her at ease. "Is that reasonable when they're also my children?"

"It is to me. Do you think I'll allow it when this house becomes mine?" He raised his voice when he said, "*I am* your first son, not Honovi!"

"No, you're my *firstborn,* not my first son." Peyton wasn't sure whether he said such things to aggravate her, or meant them as a matter of fact. "And I'm a long way from dying. Besides, doesn't Bryce inherit anything?"

He crossed his long, thin legs and hooked a foot behind his ankle. "Women are gold diggers." He tapped his palms on the arms of the leather chair. "She'll find a rich husband and won't need this estate. Probably why she's after loaded William, and Honovi makes significant money. He doesn't need mine."

"Am I a gold digger, Gideon?"

He shrugged and thrust out his lower lip. "You didn't marry a pauper. Dad had his own house and land up in Chama when you met him."

Sad at her extreme failure with him, she held back tears and petted the puppy.

"Do you want to know what else would make me less angry?"

Peyton read her son like a chirologist reads palms. "No, you're not getting a new car, or anything other than your allowance, which is bigger than most families' monthly incomes."

"Put the condo in Los Angeles in my name, at least."

She tested him. "If I were to do that, would you feel loved and appreciated?"

He uncrossed his legs, rested his pointy elbows on his bulbous knees, and webbed his fingers. "Mother, I know you spend more money on Bryce than you ever spend on me."

Peyton lifted Apollo and stood up, stretching to her model height. "Your sister earned back in prizes and sponsorships more money than we ever spent on her." She pressed closer, forcing him to push back in his seat and look up at her. "Count your blessings, not hers, and you won't feel such envy anymore. Envy is a parasite that eats you alive. And you'll soon make gobs of money as a nuclear engineer with the degree *we're* paying for while you live at *our* condo on the generous budget *we* provide."

He came to his feet, forcing her back. "When I was little, you once told me God would break my arm."

"I said that the day you gave your sister the scar on her back."

He sneered and faced the door. "Well, Mother, God never did."

"Will you turn around and look at me, Gideon?" When her son did, she said, "The day you were born was the happiest of my life."

"I believe you. It all went downhill after that, didn't it?"

"No, honey, not like you describe."

"Come on. You're honest and I'm smart. Let's not pretend we're not Grendel and his mother."

"That's cruel." Peyton chewed her cheek. She had nothing of value to tell him. "I nurtured you the best I could, but nature always wins over nurture."

"Makes no difference. Nature or nurture, it's all your fault!" He gave her a sardonic chuckle and stood taller. "I didn't lie. That's our true portrait, Mother. Paint that!"

Peyton said what was unadulterated and pure. "I love you with all my heart."

Gideon carved his marquee slasher smile. "I'm still going to win in the end," he said. "I'm just getting started."

Vacant of him, the room was still suffocating. All his life, Peyton had wanted Gideon to validate her as a loving, nurturing mother. But he was clever and sadistic enough to deprive her of that. She wound the banjo clock, crying. It had been her father's favorite possession, and he always said he believed time was for her. That's not how she felt.

six

White, like his mother was before him, sporting the same blonde mane, Bourbon was shuffling with pent-up momentum. As Peyton saddled him, he bobbed his head, itching to dash away. Long, loving strokes in key spots readied a horse for a good run, but he needed none. Finn, her American Foxhound was circling around, nudging her. She petted his soft head and said, "You want a treat, don't you, Finn?" One of her bags was always dedicated to feeding her beloved animals. They knew it and pointed their noses at it. She grabbed a few biscuits and gave them to Finn, who stood on his hind legs to take them. "Let's go," she said, ready to start her journey to the ridge.

Dressed in her favorite stretch jeans, Dubbary black riding boots, and a red linen shirt, Peyton mounted the Friesian, her eyes on the horizon. The gods had distilled the sky to cognac and Hypnotiq and crowned the mountains in crushed ginger cookies. She knew Bourbon would eventually break into a gallop, but she hadn't expected he'd do it right out of the stables or keep racing as the rocky trail rose toward the ridge. She clutched his massive muscles with her thighs. He was the fastest horse on the ranch, born to run. Finn tried to keep up, bolting at top speed.

She reflected on all the times she'd raced uphill, competing against time, against the odds, and the desire to flee.

Somewhere deep within her, she feared, this time, she'd lose.

Bourbon slowed to a trot, hoofing on prairie clover, around towers of flowering century plants covered with bees, past musk thistle, and Indian paintbrush blooming red. She'd soon reach her destination at the pinnacle, but was she ready for the summit—any summits?

Hair-raising incantations told her she was nearing her destination and propelled Bourbon into a trot. The white Friesian neighed and shook his long mane. She dismounted, her heart thundering at the sound of Willie BearClaw chanting a prayer. She left her horse to graze and joined the worshipers gathered at the top of the mesa.

BearClaw, dressed in a long tunic, half blue, half red, was looking up at the sky and fanning a burning bundle of sage as he chanted, "Hey-a-a-hay! Hey-a-a-hay! Great Spirit, hear your children. Let us hear the voices in the winds that blow in all directions."

They turned in unison as BearClaw called, "From you, East, we seek the lessons of the past, to see with the trusting innocence of children. From you, South, we seek the ways of questioning, the passion and stamina of adolescence. Show us the truth and the path of growth. From you, West, we ask to accept the responsibility that comes with marriage and family and to release us from the bondage of guilt. From you, North, we ask to walk in balance and harmony with our Mother Earth, Father World, and Grandfather Sky as we prepare for our ultimate walk."

Like a lemon drop, the sun melted behind the blue mountains, oozing streaks of gold and violet. Ricky played the flute, while Honovi and Koda added incense to the blazing fire.

BearClaw faced the sunset and bent at the waist. "To the West, we owe blood, for it is from the West we receive the blessing of family. Show us the lessons we should teach and those we should learn." He purified a knife over the fire and cut into the flesh of his left hand, dripping blood into the flames. "Blood for blood," he said, his eyes on the last rays of sunlight. "If you're going to sacrifice to the West, do it now."

Honovi, Koda, Ricky, and Layli purified knives. Peyton removed a pocketknife from her saddlebag and sterilized it as the others had done.

"Ask for what you want as you give life to the fire," BearClaw said.

She incised her left palm, contemplating what to ask. The knife had been Adler's years before he gave it to her, and it retained both their energies. She squeezed hard, dripping blood over the tongues of flame. Hypnotized by the flickering and the hissing of sparks, she asked God to bring peace to her family and restore harmony to her marriage.

"Hair too," Honovi said. "A lock is good about now."

Peyton grabbed a lock at the base of her neck and chopped it off.

Before she could toss it into the fire, he touched her arm and recited something in Ute she didn't understand. "Now. Protection for you and Dad."

She released the lock into the flames, mindful of the fears and weaknesses she wished would go up in smoke. Her flesh burned and her legs ached, but relief washed over her, and she wished Adler could feel the same baptism.

Six people stood around the fire like the six points of the Star of David—connected, interlaced, inhaling incense, bonding with the elements. Each of them had come to fuse with the universe. Each came with a plea. Peyton murmured the Lord's Prayer and crossed herself, wishing for fortification and resolution.

The sky had turned indigo when BearClaw shed his robe and cast it over his shoulder, signaling the end of the ceremony. He pulled a packet of cigarettes from his shirt pocket and tapped one out. He offered Peyton one, though he knew she never smoked. "Your heart is so heavy, it's weighing *me* down." He scratched his white stubble and the three parallel scars on his cheek, a souvenir from a bear.

Spurred by the beast thudding in her chest, Peyton marked her forehead and cheeks with her blood. The beast ran faster and faster as her breathing quickened.

"Which animal slinks through ya?" Willie BearClaw asked.

"A lioness lurks beneath my skin."

"The greatest of guardians. Not the fastest, but the deadliest." He exhaled smoke through his nostrils and sandwiched her hand in his, swaying. "When you enter the forest, you either make friends with the bear or you kill him. What you don't do is build a fence and hope he minds it."

"And you think I've built a fence?"

BearClaw had once nurtured a cub bear into adulthood. "We both raised bears, but only one of us put up a fence. You had to, I know. Problem is that others got stuck behind it."

Peyton played with her earlobe, aware BearClaw meant Adler. Her son and husband were more fused together than she ever knew.

"Time for you to seek hallowed ground," BearClaw said.

Lake Tahoe was a massive vortex, echoing her name. She resolved to visit the Sierra Nevada sooner rather than later. "Thank you, guys. This ceremony was enlightening." She craned her neck and watched the pinpricks shining above. "I'm embarrassed it's taken me this long to hear and understand."

Layli asked, "What did the Great Spirit say to you, Peyton?"

Honovi was firm. "You mustn't ask."

"It told me I've been too focused on the lessons I needed to teach Gideon, but not enough on the lessons I needed to learn from him."

"And what's that?" Layli asked.

He raised his hand, not allowing his mother to respond. "The Great Spirit spoke to the blood of its blood. It's just for you. Don't share it."

Layli grimaced. "Okay, she'll just have to tell me later when the schoolmaster returns to his office."

Though Peyton and BearClaw simpered, Honovi wasn't amused. "I'll say my goodbyes here. Our flight is scheduled in four hours."

Peyton wanted to hug him, but his stance dissuaded her. "I'll see you and Ricky in Sedona after my trip to Lake Tahoe, my special one."

He pasted a fist to his heart, got in one of the ATVs, and waited for his brother.

Peyton embraced Ricky and lingered. "Don't forget to send me every-thing you're composing, even your unfinished bits."

"Take extra care of Dad, okay?"

Growing up, Ricky spent most of his time shadowing his father and feeling safest in his orbit. "Don't I always?"

"Of course, Mom, but he's beginning to have it with the Gideon drama."

She reassured him with another hug. "I'm so proud of you and your caring spirit. Have fun in Sedona."

"Light is disappearing fast," Layli said. "You're sure you should ride back?"

Peyton gazed at Venus, outshining diamonds, and heard the instruc-tions of the Goddess of Love. "The night is clear, the moon is full, and the path is not long."

"That's a prophecy if I ever heard one." Koda laughed. "Besides, Bourbon knows the way very well. Horses are like homing pigeons." He petted the horse and Finn, who had been busy visiting each one of them. "Peyton also has this Energizer Bunny with her. I've known many dogs on the ranch. Finn can outlast them all. What's he on?"

"It's true," Peyton said, "he's always high. He must have caffeine for blood. I should've named him Espresso."

Finn looked from one to the other and spun around them, unable to keep still. Peyton reached into her saddlebag and pulled out biscuits for Finn and apple slices for Bourbon.

"BearClaw, staying up at my cabin?"

"Yeah, Layli, especially if you saved me some of your sausage and white bean casserole."

"I didn't," she said.

"Yeah, you did."

She snickered, playing with her hair. "I saved you lasagna too."

Peyton hooked her arm through Layli's and walked a couple of steps with her. "My goodness, he still magnetizes you. How do you do it?"

"Acceptance goes a long way into sobering a woman."

"Ah… acceptance… that thing I hate."

Layli tapped her hand. "Go on down, now. It's best if you make it before us. We still have to extinguish the fire before we leave, but I'll come down to make sure you made it."

Peyton mounted Bourbon, called out for Finn, and set out for the ranch. The sky glowed with the full moon, spotlighting her path. Finn bounced along, telling her all would be well on her way home. She couldn't remember the last time she'd ridden in the moonlight. Alone in the high desert, listening to nocturnal creatures exchange calls, she decided her life needed a reboot. It needed a bigger part of her old self—the youngest old self she had.

Though the day had been eventful in painful ways, she returned to the stables, strangely invigorated. She unsaddled Bourbon beneath the stars so he could enjoy the refreshing breeze on his warm hide. She hung his gear on the rail fence outside the stables and fluffed his long mane, thanking him for keeping her safe. "You're Rapunzel in need of a good brushing." A loud neighing came from the stables, followed by angry clip-clops. She couldn't understand why a horse would run out at that hour. Then she saw Gideon riding Bryce's horse, Big Red, whipping him to go faster.

"Sweet Mother of God, get off him! Gideon, you can't ride!"

He whipped Big Red harder, which made him do what he was trained to do. The Hanoverian flew over the gate, kicking high, jerking Gideon off him. His foot got caught in a stirrup as Big Red continued to dash, frantic from the abuse. She made a quick calculation. The path ahead became rugged and dangerous, with boulders and cacti protruding in enough places to kill Gideon should Big Red continue to tow him. Only one thing could stop Big Red in time. She did what she hadn't since she was Rodeo Queen at twenty-one. Peyton clasped Bourbon's long mane and mounted him bareback, using the fence for leverage. "Run, boy, run!"

She'd have to catch up to Big Red, lean over, and pull on his reins to bring him to a stop. The more Bourbon closed the gap, the more debris blew in her face. She huddled low to stay on top of Bourbon, shielding her eyes as best she could from flying rocks. She was afraid Big Red would kick Bourbon, and even more afraid he'd trample Gideon who was screaming and cursing. Flying dross cut her chin and forearms, yet she pushed her horse harder. As he came neck and neck with Big Red, she balanced on his slick hide, leaned out, and grabbed at the reins, pulling at Big Red's bit, urging him to stop. The horse whipped Peyton off Bourbon, and she swung to the ground. But she'd stopped Big Red in time, and Gideon's yelling told her he wasn't critically injured. She'd crashed to the ground and thought she might blackout as she sat up, moaning, and clasped her head, while Finn barked and licked her face. Bourbon raced past them, then turned around and trotted back, snorting, as if he understood the situation. He came to Big Red and tried to calm him down with head butts and rubs.

"You're okay, Gideon, just hang on."

"My wrist is fucking broken!"

Big Red continued to jerk with bulging eyes and angry spasms.

"What did you do to him?"

Her son's foot was still stuck in the stirrup, keeping him on the ground. Peyton shook off her tremors and crawled toward Big Red, though she feared in his state he might kick her in the head. "Sorry, Big Red, so sorry," she said. "Easy, boy, easy." She massaged his forearm to release his tension, drawing on years of handling horses. When he kept close and stopped straining, she used his saddle to pull herself up to her feet, and stroked him from mid-belly to mid-back, cooing, a calming technique Scarborough had taught her. Once the horse quieted, she found a pressure point on the side of his neck and pushed on it, releasing endorphins to ease his pains and restiveness. "Anything else broken, Gideon?"

"My wrist isn't enough?" he shouted. "Help me, not him!"

"I *am* helping you." Peyton used Big Red to dodder around him to the other side. By the time she could help her son free his foot, Adler was dashing toward them at top speed.

Gideon tried to sit up, wailing, and cursing the horse.

"Are you all right?" Adler asked. "Tell me you're all right, Peyton!"

She freed his foot from the stirrup. The way her son sat up on one elbow made her suspect he'd suffered no major injuries. "Stay still." She inspected Big Red, saw the needle stuck in his buttock, and pulled it out. "Gideon, what was in the syringe?"

"Nothing."

"I don't believe you!"

Adler brought his son to his feet, then went to Peyton. "How are you standing? I saw you fall, and it nearly gave me a heart attack."

"I may have a concussion. My left side hurts and my hamstring is sore, but I'm fine. Is my face badly scratched up?"

"Just a little." He showered kisses on her face and held her as if he thought he'd lost her. "I can't believe the risk you took. Thank God, you're all right."

"How could I not take the risk? I'm his mother, Adler!"

Surprised at her angry response, he said, "I just didn't expect what you did. That's all."

Peyton pushed his hands away. "Why not expect that from me? I would've expected it from you. Would you say that if this were Bryce?"

"No, Dad wouldn't!" Gideon said.

Adler shot him an angry stare. "Not what I meant, Peyton."

She made it clear she needed him to stand away, preferring to balance herself with Big Red's help. "Do you need to throw up, Gideon?" she asked, dizzy, clutching her head.

"I ache all over."

"You should take him to the hospital."

"You too, come on," Adler said.

Her husband gave her his hand, but she rejected it.

"Are you kidding me? Please, take my hand."

"No. The man I know would've stayed with me when I explicitly said I needed him. He wouldn't have doubted I'd do anything in my power to save my child."

"Dad, I need painkillers!"

"Peyton, please," Adler said, still extending his hand. "I don't doubt your devotion. Never."

"You fetched him rather than letting him blow off steam and look at what he did. Go, Adler… take him to the hospital."

"Don't blame Dad for your failures, Mother!"

Peyton glowered at her son. "I don't blame your dad. I blame you!"

Layli and Koda rolled up in an ATV, their faces plastered with questions.

"What on earth?" Layli asked, jumping out of the vehicle, almost stumbling before Koda could park it. "Adler, what's the matter with her?"

"She was thrown off Bourbon, trying to stop Big Red from killing Gideon."

Layli and her brother guessed the rest. They could see one horse was unsaddled and the other skittish. Peyton showed the syringe to Koda. "It's pink. Is it Fluvac? Gideon stabbed Big Red with it before he went berserk."

"Let me see your eyes," Koda said, though he was a veterinarian, not a physician. "You won't believe over the years how many people ask me to diagnose their issues and give them prescriptions. I picked up a thing or two."

"I can move everything, just banged up and nauseated. Take the syringe."

Koda held the syringe against the light, examining it and smelling its contents. "Did you steal this from my bag, Gideon? You would've had to hack the digital lock. How could you go through my things?"

Adler shouted at his son, "Answer him, dammit!"

"Yes, I did, and? It's just a vaccine." Gideon dusted the dirt from his hair. "I probably helped him."

"What else did you give him?" Koda asked.

Adler stood close to Peyton, his hands outstretched. "Please, let me help you."

She gave Koda her hand, instead. She couldn't bear the thought of being in a car with Gideon for an hour to the hospital and an hour back. "We'll take care of the horses. Take Gideon for a check-up, and I'll see you when you return. I'll stay awake in case I develop other symptoms."

"Actually, *I* should take care of the horses," Koda said. "I'll examine both of them."

"Thank you, Koda," Peyton said. "I know Fluvac can give Big Red flu-like symptoms, but is there more?"

"Unless Gideon gave him something else, he should be all right. But he's traumatized now." Koda turned to Gideon. "Did you poison him or give him something else? Bryce will be devastated if anything happens to her horse."

"Bryce would rather something happen to me than to her precious horse."

"Shut up!" his father yelled. "How could you have hurt that horse? Did you give him anything else, Gideon?"

Defiant though mauled and grubby, Gideon leered at his mother. "Was it instinct, or did you have to think about it?" He was bleeding from flesh wounds, scowling at her with mangled hair and a hideous attitude—the image of Grendel.

"Is there any part of you, Gideon, that cares about your family at all?"

Koda said, "I'll run a toxicology report, but if you tell me now, you'll have done one right thing today."

"Answer Koda!" Adler shouted.

"I only stuck him with Fluvac, Dad. I wanted to see what he's made of."

Adler looked defeated in a way Peyton hadn't seen before. "He's a horse. What are you?"

Her husband's torment melted her anger into compassion. She reached out to him, knowing they needed each other more than ever. "Adler, help me to the house?"

He scooped her in his arms, locked her to his torso, and put her in the ATV. "I'm more sorry than I can say."

Layli said, "Gideon, get in."

He scowled, his upper lip curling with a mixture of displeasure and disdain. "Then help me, dammit!"

Koda pressed his fingers to Peyton's neck, assessing her heart rate. "Your pupils look fine. You're talking fine, haven't thrown up, and have good color. No fear of brain injury. I'll take another look later, but the hospital is best. I'm no physician." When he tried to do the same to Gideon, he moved away. "I'll follow you as soon as I can, but first, I'll take care of the horses."

Layli helped Gideon into the back of the ATV, while Adler took the wheel.

He turned around and looked at his son. "Did you thank your mother for saving your life?"

"What did she do that other mothers wouldn't?"

"Most mothers aren't this capable or brave!" Layli said. "What are you talking about?"

Peyton squeezed her husband's thigh. "I saved the part of you that's mine. But the part of you that's yours, Gideon, only you can save."

He screamed as if he were being caned. "Why don't you ever call me Sorensen? It's my first name—my *real* name!"

Peyton's instinct was to snap back in his direction, but her neck hurt. "When you act like a Chase, I'll call you one. My father was loved by all. Can my son say the same?"

Adler stepped on it, avoiding another word from either of them.

seven

Layli said, "I'll help Gideon to your Jeep, Adler, and get him wipes and acetaminophen. You take care of Peyton."

He helped his wife into the bathroom, pleading to let him take her to the hospital.

"I don't need the hospital."

"At least, let me help you bathe."

"Layli will help me. You need to get Gideon looked at. I'm miraculously fine."

He stood flush behind her as she leaned over the marble bathroom counter. "Forgive me."

"Isn't that what I've been asking you to do?" She looked at their reflection in the mirror above the sink. It felt distorted. "I want to."

"But you can't?"

"What did I do to make you doubt me?"

"Nothing," he said, holding her, resting his chin on top of her head. "I'm sorry."

"Give me time to process my hurt. We both have things to consider."

"Why do you have blood streaks on your face? Not from the fall, right?"

She showed him where she'd cut her palm. "A call to courage, a sacrifice to fend off worse suffering. Maybe it worked. Gideon and I came through this alive. BearClaw led the ceremony. I used the knife you gave me to offer a sacrifice for both of us."

There was shame in his voice. "A ceremony with Willie? Is this your way of telling me I cut into you?"

"*I* chose my pain, but we need to mind each other's feelings better."

He spun her around and pressed his forehead to hers. "I'll message you every step of the way, share all I learn in real-time, and come home as soon as I can."

She nodded and let him kiss her. "I'll wait for Layli," she said, removing her dirty clothes. "Don't tell Bryce anything till she comes back from Royce's tomorrow."

"She's not in her room?"

"Lately, you've been missing more than you know with Bryce and me."

"I'll do better."

"You're spread thin, and so am I." She ran flat palms over his firm torso. "We need permanent solutions, though."

"I'll take Gideon to the hospital now." His tank was almost empty. "Keep yourself safe for me."

When Layli knocked on the bathroom door, Peyton was already running the hot water. The bathroom was vast, covered in aqua glass tiles with a large picture window that overlooked the mountains. "I'll use the built-in seat in the shower, so I'll be fine."

"I'll wait right here. You'll need me."

Peyton hobbled into the white onyx shower. "I'm super sore, oh my."

"That's why I have magic brownies. Are you concussed?"

"I don't feel dizzy or nauseated anymore, but I can barely raise my arms." A hot waterfall and linden-scented shampoo were what she needed. "I'm so frayed."

"I only feel tired when I'm around BearClaw."

"How come?"

"We should've had a life together. He's a reminder of how much I lost out on. Living should exhaust me, but it's not living in full that drains me. Ironic enough for you?"

"Did Gideon say anything to you?"

"I asked him why he's been more aggressive and out of control lately. He said he can't help himself and refused the idea of medication because it turns him into a zombie."

"We have a hopeless situation," Peyton said, running a loofah over her thighs.

"I hate to agree with you, but he admits he can't rein himself in enough."

She turned off the water. "My son needs to keep away from provocative situations. But that's all we have here. He's more sedate and reasonable when he's away from us." Peyton examined her bruised body. "It'll be weeks before I look normal again." She toweled off and slipped on a loose shirt and shorts. "When I met Adler, he was a man of the outdoors, hunting and fishing. I took it as a testimony to a healthy body and psyche. Didn't realize then how much he relied on his solitary time to cope. I should've understood that, but I didn't."

"Are you feeling lonely?"

"He's been retreating from me, not just from our stressors. I feel like I spend too much time waiting for him, even though I'm always busy." Peyton tested the tender spots on the left side of her body. "I resent it."

Layli slumped her shoulders, her eyes cast down. "I know what you mean. When the other side of the bed is tidy, it feels cold." She gave Peyton a hand as she crossed the bathroom floor. "Does Adler share your pillow? Maybe that question is too intimate. You really don't have to answer."

Peyton laughed. "You ask me about sex, but intimacy is off limits?"

"Intimacy is different. It's peeking into the soul, not the flesh."

"He used to more, at dawn especially." Peyton titled her head, smiling from the caverns of their history she kept lit with warm memories. "It's sort of an art, isn't it? We can't teach our lovers such things. They know it, or they don't. He knows it, but we're too mad at each other at times."

"It's the one thing I long for but don't find." Layli helped her onto the teak stool. "First, magic brownies and some hydrogen peroxide." She dabbed Peyton's cuts and applied ointment.

"Do you still feel that BearClaw is your soulmate?" Peyton asked.

"No doubt about it. Is Adler yours?"

Before Gideon's hormones cranked up his malice, Peyton wouldn't have hesitated to answer. "Do we get more than one soulmate?" She chewed on a moist brownie, studying her face in the mirror.

Layli brushed her hair like she used to when Peyton was a tween. "Perhaps it depends on the timing. But could your question have anything to do with your mysterious puppy sender?"

Peyton closed her eyes. "My scalp hurts, if you can believe it."

"Maybe your memories hurt more? Answer the question, missy."

"You guessed it was Ashton, didn't you?" She finished her brownie and wiped her lips on a tissue.

Layli handed Peyton her perfume and lotion bottles. "That puppy makes you extra giddy. And who did you tell me you saw last month?"

"It was fantastic seeing Ashton." Peyton stared at Layli in the mirror. "We bumped into each other at Geraint's gallery in Los Angeles. We just took a stroll, but it was one of my happiest moments."

Layli said, "I wonder if Gideon would've been different, had he been Ashton's son."

Peyton hung her head until she realized it hurt more that way. "Gideon is Harlow's grandson. I cursed him, most likely. Which is why he targets me more. Maybe I deserve it."

"Not true." Layli helped her up.

"I must've made more mistakes than I know."

"That's it. You're eating another brownie." Layli frowned, gawking. "You're nothing if not devoted. Gideon is unreasonable."

Peyton ached more with every step she took. "I wish I could sleep."

"In a little while. Sleep is good for a concussion, but only if you don't develop symptoms after a few hours." Layli led her downstairs to the living room. "Want a snack?"

"How about carbs with carbs? What do we have?"

"Who're you, Kelcy? Want bacon?" Layli made sure Peyton didn't slip down the marble staircase. "I'll check the cupboards, but first, let's get you situated."

Kelcy was waiting for them in the great room, chewing on an unlit cigar. Vibrant paintings hung on white-washed walls, complementing the rich serape and Native tribal inspired rugs and fabrics.

"Little lady, you all right?"

Peyton installed herself as best she could on a large, deep white sofa. "Just banged up. Don't worry. Harlow's daughter always lands on her feet… unless she's spilling off horses."

"Well, you'd better. I wanted to see you for myself before telling William."

"Just leave him down in Santa Fe with his girlfriend." She gazed through the wall of glass at Orion, thinking of her daughter's heartbreak. "He'll find out what happened soon enough. I didn't tell Bryce, either, and I'm ecstatic neither of them were here to see it."

Kelcy gave her his trademark puckish smile. "They say, darlin', learn to hold your bourbon."

Peyton tittered, wanted to flick a hand at him, but she ached too much. "I'm just glad my son is all right, but I worry about Big Red. He's no Bourbon."

"Koda said he'll be fine by morning."

Layli returned with a whiskey for Kelcy and a cup of coffee for Peyton in time to hear her say she feared her kids hated each other. "My brother felt closer to me the older he got."

Kelcy said, "Siblings are rarely like Koda. They're little shoplifters who grow up to accuse you of stealing."

"Don't you have a brother, Kelcy?" Layli asked.

"I did, till he stole from me."

Peyton giggled. "I think it happened to Gideon. He feels robbed."

"That's possible," Layli said. "First there were the boys, then Bryce followed. Maybe he has middle child syndrome."

"What he has is middle *finger* syndrome." Kelcy rolled his eyes. "Middle children don't stab horses with stolen needles. What are you talking about?"

"I'll fetch some comfort food."

"What are we having?" Kelcy asked. "I was robbed too."

Layli flung her arms in the air. "Three plates of munch and crunch, coming up."

Peyton's phone pinged with a message from Adler. "The doctor has seen Gideon already. He isn't alarmed but has ordered an MRI first, just to be sure. His left wrist is fractured, but the rest are just flesh wounds and bruises."

"So much for not riding bareback any longer," Kelcy said. "What you did tonight was remarkable. I hope you can take yourself off the hook now."

"Adler feels bad, and so do I, but I don't know if he'll meet me halfway."

"Your husband isn't good at halfway."

She skimmed eyes over their past. When they first met, Adler had made her come to him, and he'd done it again during the challenging phases of their lives. It was the way he sought assurance, but she was getting too old for that. She needed more brownies. "We have to bend for each other."

Kelcy rubbed the handle of his cane, as if polishing it. "If you can be flexible, little lady, nothing will bend you out of shape."

She was feeling less achy as the marijuana did its magic. "What I find hardest is knowing the difference between flexibility and stupidity."

Kelcy chuckled. "Bend, but don't end up with your head up your ass."

"Kelcy Loving!" Layli said, returning with a tray of goodies.

"What? Peyton asked, and I answered."

Peyton was buzzed to high heaven, giggling and swaying nonstop. "You're so, so bad, Kelcy."

Koda came in and stood before Peyton with his hands on his hips like a fed-up nanny. "You may not be feeling your pain much, but sit propped up and relax."

"Okay, Doc. How's Big Red?"

"Angry but tranquilized, falling asleep. Horses have a great long-term memory, though. Best to keep Gideon away from him, especially since he has upcoming competitions."

"And Bourbon?"

"Happy as a lizard on a warm rock. You didn't hurt him, or he doesn't seem fazed by it. I gave him extra oats." Koda brought his braid over his shoulder and began undoing it.

Peyton ate a chocolate truffle and offered him one. "Two upcoming competitions in Texas. Then enough of that."

"I'll go with you," Kelcy said. "Bryce can use the support, and I can use a visit to Pilot Pointe Manor. In fact, come with me. It's been a while. All of you should come down." Kelcy used his cane and the arm of his chair to hoist himself up. "Well, I'll be back at dawn."

"I'll get Kelcy settled, and I'll take care of Apollo for tonight," Layli said, then turned to her brother. "Don't ask Peyton anything now. She's not exactly in tip-top shape." She helped Kelcy stand up and took his arm.

When they were gone, Peyton whispered, "Ask me what?"

"Layli is right." Koda softened his gaze and rubbed his collarbone. "Not an ideal time to ask."

"Puhleeze. I'm contused not of unsound mind."

Koda rubbed his palms on his thighs. "I'm done working for other people. I want my own practice."

"Ah, you want clients, not bosses." Peyton felt a burning cut on her neck. "That sounds great to me."

"Well, you haven't heard the rest of it."

"Yes, I have. You want your clinic to be here on the ranch."

Koda beamed. Peyton always made it easy for him. "There are those sheds behind the stables—"

"—the ones housing old equipment. You want them?"

"I want to lease them, but I'll have to link them together somehow to make them functional. They're expertly built but on the small side. Horses take up an enormous space."

"Get an architect to draw up plans for now, but I have one condition."

Koda lifted off his seat. "Shoot."

"You're family to me, practically a little brother. I wouldn't lease the property to you. You'll have it for as long as you need it. I want you to succeed."

"No, Peyton, that's far too generous."

"Come off it. Your presence here will also benefit the ranch. You'll attract traffic and activities to a gallery and museum I want to build. Consider that in lieu of a lease, especially if you train Bryce."

"You should think longer on this."

"What's there to think about? You want to resurrect a sleepy part of the ranch, and it's exactly what I want. Besides, it could be a long time before you net profits if you also have to worry about paying for the expansion. The future of this place requires a diversified income. A clinic for equines and bovines is smart. And you'll take over the care of our stock from our veterinarian at a discount. I'd rather pay you. It's a win-win."

"What was that about training Bryce?" Koda asked.

"She's been accepted to both pre-med and pre-veterinary programs, but I think she'll choose to follow your path. What's better than apprenticing with you right on the ranch?"

"Don't you want to discuss it with Adler?"

"I will, but I know what he'll say. He loves you, too, you know. Anyhow, let's hear what an architect would propose and at what price."

Koda's eyes overflowed with affection. "Wasn't it enough you supported me in college and paid for my tuition?" He covered the divide between them and hunched over her for another inspection, smelling of sandalwood and anise. "Are you in pain?"

She let him take her pulse and examine her eyes. "I seem to know how to respond to everyone, except my youngest son. How can that be, Koda? I'm his mother, yet I understand him less than anyone in my life."

"Maybe you don't need to understand Gideon and shouldn't try to." He chuckled and bit into a magic brownie. "But I have a suppository that would knock him out for days."

Peyton heard Adler and Gideon in the hallway.

"If you change your mind and need help, call me," Adler said.

Relieved not to have to deal with Gideon just yet, Peyton said, "Glad you're back."

Adler leaned over and kissed her on the mouth, mindful of the scrape on her chin. "Are you hurting too much?"

She pointed to the plate of brownies on the aspen wood coffee table. "I'm floating about now."

Koda gave Adler a bro hug. "I'll leave you two to have a moment."

Alone with her husband, Peyton said, "How're you in all of this?"

He looked tired, his scruffy salt and pepper beard aging him. "William's car wasn't in the garage. He's not here either?"

"You're not asking me if he's with Bryce, are you?" She saw that he'd contemplated the idea. "He was thoughtful enough to take his girlfriend away."

"Girlfriend? Sounds serious."

"Could be," Peyton said, touching his hand. "Did Gideon tell you anything?"

"He wants to invite friends over for a while. Maybe throw a party."

"What?"

He sculpted his features into a question mark. "Bryce just had a get-together."

"For a celebration, like the one we threw for Gideon before he left for California, though his was more elaborate. You didn't tell him he could, did you?"

"I don't understand what you want to see happen. All his friends are from out of town, and we want him distracted, don't we? Isn't he allowed to feel at home here any longer?"

"Gideon makes it hard for *me* to feel at home anymore. He robs me of my sense of security and peace of mind. He does the same thing to Bryce. Don't tell me he doesn't strain you in the same way. I don't trust him with the house, the animals, or any of us."

"I hate when you exaggerate his behavior." Adler faced her, hanging half off the sofa. "You say you haven't given up on him, but you have."

"At least, I'm not rewarding him for his atrocious behavior. What do you want? What do you think can happen?"

He buried a hand in his hair and tugged at the roots. "Maybe if we treated him as if he belongs, he'd act like it."

"At what price?"

He furrowed his brow and raised his voice. "What do you mean?"

"I want to know what price you're willing to pay to give Gideon another chance, even though he shows nothing but increased contempt and disdain for us."

"I don't know how to answer your question, Peyton."

"Are you willing to have him poison the horses, burn down the house, what? Where do you draw the line?"

There was anger and rebellion in his reply. "You know, he's done none of those things."

"He's done enough to justify my fears."

Adler got to his feet. "I swear on my life, I won't let him hurt anyone or hurt himself."

"Now swear on *my* life!"

"What?"

She pointed to her chest. "Swear that God may strike *me* dead, not you, should you be wrong."

He knelt beside her, filled with love and rage in equal measure. "I would never, ever do that."

"You won't, because you know you can't vouch for what he'll do next. None of us can."

"What do we do? You already took the unilateral decision of cutting him out of the ranch."

Peyton eyed the Kiva fireplace that bowed out from the wall like a massive beehive. "You make unilateral decisions too. And I didn't cut him out of the will. He'll get equal value, just not my ancestral home."

He pushed off his knees into a squat. "Then we deserve each other."

She didn't stop the tears from dripping down her lips, didn't think she could stop anything. "Before Gideon, that would've been a compliment."

Adler, who seldom cried, gawked at her with glistening eyes. "You're making me choose between you."

She leaned forward and tried to pull him closer, but he resisted her. "I'm just taking away his arsenal. Why can't we see him on his turf, join him in his life? We'll continue supporting and loving him, but we establish new boundaries with him. Unless he agrees to medication and shows a genuine change in his behavior and intentions, Gideon should no longer be allowed near those he's hell-bent on hurting."

Adler looked at her with tightened lips. "I know you think you've found a reasonable solution, but what you're proposing is to exile him."

"Okay, you decide what'll happen."

He wiped his face on his sleeve and sat beside her. "It takes two of us."

"It takes two of us to do what only one of us thinks is right. This is where we've been on Gideon for years. And it's killing us. I'm turning over the reins to you, but my forgiveness is cracker thin."

He brought his face closer to hers. "Does this mean you're giving up on me as well?"

"I'm putting Gideon in your hands. I can't handle any more of your blame or my failure. Just keep him away from Bryce."

He touched her arm. "I don't blame you, Peyton."

"Oh, but you do."

"I want to try with him one more time. Can you give me that?"

She nodded, though her head felt heavier than a cannonball. "You decide. I'll just melt away in the background where you want me, but if he hurts anyone, it'll be on you." She knew he was risking more than he fathomed, but she also knew she couldn't stop him.

"You feel I diminish you, but what I'm trying to do is prop up Gideon."

"Okay," she said, looking away.

"You don't believe me, do you?"

"It doesn't matter."

"You matter to me more than anything."

His words were beginning to carry less weight. "I want to go to bed," she said, refusing to meet his eyes.

"Look at me, please… Do you think I'm a good father?"

"The best."

"Let me try to be that."

"To both children, please! Bryce needs you too. As a matter of fact, Honovi and Ricky have also been getting less of you."

"I saw them before I went looking for Gideon. I always make sure they know I'm here for them. Yesterday I was distracted, but I'll make it up to Bryce." He touched her knee. "You look like you're getting worse. What can I get you?"

"Nothing."

"I don't mean to let you down, Peyton."

"I don't mean to let you down, either."

He sighed and looked at the ceiling, fatigue etching his face and spirit. "Let me take you to bed."

Peyton huddled her face in her hands, barely able to keep her eyes open.

He kissed her forehead, picked her up and carried her upstairs, which he hadn't done in forever.

A part of her, no matter the circumstances, felt the unbreakable bond between them. "You've carried me up these stairs enough times, haven't you?"

He kissed her, and it was sweet. "And I always will."

eight

As the sun was preparing to break through the membrane of dawn, Peyton pried herself out of bed and took quiet steps. She left Adler to sleep and descended to the great room, where Kelcy was drinking coffee and reading a newspaper.

Through the glass wall, she could make out the North Star at the tail end of the Little Dipper. "There's a light here that feels like a hangar to my spirit."

Kelcy chuckled. "Your spirit is a dress?"

"A hangar for planes, silly. My spirit is buoyed by the tides of sky here." She pointed to the North Star. "I could find my path if I knew which of my stars pointed the way."

"Let your heart be that star. You often want your head or your sense of duty to lead. Maybe this time, your heart should." Kelcy checked his vintage Cartier watch. "Royce should be here any minute now. She barely sleeps."

"Does your watch date back to the Berlin Wall?"

"You're making fun of my watch, little lady?"

Peyton simpered. "It evokes memories of my dad and his love of clocks and watches, reminding me I still have his favorites in the safe." She touched a hand to her chin. "I almost forgot about them."

"It was the first really expensive thing I bought myself, the year Clinton became president and the Dallas Cowboys won the Super Bowl."

"What's it supposed to remind you of?"

"I was sure I'd made it when I could afford this watch."

"If Royce were here, she'd say pish-posh, treat yourself to a new one, but I totally understand." In the stillness of early light, they heard a noise coming from the kitchen. "And speaking of Royce, I think they're here."

"Woohoo…" Royce called out, as she always did.

"At her pace, she'll get here tomorrow," Kelcy said.

Royce was still in the hallway when she said, "I may be slow, Monopoly Man, but I don't need three legs like some people."

"No, you need four." Kelcy laughed. "Is that you or your wig speaking?"

Royce leaned against the doorway, steadying herself with one hand and fluffing her blonde wig with the other. "I can't believe I need a break already."

"Your wig is too heavy."

"Kelcy, don't think for a second I'm beyond tripping you accidentally on purpose."

"First, you'll have to catch up to me, but your wig will paste you in place."

Bryce rushed from behind her and held her tightly with one arm, the fox cradled in the other. "You said you'd wait for me, Auntie Royce."

"I didn't realize you needed me to help you walk, Bryce."

She snickered, then saw her mother and shrieked. "Your face is scraped, and you have mean bruises on your arm!" She put the fox down and helped Royce to a chair.

"I told you I took a tumble. It's just scratches, honey."

"You have good color, but it looks worse than a tumble." She rushed to her mother for a hug. "Just how did you fall off Bourbon? You're a brilliant rider, Mom."

"She rode bareback, that's why," Kelcy said.

Bryce turned to her mother, her hair in dark ripples. "But why on earth would you ride bareback?"

Peyton rotated at the waist in both directions and moved her arms up and down, ignoring her pain. "See? I'm fine and dandy."

"If you can do that," said Kelcy, "I need me some of those magic brownies on the double."

"Eat some breakfast before training," Peyton said.

"I'll go change."

The fox scurried to Peyton and rubbed her soft fur against her ankles. She tapped her lap, signaling the pup to jump up. "Big Red might be tired today, possibly getting a cold. Don't practice too much."

"Oh my God, what? He can't get sick now," Bryce said, and hurried out.

Royce leaned out of her chair, and whispered, "Lordy, now tell me what really happened."

Peyton kept the drama out. "Gideon is fine. That's all that matters."

Royce played with a stack of bracelets. "Bryce invited me to join her at her next competition."

"Then you, too, can come to Pilot Pointe Manor," Peyton replied.

Royce pulled her smooth eyebrows together. "You hick, you weren't going to invite me, anyway?"

"I wouldn't miss your wig collection for the world," Kelcy said.

"Good. I'll lend you one, now you have two and half hairs left."

"That's still two hairs more than you."

Royce laughed and turned to Peyton. "I couldn't say in front of Bryce, but you look like Barbie fresh out of the spin cycle."

"I wish. More like Barbie's mother forgotten on the clothesline." Peyton had been thinking about how to mend things with Gideon. "I need to check on my son. I'll be back."

"You're going to see Gideon by yourself?" Royce asked.

Though it was a painful subject, Peyton snickered. "Between Gideon and me, I'm the lion."

"Take mace and a taser, also a chainmail suit."

Peyton headed to the study with a plan. Since the sunset ceremony, she'd been reflecting on what she was supposed to learn from her son. Now she knew.

She had to stop seeking his approval.

It could've been the reason she'd lost his respect. Was she making the same mistake with Adler?

She unlocked the safe and pulled out the jewelry box where she kept her father's belongings. It had been years since she'd inspected his collection, and it made for a happy reacquaintance with items that held his energy. Warm memories skipped in the stream of her mind as she played with his watches and rings. How he'd polish his watches and spin them on his wrist, engrossed in thought—his private wheel of time. She chose a watch and two rings, then resealed the safe. She slipped a ring crowned with a ruby framed in two rows of diamonds on her middle finger. It was too big. She could never get Adler to wear any of her father's jewelry. Not his style. She wore her mother's emerald ring, a testament to her talent and strength. But she was facing a difficult challenge and needed her father's ring, too, a reservoir of his unwavering love and resilience. She headed to her son's bedroom, aching more with each step up the marble staircase, but her spirit was lighter.

Gideon's bedroom door was open. After a gentle knock, Peyton entered, which she seldom did when he was in it. "Awake?"

He was vaping, buttressed upright in bed, his left arm in a splint. "Maybe."

She hoped he'd make room for her on the bed, but he didn't. "Painkillers working okay?"

He held up his vaping pen. "I prefer marijuana, like my mother."

She put the jewelry she'd brought on his lap. "Your grandfather loved white and rose gold, especially studded with diamonds. I want you to have his Cartier Ballon Bleu watch and the matching ring."

"I'm confused."

"I'm giving you this special watch for two reasons. It belonged to the man you're named after, and to remind you never to allow the hours to own you."

Gideon supported himself better, took his mother's offering, and scrutinized the valuable jewelry. "I don't understand."

"Too late comes too soon, unfortunately. I don't want that for you."

"Is that how you feel?"

She thought about what her son would've accomplished if he'd used his cleverness in productive ways. "The ring is to remind you not to waste your talents." She rubbed her sore neck. "We all wed ourselves to certain priorities. Use this ring to wed yourself to something that will make you joyous, Sorensen."

He showed a glimmer of vulnerability, drooping his cheeks in a way reminiscent of his child self. "Is this a setup?"

"The back of the watch is inscribed. Read it out loud, please."

He read the inscription to himself before doing as his mother asked. In a rarely displayed softness and a dry throat, he read: "'Fear not the end, Sorensen. Fear only never getting started.'"

"This watch was a gift from your grandmother to your grandfather. She wanted him to do more, I believe. Take it as an inscription from me. You're mature enough to take an independent path. Seize it." She leaned closer, testing if he was open to a hug, but he didn't budge.

Gideon wore the watch and ring on his right hand. "They fit."

"I can replace the battery for you, and they could use a proper polish."

"I'll do it." He gawked at his mother, probing and weighing. "Is Big Red all right?"

"Would you care if he wasn't?"

He fluffed his untidy dark hair and vaped. "You might not believe it, but I know what regret is."

"How about contrition?"

He examined the jewelry more intently, deaf to her question.

"Don't take this the wrong way, but he'll be fine if you keep away from him."

He tucked his hand behind his head, wrapped one long leg over the other, and leaned back against the headboard. "Is that how you feel?"

There was enough truth in his question to make her tear up. "I look forward to the day we can enjoy each other." She ran her fingers through his hair, like she used to when he was little, and massaged his scalp. It was the one soothing touch he'd allow as he matured. "I miss picking you up and bouncing you on my lap."

"Did you also give Bryce a watch and a ring?"

It pained her to think the small fortune she just handed him, priceless in its symbolism, mattered only in comparison. "Time is the currency with which you spend your life. *Be* Sorensen."

"Thank you."

"I'm glad you like them."

He glared at her with blue, intent eyes. "I mean, thank you for stopping Big Red. I thought for sure he was going to drag me to hell."

"Well, I'd never let that happen—not to my son."

"Would you do it again, Mom?"

She flipped through the album of memories, reliving her excitement when she and Adler got married and started a family. "I wanted you so much, it changed the trajectory of my life."

He sliced his wicked smile. "I bet you regret that now."

"My only regret is your unhappiness. Let me know if you need anything."

"For the record, Mom, I got away with a mere wrist sprain. God had the opportunity to break my arm, but he didn't."

"Perhaps God was warning you. Accept the caution."

"That's not the explanation. There's simply no God. Otherwise, how would you have been cursed with me?"

"Not how I'd label you." Not wishing to be provoked any further by someone proficient at pushing her buttons, Peyton shuffled out.

Adler was waiting for her in the hallway, leaning against the wall, his face congested with many emotions. He pasted a finger against his lips, took her hand, pressed it to his heart, and mouthed for them to return to their room.

"Why did you do that?" Adler asked.

"It's what you both needed."

"I needed you to give him jewelry?"

Her eyes said he knew better. "You needed me to make him feel he belonged, and he needed me to show him he was favored."

He penned her to his body and rubbed his hands up and down her back, mindful of her soreness. "I'm sure you succeeded."

She didn't want to rob her husband of his hopes, but she didn't want to lie, either. "There's a fine line between supporting someone and flat-out enabling them. My concern is, we don't seem to know where that line is."

"In the ATV yesterday, you said you'd call him Sorensen only when he acted like a Chase." He held her gaze, divulging angular feelings. "Is my family inferior?"

"That's not what I meant. The man he's named after is a Chase. How can you think that, though? You're my man." Peyton lingered on her last sentence. Love remained, but it was becoming overshadowed by defensiveness, criticism, and stonewalling.

His fury thickened the air. "You were angry and spoke truthfully. What if Gideon were all Adler and not a Chase at all? Would that be so awful?"

"He's tall and sharp like you, but hardly anything else, and I feel he's nothing like me. He's neither of us, rather the worst version of himself." She wrapped her arms around him and kissed his heart. "I'm proud of who you are. Just not proud of what Gideon is. He doesn't feel like my father's grandson or my husband's son."

"But Bryce does?"

She stepped back and pulled her brows. "Are you telling me you don't see how Bryce is the best of us combined?"

Adler's anger whittled to sadness. "I just wish you didn't make that glaringly clear to Gideon."

"You know, it's Gideon who makes it glaringly clear to all of us." She made to leave, but he blocked her path. "I invited Father Gabriel to breakfast and want to go deal with that."

"Stay and deal with me."

She gave him no less than she wanted from him. "I'm here, but I'm tired of arguing about Gideon. He's a fraction of us, but he feels like the sum of us."

In a strained voice he seldom used, he said, "He's my only biological son."

"And I'm your only wife, and Bryce is your only daughter."

"I hear you, but I can't let go of my dreams for him. And don't kid yourself. He's tenacious like you, analytical and outspoken like you, and he argues in brevity, also like you."

She needed a change of topic. "Father Gabriel has no transportation. The truck you gave him is shot. I've been thinking we should give him another vehicle."

"Which one?"

"He needs a truck because of all the hauling to the pueblo. Let's buy him the new version of the pickup truck he has now."

"What are you trying to do, ward off the evil eye or something?" He opened the door to their dressing room. "I'll help you change and walk down with you," he said, and helped her slip on a flowy silk dress she'd bought in Hawaii.

"Thank you."

"For what?"

"For waiting for me for a change."

Adler rubbed his eyes. "I don't understand how we have a ton of ground to make up."

Those many years ago with Ashton, when other essentials were missing, love hadn't been enough. Peyton knew it wouldn't be enough with

Adler, either. "Gideon has been a chasm. Can we go back to when we rarely argued?" She looked into the golden eyes he'd lent their daughter. "Do you remember what romance is?"

"I'll fix it," he said and hugged her.

She doubted he could repair what was being crushed to dust under the hoofs of time and discord. At the sound of a puppy scratching the door, she said, "If Apollo is here, then Layli is downstairs. I'll go get some coffee and another brownie."

Peyton followed the aroma of Kona coffee and baking cinnamon rolls to the kitchen.

Layli was grabbing small plates and large mugs. "You look better, but worried."

The sputter of an old engine told them BearClaw was parking his old-timer truck. Peyton followed Layli outside and was happy to see BearClaw smoking with his windows down.

Layli said, "Your trusty rusty sounds like an industrial saw."

"Still works." BearClaw's face branched more lines than a map.

"So do our ears," Layli replied. "But not for long, it seems."

He extinguished his cigarette on his dashboard and flung the butt inside his cabin. "Peyton, you dyin'?"

She giggled, though hurt. "One day."

"Good, got something for ya." He spewed out of his truck with a vial of oil in his hand. "It's for the cuts, especially the one on your left palm."

"Thank you, but it'll heal just fine without—"

"—don't argue, woman. Apply it every day, but when your cut is healed, you must return home."

"Why, and what makes you think I wouldn't be home?"

"Because my vision decrees it."

"Decrees?" Layli cackled, her hands on her belt. "Who're you, Honovi?"

Peyton thanked him, uncorked the vial, and took a deep whiff. "Smells nice."

"Where's mine?" Layli asked, holding up her own cut palm.

BearClaw rubbed his white stubble and sighed. "You need something else altogether."

"What?"

"That casserole was delicious," he said, "but I'm hungry again, and I miss Mustang. He inside?"

"Adler went to fetch Father Gabriel," Peyton replied. "Got any oil for him? He's hurting too."

He winked at her, characteristically cryptic. "I'm giving it to you, but it's for him."

"For him?"

"I saved his life, not yours. He's my ward forever. You just get the added benefit."

"Thank you, I guess."

"At least you got oil." Layli rolled her eyes. "I got zilch."

BearClaw stepped into Layli's personal space. "You got me."

She inserted her fingers into the back pockets of her jeans and stared at her shoes. "Mikey has you."

He huffed and reached for another cigarette. "We're all interwoven like a ceremonial blanket."

"In that case, I must've been the loose thread hanging out on its lonesome."

BearClaw exhaled smoke out of his nostrils. "I mean, look at me, a chain-smoking, scarred old man. Don't I sicken you, Layli?"

"You do, but not how you imagine."

Peyton slipped into the house, leaving them to talk in private. She ate a brownie and was heading to the terrace when she spied Scarborough.

"Got a minute, ma'am?" he asked.

"For you, always. Shoot."

He was at home at Pioneer Ranch about as much as he could be anywhere, wearing a new yellow shirt with an embroidered yoke, and a blue bandana tied around his neck. "You wrestled with a cactus last night?"

"Yup, but I threw the first punch."

"I can see your wagon is still chuggin'. Sure all your spokes are intact?"

Peyton leaned on one hip and unpacked her southwestern parlance. "Not thrown off my trail yet, and you're on it, luckily. Bryce is about to take a fork in her road, with or without destiny's permission."

"Destiny is a whip that cuts two ways—by refusing our wishes and by granting them. Which is why I have a favor to ask."

Peyton thought of how destiny had once granted her the ultimate wish—a firstborn. "Seems like we ask of God, but Rumpelstiltskin answers. What favor do you need?"

"Take me with you to Lake Tahoe to see Rebecca?"

"I never could get you to visit Carmel-by-the-Sea. I never thought you'd choose Lake Tahoe instead, but that's an excellent choice." Scarborough had been part of the marrow of Pioneer Ranch for six decades, yet he and Peyton rarely ventured far together. "Well, it's about time, isn't it?"

"Lake Tahoe. Ain't it Charles Bronson's country up there in the Sierras?"

"One of nature's finest images." Peyton's eyes wandered to Rebecca, who tucked her platinum blonde hair behind her ears, watching them. "Do you ever feel you spent too much time in Abiquiú, and not enough elsewhere?"

Scarborough played with the brim of his gray hat looking down, his brilliant blue eyes like twin topaz crescents. "My track was never wide. I didn't need it to be. But it sure looked at a lot."

"Yes, New Mexico is special that way."

"Pioneer Ranch is special that way." He studied Koda, sipping coffee, engrossed in conversation. "Koda told me he'll be doctorin' equines and bovines here on the ranch."

"I think the hour chimes for all of us."

"And does it chime wings or roots?"

She elbowed him. "It chimes branches, I believe. I only want to stretch, not get swallowed up like I did in my twenties."

"But Bryce needs her bigger wings," Scarborough said. "I'll go with her to Texas, but no rider should attempt the job of a horse. She has Big Red for that, but she needs reminding."

"That would be a blessing. Thank you!"

He tapped his hat on his thigh, an old habit whenever he deliberated. "I spoke to Adler just now. He's on the terrace with Father Gabriel, reading newspapers." He chuckled. "Will you forever order them New York and Los Angeles newspapers?"

"It's the only one of Dad's traditions I keep alive. I love the crispness of a real newspaper and the nostalgia of inked headlines… I'll go see Father Gabriel and leave you be."

On her way to the terrace, Peyton received a text from Ashton that made her heart stop: *All confirmed. Can't wait to see you. Not a euphemism. I feel twenty years younger thinking about it.*

She hadn't broken her vows, but she felt culpable.

The terrace was framed by an array of foxgloves, lavenders, and roses. When Father Gabriel saw Peyton, he removed his rectangular glasses and folded his newspaper. "Child, why are you banged up?"

Adler smiled in that way that lit up his face, stood, and helped her to a chair. "Is Bryce in yet?"

Her grin was wide, the brownies doing their job too well. "Anytime now… Father, we'd love to replace your truck with a new one. God just spared us a disaster. The least we can do is provide his priest with a reliable vehicle."

"You two have always been my loaves and fishes. You already supplied my parish with solar panels, fuel, and food staples. A truck too? Let us pray." He twined his rosary beads about his fingers and brought them together, leading them into a prayer.

Bryce glided onto the terrace, exuding grace. "Father, would you bless Big Red before you leave? He's off and I need him in tiptop shape."

"But of course." He clutched the wooden cross around his neck. "What's impossible with men is possible with God."

Adler pulled out the chair beside his for his daughter. "You won the day you learned that it's you who makes victory—it doesn't make you."

She inched her chair closer and poured a cup of coffee. "I'd rather not end my career with a loss."

Her father rubbed circles on her back. "Are you afraid of losing or of quitting something you love?"

"I'm afraid I'll never find something else I love this much."

Adler hooked an arm over her shoulders and tugged her into his embrace, his eyes trained on his wife. "Time is a coin and the other side of fear is freedom."

"Quite wise." The friar stroked his salt and pepper tonsure. "Those are words God likes."

Peyton said what she needed to hear herself, "Fear chains most people to lives they loathe, but you know better than that, honey. You know how to use fear to catapult your life." She'd once had to face her greatest fears, and because she was loved, her audacity had paid off. She wondered if having led a safe life since was turning her into a coward, walking the line, afraid of her impulses.

Adler poured coffee into Peyton's cup and added cream and sugar. "Bryce, you're choosing a different direction in life when you're at the top of your game. That's moxie."

"Faith is how you starve your fears, my child," the friar said.

"Every time you've put yourself on the line, every time you've risked failure, you've grown," Adler told her. "We're very proud of you."

"I'll have more courage if you're there, Dad."

He squeezed her hand. "You don't need me."

She leapt up and hugged him tight. "But I do need you. Just because

I don't whine doesn't mean I don't need you."

Peyton gave him told-you-so eyes.

"May grace, mercy, and peace be with you," said Father Gabriel.

Gideon leaned out his second-story window and looked down at them. "Blessed be to Bryce, wahoo!" He gave a lazy clap, while everyone looked up at him with aggravated faces. "I know what you're thinking, Priest. I'm the one who makes the devil go, 'Oh crap.'"

"My son, the devil in each of us makes its own hell until we're saved by God."

Though mellow, missing his cutting edge, Gideon said, "Are you the devil, Father?"

"Cut it out, Gideon," Adler said.

"I'm merely asking the friar to clarify."

"I am God's servant and follow his every word."

Gideon chuckled, but it was unnerving. "Ever think only God shared his version of the story? Is it fair to judge the devil without hearing his side first?"

The friar worked his rosary beads. "Pride cast Satan out of heaven, Gideon."

"Seems to me God was the proud one, unable to deal with confrontation."

Father Gabriel crossed himself.

Adler rose, glaring at his son. "You should go back to bed."

"Casting Lucifer out of heaven created a formidable enemy, right?"

"For the love of God," Peyton said, "listen to your father."

"That's just it, Mother. The devil doesn't have love for God."

Adler plunged into the house.

"I'm profoundly sorry, Father," Peyton said, her fists at her chest. "I don't know what to say."

"I hate when you apologize for me," Gideon called out with a lethargic air, having vaped plenty.

Peyton pressed her temples and waited for Adler to pull their son from the window. "God punishes me."

Gideon said, "Maybe you're not so innocent, after all."

"Mom, why is Gideon's face swollen and bruised up? What really happened here last night?"

"Can I explain it later? I'm too emotional right now."

Bryce vibrated a leg. "Is he why Big Red is sick today? He did something to him, didn't he?"

As his father coaxed him away, Gideon called down, "Big Red is a wimp. One big scaredy-cat, like my sister."

"My child, whatever your brother has done, it hurt your mother the most."

Bryce snapped to her feet. "Other people have a personal God. I have a personal devil. It's unfair. I do nothing to Gideon, yet he's always trying to hurt me." She bolted back inside, leaving her mother with her face in her hands.

Peyton understood exactly how her daughter felt. Her own sister, Lexi, had once antagonized her unjustly. Yet Lexi was mellow compared to Gideon.

"I don't always understand what God is doing," the friar said, "but he can't possibly be punishing you or Bryce. God tests first and explains the lesson later."

"I'm depleted, Father."

"That only means you're a wayfarer, Peyton. Stick to the road of salvation, and you'll get your atonement."

Peyton tensed and raised her hands. "Atonement from what, though?"

"From asking, 'Why me.'"

She straightened up. Was she resentful to that degree? Was she raging against God also?

"Do what's necessary, then graduate to doing what's possible. Eventually, you'll do the impossible."

"I feel the breakers of change crashing over me, and I can't find my balance."

The friar nodded and got to his feet. "God may have children without sin, but none are without suffering." He made the cross over her. "What will you do now?"

When did her life, full of riches, become so impoverished? She thought of Ashton and said, "Go to Texas."

nine

In the heart of the Lone Star State, Peyton entered the pen where Bryce had been since dawn. Careful to conceal her concern, she kept her tone upbeat. "Showjumping has as much show in it as dance. That's why I sent you to ballet lessons for years."

Bryce was too focused on sewing her horse's braids to look at her mother. "That's the part I have down pat. It's the jumping that worries me. We've never jumped higher than four feet, nine inches, but we might have to. If not in this competition, then in the next." She hung a basket of oats to distract Big Red while she stood on a stool beside him plaiting his mane into even knots. She spoke to him, reminding him to watch out for minor faults.

"How did the practice go?" Peyton asked.

"He jumped like a demon, in spite of all the distractions." Bryce moved her stool so she could plait Big Red's forelock. "We're experienced enough, and thanks to Koda, Big Red is healthier than ever."

"His coat gleams and he's nonchalant, considering everything."

"It's the jumping that gets us." Bryce finished her sewing and kissed her horse's forehead. "He's such a good horse, Mom. Thank you for choosing him for me."

Peyton fluttered her eyes, smirking. "I know horses, and I know my girl. A horse is like a man. The fit matters."

She stepped off the stool and gathered her tools. "I bet you'll look spicy once you're done getting ready."

"It'll hurt, but it'll feel good."

At the hotel, Peyton took her time dressing. It unnerved her that being away from Adler no longer felt like a hardship. She was applying makeup with the hand of an artist when someone knocked, and the fox and puppy raced to the door.

A hotel attendant, carrying a large gold box, beamed at her. "Ms. Chase, this just arrived for you. May I put it here, ma'am?"

She grabbed her wallet for a tip. "Thank you very much."

A Lady red – amid the Hill
Her annual secret keeps!
A Lady white, within the Field
In placid Lily sleeps!

She didn't need to read the note to know it was from Ashton. Once he got under her skin, he fused with it. He'd chosen Emily Dickinson's poem—a symbol of their best days together—and timed it in perfect cadence to her needs. Inside the box, she found a red halter ruffle-trim dress by Carolina Herrera. He'd done his homework. It was sexy, the perfect fit, and in Bryce's signature color, ideal for the competition.

Peyton put it on and examined herself in the mirror. She felt young and sleek, vivacious even. And the dress matched her father's ruby and diamond ring. For a moment, she lost all guilt. When Adler called, she ignored it, muted her phone, and headed out with the puppies at her heels.

Royce and Kelcy were waiting under a marquee. Bryce, in white jodhpurs, black boots, and a bright red jacket, called, "Look at you, Mom! You haven't done yourself up like that in forever."

"Gotta look like Harlow's daughter sometime."

"I declare," Royce said. "Barbie is out of the dryer."

Everything in Texas is big, but at equestrian competitions, it's enormous. Music blared, the spectators bantered, drank boots of beer, bought flashy souvenirs, and shot videos. Royce and Kelcy were indulging in a lavish buffet.

"Glad Layli isn't here to nitpick me," Kelcy said, piling his plate with ribs, pulled pork, and cheese-stuffed brioche.

Royce pointed to the raspberry cake. "Not starting with dessert this time?"

He chuckled. "I ate some of that earlier."

"Is it any good?"

"It's pink… Don't you miss your appetite, Royce?"

She sighed, playing with her long burgundy wig. "It's like I don't have taste buds anymore. That's why, at my height, I look like a molted ostrich."

He pushed a platter of cookies her way. "Can't taste cookies either?"

"There's no joy in it for me anymore, but I can have an Old Fashioned anytime. Where's that server?" As she scanned the crowd for help, she spotted Peyton's niece, Lexi's daughter. The older she got, the more she looked like her aunt. "I think I see Margot over there."

Kelcy's eyes fell on the wrong person. "Are you blind? Margot is a ritzy redhead. This one is a dud, sort of butch."

"You're looking at a man, but I'm blind? Maybe if your neck wasn't so thick, it would twist better."

Margot swung her hips their way. She was thirty nine years old, Koda's age, chic and confident with the air of Hollywood in her every gesture. The closer she got, the more she exaggerated her swagger.

"Is it me, or is Margot confusing the field for a runway?" Royce asked.

"What's that, a chiffon train over a leotard?"

"Leave my niece alone," Peyton said, preparing to hug Margot. She hadn't expected her.

"*Ciao*," Margot said, scraping dirt off her heels on the steps leading to the dais under the marquee. "Miss me?"

Kelcy looked her up and down. "Did you forget to add a skirt to that top, young lady?"

Margot giggled as if tipsy. "This is an haute couture dress you're making fun of."

"Haute what?" he asked. "Ought to be outlawed!"

Peyton gave her a tight, warm hug. "I'm thrilled to see you, honey, but how did you know we'd be here?"

"Auntie, you're looking stellar. Texas suits you… and lend me that dress. It's lit!" She kissed Bryce on the cheek, avoiding lipstick smears. "Gideon told me. I thought I'd cheer Bryce on. Besides, I missed Koda." She studied her little cousin. "I used to think I was the prettiest of Harlow's line, but you give me a run for my money, Bryce." She pulled out a chair, sat down, and crossed her long nude legs.

Bryce handed her mother glittering accessories to put in her hair, turned around, and said, "I didn't know you spoke with Gideon so often."

"Hasn't he told you? He visits me. After all, he's my doppelgänger." She looked around. "Where's Koda? I wanted to surprise him. Haven't seen him in weeks."

"Weeks?" Royce asked. "I didn't know you kept in touch that much."

"I didn't know we owed you a report. Why so surprised? Koda and I are friends."

"Just how close?"

"Give me your number, Royce. I'll send you pics."

When they'd first met, Koda had shorn his long hair to please her, but she'd broken his heart. Now Peyton realized they were still involved. "Margot, tone it down."

"But, Auntie, if I did that, what would I be?" She helped herself to a mini sandwich. "There's a surprise for you, but I won't spoil it."

Bryce said, "I would've invited you, Margot, but I didn't think you'd want to come. That's a stunning dress."

"It's a Zuhair Murad. You can borrow it anytime, though it might be a couple of sizes too big. It's my divorce gift to myself, together with the rest of Murad's collection."

Bryce covered her mouth in shock and amusement. "You're so bad."

Margot made her fingers dance in the air. "I'm so good… to myself."

Peyton hurried her daughter away. It was time. "And, honey," she said, "let Big Red push if that's what he wants to do. Sometimes you hold him back with your fear for his safety. He knows his limits better than you ever can."

"That's what Scarborough told me." Bryce took a drawn-out deep breath and went off to the stables with a volley of good wishes at her back.

"I wonder, Margot," Kelcy said. "Did Gideon tell you his mother almost broke her neck trying to save him from himself?"

She pulled a bottle of champagne from an ice bucket. "I know Gideon can be wicked and quite the talented editor, and I know Auntie has allowed him to take advantage of her good nature."

Peyton pulled a chair closer to the pups, making it easier to pet them. "Are you saying I'm gullible?"

Margot poured a glass for herself. "I'm saying you should stop going back and forth with him. He'll pester you forever if you allow it."

Royce focused her eyes over Peyton's shoulder, zeroing in on someone unexpected. "Here comes Koda, but who's that walking ahead of him? Is that—"

"—Auntie's surprise? It is, it is!"

Peyton saw for herself and shot to her feet. Ashton Grant seemed to be materializing through fog. Though heavier than he was in his thirties, he'd maintained his exceptional looks and penetrating presence. He'd lost none of his dark hair, which was styled to perfection, but it was his smile that made Peyton weak in every muscle.

She prepared for a handshake, but he went in for a hug, and embraced her long enough to inhale her, then stepped back and took both of her hands in his. "Peyton Chase, you're always the belle of the ball."

"I wish, but it's kind of you to say." The familiar scent of the Creed cologne he still wore instantly transported her back to their intimate moments together. Notes of patchouli, pineapple, bergamot, and oak moss.

"When did you know me to be kind?" He kissed Royce on the cheek as though she were his mother. "I love you best in red," he said, eyeing her wig.

Then he introduced himself to Kelcy. "Ashton Grant, if you recall, Mr. Loving."

"Don't you kiss me. I'm a Texan, after all… And I'm old, not an imbecile." Kelcy shook hands with him and invited him to sit down. "Jimmy's son, the heir to a massive oil fortune. We met before, at Royce's way back. Did I place you right?"

"With precision."

"Sit and tell me if your dad is better. You're the one running the show now, right?"

"I took the helm this year."

Koda had lifted Margot off her feet. "What are you doing here?"

"I came to cheer Bryce on and to see you, Koda Hoarnhorse." She flashed her left hand free of a wedding ring. "My divorce is final. Missed you, horny horse."

Royce huffed. "Third divorce, is it?"

"You know what they say about the third time."

"Not a charm."

"Whoever said that didn't get charmed out of a fortune," Margot replied.

Royce sipped her whiskey. "Ugh, we don't speak of money, dear. It's garish."

Koda pulled Margot away. "We won't be back."

"I can't believe you haven't visited me in forever, Ashton dear," Royce said.

His smile was part angel, part shark. "Peyton, at least, knows why."

Excitement squalled within her, but trepidation more. "Walk with me?"

"I'll go with you anywhere," Ashton replied.

Kelcy made eyes at Royce, who was already smirking. "Yeah, sure," he said, "leave the helpless geriatrics alone."

"You helpless? Ha!" Peyton said. "It won't work, Kelcy, but I'd appreciate it if you paid the pups some attention." As she strolled away with Ashton, she said, "I thought we were doing coffee, not gorgeous dresses and jumping shows. And thank you, by the way. You always had magical timing." She stared at him, as magnetized as ever. No matter their ages, it was always the same penetrating allure, which was why she hadn't sought him over the years, though she'd thought of him. "I must ask, why now?"

"Why not now?" Ashton stopped and faced her. Kelcy and Royce were watching them more than the competition. "It's been long enough, don't you think?"

"How did you know to send me a Labrador puppy?"

"Wasn't I always very good at giving you what you needed?"

"Yes, just not what I wanted."

"I tried to give you what you wanted but couldn't."

"Wouldn't." She fiddled with her father's ruby ring. "Let's not revisit the past this way."

There was more than charm in his face when he asked, "Which way would you like to revisit it?"

Peyton shook her head. "You were always excellent at reeling me in, but you mustn't now. I'm a married woman."

"Yes, I know all about you." He raised a finger and moved close enough for her to see the copper flecks in his cinnamon eyes. "Am I so scary you wouldn't come to my house? Not even to see *The Last Start?*"

Twenty years before, he'd purchased the painting at auction for two million, two hundred thousand dollars, the only work credited to both Peyton and her equally famous mother. *The Last Start* was the treasure that made her star rise.

"I guess you *are* that scary."

Loudspeakers announced Bryce's name, and she hustled for the best view. "You and Koda are friends now? I'll never forget how annoyed you were with him when you wanted me all to yourself long ago."

"Not friends, but he grew up, didn't he? And I did too."

She cocked her head, staring at his beautiful face. "Ashton Grant, did I just hear you admit you had some growing to do?"

"Come to dinner tonight and find out. I have something important to show you."

She hesitated, her eyes on Bryce, who rode into the arena with the grace of years of training. "Look at that form. Yes!"

"You're not only a mom, but the mother of adults. Where did the time go?"

Peyton raised a fist in the air when Bryce cleared the first obstacle with ease. "When she starts off with this kind of energy, she always wins. Straight back, square shoulders, thighs against the horse, sitting firmly in her saddle, and her hands are in front of Big Red's shoulders. Perfect!"

"I didn't think I'd enjoy watching you be a mother." He placed his hand beside hers on the railing. "I might've been foolishly afraid it would change you and resisted giving you a child when you first asked me to… when it still mattered."

Peyton froze, latching eyes on him. "Parenthood challenged me." She shielded her eyes with a hand and studied Bryce's jumps. "Why didn't you have any children? You never changed your mind?"

He touched her arm, forcing her to look at him. "You must know the answer. Children weren't my thing, but I was willing to have them with you. *Only* you."

The crowd cheered as Bryce cleared yet another obstacle. He waited until Bryce completed her course, smiling and cheering each time she jumped.

"It's a clear round. No jumping faults or penalty points. It's what Bryce needs to boost her confidence for next week's big one."

"She'll win today?"

"With this score, there's only one other competitor who can unseat her. We'll see."

"You're very proud of her, aren't you?"

Peyton watched her daughter wave to the fans on her way out of the arena. "Always. Bryce makes it very easy."

"But you're not proud of Gideon."

He wasn't asking. "You know about Gideon? How much has Margot told you?"

"Not Margot."

"What? Who?"

"Tell you everything at seven?"

"Come, I'll introduce you to Bryce," she said, buying time.

Ashton was full of questions, more aware of her life than she knew. As they walked to the stables, he astonished her with one revelation after another. He'd visited Honovi's gallery in Sedona, spoken to him at length, and bought some of his artworks. And he'd heard some of Ricky's musical compositions.

Bryce was already undoing Big Red's plaits and brushing him down while he ate a bucket of carrots and pumpkin chunks.

"Already tucking him in?" Peyton asked. "Won't you come out and watch the rest of the competition?"

"Not today." She saw that her mother had brought a stranger along and jumped off her stool. "I won't shake your hand, been handling my horse as you can see, but I'm Bryce Adler."

"Ashton Grant, an old friend of your mother."

She looked at her mother with a wide grin and ran careful eyes over him.

"You have some wings, young lady."

She rubbed her horse's back. "He does all the work."

Ashton peered at her fondly. "You have your mother's features, height, and sweetness."

Peyton wondered what her daughter would've looked like had she been Ashton's.

Bryce said, "But not her warrior spirit."

"Sure, you do," Peyton said.

He touched Big Red's back. "It takes courage to launch on a horse as you do."

"Mom is a natural. I work hard at it."

"Then you get more credit." He looked from Peyton to Bryce, his eyes betraying that he knew he'd lost out on something precious.

Peyton didn't want her daughter to compare her equestrian talent with her own. She'd done that with Harlow, never believing she could be the painter her mother had been. "You exceed me in every way, honey."

"Why do I feel winning today won't make you happy?" Ashton asked.

Bryce colored and bit her lower lip, a habit pilfered from her mother. "I don't take winning for granted, but I'm not whole today."

"Certain voids last forever," he said, his eyes bonded to Peyton's, who tucked her chin down, goosebumps overrunning her skin.

"I didn't see all the scores," she said. "We should go peek."

"You go," Bryce said. "I won't bring Big Red back out again. I know it's customary, but I'm zapped."

"It's not a disqualification at this venue, but the press will criticize you for it, label you spoiled. If you're sure..." Peyton hugged her daughter. "See you out there when you're named champion."

"What's eating at her?" Ashton asked as they strolled away.

"Heartbreak, but she'll get over it."

"Some of us never do."

She avoided his gaze and scanned the scoreboard for riders good enough to beat her daughter. "I think Bryce clinched it. Too bad she's not as excited as she ought to be."

"Say yes to dinner tonight. I'll pick you up… For old time's sake, just as friends."

"Just as friends? Okay, see you at seven."

"Keep that dress on." He caressed Apollo under the chin. "I have the perfect place."

"Why did you name him Apollo?"

"Don't you remember the Borghese? You couldn't have forgotten that trip to Italy." He waited until she showed him she hadn't forgotten. "Apollo needs his Daphne."

"Daphne ran away, Ashton, then turned into a tree."

He touched her long, wavy chestnut hair. "Lucky for me, she hasn't leafed out yet."

She wondered if she was undergoing a metamorphosis, after all. But if she was, she'd prefer to do it with Adler.

Peyton settled beside her daughter, who was playing with the pups on the bed. "Don't you want to come out and celebrate your win?"

"I'm content just fooling around with these cuties and turning in early. I'm exhausted to the bone, and you should live a little."

"Ashton should be here any minute."

Bryce sat up, her eyes full of questions.

"Your dad has nothing to fear."

"This is *the* Ashton, right? He's striking and personable."

"Always was."

Bryce's eyes welled. She ran her palm over her slender arm and winced.

"What is it? It's like you're on fire."

"I can't become like Ashton, looking at William with some painful longing forever."

"Ashton has an enviable life. You can see it in how well he's aged."

Bryce buried her face in a pillow. "I know the look. It's how *I* feel. I can't survive decades of it."

"You'll make better choices. Besides, Ashton has led a happy life, despite what you might've read on him today. For starters, he doesn't have your brother for a son."

"I want to skip Pilot Pointe Manor… I can't see William."

She lifted Bryce's chin, wishing she could spare her the pain she had suffered when a future with Ashton turned to ash. "One day at a time, you'll heal and make your own way."

"Why did you choose Dad?"

She fluffed her hair, smiling from places shoved to the bottom of her chest. "Your dad prioritized me, accepted Honovi and Ricky, and wanted to start a family. He was the better choice. The best, in fact, and I loved him to the bone."

"Was?"

"We spend fewer days feeling that way now. I'm not without hope, just disappointed."

"But Ashton didn't prioritize you?"

"Yes, and no." Peyton took a deep breath. "When I met your father, he'd already made all his choices and arranged his life as he needed it to be. It was already structured with room for me. Ashton's life was entangled, and he needed me to be part of its solution, but that never works."

"You don't have any regrets?"

"Your father was lightning to my soul. But over the years, Gideon became the lightning rod of our lives. It's been a long time since I felt that quickening with your father."

"Wow, you just put it perfectly. Gideon sucks all Dad's energy, leaving what for the rest of us?"

"The thunder, but you know what Mark Twain said? 'Thunder is good, thunder is impressive; but it is lightning that does the work.'"

Bryce burst into tears. "How do I shake this sadness?"

Peyton cuddled and rocked her. "By doing the rarest thing. Savor existence, relish it, my darling. Don't just exist, live, and do it one day at a time." She knew she'd merely existed for several years now and resolved to follow her own advice.

"Without William?"

"Ultimately, we all have to learn how to be happy leading solo lives. Life is hard. I won't lie to you."

"And painful and cruel. Makes me feel weak and stupid, as if my entire happiness hinges on William when I know that's not true."

"Not weak, Bryce, but raw. In time, you'll spin your silk into the most beautiful tapestries."

"Like you did?"

She cupped her daughter's cheek. "In you, I have, anyhow."

"You lived alone for years. Were you happy in your solo existence?"

Ashton knocked on the door of their suite.

Peyton grabbed her purse and told her daughter the truth. "I painted a lot, learned to nourish myself, and made good friends. I led a meaningful, creative life, but I was also living with guilt and pain from my childhood and a breakup with Ashton. Happiness isn't the right goal. A meaningful life is."

ten

Peyton and Ashton were seated in a private corner at the restaurant, surrounded by a Himalayan salt wall illuminated with candles.

"Leave it to you to choose seafood in Texas," she said.

Ashton closed his leather-bound menu and eyed the ruby and diamond ring Peyton wore. "Cioppino for two, and a 1992 Wiltingen Riesling like the old days?"

Peyton remembered all the times they'd shared cioppino bowls at the seaside. "Do you still go to Mendocino?"

"No, and California without Mendocino is missing something. That's how my life has been without you."

"I'm sure there's hardly a corner you haven't visited or a delight you haven't sampled. I won't feel sorry for you."

"It's all in the seasoning, Peyton. What's steak without salt?"

"I'm salt to you?"

A server arrived with a large bottle of Perrier and a cedar platter towering with warm bread and truffle butter.

"You're salt, spice, sugar, every ingredient. The entire menu, I'd say."

Peyton sipped sparkling mineral water. "How do you know so much about me, if not from Margot? I know it's not from Royce, she'd tell me."

"How do you think I learned about Honovi?"

"Koda?"

"Guess again."

The server returned with their drinks and a tray of oysters. Ashton watched her squirt lemon juice on one, add a dot of cocktail sauce to it, and hand it to him. "That's the perfect oyster."

"It's how you like them."

"You remember?"

"I may be inclined to forgive, but I don't forget much."

They raised their wine glasses. "So, I'm forgiven?"

"You don't need forgiveness." She dressed another oyster for him. "Who has been enlightening you about me?"

He loosened the plump oyster with a cocktail fork and ate it. "Three months ago, I invited Margot to dinner in Santa Monica. She brought along a young man who introduced himself as Sorensen Chase Adler. I knew right away, of course."

Peyton shifted in her seat, taken aback. "Wait, he used the name Chase?"

"Yes, I'm not surprised Chase is his middle name, but Margot called him Gideon."

Peyton was lanced. She had focused so hard on seeking her son's approval, she'd missed realizing how desperately he sought hers. He withheld what he didn't receive, yet believed he deserved.

"Gideon explained everything to me. He's not shy, rarely subtle, though witty, downright hilarious."

"Gideon is funny?"

"Sarcastic and quick. Don't you agree?"

She leaned forward and lowered her voice. "What did my son share?"

"He's proud that the Chases are a founding family in New Mexico. I don't think the same goes for your husband."

"My children's father is a phenomenal man who passed down special gifts."

"I'm sure," Ashton said. "Gideon said it's from his father he gets his love for risk taking."

"Whereas Gideon means gambling at casinos, Adler would frame it differently. He's like you in that way. You both stalk, calculate, and strike only when a favorable outcome is almost guaranteed."

"Gideon might also be like that."

"So you're the guy with a butler and a private jet who's been fascinating my son?"

He chuckled. "An assistant, not a butler. Gideon loves luxury, like someone else, you know."

Ashton's aversion to children had made her fear he'd be an inadequate father, yet her son idolized him. "What impression did my son give you of himself?"

He wrinkled his brow. "Are you asking me because you trust me to tell the truth or because you don't think he did?"

"Both."

"He wants to be viewed as a prince with a perfect life. You want to know why I knew he was a difficult child for you. It's stuff he said in jest. For instance, twice he referred to himself as Peyton's baby, in reference to *Rosemary's Baby*. He spoke of activities with his father, but when speaking of success and wealth, he referred to you. He insinuated the family fell short of your expectations. Stuff like that."

"That's downright embarrassing." Peyton tucked her chin in her chest, tired of the river of pain with one too many stepping stones. "Gideon can be difficult, but he's loved, and he has a devoted father."

"He doesn't act as if he's unloved, just not adored. I think getting attention and adulation is more important to him, but that's not your style. That's cheap to you. You love and love some more and never stop."

The server brought their oversized bowls of cioppino, which gave Peyton a chance to collect her nerves. "So did you then bump into me by accident at Geraint's?"

"Gideon told me you were in town. I bribed Geraint to tell me when you were going to see him. I'd been wanting to see you again since Sedona."

Peyton patted her lips with her serviette. "Sedona?"

"In March, you were at Mariposa in Sedona." He waited until she figured out what he meant. "And so was I."

She brought a manicured hand to her mouth. "Was it you who sent the bourbon and the *boca de muerto* dessert to Honovi and me? The server only said it was from an admirer."

"Of yours, not Honovi's. But he's so popular up there, I knew you'd interpret it that way."

"Then why do it?"

"Because you love a Grand Marnier torte. Watching you enjoy it brought me happiness."

"And? There's more."

"It was a dessert I often ordered for you. I was hoping it would resurrect me in your mind."

Peyton sat back. "You were never buried."

He looked down, smiling less. "Didn't you miss me now and then, Peyton? Not even a little?"

"You wouldn't ask if you weren't sure I did. And a lot. Is that why you invited Margot out?"

"I wanted insight into your life," he said. "I followed your career over the years but couldn't tell where your personal life stood."

"And I followed yours," Peyton said. "Is that how you discovered Honovi?"

"Just about anyone in Sedona could've told me about Honovi. But when I was at his gallery, I recognized the landscapes of Abiquiú in his paintings and some of you. Not to mention the indirect tidbits Gideon shared. Putting two and two together, I figured he was one of the brothers you adopted."

"My oldest probably figured out something about you. Honovi is a seer."

"I don't believe in hocus pocus."

She knew his position on soothsayers. "What do you believe in?"

"Redemption." He leaned closer and stretched his hand her way. "Do you ever ask what if?"

She sat back and crossed her legs. "Life is harder with what ifs."

"Though you're unhappy now?" He raised a finger. "Don't deny it. I know you too well."

Peyton smiled, knowing he saw through her. "Happiness ebbs and flows, and yes, it's ebbing now. What about you?"

"Quite the opposite. After all, you're here, and I have something to show you."

She leaned forward and placed her elbows on the table. "You said as much."

"Had I given you what you wanted, I might've given myself what was most valuable. But I'm aiming for a pivot." Ashton brought something up on his phone and handed it to her. "I hope late is better than never."

She read the court documents. "You filed for divorce? You're kidding."

"I did it the day after we strolled outside Geraint's gallery. I wasted too much life away from you. I'm not going to keep doing that."

She squeezed his hand. "Ashton, I'm married."

"If I'd gotten divorced like you wanted, would you, for one minute, have entertained another man?"

Peyton would never have met Adler, though she was happy she had. "Not in a million years."

"I love how honest you always are. What a rare quality." He clasped her fingers, reminding her of how little excitement or romance she had in her life.

An alternative life dangled before her. "I can't believe you're getting divorced. Don't you have hundreds of millions tangled up in your marriage?"

"More like a few billion, mostly in shared businesses, but Dad is no longer in charge. I am. And I'm using my new power to change the future."

"Billions?"

"I should've done it those many years ago. You were always worth it." He reached for her other hand, and she gave it to him. "You're my greatest regret."

Her eyes glistened. "Ashton…"

He knew when to advance, when to retreat, and when to shift sideways. Maybe that's why he was massively successful in business. "Where to next?"

"Dallas, for Bryce's last competition, then to Lake Tahoe, to visit some new acquaintances."

"Who?"

"You wouldn't know them."

"It's a small community. I bet you I know them."

"The Elliotts."

"Ah, Mason and Rebecca," he said. "When?"

Peyton smirked. "I'm not telling you, partly because I don't know when."

"And the other part?"

She pressed up. "That's the part you get to take back to the hotel."

"Even after the court papers I showed you?" he asked.

"Because of them."

If he grinned any wider, he'd split the skin on the corners of his mouth. "My hotel or yours?"

"You never could behave, could you?"

"Not around you, anyhow."

Peyton thanked him for a serene evening as he drove her back. "The dress is gorgeous, and Apollo is a touching gift. I don't know what kept me from getting another Labrador all these years."

"The same thing that kept you from seeing *The Last Start*… or me."

Too much love. But should love be the lock or the doorway?

He escorted her inside the massive lobby. "I know you'll be busy tomorrow, packing up Big Red and shepherding a fragile daughter, but let me see you before you leave."

"No, Ashton." Peyton clasped his hand one last time. "I can't thank you enough for this evening. I needed it, but you're quicksand to my slow-moving feet, and I'm married."

"Am I to take your rejection as a compliment?"

"You should, especially after all these years, and it's not a rejection. It's a boundary. You know… that thing you don't get."

He cupped her hand and fiddled with Sorensen's ring. "What's the story with this ring? It's clearly a man's, too big for your finger."

She removed it and handed it to him. "It was Dad's. Jewelry was his favorite flamboyant indulgence."

Ashton slipped it on his left ring finger. "Regal."

When he tried to slip it off, she said, "No, leave it on. It suits you so well."

"But it was your father's."

"He'd rather it went to someone who appreciates it, and I want it to go to someone meaningful."

He stared at her. "Do you still own those two portraits you did of me?"

"I told you I'd keep them."

He inched closer. "What else of me do you still have?"

"Only what you left behind."

Ashton dropped his smile. "That would mean all of me."

The intensity of his stare shot currents through her. That handful of words elated her. She realized how denied she'd been, and that it had been partly her own fault.

He kissed her hand. "You can ask me anything, tell me anything except to leave again."

He was dangerous to her life. "Ashton…"

"I need to see you again."

She needed the same. "Better not."

"You have my number. Use it."

A familiar pang drilled into her chest. "I won't."

He shook a finger. "Don't make me send you more puppies."

She giggled, but when he lifted her inner wrist to his lips and kissed it, she agonized. "I missed you so much, but I'm going home." She turned and walked to the elevator feeling his eyes follow her and knew he'd swallowed her up, as he had so many years before.

Peyton hadn't begun to undress when Adler called. She brought him up on her tablet and saw his face, but didn't activate her camera.

He was in bed, a book on the nightstand. "I've been thinking of you."

"Do you do that often?"

"What's that meow I hear in your voice?"

She unleashed a coquettish giggle, high on a night of flirtation and selective recollection. "It's a week till Bryce's last competition, but I'd love it if you joined me sooner."

"Miss me that much?"

She removed her earrings and fell quiet, giving him time to mull over her proposal.

"Gideon is in a slump and shouldn't be left alone. And I don't feel like being in the city for a week."

What she heard was a week with her was too long. "We can run off to South Padre Island alone. Go parasailing and deep-sea fishing."

"Gideon's arm is still in a sling. He needs help. Besides, it would mean leaving Bryce alone before her last competition."

She bit her lower lip and sat on the edge of the bed. "She needs to see her parents get along more than she needs company, but okay."

At the change in her voice, he jostled. "I'll come down a couple of days beforehand."

One man had told her she was the entire menu, the other threw her crumbs and called them a banquet. "I don't want Gideon alone at the ranch. He loves California. Put him on a plane," she said, knowing he wouldn't. She glanced at her reflection in the mirror across from the bed and saw someone who constantly slipped back.

"Peyton…"

His pause was enough. "That's all right. Stay up there and stick to the original plan. I'll see you next week."

"I didn't upset you, did I?"

A message from Ashton flashed on her phone, thanking her for the evening and reminding her to call him soon. She pressed the ridge of her nose and exhaled. "I'm tired. It's been a long day."

"You mean the world to me," he said.

His compliment felt like an insult. "You've developed this habit of deferring everything until tomorrow. It's called taking me for granted."

"It's only temporary until Gideon pulls it together. We'll do something. But will you accept my video call? I miss your face."

She prepared a smile she didn't feel and activated her camera.

He took a long look at her and sat up. "Were you on a runway somewhere?"

She removed the rest of her jewelry and piled the pieces on her lap. "I haven't changed yet."

"So, you wore that dress to the competition?"

"Yes, and it was a great one. You should've seen Bryce fly."

Adler had been a navy SEAL, had owned his own IT security business, and hunted with stealth and precision. "Figured out who sent you that puppy yet?"

"I know it wasn't you." She looked down, kicked off her stilettos, and unzipped the side of her dress. "I'll turn in myself now."

"Will you wear that dress for me when I get down there?"

"Why? I don't need a sexy dress to argue with you about Gideon."

He pursed his lips and cracked his knuckles. "We have more ground to cover than I think, eh?"

"I've explained how things are, but it might be easier to explain what they're *not*."

"Life?"

"Our marriage."

"We could always fix anything."

"Like we fixed Gideon? It's time we stopped claiming everything is rectifiable."

Like a waterwheel, the days spun, repeating but not advancing. On the day before Bryce's last competition in Dallas, Peyton was sitting on a bench, sketching her daughter as she exercised the pups with a frisbee. The tip of Myriad's tail was inking darker, and Apollo was running faster. Ashton had sent her an email asking when she'd be in Lake Tahoe. He'd attached pictures he'd taken from Freel Peak with spectacular views, well clear of the tree lines. She searched for an angle to see Ashton without culpability but settled on prudence. Bryce bounded her way, which convinced her that she couldn't see him. Period.

"How do you feel about tomorrow?"

Bryce yanked a magazine from her bag. "I wish Dad wouldn't wait till the last minute to come down. It's bad enough he skipped my last competition."

Peyton took a deep breath. "Did he tell you he's bringing Gideon with him?"

Bryce held up the magazine, about to wallop someone with it. "But why? I'm stressed out as it is." She flipped to a page and pointed out a photograph of herself. "Look at this horrible picture of me. I'm criticized for being reserved. This stupid reporter wrote that I'm cold and overprivileged because I wasn't giddy enough for him. They never accuse male riders of not smiling enough."

Peyton gripped her daughter's shoulder and sighed. "I thought we didn't read negative reviews."

"I didn't realize I was in it. Anyway, I'm on edge and if I don't stop, it'll transfer to Big Red." The pups hovered around Bryce, doing their bit to soothe her. "What do I do, Mom?"

"Eat a decent meal today… take a swim… get a massage. Anything to let go." Peyton took the magazine from her daughter and tossed it in the trash. "Release and acceptance are the hardest things in life. I still struggle with them. But the sooner you learn them, the stronger you'll become."

Bryce squatted and caressed both pets, reminding her mother of when she was a toddler.

"Come, my swift one, who'll always jump high." They took their respective furballs and strolled back to the lobby. "It's all right, you know, to tell your dad you're disappointed he didn't come down sooner."

"I just want Gideon to stay away from me and my horse, and I fault Dad for bringing him here. Does he want me to lose?"

"Your dad loves you more than life itself, but he feels the need to supervise your brother, so he brings him along." She checked her watch. "They should be here any minute now."

Peyton was gazing out the window, wearing skintight jeans and a fringed cami when Adler let himself in.

"You're a sight and a half." He dropped his bag and went to her. "I thought maybe you'd meet us downstairs, but you don't seem happy to see me."

She hugged him and squeezed. "I'm not happy you brought Gideon, but I want you here, and I'm always happy to see you."

He sighed and plopped into a plush chair. "He asked to join us. I couldn't refuse him."

"But what about what we need?"

Adler was still a distinctive-looking man with a fit physique, silver hair, straight nose, and gilded eyes. "I didn't want to leave him alone at the ranch, and I couldn't tell him he's not welcome to be with us."

"He never apologized to Bryce, never admitted to any wrongdoing. How has he earned this trip?"

"What is it you want from me?"

In an airy space, Peyton felt suffocated. "Why can't you say no to him when you say that so easily to Bryce and me?"

"It's never easy." He rubbed his eyes and forehead. "When I turn you down, you don't disintegrate. He does."

She sat next to him and put a hand on his lean thigh. "You're saying because we won't harm the family, we get less of you and from you as well."

"Peyton, I've only just arrived. And Gideon is not always belligerent."

She bit her lip and poured two glasses of wine. "Keep him away from Bryce and her horse, okay?"

He glued a hand to her naked shoulder and rubbed it. There was desire in it. "We've already had that conversation. He understands."

"He was never short on understanding, Adler. It's his behavior he can't control."

He kept his hand in place, but relaxed his fingers. "I was hoping for a passionate reunion. I miss holding my wife against my skin." He turned her squarely toward him and penned her to his body. "You're my world."

She couldn't reconcile his words with his actions. "Do something with Bryce today. She's been fighting too many disappointments and needs you to put her first."

He took her face in his hands. "And do you need the same?"

Her tears surfaced, more from frustration than sadness. "I'm not that to you now."

He squeezed her face harder. "How can you say that to me? You're my universe!"

She shook her face free. "Not at all how you make me feel, but you used to."

"I'm giving you what you want, aren't I?"

"Because you're here now?"

"In part, yes."

She stood up and stepped back far enough to keep him from touching her. "So you're here for me, not for Bryce's last competition?"

"I am, but I'm also mindful of you." He stretched his spine and reached for her. "Let me hold and kiss my wife properly."

"I wish you'd stop building this wall between us." Peyton came closer and kissed his heart. "I love Gideon, but he's likely to make tomorrow about him, instead of about Bryce. He ruined her celebration lunch. He mustn't be allowed to rob her of a champion's exit."

"He won't."

"How do you know?"

"He promised."

"Does this mean you bribed him?"

Adler ran his palms over her nude arms and kissed her neck. "I miss how you used to look at me."

He had a way of subtle probing she found fascinating. "Which look is that?"

"The look that said I was beautiful to you."

"You *are* beautiful to me, but bringing Gideon here isn't beautiful."

He kissed her with open lips. "Let's close all the blinds, get in bed, and stay here all afternoon."

"Staying in bed is easy. Coming with me for a few days alone or tagging along with Bryce is harder. Aren't we worth your effort any longer, Adler?"

"Of course you are! It's unfair to even ask such questions."

"Then take Bryce out. Just the two of you. Play pool, go on a run, something. If she uses training as an excuse to avoid you, push through it. She needs you."

"I need her, too, and I will. But when I get back, will you let me make it up to you?"

"We'll see."

The Navy SEAL in him gave her a stare she knew all too well. "Not good enough."

"Right back at you, Captain."

"That's it, Mrs. Adler." He clutched her to his body, lifted her off her feet, and kissed her hard. "I think you need me to push through your resistance just as much."

"I deserve extra effort," she said, giggling. "Especially when you insist on calling me 'Mrs. Adler,' though my name is legally still 'Chase.'"

The longer he locked lips with her, the harder it was to stay mad at him. Something about the scent of his skin always revved her loins. Adler unzipped her top, ran his hands under it, and pushed her back on the bed. As he laid his weight on top of her, she felt lighter, primal, and ageless.

eleven

The bells hadn't sounded yet, but early announcements on loudspeakers throughout the stadium were hounding spectators. On that sweltering day, Bryce stood next to Big Red before a fan, misting him, while Peyton and Scarborough massaged his pressure points.

"Is he relaxed enough, Scarborough?" Bryce asked.

"Are you, jumping bean?"

"Not really."

"Right. Stop focusing on winning, and just go out there and have fun." He removed his hat and smoothed his white hair. "If I were you, I'd make my last competition my most memorable by trusting Big Red to be himself."

As she patted her horse, she was the mirror of raw nerves. "Do you know why I called him Big Red?"

"Ain't he big and red?"

Peyton simpered, loving Scarborough's directness.

"It's just a lucky coincidence. I wanted to do it with as much passion as possible and leap with greater impulsion." Bryce exhaled hard and bit her upper lip. "I can't find that passion anymore."

"What you call passion, I call guts." He fanned himself with his hat. "Can you fuel up on that?"

Peyton knew that, in Bryce's mind, stables were the best cathedrals, holy places. "You haven't told me why you're retiring."

"Everyone thinks I'm retiring because of college, but that's not it." She sipped cold water, then pressed the bottle to her neck. "I just don't want to be confined to a ring anymore."

"Do you know why I never married?" Scarborough asked. "I never wanted to be confined to a ring, either." He donned his hat and ran a hand over the length of Big Red's back. "You just ride into the sunset, kid. Circles ain't for true riders."

Bryce's eyes misted, sadness underscoring her voice. "Hasn't it been lonely riding alone like that?"

He smiled and played with his ten-gallon hat. "We all ride alone, sooner or later. If we're lucky, we meet up with someone special at the watering holes."

Bryce asked, "Would that next watering hole be Lake Tahoe?"

He tipped his hat, laughing. "You're your mother so much, it's uncanny." He turned Big Red around and stared into his face. "He's real ready, and you know how to move with him."

Peyton asked, "Are you still leaving after the competition?"

He punched a fist in the air. "I know Bryce has already won, but I'll watch every jump before hitting the road. I'll get myself ready for Lake Tahoe, ma'am."

"Enjoy the drive back in your beautiful '44 yellow Fargo truck," Peyton said. "I already confirmed with Rebecca for both of us." She turned to her daughter and said, "I'll go refill the oat buckets."

The first bell peeled. Bryce would soon have to enter the arena. She adjusted her stock tie in the mirror, and square breathed the way her father had taught her long ago.

William arrived, catching Bryce by surprise. Peyton heard her say his name and anchored in place.

"I thought you'd have changed your mind," Bryce said.

Peyton spied through a slot in the wood slabs and could see her daughter on the verge of tears.

"Why would I?" William moved closer, but Bryce shifted back. "Aren't you going to let me hug you?"

"If I touch you, I'll burn," she said.

He stared at her with red ears, clenching his jaw. "I had to see you on your big day."

Bryce's chin trembled as she cast her eyes to the hay-covered floor. "Thank you."

"I know you'll win." William stroked Big Red, bringing his hand into the light.

Peyton noticed the new ring on his left hand and covered her mouth.

Bryce looked as if she'd swallowed ash. "Are you engaged?"

"Sort of." He swept his hair out of his chocolate eyes with a sheepish smile. "Carina asked me."

Bryce expanded her eyes into gold coins. "Ah, you're running your last race as well… Congratulations, William." She gave him her back and returned to spraying down her horse.

"Bryce, look at me."

She didn't. "Please, go."

He put a hand on her back. "Not like this. Come on. I'm your William."

She dialed around, tears streaming down her face. "That's a lie, but I'll be fine."

"I only wanted to cheer you on."

"Okay, thank you. Go." Bryce faced away and waited until she was alone, then bent over, sobbing, ruining her makeup.

Peyton ran back as the second set of bells tolled. "Come on, honey, or you'll be disqualified. Find your strength and straighten your spine."

Bryce removed the platinum and sapphire bracelet that hadn't left her wrist in four years and handed it to her mother. "I can't stand this bracelet anymore." She buried her face in Big Red's neck. "Hold me up, and I'll never let you down." Though her tears dripped, she secured her helmet, slipped on her jacket, walked her horse out of the stables, and mounted him. "I'm so done with jumping. I need a different life."

"I'll be there every step of the way." Old and new pains converged within Peyton, but twin rivers were stronger together. "Now do what a Chase does, like Grandpa Sorensen would say. If you can't walk, what do you do?"

"Fly!" Bryce said and trotted to the arena.

Peyton couldn't bear to return to her seat. She watched from the sidelines as Bryce, guided by instinct and practice, went through the motions.

She seemed impervious to cheers from her family and friends and didn't respond to the fans throwing flowers in her path. She whistled for Big Red to start the course, allowing him to do what he was born to do. They made one jump after the other, but Bryce was late to register that they'd jumped five feet one inch, setting a new personal record. Someone in the stands shouted that she was now near impossible to beat. She lowered her helmet over her brow, acknowledged the crowds just enough to earn her exit, and guided her horse back to the stables as her mother pressed after her.

Peyton watched Bryce dismount, remove her helmet, and flop to her knees, sobbing. Before she could catch up to her, William appeared. He slid beside Bryce and picked her up, hoisting her onto his lap.

Peyton stood back, giving them space.

"I'm sorry, Bryce, so sorry. I can't bear to see you like this."

Bryce rolled off him. "I can't bear *you* to see me this way, either." She smiled, though she cried. "Go and be happy. You deserve that."

He looked at her as if happiness were a foreign concept. "I think you won today."

"William, I've never lost this much in my life." She got to her feet and took Big Red by the reins without bothering to dust off her white jodhpurs.

"He's a bona fide prize horse now," he said. "He proved his mettle, like you." When she turned away, he said, "Don't go."

She gave him her profile. "I haven't. You have." She dabbed at her eyes with her wrist. "I mean it when I say no regrets." She led her horse to the stables, not once looking back at him.

William plastered his vision on Bryce, unaware that Peyton was standing beside him. He jumped when she spoke. On another day, it would've been funny.

"I'm a terrible man." He dusted his jeans but was on the verge of tears.

"It's time I reminded you of something you might've forgotten. Do you remember when Bryce would sit up in her crib crying at night?" His befuddled eyes told her to continue. "You were visiting us when I was training her to self-soothe and go back to sleep by herself."

"What am I supposed to remember?"

"For a few nights, I'd hear her cry, but she'd soon quiet down. I thought I was succeeding in training her until I caught you sitting in a rocking chair with Bryce in your arms. You heard her cry, too, and took it upon yourself to rock her back to sleep." She touched his handsome face. "You tried to take her tears away back then, also, but she's not a baby anymore."

He swept his hair out of his eyes and sucked in his cheeks. "I see that."

"You're allowed to make your own choices and love whomever you want. But I hope you figure out what Bryce means to you. Keep away if Carina is the one. You're giving each other pain now. I love you both too much to stand by and say nothing."

He leaned into her for a hug only a mother could give. "Pioneer Ranch is my home."

She gave him a tender embrace. "Of course, and it always will be, but perhaps Bryce isn't. Let a few months go by. Allow her pain to deaden."

"And what if Bryce *is* home to me?"

"Then, you'll know. Distance destroys weak relationships, but it bolsters strong ones, as strange as that may seem."

"Why aren't you mad at me?"

"There's nothing to fault you for, honey. Bryce loves you beyond the bonds of friendship and family, but that doesn't mean you have to change your path in life. In time, she'll feel differently."

"I just want to go after her."

"Because you don't clearly understand your motives yet, I advise you not to."

He tucked his shirt in his pants and dusted them one more time. "Grandpa called me an idiot when I told him I got engaged. Am I making a mistake?"

She raised his hand closer to his face, forcing him to look at his engagement ring. "Honey, only you know. Nothing reveals better than time."

"You don't like the ring?"

"Is it platinum and sapphire?"

He gave her a hangdog chuckle. "It matches my bracelet pat."

Peyton kissed him on the cheek like she used to when he was small enough to climb on her lap. "The ring should match the bride."

He stared at the ground and played with his bracelet. "Is that what I did?"

"Until you know for sure what's in your heart, stay the course."

He nodded and thanked her for being there for him. "I plan to meet the architect coming for Koda's clinic. I have questions of my own for him."

"Come up like always. The ranch is your home too. Besides, Bryce won't be there."

"Why not?" he asked in alarm.

She could see how conflicted he was and patted his arm. "She wants to spend the summer in Sedona before continuing to Berkeley. It's her way of avoiding Gideon. The ranch is all yours."

"Will I see you, at least?"

"Of course. I'll be back in Abiquiú after Lake Tahoe and Sedona. I have my own requests for the architect."

"That's a relief." He relaxed his shoulders. "And Bryce?"

"She's only beginning to discover the depth of her strength. She'll be all right."

"What about you?"

"I always think of something." She gripped his chin, though he was too old for it. "Put on a brave face and don't let the others know how upset Bryce is."

"I can do that."

She pictured little William clutching her leg and resting his cheek on her thigh. Now he towered over her. "You deserve the best."

"After all this, I won't come with you to dinner tonight. Is that okay?"

"I figured." She hugged him, realizing the children were old enough to spread far, making her an empty nester. How depressing. "I may be Bryce's mom, but I'll always be here for you." She waited until he disappeared around the bend before heading to the stables.

Peyton was helping free Big Red from his tack and pack away his things. "Is there anything other than dinner you want to do this evening?"

"I don't feel like food," Bryce replied.

"You were flawless out there today. I've never seen you ride with so much abandon."

Bryce chuckled, but there was pain and anger in it. "It's ironic how I perform best when I'm not there. The entire obstacle course was a blur."

"Not what it looked like. It was quite an accomplishment. You did it your way."

Bryce scrolled through her phone, then handed it to her mother. "I can't be idle all summer. I want to register for Hatha yoga teacher training in Sedona while I'm up there. Maybe I can get a job teaching yoga while I'm at Berkeley."

Peyton examined the website. "It's a great idea, though it seems intensive."

"I don't want to be in Honovi's hair all the time, and I can use a rigorous spiritual immersion." She sobbed and blew her nose on a rag. "Something has got to help me stop wanting to rip my heart out of my chest."

Peyton hugged and rocked her. "Okay, I'll transfer the tuition money to your account."

"You'll come up to Sedona and visit me, won't you?"

"Already booked a hotel. I'm coming to Honovi's festival. Your dad will definitely come, I'm sure."

Bryce stomped her foot, making Big Red shift. "I don't want him to come if he's bringing Gideon again!" Her face contorted and her neck strained. "I bumped into my horrible brother at breakfast this morning. He wished me good luck by telling me to break my neck."

"I have no words."

Bryce undid her clips and chignon, then fluffed her hair. "What if I dyed my hair a vibrant red?"

She knew her daughter needed an outer change to thwart the inner stagnation. "Tell you what… we'll book a double appointment. You'll go red, and I'll go beach blonde. What do you think?"

"You've had chestnut hair forever."

"Time for a change. Blonde would suit my complexion, don't you think?"

"Let's make an appointment right now."

While Peyton scheduled a hair appointment at her favorite salon in Santa Fe, Bryce applied lip gloss, ready to look the part when she was called out to accept her prize. "There's a popular saloon here. Can we go there instead of dinner? I want to dance, not sit at a table."

"It's your night. Whatever you want." Peyton thought of what she wanted. It was lofty and not within her control. But she'd been here before. The fruit may have hung high, but she rode a tall horse.

twelve

The saloon was a hole in the wall with wood panels and leather, smelling of liquor-soaked stools.

"Is this the place where you can check out, but never leave?" Royce asked, once inside the shabby saloon.

"Shush…" Kelcy pointed with his cane to a horse's butt taxidermy mounted above the bar. "They have whiskey by the bucket here for just about any jackass." He chuckled. "They'll yank that tail if they think you're full of horseshit."

Royce said, "You better leave now then, Kelcy, or that tail is coming off tonight."

Adler opened a tab for food and drinks and ordered a round of bourbon shots and beers. "The problem is you never get drunk, Royce. If you did, this bar would look like the Ritz."

She shook her head, smirking. "Lordy, with so many jackasses, it already is the Ritz."

Bryce commandeered the dance floor, in denim shorts, a cow-printed bustier, studded boots, and a teardrop cowgirl hat with upturned sides.

"Karaoke!" Peyton clapped her hands, headed to the DJ, and put her name on the list. It had been a while since she sang.

While Koda dove into the menu, Margot joined her aunt. Though in the heart of Texas, she was dressed like a Hollywood star, braless, in a micro black dress and six-inch heels.

"I've been watching you for a while now, Auntie. That old spark you had only comes out around Ashton." She shook her long fiery red hair and flashed a deviant smile. "I'm trying to solve your problem here."

"I have a problem?"

"I've been divorced three times, so that makes me an expert. You need a different life now. It's about time. Your problems are multiplying like rabbits."

"Honey, I know you're cutting to the chase, but big reasons break up marriages. Gideon will be too busy with work after his graduation. Perhaps we won't have such big problems after that."

Margot did a twirl, her arms outspread, though country music wasn't her genre. "Big reasons have their origins in a succession of smaller choices. They're like corn kernels put to heat, eventually they blow up and overflow the pot into the divorce lawyer's office. Ask this practiced plaintiff."

"Wow… not at all what I thought I'd be discussing tonight."

"Auntie, the flame of marriage goes out gradually, then suddenly." She danced some more and gestured for Koda to bring her a drink. "Ashton only entertains me when he has a bunch of questions about you." She touched the tip of Peyton's nose. "Adler never asks me a thing."

Peyton's anxiety strummed louder than the music. "Maybe Adler has nothing to ask. We live together."

Margot kissed her on the cheek. "Okurrr… here's the thing… because he lives with you, he should ask more questions, not less. But what do I know? None of my marriages lasted longer than three years." She danced toward Koda, who carried four shots and lime slices.

To the romantic song "Your Man," Peyton downed a shot of bourbon and followed it with a sip of beer, her eyes on her husband.

"Dance with me, Mrs. Adler." He led her to the dance floor, keeping her flush to his body. "How long before you leave for Lake Tahoe?"

"End of this week, same day Bryce leaves for Sedona." She smiled, though her next question was heavy. "Why don't we go out much anymore, or ride like we used to? What's stopping us?"

"You sleep facing away from me more often than you used to. When you're gone, you don't call me much. When I'm gone, you don't leave tender little notes in my stuff or spray your perfume on the collar of my jacket. The small affections that made the big hurts tolerable are gone."

"The energy for such little nothings requires everything," she said, not sure he'd understand.

He pulled her closer, crossing his arms tightly around her. "You don't miss me anymore."

It wasn't the pure truth. She missed parts of him, aspects of their life together now pitched to the back. "I don't miss fighting, and I prefer when you're with me, not camping away or staying behind."

Fear, which she rarely saw in him, peeked out. "So long as Gideon is elsewhere?"

She was aggravated by the direction Adler was taking the conversation but maintained her warmth. "You're thinking if I can send my flesh and blood away, I could do the same thing to my husband." His body felt heavier now that she'd laid that hulking thought on his shoulders. "I don't want to stop seeing or loving my son, but I prefer to interact with him on his territory where he feels more secure and less threatened, lashes out less. But can we just talk about us?"

"Yes, Mrs. Adler, we can," he said, twirling her on the dance floor.

She looked into his eyes and stopped dancing. "Before Gideon there was you, and after Gideon there'll be you. We're bigger than parenthood."

He cuddled and kissed her, but it wasn't consoling. "I really needed this."

"Sure you won't come with me to Lake Tahoe?"

"I promised Gideon a hunting trip with his buddies, but you can postpone your trip for a while and be at home with me."

"There are other places to experience, Adler, and I'm getting older by the second." The song was over, and with it, her patience. She joined the others at a rustic table with a bucket of peanuts at its center and shells all over the floor. "Time to celebrate Bryce!"

Toasts in Bryce's honor were abundant, but her smile was gaunt, her gaze fixed on the empty seat that was meant for William.

"Winning keeps us going when losing makes us stop," Peyton said, "but a crown is worth stopping for." She raised her cocktail aloft. "To Bryce's big win today."

"Da'ohdlą́!" said Koda, raising his glass above his head.

"Da'ohdlą́!"

Margot climbed on her stool, making Koda so nervous, he stood up and gripped her slender legs.

"Why're you acting like a showgirl?" Royce asked.

"Because she can pull it off," Gideon replied, joining them. He reached for the drinks tray and quaffed a shot of tequila. "Hey, Royce, ever considered a half-white, half-black wig?"

She shot him a challenging look. "Fancy a skinning? I can always use another coat."

He scratched his nose with his middle finger, then sent Margot flying kisses. "Glad you came, cuz. It's no party without you."

"Or you." Margot leapt off the stool, counting on Koda to catch her. She searched her purse for a blue box wrapped with a white ribbon. "Bryce, I have something special for you. They go perfectly with what you're wearing right now."

Bryce held up the white gold and blue diamond earrings for all to see. "These are showy and dazzling. Thank you, Margot."

"You're a woman now and need to dazzle and razzle."

Gideon rolled his eyes. "Women who dazzle don't get overlooked, do they? I mean… that Carina, wow!"

"Gideon, never underestimate Harlow's daughters." Margot turned to Bryce and said, "I don't have your courage. I never would've attempted anything as daring as showjumping. Perhaps that's why I kept myself on a treadmill. Go and break all the horses you can."

Adler asked the server for another round of drinks. "We don't break horses. We nurture them."

Gideon glued his eyes to the server's derrière. "Yeah, I'm sure horses think bits shoved in their mouths are very nurturing."

"Don't be rude to your father," Peyton said. "He's your top ally."

Gideon banged on the table, spilling his drink. "Why is any challenging question immediately labeled rude?"

Bryce slid off her stool. "Can I have one decent evening with my family without you ruining it, just one?"

"Now be honest, sis. I'm not the one who's ruining your day with *your* family. Mr. Perfect did when he reminded you, yet again, you're not worth his time."

Adler gritted his teeth. "Gideon, apologize to your sister."

"You know, Dad, I don't want Gideon to apologize to me." Bryce gawked at her father, her lower lip trembling. "I want you to stop forcing this illusion of a happy family. I don't love him just because he's my brother, and he sure would love to see me break my neck."

"Cheers to that." Gideon chugged his beer, then pushed back from the table. "All your love goes to William, but who's he giving his love to? Not you!"

Adler snapped to his feet. "When will you learn that love multiplies and hate divides?"

"Blah, blah, blah… Dad, you're sounding like an old man."

Margot said, "Gideon, you really mustn't be worse than me."

Adler glared at his son but touched his daughter's arm. "Bryce, I'm sorry I can't seem to find a balance. I'll figure it out."

She gritted her teeth and her eyes welled. "I'm fed up. I thought you'd protect me better! Why don't you?"

Peyton felt torn from limb to limb. "I'm so sorry, honey. You're right." She got off her stool and hugged her daughter. "But I swear to God, we will."

"You've been safe and sound since we arrived. Haven't you, Bryce?" Adler replied, lancing his wife with dagger eyes.

With another argument on the way, Peyton swilled a shot.

"We're all family," Kelcy said. "And now fries are here, I feel even closer to you. Let's eat."

"Play pool, Dad?" Gideon swilled another shot and snuck a slasher smile at his mother as his father prepared to join him.

Peyton knew her son was showing her who won, but said nothing.

Margot drained her cocktail and asked for another. "Bryce, the best way to get over a man is to get under another sizzling one."

Kelcy almost choked on his fries. "Don't say that to her, dammit!"

"It's true. Ask Royce."

Royce flitted her false eyelashes and tapped her long, polished nails together. "A woman gets over a man by getting over herself."

"Auntie, thank you for the do-si-do, chawbacon experience, but time for real fun." She stood up and extended her hand to Koda. "Let's show Bryce a thrilling time."

Peyton gave her niece big eyes. "Not under or over anyone, okay?"

Margot started toward the exit, pulling Bryce by the hand. "We'll keep it rated PG 17… not!"

Kelcy brought the plate of fried cheese closer. "Little lady, you raised that doll quite right. It pains me how much she's hurting. What's my grandson thinking?"

"It's not William's fault he's lovable."

Royce dropped a shot of bourbon into her beer and watched it foam up. "Kelcy and I are wondering if Adler isn't making a point about Gideon you might be missing."

"Like what?" Peyton asked.

"Maybe he's afraid if he sends his son away, it would be as if he's giving you permission to send *him* away."

Kelcy added, "We think Adler is afraid one unraveling would lead to another. Instead, he does the opposite and keeps Gideon glued at the hip because he wants you with him always."

Royce smacked her lips. "I think she got it just fine with the way *I* said it."

"You're woman-splaining, Ms. Wig!"

"Why on earth would Adler think I'd walk away from him? I love him."

Royce gestured big. "I don't know what could worry him. A daughter who wants to be gone before leaving for college, a son who minds no one, and a wife unable to smile from within, who looks her best when she's not around him. I mean, what's he got to worry about?"

Kelcy said, "And a wife with ambitious plans that don't need his help."

Royce stabbed a finger at him. "You're doing it again. I explained it just fine the first time."

"That's because you keep stopping short like a terrible driver."

Peyton wavered between laughing and crying. "He turns me down when I ask him to come along." She removed her black cowgirl hat and ran her fingers through her hair. "Is this all you two do, dissect Adler and me?"

"And Bryce and William, and Koda and Margot," Royce said. "We'd be bored otherwise."

Kelcy smothered a laugh. "Little lady, we may be a couple of bozos, Statler and Waldorf, but we have an advantageous view from our balcony."

Royce made a disgusted face. "We're Muppets now? Pray tell, which one am I, Statler or Waldorf?"

"Royce, you're getting distracted. We're here to enlighten Peyton, and I could've called you Miss Piggy, but I didn't."

Peyton cracked up, if only to keep from feeling overwhelmed. "I used to know what interested Adler. Not anymore."

"Don't just throw in the towel like Royce."

"What, me? I'll deal with you later." She made a choking gesture and turned to Peyton. "Darling, you're angry with your husband. It makes it harder to reassure him." She carved a wicked grin. "You could also just go to SoCal for a month… or a year."

"Really, Royce?" Kelcy piled his hands on his cane. "Peyton darlin', I know you're exhausted, but you have to push harder than ever."

"Have to?" Peyton asked in a glum voice. "Adler wasn't the one who sent me Apollo."

"We know!"

"What don't you two know?"

"What to get for dessert." Kelcy probed his pocket for a cigar. "Do they have carrot cake?"

Royce hunched forward, her chin creasing in folds. "Does your stomach have a bottom?"

"Does your meddling?"

Adler returned with a tired face. "I put Gideon in a taxi, but he'll probably take it to some bar."

Peyton asked, "Whatever happened to his promise to you?" Kelcy gave a fake ahem, but she ignored him. "What did you say to him after that performance?"

Adler hooked a foot on a stool's bottom slat. "I shrunk the maximum he can charge per month on his credit card, which could make him retaliate worse."

Royce rolled her eyes. "I can't believe he has access to any credit at all."

Kelcy said, "My son, Charles, is now in charge of everything. When he first got out of college, I gave him a sizeable sum and told him if he doubled it in three years, I'd match that, but if he didn't he'd have to work for someone else and wreck their business, not mine."

"We only helped Edward get a suitable position," Royce said. "He made a success of it on his own," Royce said. "Don't be afraid to toss Gideon into the deep end of the pool."

"He's tall enough," Kelcy said under his breath, flicked his gold lighter, and lit a cigar. "Who's up for shots and darts?"

"There's no smoking here, Monopoly Man."

He pressed himself up, using the table and his cane for support. "You can catch way worse than secondhand smoke in this joint. Come on, Adler, join me."

Adler leaned into his wife and spoke in a low, lacerating tone. "Thank you for never showing a united front with Bryce."

"Adler! That's really unfair."

"I love her too," he said and followed Kelcy.

Peyton pursed her lips and looked at Royce. "We're constantly angry with each other."

"Darling, can you be this unhappy forever and do nothing about it? Adler knows you'll find a way out, even if it's through him. You're still young enough. No reason not to seek a different situation."

"I'm committed."

"Yes, until you're not."

"You stayed married all those years."

Royce chuckled. "Because I was committed to affairs as well, not just to my husband. I had fun, found other ways to be happy. You don't, and you're working very hard for very little."

"It's not little, Royce. I have a whole, full life."

Royce hooked her wizened eyes to Peyton's. "Deduct Bryce, now she's going away to college. What do you have left, a husband who loves to hunt and fish away from you?"

Anxiety clawed at Peyton's liver. "A whole life."

"But not a full one."

Peyton had no answer, except to look forward to small things. When did small things become the only big there was? But there was one exemption, and now he wore her father's ring.

thirteen

Peyton stood on a paddleboard, awestruck by the crystal water. Though she'd visited the lake before, she never lost her wonder for it. Tahoe, the largest alpine lake in North America, a massive vortex, soothes the nerves, heals the spirit, and wings dreams.

Rebecca paddled next to her. "Ashton made me promise I'd tell him the exact day and time you were due to arrive, under pain of death."

The breeze was refreshing under the relentless sun, and news of Ashton was enlivening. "Ashton has always been prone to exaggeration."

"I don't think he exaggerates how much he needs to see you."

"It's really not what you think." Peyton longed to listen to the lulling of her paddle slicing into pristine water, but her hostess preferred to chat. "I can't tell you how enjoyable it is to step right off your own causeway onto a paddleboard. This is such a treat. Thank you for suggesting it."

"Why don't you own a house here?" Rebecca asked. "Ashton does."

"It never occurred to me. I have a house in Carmel-by-the-Sea for stunning beaches and sunsets, and a condo in Orange County, which our son lives in. I prefer the sea to a lake, but I'm open to change and Lake Tahoe has a unique feeling."

"Thank you for bringing Scarborough. Few people understand an open marriage, but you don't judge, do you?"

"My sins are many… Ask Father Gabriel. Besides, Scarborough is ecstatic to be here."

"How do you do it, Peyton, the same man year after year?"

"It's in my nature, as simple as that. Not to mention Adler gets me, senses my deepest feelings and thoughts. He might mull over them for too long, but it doesn't change the fact that he comprehends."

Rebecca sighed. "Never had that. I explain but get little validation." They came to a moored boat, paddled around it, and angled for the shore. "I invited Ashton to dinner. He made me."

To speak of him was enchanting, but to hear that he wanted her was mesmerizing. "Once, a long time ago, Ashton felt like all my vital organs combined."

"And now?"

"Now I'm married to someone else."

Rebecca said, "Mason is like an appendix, yet I want him around. Is Ashton really just in your past?"

Peyton stuck out her tongue and sprayed her with the paddle. "It's all I'm telling you, Rebecca Elliott."

She adjusted her bikini, then tapped her paddle on the water's surface, playfully spraying Peyton back. "Scarborough just loves you. You're his family, through and through."

Peyton pressed her sunglasses higher on the ridge of her nose. "He was never what you call a fair-weather friend, quite the opposite—the best of family. I can't imagine Pioneer Ranch without him. It was a shock when he left the upper cabin on the property. We were happy for him, but it was an adjustment."

Rebecca stretched her back, raising one arm up in the air. "I don't have love affairs, just sex affairs, but because Scarborough has been down in New Mexico or in Texas, we've spent a lot of time video calling. With sex put on hold, it feels like love."

"Is that bad?"

"It's more complicated this way. I prefer simple and untangled."

"Ah, like Scarborough. He's an old cowboy, rustic living and attitude, nothing like polished, sophisticated Mason."

"And that's his charm. He's refreshing, and he turns me into someone earthy, more beached, not so adrift."

Peyton conjured images of him polishing his classic yellow truck and riding his vintage Indian motorcycle without a helmet. "He is constant."

"I asked him to stay a while longer," Rebecca said. "But he won't stay where Mason lives, he said."

"And?"

"He didn't answer me beyond that. Don't know."

Peyton hid her suspicions of Scarborough's tight-fisted nature, and he wasn't the type to allow a lover to pay for his stay. "How do you remain close to Mason when you're with someone else?"

"It's like asking how you enjoy your appetizer when you also ordered an entrée. My answer is I order dessert too. Mason and I function best by expecting less from each other, but more *for* each other."

She hadn't heard an open marriage explained that way before. She thought of Adler's reaction, should she have an affair. He'd never forgive her. "I'll attend to your Mary Cassatt tomorrow. I brought my restoration kit. From the videos you sent me, it's a minor job."

Rebecca swirled her hand like a princess. "Bill me anything you want."

"Don't be silly, Rebecca. It's my gift to you."

"That's beyond generous. You must charge me something."

Peyton secured her paddle and raised a hand to keep her from arguing further. "What time is dinner?"

"Eight, so you don't miss the sunset."

"I'll bring something nice."

Rebecca gave her a crafty smile. "I'll bring Ashton."

The pink evening sky rolled in, filled with Western tanagers, hot-air balloons, and tourists feasting on panoramic views of Lake Tahoe and the snowcapped Sierra Nevada Mountains. Peyton's fuchsia mermaid dress had a bare top with crossed spaghetti straps. She accessorized it with confidence and excitement. As she drove through Incline Village with Scarborough in the passenger seat, they cut to Shoreline Circle, tracing the edge of the lake to Rebecca's chic three-storied modern mountain house. They trundled between coniferous trees, interrupted by turquoise water, pale sky, and Bavarian architecture.

Scarborough asked, "Why do you reckon Rebecca lives in such a grand house when she ain't got a brood?"

"Maybe it's compensation, and maybe because the Masons can afford the best."

He tapped his hat on his thigh. "I asked her if she gets lonely in that palace of hers."

"Many rooms insulate from loneliness as much as one could."

He chuckled, ruminating. "Sort of what she said."

"She likes you."

"I'm too old not to know these affairs die young."

Peyton rolled up her window and scanned her phone for a security code that would open the gate. "Let's just have a great time."

He shook his head as she parked the rental car in Rebecca's semicircular driveway. "Funny how people from opposite sides of the gully can be alike."

"I've been to four continents," Peyton said, "and I've found people are the same everywhere. Some shop discount, some don't. Some eat spicy foods, some don't. It's a Western movie out there with friend and foe about everywhere."

"Rebecca tried to give me a watch by some fancy brand… err… Gussy or something like that. I couldn't let her."

Peyton snuffed a laugh. "Do you mean Gucci?"

"I mean, expensive and nothing my wrist would ever get used to."

"Okay, but maybe you should let her gift you. You make her happy. Her way of showing it is to give you something nice."

He prepared to open the car door. "Ma'am, she gives me more than a cowboy can carry in anything but his heart."

"It's what we all say about *you.*"

He smiled and nodded. "Ma'am."

"You've got to call me Peyton."

"I will."

When Rebecca opened the door, Ashton was standing behind her. He shook hands with Scarborough, while his cinnamon eyes devoured Peyton.

"I hope you're starving," Rebecca said. "I ordered a feast."

Peyton handed her the Asti Spumante, lobster salad, and smoked garlic sourdough bread she'd brought.

"Sacher torte also? It's too much, Peyton."

"The torte is from Scarborough, actually."

"It's been my favorite, ever since I had it at the Sacher Hotel in Vienna." Rebecca stole Scarborough away and left them with drinks.

Ashton grinned like a kid with a secret. "You're blonde!" He hugged her and ran his hands over her back.

She could feel how much he wanted to kiss her. "I have something for you." She squeezed his hand, noticing he still wore her father's ring. "You must stop showering me with presents."

"I hardly did that, and don't you know me? I love giving you beautiful things."

She held up a gift bag, currents of longing and excitement electrifying her. "I got *you* something."

"But you never have to." He invaded her personal space. "Your company is gift enough."

Peyton strolled to the upper deck facing the vibrant lake.

Stirred and giddy, the man who had everything followed her with his gift. "This is a Hasselblad 500C. A genuine classic film camera."

She faced him, her arms twined behind her, the lake at her back. "I hope all your other cameras are digital."

"They are. It hadn't occurred to me to get a classic camera with real film, but I should have, considering how much I love vintage photos."

"I'll never forget how enraptured you were at the American Museum of Natural History in Manhattan."

"I was enraptured by much more than the museum." He stared at her as if he had never seen her before. "Still am. You're stunning as a blonde. It brings out the green in your eyes and the gold in your skin."

Being made to feel beautiful was more important than whether she was or not. "Do you know why I'm here?"

He plastered a hand to his chest, chuckling. "To see me, of course."

"Walk with me." Peyton led him to the sitting room where she'd seen three of her mother's paintings earlier that day. She pointed to *The Girls* with its gilded light and detailed textiles. "I remember Mom painting this one. It was a stage in her life when detailing beadwork and designs on baskets and blankets had become essential. She'd painstakingly use magnifiers and extra-fine handmade Japanese horsehair brushes. It took her a long time to finish this one. I have a picture of us with *The Girls* in the background, when it was still unfinished. I can't wait to feature them side-by-side—the painting and the photograph—at the museum I hope to start."

He stood close enough to touch his elbow to hers. "You're here to buy them back? Clever, clever Peyton."

"Why does that make me clever?"

He took her shoulders and turned her to face him. "My mind is drifting to *The Last Start* at my house in Malibu. You're giving your mom her new last start. You must realize that."

"No, but you're dead right." If she'd thought him gorgeous a minute before, she thought him perfect now.

"Museum you said, where?"

"My idea isn't fully formed, but a combination of museum and gallery on Pioneer Ranch, for the three generations."

He stroked his chin. "How many have you located?"

"Five, besides these three, so not much."

"Ah, you need a professional to help locate the rest."

"I can't ask that of you, Ashton."

"I'm volunteering, and I'll bet many of them belong to my acquaintances. You'll be needing introductions." He chuckled with inner satisfaction. "I know everyone."

Peyton raised her eyebrows. "Leave it to you to have befriended every member of the hundred-million-dollar club."

"It's what I really do for our business, Peyton. I'm the face of the company. And since we found new reservoirs in the Delaware Basin, the biggest accounts seek me out."

"I know. I read about your role with the Permian Basin and the huge oil extraction there."

He inserted his hands in his pockets, regal and meticulous in his appearance. "I just remodeled my house. Come tomorrow and give me your opinion. I'll text you the address."

Ashton knew style as intimately as doves know white. "I'll have to bring Scarborough."

"What are you, five? Need a chaperon?"

"I'm pragmatic and prudent."

"Nothing will happen that you don't want to happen."

She nudged him. "I know, silly."

He huffed and went inside to grab the drinks they'd left on the bar. "When did you become uptight?"

"You love blurring all boundaries," she said. "I don't."

He added a maraschino cherry to her cosmopolitan before handing it to her. "Who's taking care of you?"

"Many do."

He shook his head and stared. "No one is. Whatever goes on in your life, *you* think it. *You* plan it. *You* execute it. And I doubt you get applauded for it."

She sipped her cocktail and turned away, concealing how much she agreed with him. "That's the curse of the independent and strong, but I'm loved and valued."

"And nurturing like no one else."

She spun around in time to see regret baked into his expression.

"Did you bring Apollo with you?"

"He's getting spoiled as we speak at the dog lounge back at the hotel. Scarborough doesn't approve."

"Bring him with you tomorrow. We'll take him out for his first sailing experience."

"Let me guess. A sloop, a fifty-footer, with exceptionally tall sails."

He placed a hand on her neck. "You always knew me well."

She retreated, keyed-up. "Ashton, I don't want to play with fire."

"I'm inviting you to play with water. Don't be childish."

"I don't want to hurt you, and you sure can hurt me."

He took her drink, put down his own, and pressed her hands. "Don't fear me, please. I just want us to spend time together. That's all."

"Okay, I'll go sailing, but not till the afternoon when I finish working on Rebecca's Cassatt. And this time, you're teaching me how to sail like a pro."

He etched his heart. "This time you get everything you want, exactly as you want it."

Silence sat between them like down feathers, cushioning the moment, as she re-grouped. What did she really want? And at what price?

Rebecca and Scarborough returned with a tray of hot hors d'oeuvres, intruding on silence.

"I hear history rhymes," Rebecca said, which made Scarborough fidget. "What did I say? It's true."

Scarborough picked a pastry pocket filled with shrimp. "So long as it doesn't rhyme with hitch." He popped the warm pastry in his mouth. "This tastes like something Ms. Chase makes."

Peyton sniggered. "You say that about everything except barbeque or a ham sandwich."

"If it ain't like Grandma made it, it's like Ms. Chase makes it."

Ashton said, "Mason told me he'll be in Thailand till mid-August. Does that mean you're here by yourself for a few more weeks, Rebecca?"

She winked at Scarborough. "I hope not alone. It's a huge house."

From Scarborough's awkward stance, Peyton knew otherwise. She watched the sun ooze gold over the lake, staining the horizon cherry. She thought of how she increasingly spent nights alone. There was a time when sunsets and sunrises were her time alone with Adler. But so much had changed. "I could paint this exact sky."

Ashton moved toward her, his eyes on the chair beside hers, but Scarborough beat him to it.

Rebecca asked, "Are you sure seven is not too early for tomorrow?"

Peyton replied, "Mary Cassatt deserves losing sleep over."

"I don't know how to thank you."

"You can sell me Harlow's paintings."

Rebecca laughed, then her eyes turned intense. "You're serious, aren't you?"

Ashton walked over and nudged her. "Sell her at least two for a museum she wants to start for her mother."

Peyton said, "I'll give credit to you and Mason in the dedication plaque."

"Sell them?"

"I'll replace them with impeccable replicas."

Rebecca took a seat. "Even if I agree, Mason might not."

"Come off it," Ashton said. "Mason does whatever you want him to."

"A museum, you say?"

"Yes, for Harlow and Honovi too."

"I adore Honovi."

Ashton ambled to the bar. "You know that glass house you wanted, Rebecca, the one you couldn't get a building permit for?"

"What about it?"

"I can get it for you if you sell the paintings to Peyton at a fair price."

"Well, I like those paintings, but that glass house is a dream of mine."

Ashton mixed a batch of cosmopolitans. "And any replicas Peyton provides should be part of that fair pricing, not above and beyond it."

"I'll talk to Mason." Rebecca held out her glass for a refill. "But why didn't you offer to help before?"

"Political currency is valuable," Ashton said, "but Peyton is priceless."

Lost for what to say, Peyton massaged the faint scar on her left palm. "Thank you both."

"Want to negotiate peace between Palestine and Israel next?" Rebecca asked.

"Then we have a deal?"

"I'll have to talk to Mason, but yes." She finished her drink and invited them to the dining room. "Scarborough and I will open a couple of bottles. Join us when you're ready."

In a patient, hushed tone, Ashton said, "You're a terrible negotiator. You offer too much, too fast."

"That was remarkable."

He touched her cheek with the back of his fingers. "Remarkable is being with you after all these years and feeling as if time hasn't passed at all."

She felt the quagmire that lay ahead, but decided sailing would be one way not to think about it.

Peyton picked up her puppy and called Adler as she headed to her room. When he didn't answer, she took it as a sign and made another call.

"What are you bored in Lake Tahoe or something?" Layli asked, working her sewing machine.

"Isn't everyone who comes up here to the end of the rainbow?"

"Uh-oh, you've got that voice going on."

Peyton could hear her snipping fabric. "What voice?"

"The save-me-from-myself voice. What's the matter?"

"Two words—Ashton Grant."

"I need to stretch my legs for this one, so let me move to the sofa," Layli said. "Two words, you say? Hell, that's an entire library."

"Isn't Adler home?"

"Can't tell you. I've been up at my cabin all day. But let's go back to Ashton. He's with you?"

"Not *with* me, but up here." Peyton bit her lower lip. "He's taking me sailing tomorrow."

"And you feel guilty about that?"

Apollo rose on his hind paws and tucked his head under Peyton's chin. "I feel weak, tempted to forget all my obligations for just five minutes."

"Do you know why you called me of all people, Flower Child? Because if I could be with BearClaw, I'd drop everything for him."

She took deep breaths and ran her fingers over her lips.

"Mark a line in the sand and don't cross it."

"We're going to be on water."

"Cut it out. There's nothing wrong with going sailing with whomever you want."

"Then why does it feel wrong, Layli? Not going makes me feel cheated, but going makes me feel like a cheat."

"That's a ridiculous declaration, if I ever heard one. Have fun and stop blowing this up."

She lay on the bed cuddling the puppy. "Ashton is helping me buy back Mom's paintings. He's ten times busier than Adler, yet he's making time for me. I find his efforts magnetizing."

"He clearly wants you. The question is, what do *you* want?"

"Oh God, Layli, how am I this weak?"

"You're not weak. You're hurt and neglected. My advice is to enjoy yourself but remain disciplined, and from the looks of things, Ashton isn't going anywhere, though some of us scatter seed to the wind."

"Won't that waste it?"

Layli yawned. "It might, or it may just grow new plants, Flower Child."

"Lots to think about, but I'll let you go to bed."

"I adore Adler, and hope you can figure things out with him," Layli said. "But it's better to regret what you've done than what you never dared to try."

fourteen

Peyton was standing at the embankment of her September years, but adrenaline crashed over what's dry and quiet as she walked along the dock with Apollo. Ashton was waiting on a handcrafted vessel with tall sails, waving. As she picked up her pace, nostalgia crisscrossed with enthusiasm into a new pattern of life.

Holding her puppy in one arm and her bag in the other, she sprung toward her target in the afternoon sun, feeling as young as ever. "I stopped to get a life vest for Apollo and chocolate chip cookies for you."

He took her bag from her. "Dogs can swim, you know." He gave her a side squeeze as they moved toward the boat and a hand as she boarded. "Good—rubber soles. The first time I took you sailing, you slipped and slid in leather sandals."

"Live and learn." She gave him an approving look. They were both wearing athletic shorts and tank tops. "Your tan says you're sailing daily."

"I have tan lines, all right. Want to see?"

"Ashton, you're incorrigible."

"I'm a Grant, darling."

Her eyes roamed about the boat's inlaid wood and hand-stitched marine leather. "I was wrong. It's a much bigger vessel than I thought."

"Again, I'm a Grant, darling." He uncoiled the rope from the cleat and released the sleek sloop into waters the color of Curaçao liquor. "Ready to tack?"

"Aye, aye Captain! What's my first lesson?"

"Mine was learning how to capsize my boat."

Peyton loved the sound of the boat slicing through the water. "For real?"

"Yeah, it was small, like me at ten. There was a significant possibility of facing overpowering waves. I had to learn how to capsize my boat and recover it."

Peyton wished she'd learned how to recover her capsizing marriage. The dog wiggled in her arms, itching to wander and explore. She put him down but kept him on a leash. "I didn't know you'd learned to sail at such a young age."

"People like us don't just grow up. We grow out into the latitude and altitude of this world. But you don't need me to tell you that."

She remembered how he used to categorize people. "Us, as in the wealthy?"

"I'm not as chesty as I used to be." He squinted at her. "Us, as in the educated and daring, but affluence helps."

Ashton tacked the headers upwind, sailing faster. "Come sit by me and feel the powerful tug on this tiller."

Apollo bounced and wagged his tail fast, enjoying the wind tousling his fur. He yipped and tried to eat the spindrift, which made them laugh.

Peyton cozied up beside Ashton, aware it was more than enough and gripped the tiller. The muscular resistance that made a boat obey its sailor opened her eyes. She blamed her husband for restricting her ability to navigate her life as freely as she once had. For the first time, she realized the extent of her resentment. But it wasn't all his fault. Some of it was hers, for waiting too long to express the depth of her unhappiness.

"What are you thinking?" He was close enough to make her blush, spellbound by the strong breeze and sunshine.

"I want you to help me bring the museum to life."

He brought his face to within inches of hers. "What if other people don't like it?"

"I'm fed up with what other people like and don't like." She glowed with determination.

"Hold that attitude. I'll be right back." He left her to steer the boat into the wind while he retrieved the vintage camera she'd given him. He aimed the lens at her, capturing candid shots as she laughed and swayed under his watchful gaze. "You look happy, Peyton."

"I *am* happy." She spread one arm and lifted her chin to the sky. "I feel free, young, and fast."

He kept adjusting the lens and photographing her. "It's possible to race faster than the wind, but you'll have to keep on your mark."

She took his layered meaning. "And my mark is?"

He lowered the camera. "You tell me, Peyton."

"Did you sail for weeks and weeks like you used to dream of doing?"

"Yes, after you got married."

"Oh…" She rubbed her lips together and gazed at his expressive face. "What did it teach you?"

As he reflected, bobbing with the waves, the horizon claimed his vision. "That we complicate everything. We're not as important as we think we are, but we can achieve more than we believe we can, and we're never as alone as we imagine."

Peyton watched him relax into his water world.

"It's ironic, but simple. Sailing taught me to be still, but not to confuse motion with progress."

"When did you become a philosopher?"

He leaned in as if he were about to kiss her. "You didn't ask me about the gift I have for you."

"Everything you do, Ashton, is a gift of sorts."

He touched the sails, assessing their resistance to the wind. "Would you consider a sailing trip to Hawaii on a two-hundred-footer, fully manned?"

"What, just the two of us?"

"And a full crew, and a chef, not quite alone."

"How could I?"

"I'm only asking if you'd consider it."

Every pulse in her body said she would. "I can't, Ashton."

He took her hand and slipped his fingers between hers. "Think about it."

Peyton squeezed back. "Do you remember what you told me when you first took me out sailing?"

"I don't know. Don't drown?"

She threw her head back and raised her feet off the deck. "You told me to be conscious and respectful of the boom, especially during a tack or a jibe, to avoid getting knocked overboard."

"Makes sense."

She sighed. "I don't want to get knocked overboard by it now, so to speak, or let that happen to you."

"Okay." His body language showed her he'd just begun. "Can you sing at least?" He disappeared below before returning with a Lowden guitar. "Sing 'Leather and Lace.'"

It was a song about belonging with someone from day one—a test. The last time he'd requested it, she'd refused.

What he told her made her heart ache. "When we met at my polo match those many years ago, we sparked so fast, if I hadn't already been married, I would've asked you to marry me only a few days later."

Peyton picked up the guitar and tested the strings. "I would've said 'yes' in a heartbeat." The guitar was tuned to perfect acoustics. "'Leather and Lace' is about a man who walks into a woman's house and never leaves." Adler had done that, and she hoped he'd stay forever.

"Hmm… Is that the mistake I made? I should've walked into yours?"

Peyton struck the first cord, singing with more tenderness than power. The longer she sang, locking eyes with him, the deeper he smiled.

"Now sing *Queen's* 'Love of My Life.'"

"Bribe me."

He ran a hand over her neck and bare shoulder. She closed her eyes to more than reality, to blind herself to a future without the exquisite power of such a touch.

"Coffee and cookies?" he asked, snapping her back.

Peyton topped his hand with hers. "Coffee at sunset, while sailing? What can be more glorious?"

"What's better, you ask? Coffee at sunrise, sailing to Hawaii."

Peyton shook her head, tittering. "A Grant, through and through."

The day before they were due to return home, Peyton and Scarborough were sitting in a manicured courtyard. "The hotel and car have been paid in full for two more weeks," she said, removing his only obstacle to staying.

"Are you sure? It's mighty generous of you, and I'd be lying if I didn't express how much I'd appreciate more time with Rebecca, but your wagon is buckling as is. I don't want to add to your load."

"You? Never, and it's not that kind of load."

He pushed his hat back, past his hairline and huffed.

"Spit it out, cowboy."

"It's none of my business, ma'am, but since we won't see each other for a stretch, I have something to get off my chest."

Peyton softened her look and waited.

"That fella, he ain't all bad, but when he was made, God forgot to put the quit in him. I admire such grit, but I reckon Mr. Grant will keep charging till something is gutted right."

"You're worried for me and Adler?"

"They say don't feed the bear."

"The only starving creature here is me, and maybe that's my fault. I'm worried about us, too, but we can still repair things." Peyton wasn't sure if her words were based on truth or habit.

"Everything has its limits and forgive me, but I'm seeing you reach yours."

There was enough truth in his words to make her stare at her shoes. "Adler is meeting me in Sedona. It's always been lucky for us."

He nodded, though his expression lacked optimism. "You take good care of yourself now, you hear?"

"Be happy," she mumbled, and was about to leave when Tansy called.

Scarborough saw Tansy's name flash on her phone. "What in the tarnation…"

Peyton put her on speaker. "Is everything all right over there, Tansy?"

She was sobbing. "I'm quitting, Ms. Chase. I respect you too much not to tell you, but I can't take it anymore!"

Peyton found the closest bench and plunked herself on it. "What did Gideon do?"

"He's not even half my age, but he called me names and dumped food over my head because he didn't like it. I'm only crying because I didn't deck him one, which I should've done, but I won't take abuse from him anymore."

Peyton closed her eyes and steadied her voice. "I understand why you want to quit, but please don't. I'll be back in a week. Take a paid vacation in my absence and relax. I'll include a bonus for your troubles. And I'll handle Gideon."

Calmer, but sniffling, Tansy replied, "You mean the world to me, but no one is handling Gideon."

She wanted to rage and break everything in sight, curse, kick and condemn, but she pulled it together. "You won't ever have to be at the ranch with him again. You have my word on that, and I'll make it up to you. A thousand apologies, Tansy." Her voice shook, and she dug her nails into her palm. "I'll handle things differently this time, not only for your sake. Was Adler at home when this happened?"

"No, he's burying his horse as we speak. I left without cleaning up anything. Sorry about that."

"You have nothing to apologize for, but did you say Lightning died?"

"Yes, and Mr. Adler insisted on burying his horse himself."

She had more questions, but Tansy was upset enough. "I'm very sorry this happened to you. My son is… my son is…"

"It's all right. I'll be back in a week."

"Okay, Tansy, thank you for calling me. Sorry again."

Peyton looked up at Scarborough with sorrow in her bones and pressed her temples.

He doffed his hat and stepped back. "Can I get you anything, ma'am?"

"Yeah, a different son." As she dashed away, she called Adler, but he didn't answer. Her blood boiled at the thought of Gideon's behavior toward a woman who had been cleaning up after him all his life. Especially since she thought Adler should've sent him back to L.A. She dialed Gideon, but again, no answer. About to explode, she drove to Ashton's house.

Peyton came to a stop, and the gates swung open for her.

Ashton pierced through the front doors and rushed down the wide Röcka steps, meeting her in the driveway. He could see she'd been crying and opened his arms before reaching her. "What's the matter?" He helped her out of her car and huddled her in an embrace, then guided her into a bright blue and white room with a tall ceiling. "You just sit. I'll get you some water." He returned with a box of tissues, a chilled bottle of Voss water, and a glass. "The kitchen is mixing drinks for us. Take your time and breathe."

The housekeeper discreetly left cosmopolitans on the coffee table.

Peyton said, "I called my son to tell him to get out of my house this instant, but he didn't answer. I'm sick and tired of feeling helpless in ways foreign to me." She canvassed her face with her palms. "It's come to this. Oh my God! It's down to chasing my flesh and blood out of the house he grew up in."

He squeezed her bare knee. "I won't ask what he's done, but it's best you didn't find him under the circumstances."

"He's ruining what makes the ranch a home for us." She galvanized her strength and scoured her brain for a solution. "Can you get him a job in nuclear engineering? Remember, my son is pompous."

Ashton rubbed her leg, contemplating. "I'll get him out for you, but it'll take a couple of days."

"How?" She blew her nose and mopped her eyes.

He handed her a cosmopolitan and waited until she took a good gulp. "I know a private contractor for the Air Force in L.A. He'll make Gideon an offer he can't refuse, and he'll never know why he's getting it or how."

"You'll do that?"

"Peyton, what wouldn't I do for you?"

She sobbed again and reached for more tissues. It wasn't the first time he helped her in life-changing ways. "Sorry, I'm such a mess."

"Never apologize for giving meaning to my relationship with you. This is a cheap solution for an expensive problem."

"What if he fails?"

"My guess is he'll succeed, but it doesn't matter either way. I'll set it up through a recruiter—appeal to Gideon's ego." He grinned. "I know how a young narcissist feels and thinks. He has one more semester left, so I'll make sure that they work around his classes."

"I feel bad, asking you for help when I have nothing to give you in return."

He shook his finger and cradled her face, which he hadn't done in forever. "It's okay to need me. I need you, and I'm not afraid to admit it."

The sunny living room overlooked the lake's crystal-clear waters, but Peyton's spirit was extinguished and her outlook grim.

"I'm not putting pressure on you. Just stating a fact."

"I know, and I should go." She moved her eyes to the entrancing horizon where boats sliced through the water and walked toward the view. One of her paintings was hanging on the wall to her left, a beach scene with dancers around a bonfire. She looked back at Ashton, holding her breath, then saw another of her paintings, cowgirls repairing fences, laughing, wind sweeping through their hair. "How many do you have?"

"Let me show you the house." He led her from room to room, watching her expression. Every room had at least one of her paintings. They were among her largest, full of her signature emotive faces and bodies in motion. "I never seem to get over the light in your paintings."

"You filled your house with my paintings!"

"I filled them with *you*." He wiped her relentless tears, then took her by the hand as they went upstairs. "My favorite is above my bed."

They stood beside a king-sized bed in a vast room overlooking the lake. The tableau, titled *Modern-day Lady Godiva,* depicted a nude woman with wavy chestnut hair, riding a black stallion bareback, her arms splayed, enraptured and free.

"I thought it might be the portrait I had done of you."

"This is a self-portrait, isn't it?" he asked. "Geraint denied that because you didn't want it sold as such. But I knew better."

She had no words.

"You should see my house in Malibu. I had to have you at all the places I call home, so yeah." He stared at her with deep love and longing, took her face in his hands and kissed her until she began to cry, then he lifted her and placed her on the bed like a bouquet. She attempted to rise, but he pressed her down. "I just want to hold you, Peyton."

She craved his embrace, yearned for the solace Adler used to represent.

He drew her close, planting gentle kisses on her face. Guilt tugged at her, urging her to leave, but the intoxicating notes of musk, patchouli, and bergamot in his cologne held her captive. She clung to him and balled his shirt.

He pulled tissues from a silver box and handed them to her. "You can also just keep using my shirt if you prefer."

She giggled, kissed the side of his neck, and lingered on his lips.

"We were once happy together, weren't we?" he asked.

"Ecstatic, until everything turned excruciating."

"None of those obstacles exist now."

Peyton thought of her children, of Adler's loyalty, her steady life on the ranch, and everything that made it a hearth. "I don't know how to thank you for sparing us having to kick Gideon out. Your solution is brilliant."

"It's actually yours." He tucked her blonde waves behind her shoulders and ran his fingers down her back. "Pragmatism is something we have in common."

"We have a bunch in common, but I should go."

"Stay." He lowered his voice. "Let me keep you awake all night."

"Ashton, stop chipping away at the little resistance I have left. I want so much to stay, to go with you to Hawaii, but I have a family and obligations. I can't."

He kissed her with parts of him she'd missed. "Will you let me call you soon and see how you are?"

"I'll call you." She read how reluctant he was to leave the ball in her court. "Tomorrow I'll call, I promise, but let me be the one to do it."

"That's just it… *Be* the one."

She got to her feet, and he followed suit. "Thank you. I haven't felt such relief in forever."

He hugged and swayed her, reminding her of life before she became a family, when she was traveling solo, still mapping her future. "I don't want more regrets. I can't die feeling like I do now."

A spark of desire urged her to pretend all obligations away, to stop being the responsible matriarch and flag bearer, to live. "I'm not going anywhere, but of course I am."

He walked her to her car and kissed her lips. "Call me."

"I'm going to sleep better tonight thanks to you, Ashton."

"Thanks to you, I'm going to sleep worse."

That afternoon while she was packing, Peyton received a video call from Bryce, who was sitting on a sunny balcony. "You look fuller, honey, more adult and lustrous. Sedona suits you."

"Getting away from Gideon suits me. Maybe ice cream does as well." She held up her tablet to show her mother the view.

The red rocks stared down at Peyton like guardians of time, judging the human race. "I never tire of those rocks."

Bryce hooked a hand to her hips and tilted her head. "What's your secret, madam? Why art thou aglow?"

"Change away from Gideon suits me." Peyton snickered. "Since you're on your balcony, I'll sit on mine, then you can tell me about the new guy you met." She savored the view of Lake Tahoe's churning waves.

"Things with Matt are fine." Bryce played with her vibrant, thick red hair. "I stayed over last night."

From her daughter's demeanor, Peyton knew Bryce's first foray into sex had been a disappointment. "The first time is never great, especially if you're not in love with the guy. It's okay to experiment sometimes."

"No one is William, Mom, nor ever will be. But I need to move on."

Peyton raised her eyebrows. "Don't be too keen on Margot's advice. She's a social arsonist."

"Maybe that's better. She's happier than any of us."

"Is that why you sped things up with Matt?"

Bryce bit her lower lip but seemed sure of her reply. "I'm forcing myself to see how the world is not one person or one thing."

"Have you had any contact with William?"

"He messaged me… I almost didn't reply, but then I did."

"Gideon is leaving for California if you want to return to the ranch. He'll be getting recruited soon. I suspect he'll be happy about it."

Bryce narrowed her golden eyes, her mouth slightly agape. "Who would want to recruit him?"

"It's through a friend, but Gideon will never learn that."

"You look more relaxed than I've seen you in a long time, Mom."

She thought of the museum and gallery she wanted to build. "With Gideon moving out and Harlow moving in, things are looking up."

Adler's video call interrupted them.

Peyton said her goodbyes, stepped inside, and brought him up on her tablet. "I'm sorry you lost Lightning."

He didn't smile, his wrinkles etched deeper in his face. "How did you know?"

"Tansy told me when she called."

"Tansy? She never calls."

She adjusted her screen to maximize the angle. "Didn't you see the kitchen after Gideon dumped food on her? It was a mess."

He tossed his head back. "The kitchen was clean. I thought she was gone for the day."

"Ah, Gideon did the cleaning himself, didn't want you asking questions. Why didn't you take him with you to help with Lightning?"

"I could tell he had no interest, and I didn't want negative energy. The crew helped. At least Lightning went out on his own terms. Besides, Gideon has a couple of friends visiting."

Peyton didn't want Gideon partying at her house. It hurt her how Adler overruled her wishes. "You shouldn't have had to bury him alone. I'm so sorry."

"I feel like all I do is hold water through open fingers. Is Tansy coming back?"

"Not while Gideon is there. I've arranged for him to get a job in California that'll get him out of the house willingly."

Adler frowned and moved closer to the screen. "Why will he accept it?"

"He wants a new car, more money, and control. He'll take it."

"How did you pull off a job for him from Lake Tahoe?"

"Long story. Tell me how you're doing."

Adler stretched his neck and smoothed a finger over his brow. "Not great. I miss you, and I don't like how my conversation with Bryce went."

"Oh? I spoke to her just now. She didn't mention it."

He cracked his knuckles. "I couldn't learn anything meaningful about her time in Sedona. She's angry and distant."

"But you understand why, right?"

"I thought once the kids were grown up, it would get easier. Nothing feels easier."

"Right."

"How're you?" he asked, studying her with predatory eyes.

"Packing."

"You too? Come on, talk to me."

"I'm not great. But the prospect of Gideon vacating our house on favorable terms so he can't insult Tansy or challenge us every moment of every day is a relief."

"How did you devise the idea of a job for Gideon?"

Peyton knew her husband well enough not to mistake his subtle approach for letting up. She pointed to the bar. "I'll be right back."

He watched her walk to the bar and return with a bottle of water. "What's so bad you can't get yourself to tell me?"

She maintained her best poker face, effacing all emotions. "I bumped into Ashton when I was distraught and mentioned my ordeal with Gideon. I asked if he had a job for him. He proposed the solution via a connection of his."

Adler ran a tongue over his teeth and brought his screen forward as if he needed her to read him better. "Ashton Grant?" When she nodded, he said, "I won't get into his motives for now or what could've prompted you to get personal with your ex. But I want to know why you'd want to farm out our problems."

Anger pitted her reply. "I found an ingenious solution. It's the least provocative solution we have. Would you have asked Gideon to leave?"

"We'll never know now, will we?" He staked his elbows on his knees and sighed. "This unilateral decision of yours, does it trade short-term happiness for longer-term misery?"

She stood up and stepped back. "All we have is misery. Are you happy? I'm sorry I didn't run this solution by you, but when I consult you, you tie my hands."

He gawked at her. "But Ashton Grant doesn't?"

"This is not about anyone else. It's about us getting stitched up at every turn with Gideon. Can you please see this as a positive outcome?"

"Is it?" he asked in an even tone, but it felt like a shout.

It wasn't his anger that worried her. "Adler, please. This is good news, and I'm sorry my behavior hurt you."

He crossed his muscled arms over his wide chest. "You didn't come to me."

Fatigue and frustration capped her at the knees, and she flopped on the bed. "A solution presented itself, and I took it. We aren't giving each other enough right now, but I'm doing my best."

"Have you lost faith in me?" he asked, with a Navy SEAL's alert posture.

"I feel hopeful." She owed her optimism to Ashton, but it ought to have been because of him. "Gideon will accept, and we'll do what we must to reconnect."

He winced and caught his breath. "Are we so far gone in your eyes we need reconnecting?"

"Please, don't parse my words. I'm saying I want to spend time focused on you alone, on us."

He adjusted in his seat, cracking his knuckles. "Answer me this. How likely is Ashton to pop up again soon?"

"I can't control where Ashton will be. Seriously?"

"It's that high a likelihood, is it?" Though he rarely raised his voice, his tense stance and focused features said it all. "Is Ashton a problem I need to worry about?"

"That's not a question you need to ask," she replied, though unsure.

He exhaled and shifted in his seat but grew less tense. "What don't I know about Bryce?"

Peyton smiled, admiring how little he missed. "She went out on three dates with the same guy."

"Who is he?"

"I only know he's handsome, super athletic, and fun, but simple. She underplayed it, and that's fine. She's still agonizing over William."

"Like you were over Ashton when I met you?"

His question felt like a slap. "I met you four years after Ashton and I ended things. So no, not the same."

"Some people find twenty years not enough."

Peyton stared at the horizon and bit her cheek. Her husband exaggerated, but there was a kernel of truth in his words. Her love for Ashton no longer blazed in the winds, but its embers had survived. "I thought choosing you, having children together, and sharing small and big moments would be enough."

"I didn't say it hasn't been." He pinched his forehead. "Oh God, the dreaded third date."

Peyton was grateful for the change of subject and took it as an olive branch. "Sex is good for her… or rather, living according to her age is."

"Ouch. I don't want that picture at all."

She thought how they once spent most nights in the nude. What a rare occasion that had become.

"Will you be my third date in Sedona?"

Peyton knew he was asking a bigger question, but she was too exhausted to deal with heavy subjects. "You only want me for my body."

"It was in your vows, and I have it on video."

"Was it?" She twiddled with her hair, thinking how little they played now.

"Ma'am, I'm at your service."

"Now you're talking, Blake."

"Finally!" He pressed his face to the screen. "I was wondering when you were going to call me Blake again. I miss it when you don't."

"Blake, Blake, Blake…"

He looked at her with a softer gaze. "I miss you not being angry with me. I miss long stretches of peace. Where'd they go?"

She wanted to tell him he had allowed Gideon to become the vampire of their lives. "We need the change."

"I'll pack right now. Did you book that room with a tub the size of Rhode Island? I'm planning on packing lightly."

"I always found soaking in the nude with you tantalizing."

He looked at her with knowing eyes. "Let's cut our visit short and return here for some one-on-one."

"But Sedona is breathtaking."

"So is Abiquiú."

Peyton needed time away from the ranch, but she understood that her husband needed a concession. "All right," she said against her wishes and hung up. She strolled the length of the room, reflecting on how her troubles had rooted. They still had so much to work out. She could see the blueprints that would restore her marriage, but the sheer effort it would take made her want to sail to Hawaii.

fifteen

Pioneer Ranch without Gideon was serene. With her brother gone, Bryce stretched on a chaise lounge by the pool, petting her fox and sipping iced tea.

Alone in her studio overlooking the pool, Peyton sat at her easel, watching through the open window, lamenting Bryce's upcoming move to Berkeley. She dreaded the quiet winters on the ranch.

Mother and daughter flinched at the sound of William's voice. Bryce sat up and covered her body with a towel. Neither had expected him, though it wasn't unusual for him to show up unannounced.

"Can I join you?" He sat beside her with a hand tucked behind his back and bent down to pet the sweet-natured fennec fox. He scratched the top of her head and the soft spot under her chin. "How're you, Bryce?" He trained his chocolate eyes on her.

She clutched the towel higher. "Fine, fine. You?"

"Yeah, fine, fine."

Peyton stared at them, glad they weren't aware of her.

In the weeks they'd spent apart, William had grown a beard that added maturity and distinction to his face. "I hear you're leading yoga classes down by the lake."

"I earned a certificate, so practice."

"You're a redhead now."

"You say it like it's a bad thing."

He picked up Myriad and put her in his lap. "I like it a lot, but you don't need any improvements, Bryce. You never did."

Her cheeks turned tomato red. "Change is good."

"I don't want *everything* to change."

The angst in his voice was hard for Peyton, who loved him always.

"It does, William, and some of it is your choice."

"Why did you get a big tattoo?" he asked in a sharp tone. "It's not like you."

She cocked her head, frowning. "What?"

He thrust the magazine he had rolled up behind his back. "I saw the pictures! I was so shocked, I had to buy the print version."

In Sedona, Bryce had agreed to a photo shoot for an equestrian magazine with the Red Rocks in the background, befitting Big Red. It was a three-page spread in honor of her championship. "I don't have a tattoo."

"It's all up your leg, thigh, and hip." His ears turned scarlet as he splayed the magazine open. "I don't know why they put a showjumper in practically a bikini. How does this make any sense?"

"Did you come here to yell at me?"

"Show me," he said.

"What? No." She tightened the towel around her legs. "There's nothing to see."

"What? You show the whole world, but not me?"

"Fine!" She flung the towel with one swoop, exposing her defined thighs. "Here! I told you. It was body paint Honovi sprayed on me to give me a chance to test out the idea of a tattoo."

"Well, I don't want you to get one."

"Come again?" She jumped to her feet and wrapped the towel around her waist like a sarong. "By what right?"

He brushed his hair out of his eyes and puffed. "Sorry, but don't, okay?"

"No, it's not okay. *I* decide. Besides, what Honovi created was like magic. You should read the fan mail."

Peyton was proud of her daughter's assertiveness, happier than ever that Layli had mowed Vegas Rose's hair with her arrow. It taught Bryce to mow her path.

He stood up and gazed at the melted amber skies. "Come riding with me… or play tennis… anything."

There was sadness in Bryce's voice when she said, "You should ask your guest, not me."

"I'm here alone," he replied.

"I want to, but—"

"—no, none of that. For weeks you've avoided me. It may be selfish of me, but I miss you too much."

Bryce's tears came faster than her mother could blink. "What did you think would happen?"

"I don't know, but my world doesn't feel right anymore." He pointed to her body. "I wouldn't spoil this perfect skin with tattoos."

Bryce pulled her eyebrows together, her lips quivering. "Don't confuse me, then leave to plan a wedding. I can only take so much."

"I'm not planning a wedding."

"But you're engaged!"

"Yes, but we haven't set a date or planned anything." He made as if he would touch her but didn't. "Come riding with me. See the architect. I want to hear your input for a future of Thoroughbred horses and a more productive ranch like we always envisioned."

Peyton heard someone call her name, and it sounded agonized. She followed the voice deeper into the house and found Scarborough keeled over on the sofa. "What's wrong?" She saw his pale lips and sweaty forehead and screamed at the top of her lungs for William and Bryce. "I got you." She thought of dialing emergency services, but they lived too far out for that.

William tore in with Bryce at his back.

Peyton said, "William, get Koda… Bryce, grab Aspirin."

"What's wrong with Scarborough?" Bryce asked.

"He's having a heart attack. Kitchen, extreme right cabinet, where the medicine caddy is. Run!"

Red in the face, clutching his chest, Scarborough said, "You're fussing too much."

"I can't lose you, Scarborough."

Bryce returned with an Aspirin bottle and a glass of water.

William called Koda, pacing. "Koda says to put a couple of pills under his tongue."

"I'm not dead yet."

"Sorry, Scarborough. I didn't mean to speak about you in the third person," William said. "Koda is bringing his truck around."

Scarborough grunted. "The hospital is far. I won't make it."

"You're not gonna die." Bryce knelt beside him and helped press him up and back.

"I want to die here, at home."

Peyton's tears trickled. "Keep breathing. I still need you."

Scarborough fixed his brilliant blue eyes on her. "Peyton, you don't need me anymore, but you'll miss me, darlin'."

For years, she'd begged him to call her by her first name, and for the first time, he did. It made her realize how ill he felt. "You enrich our lives and make us better people."

Koda's steps thumped on the marble floor as he flew toward them. "Let's go. No time to waste."

"No." Though he labored, Scarborough continued, "Having you all around me has been the greatest gift of my life."

"You need a hospital."

"I'm done. Koda, you listen now… The house is paid for, the motor-cycle roars like a filly in heat, and the Fargo truck is a fair bride."

Koda took his hand and squeezed it. "What are you saying?"

Memories of young, nimble Scarborough coursed through Peyton's mind, images of him in every decade. "Have a sip of water, at least."

Scarborough kept his eyes on Koda. "Since you're hell-bent on follow-ing in my footsteps, all I have in this world I leave to you."

Koda's eyes welled, and his jaw shivered. "No, you didn't… Scarborough, what?"

"You're the closest to a son I ever had. The view from the house is mighty good. Just don't pull down that porch when you update that ratty-tatty place. I built it with my daddy's old barn wood."

"Just stop it and let us take you to the hospital."

Scarborough raked one face after another, smiling through his agony. "I'm the luckiest man to have kept you all snug in my chest. It's you who kept my ticker going this long, but it's time now. I know it."

Peyton sandwiched his hand between hers, relentless tears coursing down her cheeks. "We love you."

"I'm mighty proud of you, Peyton, like your daddy was. You did right by me always. I couldn't have asked for more."

"But I'm not ready."

"No one is ever ready, but wise riders keep their boots by the door. The doctors already did all they could. They told me it was bad. Tell Stands-With-A-Bow I'll miss her coffee as much as my saddle." Scarborough gasped, and his hand grew heavy and limp. An eerie rasp escaped his throat, his chest collapsed for the last time, and his jaw slackened.

Koda checked his pulse, then closed his eyes and kissed the top of his head.

Bryce cried, "Aren't you going to perform CPR on him or something?"

From the power of his ancestors, Koda unleashed a chant full of sorrow, leading Scarborough's spirit on its next journey. Bryce hugged her mother, and William hugged them both. Koda seemed like he'd never stop chanting.

Peyton's phone rang. "Honovi?"

"I'm coming home, Mom. I know how deeply you loved him."

"When you said death was near, did you know it would come for Scarborough?"

"Yes, which is why I told him to stop playing it safe for once."

"Dearheart, I'm glad you're coming home. We need each other extra now."

"I know. Ricky will meet me at the airport, and I'll let BearClaw know. He'd want to come down. Got to tell Rebecca as well."

Peyton was beyond asking Honovi how he knew anything. He was Honovi, after all. "He loved Easter lilies. We'll have to get lots of them."

"Yes." Honovi understood. "From death, life."

Peyton kissed Scarborough's cheek and removed his boots.

"What are you doing, Mom?"

"You're too young to know this. It's traditional to hang the boots of a beloved buckaroo until they fall off on their own. No cowboy was more cherished than Scarborough. His boots will go on the fence by the front gates, as he deserves."

Like carved obsidian, figures shrouded in black thronged around Scarborough's body at the Big House. Peyton insisted he'd be laid to rest in the family mausoleum, in an ornate sarcophagus covered with friezes of early settlers, their wagons, horses, and the lanterns that saw them through many dark nights and darker fates.

Peyton and Adler were standing over Scarborough, touching the brim of the hat that rested on his face. Makeup isn't for genuine cowboys. She'd asked for him to be dressed in his favorite pair of jeans and boots, and his red plaid shirt and yellow bandana. "I don't understand why people dress their dead in new clothes, rather than their most comfortable ones. It's called eternal sleep, after all. We should all be buried in our pajamas."

"Who wears pajamas anymore, sweet Pey?" Adler rested his cheek on top of her head. "Sorrow makes people seek perfection, but healing requires authenticity." He kissed her on the lips. "You can't die first. Promise me."

Peyton thought of a life without Adler. Despite all the fighting over Gideon, she still felt an all-encompassing, profound love for him. "You can't die first, either."

He patted Scarborough's laced fingers and inserted a cross under them. "He sure invoked the Lord, but he never told us which one."

"There's only one, regardless of what people choose to call him. Will you invite those outside to hear the prayers? We'll be riding to the cemetery soon."

Matt tumbled into the house like a drifter. Bryce was gawking at him with a confused expression that made Peyton beeline to her daughter. "Did you know Matt was coming from Sedona?"

"He didn't even text me. I told him about the funeral, so he'd leave me alone, but here he is."

"In time for the comfort prayer before the procession." Peyton made bolstering eyes at Bryce. "Today is hard, honey. Do what works for you, not for your visitor."

Matt joined them, underdressed and bright-eyed. He had a strong jawline, high cheekbones, unblemished skin, and tall stature. He hugged Bryce but didn't pick up on her lack of enthusiasm. "Sorry, babe. Where do I put my backpack?"

Bryce led him away, leaving Peyton to stand with Royce, close to Scarborough's coffin, waiting for Father Gabriel's homily.

The Franciscan monk wore a white alb, purple chasuble, and a stole over his gray robe. "Receive the Lord's blessing," he said, flicking holy water. "The Lord bless you and watch over you. The Lord make His face shine upon you and be gracious to you. The Lord look kindly on you and give you peace. In the Name of the Father, and of the Son, and of the Holy Spirit."

"Amen," replied the gathering.

"I'm next in line," Royce said, huddling on Peyton's arm. "At my age, I should've gone first."

"Hush, I can't hear of you leaving me. You're the queen of Abiquiú who knows way better than me. You're sticking around."

Beyond the wide doors, Peyton saw Bryce hustle toward her.

"Am I mistaken, or is your Ashton coming this way?" Bryce whispered.

"Don't call him that, honey." Peyton saw him looking around and dreaded Adler's reaction. "Oh God, he's really here."

Royce pasted her glasses to her false lashes, elated to see someone akin to her own heart. "It's a funeral. Lots of people are here. Why can't Ashton come to support you?"

"No, he's here for Scarborough, not me," she replied.

"Pish-posh, funerals are for the living, but that's a good point. Say *that* to Adler when he gives you a sourpuss."

Layli slinked toward them and inserted herself between Peyton and Royce. "That's Ashton Grant, isn't it? No one over fifty is allowed to look that good. God, how prestige wreathes this man."

Royce waved to him. Once he was within earshot, she did a cute shimmy and gave him her cheek. "Staying with me like in the old days?" She accepted multiple kisses and tapped him on the arm. "You make me think of better times and better men."

"Wish I could, and I missed you plenty. This was a necessary detour." He gaped at Peyton then spoke to Layli. "Did you know Peyton refers to you as the spirit of the ranch?"

"This place has its own spirit," Layli replied. "None of us are grand enough to add to it."

He smirked and leaned into Peyton for a kiss and a hug, sending her temperature north. "I'm sorry, ladies, for your loss. I know how important Scarborough was."

"How did you know Scarborough passed?" Peyton asked.

"From Margot. She offered to let me fly her here."

Royce rolled her eyes. "How kind of her. That girl wants to rule the world."

Ashton adjusted a Patek Phillipe platinum ruby wristwatch, the perfect match for the ring he still wore. In his elegant, tailored suit, polished leather boots, and sophisticated air, he reminded Peyton of her father, who had never met him, which she'd always regretted. "Margot is different, all right," Ashton said. "She should walk in any minute now with Gideon, I imagine."

Peyton stretched her spine, scanning the room for her son. "You brought Gideon? He never replied to my messages."

Ashton offered Peyton his arm. "Can I steal you for a second and tell you all about it?"

Royce shoved her toward him. "Take your time, darling."

Peyton searched for her husband, but he was nowhere to be found. "Friends can steal each other."

"Does that apply to lovers?"

The modulation in his voice and the gentle craning of his neck forced Peyton's gaze to the horizon. "Behave yourself."

"No way," he whispered, as they pierced the fresh air. "Margot showed up with Gideon. I brought them both, as requested."

"Why is Margot here?"

"For the same reason I am. Koda is here."

Roses perfumed the air and Western meadowlarks chirped in the Douglas-fir. It was a perfect day for funerals and feuds. "You're after Koda as well?"

He laughed but rearranged his features in an empathetic expression. "I'm sorry. I know you've been grieving."

Dozens crammed outside, drinking and greeting each other, as saddled horses were lined up.

Ricky found them and acknowledged Ashton as another mourner. "Have you seen Dad?"

Peyton was too focused to see her husband approach them with Finn at his feet.

Adler knifed eyes at Ashton, his hands on his hips. "Are you here with more plans for my family?"

"What's going on, Dad?" Ricky asked, wide-eyed.

Adler placed a palm on their middle son's chest, but kept his gaze fixed on Ashton. "This is between Ashton and me."

The moment pressed on Peyton. To soften it, she stroked Finn's head. "Ashton just told me Gideon is here. Let's go find him."

Not budging an inch, Adler's veins bulged, and his color deepened. "My wife tells me you're Houdini to our youngest son. One minute he's here, then he's gone for a job, then he magically shows up back here without warning. All thanks to you."

Ashton rocked on the heels of his Lucchese boots, grinning. "Happy to support an old friend."

"Friend?" After a pause and an orchestrated nod, Adler burned his wife with a heated stare. "Friends are like Scarborough. The man we mourn today."

Ricky stiffened his back, red in the face. "Hey, man, maybe you should leave," he told Ashton.

"I knew Scarborough," Ashton replied. "I'm here out of respect, not to mention bringing Gideon back to his father."

Adler grabbed Peyton by the arm, unnerving her, though he spoke to Ashton. "You and I know exactly why you're here."

She could see Adler's next thought would be even less friendly. She eased her arm out of his grip, gave him a stern look, and touched Ricky's back. "Thank you, Ashton, for bringing Gideon and Margot to us, but it's time to check in with the friar."

Adler led with his right leg, every ounce of the captain in him on alert. "I'm assuming we won't be seeing you at the cemetery."

Ashton flashed a stony stare. "I wouldn't miss the local yokels for the world."

Ricky's expressive face contorted. "Dad, are you okay?"

William swooped down on them like a determined hawk, throwing a thumb over his shoulder. "There's some guy with Bryce… err… long hair, weird sandals, dressed like he's hitchhiking cross-country. Who's he?"

"The guy who looks like a mixed martial arts fighter?" Ricky asked.

Ashton chuckled. "Who wears sandals on a ranch?"

Peyton made big eyes at him, hoping he would leave, but Adler kept the conversation going.

"You mean Matt showed up uninvited all the way from some faraway place as if we're having a party instead of a funeral?"

William asked, "Who is this Matt?"

Gideon overheard as he approached them. "Oh yeah, Bryce is having sex finally. Didn't you know?" He was dressed for a rave in jeans and a red graphic T-shirt. "Must be hot if Matt came all the way from Sedona."

"Hey, watch it!" Adler said. "Don't you ever disrespect your sister like that again!"

"I'm only voicing the truth like Mom always taught us to do."

Ricky said, "Mom didn't teach us to be assholes!"

Gideon curled his lips down in a disgusted grimace. "Who asked you, dork?"

Peyton seethed. "Can we focus on the funeral?" She looked at William with a softer gaze. "Matt is being supportive, like most people here. Why don't you and Ricky prepare to ride out to the cemetery? We'll talk over a cocktail when we return for repast."

Ricky and William anchored themselves behind Adler.

Gideon pressed closer to Ashton, admiring him in a way Peyton had never seen before. "Can I borrow it again?" he asked Ashton with a happy bounce. When Ashton handed him his phone, Gideon held it up to show his father. It was custom-built, cast in white gold. "This is 'the instrument,'" Gideon said, with glassy eyes. "No one calls it a phone. This red button here connects to a concierge twenty-four-seven. Ashton can get a last-minute reservation to anything—concerts, first-class tickets, runway shows, you name it—by just pushing this button. How awesome is that?"

Disappointment coated Adler's hard face.

Her husband deserved significantly better. "Give Ashton his phone back, please," she said in a mama voice. Peyton stood between the two men who had her in common. Ashton looked at her with apologetic eyes, and Adler with angry ones. "It's time to ride out with the procession."

Scarborough's coffin was draped with the flag of New Mexico—bright yellow with the red Zia sun in the center—and transported in a glass carriage. Men in Western suits and cowboy hats mounted their horses, as did ladies in elaborate Kentucky Derby hats. Laden with flags, flowers, and burning sage, the mourners prepared to ride to the cemetery. In the tradition of honorable cowboys, Koda spearheaded the funerary procession on foot, leading Scarborough's saddled horse without his faithful rider. Behind the carriage, the family rode, their boots polished, their horses groomed, and their hats chosen carefully for this auspicious day. As infirm as he was, Kelcy insisted on riding, though he had to be steadied. Bryce and William flanked him, riding their own primed stallions.

On a path with vast, wild vistas of mountains like camel humps and pouncing cats, the procession moved at a slow pace. Ricky played a Native flute and Honovi carried burial feathers. They wore Western suits and had woven beads into their hair to honor a man they considered a friend and mentor.

Kelcy said, "Peyton, I'm counting on you to speak for all of us."

Mounted beside Adler, behind Scarborough's carriage, Peyton twisted around and nodded.

Though it was a hot day in the middle of summer, an unexpected breeze and soft clouds filtered the harsh sun. When they reached the cemetery gate, Puebloan locals awaited them, chanting and calling on the Great Spirit, carrying woven baskets of food to leave at Scarborough's burial site.

Peyton budded a delicate smile and bowed her head to them.

As if the mourners had practiced their roles, they knew what was expected.

Before the coffin was carried inside the family crypt and eased into its sarcophagus, Peyton stood facing the mourners with one hand over her heart, the other twined with rosary beads. Adler stood several inches taller than most, prominently positioned in the foreground with the kids. Gideon stood in the background with Ashton, like a focal point, as though Peyton had sketched a composition of her life.

"Death can make us afraid," she said, "forcing us to reflect on our own mortality. At funerals, we mourn our loved ones from long ago. When my father died, I told myself he'd gone on a long vacation, and that in death, he'd have no delays or cancelations, and no one would lose his luggage."

Some chuckled; others sniffled.

"Scarborough was dear to us in ways I can't describe. He never had children, but he was the best family member and friend. He often said, 'If a man doesn't have a reason to die for, he ain't fit to live.' He lived because he loved and was loved. Even the undertaker is sorry." She splintered a sad smile. "As true a cowboy as I ever saw, Scarborough never complained, but no one is immune to pain and sorrow. In death, we're free of anguish, free of everything but the love we leave behind." Peyton bowed her head, her nose burning. "All that sweat, insightful advice, and his assurance that we can overcome wasn't wasted. It lives in us and in our children." She crossed herself, kissed the rosary, and left it on top of the coffin. "Thank you all for coming. I'll leave the rest of the service to Father Gabriel."

Gideon stepped forward and raised his voice. "I have something to say."

"No, you don't," Peyton said, with admonitory eyes. She saw her other children aim to intervene and held up her hand.

"Scarborough was a curmudgeon who spoke in quotes," Gideon said, "an employee, and you're burying him in premium space in the family mausoleum. You didn't even consult us!"

The mourners mumbled and frowned. Peyton struggled to hide her shame. She looked at Adler, who took big steps toward their son.

"That's enough, Gideon," Adler said. "Scarborough was an honorable cowboy. We were lucky to know him."

"What's so honorable about shoveling horse shit all day?"

Peyton detected Ashton peeling away from the crowd and discouraged him with a headshake.

He had only to utter Gideon's name to get him to yield. Adler no longer stared at his son. He gawked at his wife with livid, accusatory eyes. She knew he felt humiliated, but didn't know how to remedy the situation, except to invite Father Gabriel to assume the reins.

Layli flashed concerned eyes, but it was Royce who made sure Ashton didn't overstep again, however well-meaning, and called on him to escort her back to her carriage.

Once the casket bearers had carried the coffin into the mausoleum, guests remounted their horses or climbed into their carriages and prepared to head back for green chili pork, stuffed sopapillas, and the best New Mexico barbeque.

Ashton reappeared and took Peyton aside. "I'm leaving, but when can I see you? Scarborough isn't the only thing dead around here. You deserve way better." He brought his thumb to his forefinger—his habit when he was angry. "I'll slip away without returning for the repast, but come back to California soon where you're appreciated, not admonished."

Peyton had business in Orange County. "If I can, I'll call."

"Please do," he said and didn't relax his face until she nodded. "Gideon asked to leave with me. If that's what you want, I'll also entertain him."

Peyton played with the brim of her hat. "Gideon is already charged up. It never ends well when he is. Take him with you, though it'll bother Adler."

"What would bother me?" her husband asked, appearing with unsettling stealth.

Peyton stiffened. She wished he'd stop waylaying her, but she knew it was grief mixed with anger and external threats.

"We should get going," Ashton said. He pulled his phone out of his pocket and gestured for Gideon to follow. "Sorry for your loss."

When Adler caught what happened, he looked like he was about to gut Ashton. "What the hell?" Ire flamed in his golden eyes. "Is Gideon leaving with him?"

"It's best."

"Stay here!" Adler hollered to his son, who was standing a few feet away.

Flushed, gnashing his teeth, Gideon gusted closer. "I want to go with Ashton, Dad!"

Adler stabbed a finger at Ashton and spoke to him as though he might not understand English. "Gideon is *my* son. Peyton is *my* wife. Abiquiú is *my* home. Do we understand each other?"

"Hey, man, the boy asked. Pardon me for being accommodating." Ashton stepped back and gave Peyton a respectful nod. "No one can take from us what willingly stays. No one!"

Peyton touched her husband's torso. "Please, Blake, people are watching."

"My son stays here with his family." His tone was even but full of rage. "That's that!"

Gideon stomped his narrow foot. "I'm not a baby, Dad. *I* decide where I go and when."

"This will not help you," Honovi said.

Ricky thrust his neck out. "Why must you always ruin it for Mom and Dad?"

"You're not my brother." Spit sprayed from Gideon's mouth. "Both of you, fuck off!"

"How can you say that to Ricky?" Adler asked. "He's been our son longer than you have, Gideon."

"I didn't want to be here in the first place, but Margot dragged me. Now I have to fly commercial?"

"You weren't planning to be with us on such an important day?" Adler asked.

"Why would I give a damn? Scarborough was a grumpy fart who hated me."

"Enough airing our laundry in public!" Peyton raised her hands. "Gideon go if you want to." She eyed Ashton. "Thank you, and so sorry. I'll see you another time."

Adler balled his fists, watching Ashton parade away with their son. "I'll see you another time?" He glowered at her with fiery sparks. "You brought this on us, Peyton. You did!"

If a grenade had lodged in her chest, she would've been less horrified. "I brought what on us? Safety for everyone? We're mourning, and you pushed me to appease Gideon. I did! If that's what you mean, you're right!"

Honovi said, "Mom… Dad… please!"

"Honovi is right," Adler said. "Not the time or place, but this is not okay. Not by a long shot!"

She lowered her voice, but it cut. "What's not okay is the way you thrust Gideon into our midst and twist my arm. It's not okay how long you disappear in the woods, and how you go nowhere with me even when I ask." Peyton flounced away, crying. Her life had become intolerable. She was either helpless or blamed.

sixteen

The Big House was still buzzing with tipsy mourners when Peyton stole into the study, hoping to hide. She spied Koda's boots pointing toward the ceiling and slid back to childhood memories of lying on the rug, listening to her father recite poems. "You beat me to some quiet, I see."

Koda lifted his head off the floor, sad and nostalgic. "I thought your father would live forever somehow. I thought the same of Scarborough."

Peyton plopped into a leather armchair and piled a leg over her knee. "Margot took the room at the end of the hallway. Where're you sleeping?"

His grin couldn't have been bigger. "Is this your way of asking me if I'm with Margot?"

"I don't know what I'm asking, but I haven't seen her yet."

"She was in a mood, so I sent her to my room, but as always, she does whatever she prefers." He rose on one elbow. "Margot is like a Lucchese boot that's too tight in the arch. But damn if she's not too precious to chuck."

"You mean these boots *ain't* made for walkin'?" Peyton chuckled. "You leave them in the back of the closet, can't really wear them, but can't give them up either?"

Koda chortled and made tents with his legs. "You can wear them lying down. Does that answer your question?"

She drummed her fingers on the arm of the chair. "Some relationships can resume where they left off."

"I saw Ashton Grant. If it weren't for you, he wouldn't indulge Margot as he does. You know that, right?"

"Or Gideon. I feel bad." She stretched her legs out, relieving the tension in her feet by pointing them up and down like a ballerina. "I need a new adventure, Koda, or I'm going to wither away."

"You can have anything, but not everything."

Peyton shook her head, pressing her tongue to her cheek. "How do you always welcome Margot back when she never stays?"

"How do you welcome fair weather when it's always followed by winter?"

"Touché."

William tore in. "I'm… I'm—"

"—you're angry what's-his-face is here," Koda said. "Just come join us."

"What? No… Okay, yes. I mean, is this guy Bryce's boyfriend, boyfriend? Like, with that hair? He has locks like a girl!"

Koda swung his raven hair behind his shoulder blades. "Hey, some women love long hair."

Peyton pointed to the chair beside hers, and William tossed himself in it. "She's having fun, and God knows she needs it."

"Fun?" William gritted his teeth. "What does that mean?"

Koda released a belly laugh, rose off the rug, and slumped on the loveseat opposite them. "You can't have your cake and complain about Matt too."

"She's too young."

Peyton said, "She's eighteen soon."

"Exactly." William hopped to his feet, pacing like a colt itching for a run. "Not old enough for Matt or anybody else."

Koda chewed on the corner of his index finger. "But she's old enough for you?"

"What do you want from me, man?" The usual sweetness in his voice had drained fast. "I care about Bryce, okay? This guy doesn't deserve her."

Peyton's mind flew to the day Ashton told Adler that he didn't deserve her.

"Who does?" asked Koda with a placid voice. "Who deserves Bryce?"

William thumped his foot and played with his trimmed beard. "Not this guy. Bryce is very special, so no, no. When is he leaving, anyway?"

Peyton stretched out of her chair, amused at how perturbed William was. "That's most likely up to you, honey."

"Me?"

Koda stood up and placed a hand on his shoulder. "Some people are like the sun. They need to see and be seen every day. Some are like the stars—happy to peek out for a moment, just to dazzle. Some are like black holes. They're elusive, suck the life out of you. And some just marry Carina."

Peyton knew which was Ashton, but worried that Adler, as bright as the moon, was getting eclipsed by Gideon's burning rays.

William looked like he was about to scream. "I'll spend the night at the casita with Grandpa. I need to think."

She pulled William into her embrace in a way she'd never been able to do with Gideon. "You're loved no matter what."

"You don't know how good it is to hear that."

"She knows." Koda flung his arms into the air. "But what am I, mincemeat?"

"You're the new Scarborough now," Peyton said, hugging him. "You'd better catch up on everything cowboys say. I can't live without dusty trails wisdom."

Koda burst into tears. "I really miss that old man. I regret not having come back to see him more often."

"He knew how you felt about him. We all knew."

"Still," Koda said through sniffles. "Are there any chocolate chip cookies?"

She lobbed a kiss on his cheek. "And cake."

"I miss your key lime pie," William said, grief punctuating his words. "I've been feeling nostalgic lately… like all the time. What's wrong with me?"

"I'll just have to make you my best key lime pie soon, won't I? Too much change lately for all of us, yet not enough is changing. Strange." She grasped William's arm with one hand and Koda's with the other. "We also have magic brownies."

Peyton prepared for bed with as much care as always. She showered, moisturized her skin, and switched on the essential oil diffuser on her nightstand, filling the air with the scent of bergamot. Now that life on the ranch had changed forever, she needed to cling to her old routines.

Adler was already in bed, his hands clasped behind his head, staring up at the night sky with its velour vastness, embroidered with stars, dreams, and nightmares. She slipped under the covers but kept to her side.

"I'm failing my family," he said, not attempting to pull her closer.

She took a moment to reply, careful not to lie or exacerbate the situation. "We just can't catch a break."

"Ashton is, though. He's catching breaks all over the place."

"He popped back into our lives, but he's not the problem."

Adler sat up. "He popped back into *your* life. His interest is in you alone. And you contrived to send my son away without consulting me!"

"*Contrived? Your* son? I learned about it like you did, but I judged it a good idea. Leave your ego out of it, please."

"You want Gideon gone all the time, replaced by some exciting new life. Do you deny it?"

Peyton shook her head. "I want Gideon where he's happiest and least threatening."

"He's my son, not Ashton's, but maybe you wish he were."

"Why aren't you taking me at my word anymore?" Peyton didn't think discussing it further would tame the situation. "I lost a close friend, have to contend with a very challenging son, and most days, I feel depleted and unhappy. I could use your support."

Adler rolled away from her. "Maybe I can't be as supportive as Ashton. Invite him back."

Right or wrong, she blamed him, as he blamed her.

As if life's fast-forward button was stuck, the ranch felt gloomy and stagnate. Peyton and Kelcy were on the terrace, sharing a warm breakfast. Hummingbirds zipped to feeders, a family of deer hurdled in the distance, a Bighorn sheep bleated, and the air smelled of freesias and strong coffee. Tension still girded the ranch. Peyton wanted it eased. When Adler glided onto the terrace, she filled his coffee cup and asked whether he wanted one croissant or two. "Got that sausage you love from Kaune's Market and scrambled the eggs myself. They're fluffy like you prefer."

He sat beside her and spread a napkin on his lap. "Thank you," he said in a dry voice.

"The missus likes you," Kelcy said. "She's always cooking for you, isn't she? It's when the wives stop cooking that you'd better watch out."

"I keep hearing Scarborough in my head summing up life," Peyton said, changing the topic.

Kelcy did his own summing up. "It goes on." He hummed, chewing bacon, and buttering a warm biscuit. "When I'm gone, I want you to eat lots, drink more, spend my money, and get on with it."

"*Your* money?"

"You might not believe me, little lady, but this ranch will one day be Bryce's and William's. I know it in my soul."

The sun breached the top of Pedernal Peak, scattering spots of sunshine on Pioneer Ranch like coins spilling from a satchel. Adler ate, while Peyton cradled a mug of coffee, savoring the morning dew and the soft light on her skin until Matt banged on the glass doors, then stepped out, shirtless.

Peyton winced at the fingerprints and jarring noise.

"Doesn't he have a job to return to or something?" Adler whispered.

"Son, are you going swimming?" Kelcy wiped his white chevron mustache.

"No, why?"

"You're in big ranch country. Get some horse sense and put on your clothes."

Matt flexed his pecks and bulbous biceps. "I'm getting some rays before going riding. What's wrong with chilling?"

Peyton hid her grin, but her husband couldn't. "You ride?"

"Bryce will teach me."

Kelcy huffed. "You a pig or a hog, son?"

Matt displayed his usual quizzical look. "I don't understand most of what you say."

Adler handed Matt the coffee pot. "Pigs get fat, hogs get slaughtered."

"But I'm lean."

Peyton shook her head and gave Kelcy a look that told him to stop teasing the man-child. "Please, enjoy breakfast, Matt. There's plenty of food, and we can make you pancakes."

"It's why he's never leaving," Adler mumbled.

Kelcy downed the last of his coffee and held out his cup for a refill. "The lean run fast. Get my drift?"

Matt flashed a blank stare.

"Forgive me, not everyone speaks Texan."

"I speak Mexican, though."

Adler smirked. "Do you mean Spanish?"

"*Si, señor.*"

"But we're in *New* Mexico."

Matt reached for a biscuit, chewing faster than he could swallow. "Then why are there so many Mexican foods here?"

Bryce came out of the house with a shirt slung on her arm and pelted kisses on Kelcy's cheek.

"We were discussing how your guest is all gussied up this morning," he said.

She dropped the shirt on Matt's lap. "To prevent the chair from scratching your back," she said, though Peyton knew it was for their benefit. She grabbed a wedge of watermelon and flumped into a chair.

William pierced through the doors. His eyes fell on her first, lighting up, pulsing with excitement, but when he saw Matt, he gave a curt greeting and backtracked.

"Don't leave," Bryce said.

William paused, his broad shoulders and athletic physique filling the doorway.

"Bryce, you just got here," Matt said when she rose. "Don't you want to eat breakfast?"

She said, "William, the biscuits are still warm, your favorite."

"I'm not hungry," he said and retreated into the house.

"Go after him, doll." Kelcy pointed a menacing finger at Matt. "And don't you say a word."

When William melted deeper inside the house, Bryce excused herself and tracked him.

Matt spoke through a mouthful. "Something wrong?"

Kelcy gave a devilish smirk. "Nope, something's right."

Peyton didn't think so and followed them.

Bryce caught up to William in the kitchen and grabbed him by the forearm. "Will you wait?"

Peyton stood back in the corridor with eyes on them, fearing an escalation.

"What?" he shouted.

"I hate to see you upset."

He stared into her eyes, a hybrid of anger and yearning incising him. "And I hate to see you with that guy. I thought he left already."

Bryce inched closer. "You hate seeing me with Matt or with anyone?"

He tucked his chin into his chest. "I know I'm being selfish. I'm sorry, but it hurts."

It took everything out of Peyton not to intervene.

"I never want you hurt, dear William."

He took her hand and ran a finger over her wrist. "I wish you hadn't taken off your bracelet."

"I wish *you'd* never taken off."

"Did I do that?"

"What are we to do, William? Where do we go from here?"

Peyton asked herself the same question. She loved her husband, but she no longer loved her life. Worse, she longed for the fun and peace Ashton brought.

William cuffed Bryce's waist and pulled her toward him in a way he never had. She raised her face to his, but his phone rang, ending the moment.

"It's Carina."

There was no hiding how hurt Bryce was as she stepped back.

He sighed. "Damn… must be about that show in Houston. I promised I'd go."

She swallowed hard and looked at him as if he'd stabbed her. "This is what we're doing, then?"

He extended his arm, attempting to grab her and explain, but she'd already scuttled to the backdoor.

"Bryce, come on…" When she kept spearing away, he shouted, "The architect will be here soon. Where're you going?"

Peyton gestured for William to stay put and followed her daughter down the path toward the stables.

"Don't go riding like this. It's bad for you and Big Red."

Matt showed up with a heaving chest, having run down from the Big House. "Together we're fire, babe. Tell me again why I'm being shipped back to Arizona?"

"You're not a child being dispatched somewhere," Bryce replied, covering Big Red with a saddle pad. "You're going home."

"You practically packed all my gear, babe."

Peyton snickered but kept quiet.

"I told you. I'll be taking possession of my apartment in Berkeley soon, and I still have lots to do."

He fondled her horse, but it only irritated her further. She flicked his hand away, reminding her mother of how quickly disgust sets in when a woman has made up her mind. "When can I come visit you in Cali?"

"No one in California says 'Cali.'" She saddled her horse. "The path to veterinary medicine is tough. I won't have time for visitors."

"Christmas then?"

Bryce jolted him with a frustrated stare. "Matt, I told you back in Sedona we probably won't see each other again. It's been nice, but I have lots to deal with."

"Are you dropping me? I can move, and I like Cali. But we're vibin'. Why wreck it?"

"I don't want a roommate or a relationship. I just want to study and teach yoga." She glanced at her mother. "Matt's flight is this afternoon. I can take him, but…"

"I'll make sure he makes his plane." Peyton extended an arm in his direction, herding him away from Bryce. "We have a stereoscopic video game you haven't tried. Let me show you."

"A what?"

"It goes bang-bang."

Assured Matt was on his way to the airport, Peyton returned to her studio with a large mug of strong coffee and Apollo who curled up in his basket, nibbling a bone. She streamed mood sounds of lulling waves, longing for Carmel-by-the-Sea, and donned a smock. With surgical finesse, she lined up mixing knives and brushes. She'd been light on inspiration lately, but sorrow had erupted the volcano of her talent. She wasn't at her easel long when William burst in, speaking too fast.

"Bryce snuck in by the back stairs—as if I don't know her ways—and locked herself in her room. I tried to say goodbye, but she pretended she wasn't there, even though Myriad kept yipping."

Peyton knew how her daughter felt. Hungry, but unable to eat. Tired, but unable to rest. Angry, but keeping quiet about it. Through her large windows, she watched the sun dissolve behind the mountains into smudges of blueberry and peach streaks. "What do you want Bryce to say or do that she hasn't yet?"

William paced, his hands on his hips. "I want to say a proper good-bye, and we never finished our conversation."

"What will that do for you?"

He breathed hard, his chocolate eyes saturated with emotion. "If I miss Bryce's birthday, it'll be the first time in over ten years."

"I was only a year older than you when I fell madly in love for the first time. It takes its toll."

He looked about to cry. "I never want to hurt Bryce, but I know I am."

She got off her stool and hugged him. "If love doesn't heal, it wounds."

"I'll call her." He lingered for a moment, unable to vamoose. "Ask her to pick up when I call, okay?"

"I'll try."

Surrounded by hurting loved ones, Peyton poured her own pain into a portrait of Scarborough. Since her father's passing, blood and paint had been the theme of her life, the only constant. She worked through dinner, engrossed in bringing out Scarborough's essence in shades of blue, red, yellow, and green. It would be a kaleidoscope of colors assembled into the handsome features of a cowboy she'd adored all her life, the first work that year that felt right.

Past midnight, Bryce walked into her mother's studio, barefoot, cradling Myriad and crying. "Am I interrupting?"

"It must be about William," Peyton said, stretching her pinched lower back.

"I know he's not mine to keep, but I can't let go. How do I let go, Mom?"

Peyton removed her rubber gloves and wiped her daughter's tears away. "You're hanging on because what you seek is far."

"What's a long way off?"

"Arriving."

Bryce rested her chin on top of Myriad's head. "I don't understand."

"For years now, you've trained to jump hurdles and arrive at your goal swiftly and flawlessly. You may not believe it yet, but you treat everything as a series of obstacles to surmount expeditiously with a likely reward at the end."

Recognition flickered in Bryce's golden eyes. "But that's not life."

She summed up her own history. "Life has no end goal… the obstacles can't always be hurdled… maintaining pace takes strategy… and often sweat and pain are met with failure and disappointment."

"You're telling me to grow up?"

Peyton said what she herself needed to hear. "Change is a death of sorts, and death is no more than a change of worlds. There's no arriving, and there's no departing."

Bryce struggled to push down a groan. "How long will this pain gnaw at my insides? Just how long?"

She kissed her daughter's wet cheeks. "Grief takes however long it takes."

Bryce mounded one foot over the other. "I'm afraid."

She looked out at the snaking Chama River illuminated by the moon into a giant silver dragon. "You fear your choices, not what's happening."

Irritation enmeshed Bryce. "It's my choice?"

"Suffering is a choice. Healing is too."

"My head gets it," she said, and sat cross-legged on the sofa. "Why can't I believe it?"

Peyton sat beside her. "It'll eventually move into your heart. Only then will you believe it."

"Will you and Dad be okay?"

"It depends."

"On Ashton?" she asked, surprising her mother. "I like him, and when he intervenes, he actually makes things better, keeping Gideon away. When Dad does, he makes things worse."

She didn't want to be unfair to Adler or encourage their daughter to harbor resentment toward him. "There's no history with Ashton, and no challenges or failures. Only positivity, in part, because you only just met him. It's not a fair comparison. Your father would lay down his life for you. And if Ashton wasn't worth billions, Gideon wouldn't have been seduced."

"You're right… I'm sorry. But I'm ecstatic you'll only be a couple of hours from Berkeley. I've never lived alone before. I wish you'd move to Carmel, so I can see you most weekends."

Peyton wished for the same, at least for the remainder of the year. But Adler wouldn't agree to leave New Mexico for that long. "We'll get to celebrate your birthday together in Carmel."

After Bryce kissed her goodnight, she cleaned her brushes, lathered her hands with grapefruit soap, and sought the stars.

Tuned into the symphony of owls, crickets, and fireflies, inhaling the aroma of jasmine, Peyton sat on the terrace in the dark, meditating, and cuddling Apollo. Approaching footsteps snatched her attention. Adler came out and smiled, then paused, as though he'd rather not have found her there, and it hurt.

"I can leave, if you prefer," she said.

"You might not believe it, but I love you near." He didn't move to sit down or acknowledge the dog who ran to him. "I'm just not sure the reverse is true anymore, especially since you didn't come to bed with me."

"Would I be asking you to come with me to California if I didn't want you around? But I can't stand that you blame me for everything that goes wrong, and give me no credit for what goes right."

He sighed. "Not much has been going right."

"It might if you come with me to Carmel. The ranch is in Layli's perfect hands. We can reinvigorate our marriage there."

Though the darkness concealed his expression, Peyton felt his anger moor between them.

"We have to pack up Bryce's car tomorrow."

She knew her husband well. He was buying time to consider her proposal. "Luckily, she's shopping for most everything for her place there. We'll load up her car first thing." They'd driven Gideon to his first semester in college. She expected no less for Bryce.

He sat beside her and continued to ignore Apollo, who rubbed against his chair. "Did I hear you talking to Gideon on the phone earlier?"

Peyton rolled a ball for Apollo to fetch. "I finagled a dinner out with him soon."

He leaned back in his chair, stretching his neck in a way that told her he was about to propose a challenge. "The four of us haven't had dinner alone in ages."

"Not the four of us." She met his gaze. "Just Gideon and me. You're not invited."

"I don't need an invitation," he said and changed moods.

"Geraint is insisting I pick up a commission from a key client in person. While I'm in the area, I want to see our son."

"Is that a no?" The Navy SEAL in him hauled her over his lap, grinning as she fought him and lost. "Give into me, already. Unless I release you, you're not going anywhere." It was a game he loved to play, one she usually enjoyed, and he always won, but today it irritated her. When she quieted, he clasped her cheeks and squeezed, fueled by love and disappointment. "Why not drop off Bryce and come back here?"

She shook her face free but slackened on his lap. "I have an obligation to Geraint for a live demonstration in Carmel. And I miss California. We're here for a sizeable chunk of the year, as it is. And we don't have to stay here to be safe."

"I think we can fix things best here."

Adler was coaxing her to him, an old habit, but it felt like punishment, as if he were testing her in ways she'd already proven herself. "We need the change."

"Hmm…" he said, in a tone that told her he wasn't done testing. "Why not do dinner with both kids next week?"

Tension boomeranged. Peyton tried to get off his lap, but he held her there. "It's untimely for Bryce, precipitous even. Please, let's not push it."

Adler sighed and ran his hand through her blonde strands. "I just want one happy evening alone with my wife and kids. Just one."

"In an ordinary world, it would be a simple request, but it would be unwise and hurtful to Bryce. If Honovi and Ricky were with us, it might soften the blow, but just Gideon and Bryce creates a combustible situation."

Adler sharpened his features.

"Don't you miss Carmel? Just the two of us. I have to fulfill that live demonstration. Besides that, it'll be beach, hiking, gorgeous sunsets. Why not?"

"Why are you stopping in Los Angeles again?"

She massaged his scalp. "I agreed to repair a painting for one of Geraint's top clients in Calabasas. I figured I'd also see Gideon—on his turf."

He ran his fingers over her lips, softening, but resolute. "Deep-sea fishing for me?"

He seemed about to agree, so she kissed him with her indulgent self. "And whale watching and Meadows Trailhead and grilled sea bass on our patio facing the ocean. Everything you love."

He cuddled her, emotion straining his voice. "If I come, can we skip entertaining?"

"Come with me to Carmel, and we'll do only what you want."

He pulled her face to his and kissed her for a long time. "I prefer it when we're alone."

"Let's go be alone in bed then," she said in a coquettish voice.

He slipped his hand between her thighs. "As my wife commands."

seventeen

The family had packed Bryce's car to the hilt and was standing in the driveway. Peyton was glad the trips up and down the many flights of stairs were finished.

Bryce saw the overflowing backseat and shrieked. "Oh no! I didn't leave room for Myriad or her things."

Peyton said, "You're driving with Dad and I'm flying with Myriad and Apollo. I'll meet up with you in Berkeley."

"You're sure we can't meet you for dinner on the way?" Adler cocked his head and crossed his lean arms over his broad chest. "It's not a big detour."

"You and Bryce need time alone. I need time with Gideon. You'll take at least two days on the road. Enough time for me to see him and pick up the commission I accepted."

Adler wrapped his arm around his daughter and lifted her off her feet with one arm. "Imagine, two days of listening to Dad's stories."

"Just don't tell me again about all the different fishing hooks."

He squeezed her until she protested. "You mean the treble, the Siwash, the Aberdeen, the octopus, and—"

"—oh my God, cut it out!"

Peyton caught movement on the landing and looked up.

Layli stood at the top of the stairs in ironed jeans, a topaz blouse, and her trademark silver and turquoise belt. "Are you coming or what? The coffee is getting cold."

Peyton climbed the massive granite stairs, and they strolled to the great room. "Adler will spend the rest of the summer with me in Carmel."

"That's like six weeks. Happy about it?"

"A part of me wants to mend things. Another part wants a new start away from the resentment, contempt, and lack of forgiveness. I'll do my best, but it'll be a test for us, for sure."

Layli poured coffee, infusing the room with a nutty aroma. "What are you hiding? Fess up."

Her thoughts winged to Ashton. "I haven't told Adler yet, but while I'm in Calabasas, I'm meeting up with an art investigator Ashton referred me to. A guy who finds uncatalogued paintings. He investigates who bought them, where they're keeping them, what they paid for them, and such."

Layli pressed her tongue behind her upper teeth. "Ashton, eh? Is he the art investigator, by any chance?"

She tapped her feet. "I can use all the help I can get."

"Is that why you haven't told Adler?"

"We're having a somewhat peaceful stretch and I don't want to spoil it."

"At Scarborough's funeral, I saw how Ashton looked at you. It's something. The man wants to help you as much as he wants to help himself *to* you."

"The museum and gallery are my new adventure, the one big thing I'm looking forward to. Ashton is an ally."

"But Adler isn't." Layli dunked a biscochito cookie in her mug. "I'm not judging. Just tell me your eyes are open."

Peyton widened her eyes to their extent. "Happy now?"

"Happy about what?" asked Adler, walking in. He took a biscochito and ate it whole. "When're you having dinner with Gideon, Mrs. Adler?"

"The day I arrive, why?"

"We can leave a day earlier and join you."

Peyton ran a finger along the rim of her cup. "Did you consult Bryce?"

"It's one lousy meal."

"Don't push. Besides, I have a schedule to keep. Let me do this my way."

He stared out the window. "Isn't that all you've been doing?"

Incensed, she said, "If it were just us and Gideon, I would relent. But Bryce was emphatic. She doesn't want to be with Gideon. We promised."

"*You* promised. Sanctioning rifts between the kids isn't what I want." He grabbed a napkin and wiped his mouth. "I'll go check on the horses."

"We have wranglers for that, and why can't you understand just how much Gideon hurts his sister?"

"I know what we have and *don't have*, Peyton," he said, and left.

Layli slotted her fingers together. "That went well."

"He keeps pressing me on this point. I don't get it. Bryce doesn't want to be anywhere near her brother. I don't blame her, and I need to make a point to Gideon. What's this about?"

"Adler is an alpha male who doesn't get to lead anymore. He's not used to having so little control over his family."

Peyton scooted to the edge of her seat, tension fusing her spine. "No one has control here. We're barely surviving."

"The big decisions have been yours. It's an adjustment for all of you."

"What's been my decision? You mean Gideon getting a job?"

"All of it." Layli counted on her fingers. "Gideon's job, Koda's clinic, the Thoroughbred business, and the museum. Maybe you're facilitating those things, not hatching up all the ideas. But to Adler, it's like he's not the head of his family anymore. Even Bryce's major is your idea. Now he might approve of it, but it's all driven by you."

"It's not my fault. He's been passive or makes impossible requests. Things used to be easier. I only want peace in my home."

"The problem is you used to agree on more. Give a little."

"I am." Peyton darted up and paced. "He asked me to cut my visit with Honovi short in Sedona and return here. So, I did, though I'm restless and prefer to be away. But what good did that do us when he's either withdrawn or forceful?" She tipped her chin, restless from too many challenges. "I'm giving way. But I won't force Bryce to spend one more moment with Gideon. No, I'm not giving anyone that!"

Despite the traffic, smog, and noise, Peyton found Los Angeles as addictive as cocaine. Business and connections with the art world brought her there often.

Busy and hot, energetic and dynamic, the City of Angels embraces everyone who walks her streets and dares to sit at her table. She's the temptress, the vamp. Also, the savior and deliverer.

Peyton checked in at the lavish Bel-Air Hotel, a resort built in Spanish architecture, surrounded by bougainvilleas and laurels. She settled the pups in her modern, airy room and phoned her son, who didn't answer. A few texts and calls later, he called her back, apologizing for having to change their plans.

"But I'm in Calabasas tomorrow, Gideon," she said, sitting on a chaise. "It's business. I said dinner tonight, not tomorrow."

"I just started this job and can't say no to staying late. Come on, Mom. How long can your appointments last?"

"I planned on heading up to Berkeley in the afternoon and already booked a flight."

He gave his mother his most angelic voice. "I'm sorry I messed up. Please, stay and meet me at 71Above, at six. A buddy of mine flies a chopper. He'll take you afterwards, I swear."

"Gideon, I'll have valuable art to transport and two pups. A chopper flown by a pubescent won't do."

"Then you'll catch a flight the next morning. It's a minor delay." She could picture his body language when he added, "When was the last time I asked you for anything?"

"Do you remember that time you wanted to go hunting with Dad, but he wouldn't take you because of school?" Peyton bit her lower lip, waiting for Gideon to acknowledge the reference. "You were upset and kept asking to sleep in a tent outside like he was doing?"

"Yeah?"

"I put one up for you. Then, you didn't want to sleep alone outside. You came to get me, even though I hate the cold and the hard ground."

"I remember."

"It took me forever to fall asleep. By morning, I was freezing and had a crick in my neck and a headache. But where were you?"

He laughed and clapped, as if he had just won at poker. "I didn't like it much and went back to my bed."

"Exactly."

"I'm not nine anymore, Mom. I'll be there, I promise."

"Let me see if I can change my flight, but this is not cool." She tossed the phone in her lap in frustration, realizing her son had told her they would meet at a restaurant where reservations were hard to get. She thought of calling him again, but she still had to rearrange her flight to San Francisco and figured he'd tell her about it the next day, giving them something to talk about.

It was a dry day in Los Angeles, borrowed from paradise. Peyton was dolled up in a white summer dress and floral stiletto sandals for a professional consultation with a new client and a meeting with the art investigator.

Today's calendar was about fine art and the efforts to restore and preserve it. She dropped off the pups at a pet lounge, then drove to see the client, who had a Fede Galizia painting requiring her expertise.

Elegant and confident, she cleared two security gates before reaching the front steps of the architectural masterpiece known as La Maison des Fleurs, a mini castle wrapped in Italian limestone on an acre of lush grounds. She walked up the long staircase leading to a wrought-iron and glass door, carrying a bag designed to transport precious art.

"Ms. Chase, nice of you to come," said the tiny figure who stood at the wide entrance. The lady of the manor held out her arthritic hand, wearing fuchsia slacks and a Hawaiian shirt. "I hope you like churros and champurrado." She seemed older than her heritage house.

Peyton cradled more than shook her client's hand. She'd expected a housekeeper to answer the door and hid her surprise. "Mrs. Velasco, it's a privilege to work on any Fede Galizia, and I love churros and champurrado."

Mrs. Velasco struggled to look up at Peyton, who towered over her. "Come in, please. We're sitting in the red room."

"You're a lady of uncompromising standards," Peyton said as they passed through a foyer flanked by staircases and domed with stained glass. She stared through the French doors at a white bridge crossing a long infinity pool overlooking the valley.

"Why?"

"Polished floors, gleaming chandeliers, immaculate surfaces, fresh flowers, and a pot of champurrado still steaming."

"What're you, Sherlock Holmes?"

Peyton snickered, gesturing toward the damaged painting on the wall. "Maybe Doctor Watson." As she slipped on her white gloves and prepared a magnification loupe and a portable light, she asked for permission to remove the painting from the wall. She was astonished at the harm someone had inflicted on such a valuable work.

"When I first bought it, it wasn't covered with markers and whatever that black goop is, and it sure wasn't punctured with a screwdriver." Mrs. Velasco eased into a low, plush seat, and poured the chocolaty hot drink, her veiny, manicured hands splotched brown. "My demonic grandson and his friends did that. I left him down here just one night, and he damaged some of my favorite things, including the grand piano." She took a sip of champurrado and smacked her lips. "People can't understand the burden of such a child. It's easy to judge me for throwing him out, but until you have—"

"—sorry to interrupt you, but I understand how you feel, and I don't blame you for protecting yourself and your property."

"Forgive me, but how can you understand? Everyone thinks I'm a witch." Mrs. Velasco patted the seat next to hers. "Do that later. Come sit by me."

Peyton put down her tools, removed her gloves, and reached for her dainty cup. She took a sip, fortified by the rich, chocolaty drink.

The lady of the house adjusted her oversized, round glasses and gawked at Peyton. "What might you know of out-of-control imbeciles?"

Peyton crossed one long leg over the other, and let her features loosen into the sad state they'd grown well accustomed to. "I have a troublesome son who's done worse than damage valuable paintings. He was loved, nurtured, educated, valued, yet he was always a colossal task. I speak experientially about the trials of willful children. You're never sure you're doing the right thing with them, even after you've tried everything you could."

"Willful, my foot. Wicked, diabolical, looking to put me in an early grave… at least mine is." Mrs. Velasco flashed a quick smile. "Churro?"

"Not yet, thank you." Peyton returned her cup to the tray, feeling fortunate to discuss Gideon without guilt or shame. "My son goes through phases. I'm not excusing his behavior, but it's like he's compelled in some hard-wired way."

"Well, my grandson must be half Lucifer's, and nothing like me or my late husband."

"Will you never let him back here?"

"Not even when I'm gone. I have more deserving nieces and nephews. Why not leave it to them?" She leaned back, engulfed in the Louis XVI sofa. "I'm too old to give a damn what others think. He's banned, and that's that, but that doesn't mean he's not enjoying my money. His rent, his car, even his weed is on me, but not come next month. I'm cutting him off. He doesn't believe me, but he will."

Peyton thought of Gideon and his cryptic call the night before. "Nobody is problem-free, are they? Which is why I don't envy anyone for anything. People pay in ways we can't always fathom."

Mrs. Velasco crunched her churro. "That's something Harlow would've said."

Peyton froze. "You knew my mother?"

"That's partly why I wanted to see you. How I loved her! Geraint said he'd pick up the painting and get it to you, but I insisted on meeting you." She gazed at the horizon for a while, as if expecting memories to arrive from another continent. "We were shocked when she packed it up, moved to the country, and married an intellectual."

Peyton's parents were very different from one another; the match never made sense to her. But attraction and love are hardly built on sense. "Love is great, but some things are above it."

"Commitment?"

"For one, but also integrity, and Dad had plenty of that." Adler too, who shared Sorensen's honorable qualities and strong Catholic faith.

"Your father helped Harlow stay grounded, and she needed it." She chortled, her eyes cast down. "Harlow was groovy, fab, and adventurous in her day. I have one of her paintings in my bedroom." She scrutinized Peyton with a careful gaze. "You're choice, like she was."

"Thank you. You're kind to say that, but wow, which painting?"

"I can't remember. The title is on the back. It's a woman reading old love letters."

Unable to contain her excitement, Peyton's voice squeaked. "May I please see it? I can't imagine which one it is. There's no complete inventory of Mom's work. We have a good idea, but there's no catalogue raisonné."

"That's unfortunate. I bought the painting at her opening exhibit in L.A. a million years ago, before she shifted to Native Southwestern themes." Mrs. Velasco sniggered until she coughed. "It's upstairs, the last bedroom on the right. Take your time. I'll be here when you're done."

Peyton thanked her client and hustled out of the room.

The painting on the wall opposite Mrs. Velasco's bed had all her mother's hyperrealism, attention to detail, texture, and geometry. She'd never seen it, and her nose burned, happy tears pricking through. She ran a finger over it, although she would've frowned if anyone else had done that. How far she'd come since her own debut exhibit in L.A. She removed the painting and took pictures of the front and back. A bronze plaque gave her mother's name and the title of the work, *Retrouvailles*, the name of the gallery that sold it, and the date. She was spellbound, wondering what her mother was feeling when she created such a tender work.

She returned downstairs to her client, elated by this serendipitous day. "I can't thank you enough, and I hope you don't mind, but I snapped a few photos of the painting so I can study it later."

"Sure, sure."

"It's titled *Retrouvailles*. I wonder what Mom was rediscovering." Peyton played with her hair, preparing to make a request. "I'm sorry to be asking, but I can't help myself. Would you consider selling me Mom's painting? I'm creating an homage to her, a gallery and museum."

Mrs. Velasco wasn't surprised. "Not yet, but at some point, perhaps. You know Ms. Chase, in honoring your mother, you honor yourself. Clever of you."

"Kind of you to say. Please, don't sell the painting to anyone else."

The woman studied her with a sly smile. "And have you settled on what it is you're rediscovering?"

She didn't hide how struck she was by the bullseye question. "I stand in the middle of my own *retrouvailles*. I'm torn, confused, unsure. You name it."

"And?"

"I'm unearthing riches, polishing them off, and finding they glimmer more than ever. Yet my life, without the stress from my son, is already a treasure."

"Sometimes oldest is best." Mrs. Velasco slivered a risqué smile and winked. "Your honesty today, Ms. Chase, is worth more than the Fede Galizia. Thank you."

"Thank *you*. You gave me plenty to think about." Peyton appreciated her client's patent mind. "I sometimes forget that Mom spent many years around these parts. Silly as it is, in my memory, she was always at the ranch. Born the day I was."

"Those were the best of times, when we were carefree, from party to party." Mrs. Velasco took another bite of her churro. "On the inside, I'm young, free of my demented grandson, able to dance and keep up with the best of them." She wiped her lips and spoke in an unwavering tone. "What will you do with your son?"

"His father and I disagree on what should be done. I think we should help him in his own life, but keep him away from the family home."

"You mean keep him away physically but close emotionally?"

Peyton nodded, relieved that Mrs. Velasco understood.

"Bull," the lady said. "If he's anything like the little monster I have, he's gangrene. You cut him off completely, or he'll metastasize to every member of the family."

Peyton resisted tears. "I love him, though he pains me."

"That's exactly what my daughter said until her son brought her to her end and trained his evil eye on me after that."

"His father would never forgive me."

"Seems to me his father needs to forgive himself. It's because he hasn't, he can't extricate himself from his son. Is he the older one?"

"The older of two biological children. We also have a daughter and two adopted sons."

"Ah, even more the reason your husband hasn't cut the cord." She pointed a bony finger at her own chest. "I know. I've seen it in my daughter."

"Thank you for your insight, Mrs. Velasco." After a moment of silence, Peyton said, "Your painting needs—"

"—I don't care, dear. Take it and bill me whatever. I know it's a sizable sum, but I can't be bothered with such details."

Peyton scooted to the edge of her seat. "What do you do if you can't forgive yourself?"

"Do you have a picture of your husband?"

She shared pictures of Adler she kept on her phone. "This one is my favorite," she said of a candid, up-close photo of him in a bathing suit.

"It would be mine, too, with this much man." She pushed her glasses back. "Very handsome, bright, but oh, so stubborn." She handed the phone back to her. "He's a lion and you're one too. I see it… Those who claim they can't forgive themselves are self-righteous in ways they don't realize." She began to rise, which spurred Peyton to help her to her feet. "Those with true humility always forgive. Tell your husband his pride is killing his *pride*."

"I never thought of him as lacking in humility."

"That's what his photo suggests. He still wants to be the hero. We can't be heroes to our adult children, not if we want to keep them grounded and able to cope."

"You can tell all that from photographs?"

"Dear, people are always revealing themselves. We only have to look." An impish smile deepened her wrinkles as she bore into Peyton. "I see you too. Are you afraid?"

Peyton pasted her eyes out the window on a fountain, spraying tall from the center of the pool. "I'm afraid of many things, but not of being seen."

"I didn't just get you here for the Fede Galizia, you know." Mrs. Velasco reached for a remote control and brought up a video of a mansion on a large screen. "That's Atalaya, my house on Seventeen-Mile Drive in Carmel. I know you live there, so you understand."

Carmel teemed with multi-million-dollar homes, but Atalaya was a masterpiece of science and art, an architectural wonder. "I love thoughtful architecture," Peyton said, "especially houses with three-sided patios. What a chef-d'oeuvre! Breathtaking. Easy to fall in love with a glass house ribbed with exquisite wood. Who designed it?"

"Ernesto Pellier. Not even Frank Lloyd Wright was that famous." She shimmied with delight. "It took three years to approve the design and four to build it because the materials and craftsmen were sourced from four continents. It's my pride and joy."

Peyton wasn't sure why Mrs. Velasco was showing her Atalaya, but she savored every room. "May I tour it in person, since we're neighbors in a way?"

"Tour it? You'll be doing more than that, dear, if you agree to my commission."

Peyton straightened her spine. "A commission for Atalaya?"

"It's too valuable to bequeath to one person. I created a foundation and I intend to give it to them, to house the best of my art collection. Atalaya needs a massive tableau of a local landmark. I want it to say Monterey Bay, but with flair. Can you guess what I'd prefer?"

Peyton snickered, excited and surprised. "Hmm… You're making it too easy. The Bixby Creek Bridge? I never tire of it, and it says Monterey like nothing else."

"I knew you were the right choice the minute I saw your website. That's exactly what Atalaya needs. Now, how will you present it?"

She had no clue. "What if I pay your house a visit, see where you'd like the painting hung, understand what surrounds it, then put together a composition for you to preview?"

"Will it be abstract or figurative?"

Peyton chose what felt right in her gut, but it wasn't a style she often used. "As a child, I painted bridges and rainbows more than anything else, usually disguised as jaws or ribs. Until now, I hadn't realized why. I may view myself or my role as a bridge. I'm channeling Salvador Dalí fused with figurative in my *sfumato* specialty."

Approval spread across Mrs. Velasco's face. "I look forward to your study, but if it's not from the soul, I'll know it, and I'll be disappointed. Your work shines best when it's from your spirit, not your intellect. I can always spot the difference."

It had been a while since she'd painted with soul alone. Peyton pressed her hands together as if preparing to clap. "I can't recall the last time I was this thrilled about a new painting. Thank you so much, Mrs. Velasco!" From the lady's change of posture, Peyton knew it was time to conclude her visit. She removed a linen cover from her bag, secured the Fede Galizia in it, then slipped it inside the padded hardcase she'd brought for it. "I'll return it to you as good as new."

"I saw a bunch of 'before and afters' on your website. You're a magician."

As they walked together to the front door, Peyton said, "Thank you for the treats and frank advice, and for a dream-come-true commission."

"At my age, dear, joy is the ability to slap as many people with the truth as possible. Most, however, never come back." She snickered like a little girl. "Which is probably why I'm keen on it."

"You give me hope, Mrs. Velasco. I'll be in Carmel for a stretch and will visit your house soon. Thank you very much."

"And you give me substance, dear. Funny how scary substance is to the sheeple." She seemed to think twice before saying, "Your husband has to forgive himself, shed his pride, and stop desiring to be the hero. But you have work to do."

"Oh?" Peyton held her breath.

"Your son is not your failure, Ms. Chase, nor is your daughter your success—which I suspect she is. They don't reflect on you the way they did when they were children. Learn to desensitize yourself to their choices. They stand apart from you."

"I know our children are born *through* us, not from us. But it feels bad anyway."

"You understand it, but do you believe it? Truly believe it?"

"I don't know."

"At least you're honest. My sense is you need a reunion—a proper retrouvailles."

Peyton thought of the first time Adler held her hand, and the immediate bond that seared them together. "You hit the bullseye. That's how I feel."

eighteen

Hector Strongman, the art detective Ashton recommended was a slender man in a slim, fitted suit, and a thin mustache with bleached teeth stacked like sugar cubes. They met at a café bar decorated with profuse greenery. Pothos and string of pearls plants dangled from the ceiling and along the wall, bringing the outside in. Over drinks, he satisfied her list of questions and concerns more thoroughly than she'd expected, and they discussed plans, fees, and expectations.

"I've located five of your mother's paintings so far. At least three owners are willing to sell… with some coaxing and finessing, of course, which is my specialty."

"It's now feeling real," Peyton said. "A good chunk of Harlow's paintings under one roof. Don't forget, please, that I don't mind paintings on loan if outright sales can't be arranged. How often will we touch base?"

"Pretty regularly. Mr. Grant was explicit in his instructions. He insists I prioritize you above my wife."

Peyton's eyes almost leapt out. "He said that?"

"Word for word, and Mr. Grant never asks twice. Not in my world."

She knew Ashton well enough to realize he had already moved beyond discretion. She knew she'd emboldened him by going to his house in Lake

Tahoe and wished she hadn't. "You're quite the find, Mr. Strongman." She rose and extended her hand. "I'm happy to be working with you."

"That's a relief," he said, with a handshake. "I can't have you otherwise."

Reassured and excited, Peyton said her goodbyes and unleashed her thoughts in a different direction. She wanted to placate her son and raise her chances of a positive outcome, so she texted him: *happy it'll be just the two of us, Sorensen. All my love xxx*

Her son knew how to trap her, and she drove to dinner, promising herself she wouldn't take his bait. Not having eaten all day, she looked forward to the panoramic views from 71Above and their acclaimed sashimi and Japanese wagyu.

Perched on the 71st floor of the U.S. Bank Tower, the highest restaurant in Downtown L.A. was abuzz with fashionable diners, panoramic views, floor-to-ceiling glass, and honey-colored woodworks—an architectural sculpture on stilts.

She'd arrived on time, but her son was nowhere in sight. A petite receptionist with beach waves and a dress the size of a napkin asked her for her reservation.

"Gideon Adler for two?"

The receptionist moved her eyes from the screen to Peyton. "Sorry, no such reservation."

"Hmm, try Chase instead, please?"

She gave a shallower smile. "No, sorry. No such reservation, either."

Peyton frowned, wondering if Gideon had played some trick on her, but was soon distracted by the appearance of a fashionably dressed man with the demeanor of a manager. He whispered to the receptionist, and she apologized.

"Please forgive the confusion, Ms. Chase. Your party is here." He grabbed a menu. "Allow me to escort you to your table. A cosmopolitan is already chilling for you and a chocolate soufflé has been preordered."

Puzzled at the copious attention, she led the way as bid, with escalating apprehension.

"Is there anything I can get you right away?"

"Not yet. Thank you." Everything became clearer when she saw Ashton stretch out of his seat with a broad smile and a fresh haircut.

He stepped forward and hugged her. "You make my days," he whispered.

She was electrified, thinking of the way he'd held her at his house in Lake Tahoe, and she longed for youth and fun. "No wonder we got a table fast. It's for Ashton Grant." She leaned over and gave her son a kiss on the cheek, but he was unmoved.

Ashton helped her into a seat and placed his hands on her shoulders. She wanted him to leave them there all night. "I told Gideon he could use my name, but he insisted I come along. You should've told me yourself."

She shot her son a discreet, disapproving look. "Yes, I should've. Thank you. This is exquisite." She sipped her cosmopolitan, and Ashton signaled the server for another round of cocktails—a Bellini and a god-father. She knew the godfather was for Ashton. "You're not of age yet, Gideon, a Bellini?"

He smirked and gave her an innocent shrug she hadn't seen in a while. "Whenever Ashton orders for me, no one asks for my ID."

Ashton touched her forearm with a familiarity that made her uncom-fortable in front of her son. "Sorry, do you oppose it? I don't mean to overstep."

"Not oppose. At seventeen, when at home, the kids could have a drink. It's why they drink in moderation, but we're out now." Hurt that Gideon had avoided being alone with her, she busied herself with her serviette, trying to hide her face. There was a time when Ashton awakened in her arms and spent days on end in them. Had fate spun one less knot for her, she would've been sitting today with him and a son they shared.

"How often do you two do dinner?"

"I know that tone," Ashton replied. "Not much. But Gideon said you insisted I join you, so I couldn't refuse."

"You're a wonderful friend to me and my family. I'm happy you're here."

"Is it true you dated Ashton before Dad?" Gideon wore a leisure suit and Prada loafers. In his element, away from the ranch, he shone. "Margot said you almost married him." He accepted his drink before the server could place it on the table and took a long draft. "Keep them coming."

Displeased by her son's rudeness, she gave him eyes full of warning, which he ignored, as usual. "I got to see one of your grandmother's paintings today, by chance."

"Riveting." Gideon raised his glass, gesturing for a server busy at a different table. "More."

"Servers are not servants. They work very hard. Please, be respectful, as I always taught you."

He glared at his mother with eyes of glass.

Ashton said, "It's a small request."

Though she had expected it, her son responding more readily to Ashton pained her. "Happy to be graduating soon?"

"It depends on how big your gift will be."

"How's the job?"

"Boring, like life on the ranch." Gideon picked up his mother's cosmopolitan and poured it down his throat.

"Why are you drinking like a maniac?" Peyton reproached herself for thinking she could still reach her son.

Ashton scanned the menu. "I recommend the tartare, for sure."

Gideon checked the watch his mother had given him, asked to be excused, and pushed his seat back too far, intruding on the patron sitting behind him.

"I can see why you struggle with him," Ashton said. "I'm sorry. Maybe I should leave."

"I should apologize to you. Gideon is being so rude. I must bring out the worst in him. I tried so hard all his life." She shook her head, holding back tears. "You improve things. Please, stay."

He squeezed her hand like old times. "It's obvious from how suave and witty he can be that he was nurtured and encouraged. And from the way Bryce looks up to you, you're a remarkable mother. Is it always this contentious?"

"This is a vast improvement." She bit her cheek hard enough to hurt. "I came here to validate him. It'll fail like all my attempts, but we're here. And thank you for Hector. He's a find and a half. He's—"

"—strange," Ashton said, interrupting her, his eyes fixated on the person who stood behind her.

"I didn't find him strange, rather—"

"—no, Peyton. I'm not sure I understand, but your husband is right behind you."

She twisted around. "Adler?"

He flashed an intense, incensed glare, burning with frustration. Bryce was at his back, but Gideon had disappeared.

"I'm flabbergasted!" She rose out of her seat. "Where's Gideon?" When Adler kept staring at her, stone-faced and seething, she turned her attention to Bryce. "Honey, how come you're here?"

Bryce teared up and shook her head. "I think we should step out to the lobby."

Silent but fuming, Adler turned on his heels and bolted toward the exit.

Peyton grabbed her purse and apologized to Ashton. "Gideon, no doubt, did this. I'll call you and explain later. I'm just horrified. Sorry, I have to go." She made to leave money on the table, but Ashton wouldn't have it.

"Peyton, please don't avoid me like last time, okay?" He gripped her wrist until she promised she wouldn't. "You have no reason to feel guilty. None."

She and Bryce dashed to the elevator where Adler was still waiting. If they hadn't been on the seventy-first floor, she was sure her husband would've taken the stairs.

"Where's Gideon?" she asked.

Adler kept mute.

Inside the elevator, she said, "You have no reason to be angry with me. I came here to see Gideon, but he brought Ashton with him. What was I supposed to do?"

"Leave!" he yelled. "You were supposed to leave!"

"That would've been extremely rude." She calculated for what felt like a year. "But why are you here? We said we'd meet at Berkeley."

"Sorry to have crashed your date. Is this why you denied me time with my kids, to spend it with Ashton instead?"

"You can't actually believe that." She saw how upset Bryce was and touched her arm. "It was an innocent dinner. How did you know to meet us here?" Adler exited the elevator and pressed forward as she hurried behind him. "Let me guess. You told Gideon how you wanted the four of us to have dinner, right?" She struggled to catch him. "Will you wait a minute?"

He stopped and spun around to face her. "The only thing I asked for was dinner with my family alone. You refused me, but you didn't refuse your ex!"

Bryce sobbed, as though she'd been shanked, which made Peyton hug her. "It's okay. We're okay."

Adler shouted, "No, we're not okay!" He took the keys from his pocket and raced off.

Peyton knew pursuing him would be fruitless and turned to Bryce. "There's no point in trying to reason with your father, and I don't want a scene in public. What happened is—"

"—of course I know what happened, Mom. Gideon connived to get us all here so you and Dad would clash. I'm not crying because you're fighting. Dad insisted, though it made no sense. You would've told us your-self if you wanted us here. How could he be this dumb?"

Peyton slumped her shoulders. "Your dad is far from dumb. He's desperate to repair us, but he can't."

"Does he really think you're having an affair?"

Peyton wished she could sit down. "I'm sure of only one thing. Your dad wants something to target because problems can be solved, but we don't have a problem, do we? We have a relentless state of being like a never-ending hurricane."

Bryce wiped her nose on a saturated tissue. "I'm sorry we ambushed you this way. I messaged you when we detoured. Didn't you get my warnings?"

Peyton slapped her thigh. "With so much going on today, I had my phone on mute. I didn't even realize, but thank you for the warning, and I'm sorry to frazzle you this way." She cradled her daughter again. "You still have to get to Berkeley."

"Can I fly with you?"

"No, honey, that'll make Dad feel abandoned." She led her daughter by the arm. "Can you find the car from here?"

Bryce assessed their location in the parking lot. "I think so."

He was behind the wheel, his chest heaving.

Peyton opened the car door. "Nothing wrong happened. I didn't invite Ashton. Gideon wanted to cause mischief, and you fell for it."

"You always blame him for everything! Was it Gideon's fault you accepted gifts from Ashton? I'm not stupid, Peyton. I know where Apollo came from. And you didn't just bump into Ashton at Lake Tahoe."

She stared at his unforgiving profile, exasperation replacing guilt. As Bryce slipped into the passenger seat, she asked her, "I'm assuming you're spending the night here, yes? It's too far to drive to Berkeley."

"Yes, Mom, at the Bel-Air, where you're staying."

"I'll see you there."

Adler bleached his knuckles on the steering wheel. "It's okay, Bryce. Go with your mother. I know you want to."

Bryce hesitated, torn.

"It doesn't hurt my feelings. It's okay, go. I'll see you at the hotel."

"Thank you, Dad," she said, and hopped out of the car.

They watched Adler drive off, unnerved like on any occasion courtesy of Gideon.

"Gideon hates us, doesn't he?"

"He really must. Who does this to his own parents? He even risked his relationship with Ashton." Peyton texted him one line: *I came here for Sorensen but found only Gideon!* "I can't even leave him a voicemail. I know he never listens to them."

"What will you say to Dad?"

"I hope we don't say another word to each other tonight."

They picked up the pups and headed to Peyton's hotel room, who was dreading another confrontation. They crossed the hallway, one more frazzled than the other.

"What if Dad has more to say?" Bryce asked. "Maybe I should stay with you as a deterrent."

"That's not your job, honey. Too much to ask of you. Whatever it is, I'll handle it alone." She was relieved when she found the room vacant. "Looks exactly as I left it."

"I thought Dad would've beat us here."

Confused, Peyton phoned the front desk asking if they had given him access to the room. The Adlers had been staying there for years, and the staff knew them. "Wow," she said. "Your father checked himself into a separate room."

Bryce touched her mother's arm. "Maybe it's for the best."

Never had Adler done anything this cold and distant. Not in over two decades of marriage. "I think you're right."

nineteen

Peyton flew and Adler drove with Bryce, but they beat her to the Ritz Carlton in San Francisco. She checked in and headed to the room she assumed she'd be sharing with Adler, ready to discuss the night before. But the room was empty. She got the pups settled with toys and snacks and called her daughter.

"I'm all checked in. How about you?"

"Dad went somewhere. I'm in the next room." Bryce knocked on the adjoining door.

Peyton let her in and changed into jeans, a pink silk blouse, and wedge sandals. "Did your dad get his own room again? They told me at the front desk he already checked in, but his things aren't here."

"I didn't realize." Bryce sat on the bed and beckoned the furballs to her. "He barely talked to me the whole way. Thank goodness for headphones. I had nothing good to say to him, either, but he apologized. I couldn't read him, though. He was closed off, but said it was bad judgement. I wasn't sure what he meant exactly." She cooed to Myriad and Apollo and tried to get them to jump. "Are you and Dad in trouble?"

"In worse shape than we've ever been. I used to think everything is fixable, but I don't know anymore."

"What are you gonna do, Mom?"

"I think it's time to stop doing. Period."

"Can Dad really believe you're having an affair?"

Peyton watched apprehension drain the color from her daughter's face. "This is about not feeling appeased enough, as if mollifying him would morph Gideon from foe to friend. Did your dad get hold of him?"

"I don't care about Gideon. If I never hear his name again, I'll be ecstatic."

That her kids were at each other's throats was excruciating and disturbing. "How did he convince you to come to dinner with Gideon and me?"

Bryce grunted in a rare bout of anger. "Dad didn't ask me. He just told me what we were doing. I couldn't talk him out of it at all."

Peyton swung her purse over her shoulder. "Let's drop off our babies and checkout the furniture stores."

"What about Dad?"

"If he wants to see me, he can call me." Peyton's phone flashed with a text from Ashton: *I want to know how you're feeling. I can talk at length after seven. I'll call.* For the first time, she felt no guilt at her reviving relationship with him and decided she'd take his call, even if she had to go elsewhere to do it.

Three furniture stores later and a visit to Crate and Barrell for kitchenware gulped the afternoon. Adler never called.

By the time they returned to the hotel, the sky was lavender, traffic had died down, and Peyton could no longer sustain herself on coffee and adrenaline alone.

"I'm starving," she said. "I looked forward to that Wagyu beef tartare last night."

"I'm hungry too. Should we call Dad?"

"Absolutely not. This one is on him."

They freshened up and went to the hotel restaurant, Parallel 37.

"They have your Wagyu tartare here. What do you think of that?"

Peyton puckered her lips. "I think it's good karma. I must be iron deficient the way I keep craving raw meat. What looks better to you for an entrée, pumpkin risotto or sea bass?"

"I'm going for the cheeseburger myself, if it's okay to join you," said Adler, standing at their table. "The hotel manager told me where to find you."

Peyton gestured for him to sit in the leather chair beside Bryce, but he walked around and slipped onto the bench beside her.

Bryce asked, "Should I give you guys a minute?"

"Stay." Her father stroked her hand. "I want to speak to you both." He waited until the server took their order. "I stayed away because I needed clarity of mind and soul. Sorry if I worried you." His wrinkles had deepened from stress and lack of sleep, aging him. "I overreacted yesterday and was embarrassed by my behavior. So, I kept to myself until I regained my senses. I was afraid I'd say and do the wrong things again. I should've known better, but I didn't."

Peyton felt empathy for him, but she banked her anger. "We never could love Gideon out of his nature. It's none of our faults." Mrs. Velasco's words resonated in her chest. "Do you think you need to forgive yourself for what you believe contributed to his behavior, and forgive me too? We might not have handled every situation perfectly, but we did our best. Can you accept that only he has the power to improve himself?"

Adler looked at his daughter, his eyes identical to hers. "Honey, I'm sorry so much of my energy goes to your brother. I'll do better. You're the apple of my eye. You know that, right?"

"Dad, we've been here before. We're back to saying things we don't do. I know you want us to be one big happy family, but I'm never happy when Gideon is around, and the feeling is mutual, believe me. Please, don't force me into any more situations with him. Okay?"

"It breaks my heart you never could get along, but it's not your fault." Adler ran a hand through his silver hair. "I'm in the danger zone, wanting something too much. If hunting and fishing taught me anything, it's not to turn into Ahab. I'll work on that, I promise."

"Carmel-by-the-Sea is a perfect place for mending bodies and spirits," Peyton said, though her hopes were muffled. "We need more vitamin sea."

"You won't like what I'm about to say." Adler sighed and wiped his tired face. "I should do what I know best to get myself centered again. Adults need reboots as well. I've been on my back foot for too long, and I know only one way and place to recalibrate."

Peyton heard something else. To heal and fortify, he'd have to get away from her. What he needed came at her expense, but she wouldn't stop him. Not when he wouldn't meet her halfway. "You're going into the wilderness again?"

He mustered a feeble smile and stroked his hatching beard. "A few weeks of grit and grime in Northern New Mexico will put me right. Can you spare me for that long?"

Peyton pictured all they'd miss together: walks on the beach, intimate conversations, cuddling on cool nights by a roaring fire, and reconnecting under sheets.

"It's what I need."

She waited to see if he'd ask her what she needed. But he didn't.

Bryce cocked her head and pushed her thick red hair behind her shoulders. "It's none of my business, but why can't you hunt and fish on Hastings Island or at San Bablo Bay? Why go back to New Mexico?"

Plates garnished with flowers and sculpted vegetables arrived. Adler waited until everyone tasted their food. "It's not about hunting or fishing. It's about getting baptized in the dirt of my youth… a cleansing I can only do in my home forests, in the rivers of my forefathers. Those woods know me. They saved me many times before, and they'll do it again."

Bryce discreetly texted her mother that her father would miss her birthday, but told her not to remind him.

Adler eyed his burger. "William called me, asking if we're still on the road. He said he can't reach you. Are you not talking to him?"

Bryce grimaced and played with her risotto. "I've had so much to do."

"Well, he thinks you have some future business plans together."

"We all need to hit pause, Dad. I can only deal with one day at a time."

Adler wiped the corners of his mouth and gulped beer. "Did you get everything you wanted today?"

"Pretty much. Whatever's left, I'll get it on my own later. The furniture will be delivered tomorrow. I'll move in then and liberate you. Besides, Mom is two hours down the coast. I'll still see her."

The server returned to ask about dessert. Adler ordered croissant bread pudding to share.

"What about Gideon?" Peyton asked.

"It didn't seem like it yesterday, but I was mostly angry with him, and I would've directed my anger at him if he hadn't disappeared. I must've done something horrible if my son thinks he can turn me against my wife and daughter." He quaffed his beer and stared into the bottom of his glass. "I need to figure out how I could've given him that impression." Adler sat upright. "You're still going to Carmel for the rest of the summer?"

Bryce excused herself, leaving her mother to be frank.

Was her husband asking her if she'd sacrifice even more for what was unlikely to mend? "Carmel is where *I* get baptized and renewed. We established that long ago—my coast, your mountain." When they first met, Adler feared he'd be too little for her, and she'd be too much for him. Now she wondered if he hadn't been right, after all. But they'd been good together for two decades. Why now?

"I may not get to join you at all."

Peyton could see he weighed her, made sure her tone was measured. She knew he wanted her to demonstrate her commitment by waiting for him in New Mexico. "My first choice is to be together. But since you'll be in elk and bobcat country, I prefer to spend my time by the sea."

He ordered a double bourbon and avoided her stare.

"You don't like my decision? It's the one we made together. Last I looked, we were spending the rest of the summer in California."

"I can't remember the last time none of us were home, when not all together."

Peyton understood his angst. "It's not a bad omen. It means the kids are grown up and their parents are busy leading interesting lives."

"Is that what we're doing?" he asked, unmasking his sadness.

"We change the narrative, we change our lives." Adler's medium was the wilderness, but Peyton's was paint. She'd have to use it to change her own narrative. And now that she had a massive commission from Mrs. Velasco, she knew she would. "Did you check yourself into a different room again?"

Guilt coated his face and strained his voice. "Yes, but I can still join you."

Overwhelmed by the pain of rejection, she clasped her arms, sinking her nails deep into her flesh.

"Would you rather I didn't?"

"I couldn't say in front of Bryce, but why didn't you at least inform me you'd be sleeping elsewhere? For two nights too. It's mere courtesy. A little respect after all these years."

"I don't know."

"I do." She shook, shocked at the degree he took her for granted. "You wanted to punish me, and you're just getting started. That's why you're going back on your word, isn't it?"

"I'm not the one going on dates!"

"So, you think I'm interested in another man, and what do you do? You leave me alone again. Good plan."

He balled his fist and seemed about to bang it on the table but didn't. "Maybe I trust my wife to respect her vows!"

Anger calcified her spirit. She stood to leave, if only to avoid raising her voice, but he clasped her wrist.

"Come home and you won't be alone so much. Maybe if I knew you were there, I'd cut my camping trip short."

"When did just waiting for you like a moron become so satisfactory? Is this my value now?" Peyton said what she thought she never would. "You were right checking into another room. I prefer it that way."

The look he gave her was pure rage and pain. "You do know what you're asking, right?"

She knew she'd risked too much. "No, Adler, it's you who did the asking when you left me concerned and alone. Instead of making amends and taking responsibility, you ask me to sacrifice more. And instead of starting the healing, you add salt to new and old wounds."

"This is not about you!" he said.

"But it ought to be. At minimum, it should be about *us*. But it hasn't been, and I wonder if it ever will again." She struggled to suppress the urge to scream. "All the ways I've tried to reconnect with you won't work until you're able to let go of your idea of what a family or a son or being a father is."

Bryce returned in time for dessert, which made her mother sit down. She dipped a spoon into the croissant bread pudding and savored it, studying her parents. "So nice to eat together." She plopped another spoonful in her mouth and sighed with pleasure. "My God, this dessert should be illegal."

Peyton knew her daughter was trying to pacify them, pretending the tension away.

Her father asked, "What do I tell William if I see him?"

All delight erased, Bryce put down her spoon. "I'll see him at Thanksgiving. I'm sure he'll be back at the ranch then."

Peyton knew the foundation of her marriage was rupturing, but she hadn't thought it could lose its flooring altogether. She excused herself, walked into the lobby, and called Honovi. She tucked into a quiet corner, a sinister feeling worming in her heart.

Honovi answered right away. "Why do I feel like your chest is cracked open?"

"Because it is." She teared up and covered her face with a hand. "But I feel better when I hear your voice. How're you?"

"I'm not the one with a trail of tears. And now I feel your energy, I think maybe I have a message for you. I'm unsure, but something dark may be coming. More ominous than anything I've seen before."

"Dark how?"

"It's dense and menacing, disturbs me. I prefer to ignore confusing messages, but I keep seeing things. And now you called, Mom, it feels related to you. I don't mean to frighten you, but I have to caution you. Please be extra safe in everything you do."

"Honey, some things are inevitable." Peyton feared that her son took too much upon himself. "Just because you can see the train coming doesn't mean you can stop it."

"Stay close to home. Don't let in strangers. Don't venture far alone. Okay?"

Fear started at her legs and coiled upward like a constrictor snake, but she forced a smile. "I will. Are you all right, though?"

"I've been meditating extra and feel a pull to the sea. I see us in Carmel before the holidays, painting together."

"Words can't describe how proud I am of you. So I'll just have to paint it."

twenty

Peyton arrived at Carmel-by-the-Sea, ready to throw herself into her art. The house on Santa Lucia Avenue featured a bright living room with a thirty-foot vaulted ceiling and wall-to-wall windows that framed the bay and lagoon, a two-tiered garden with a spacious travertine patio, and a bright studio with all-encompassing views. She placed her luggage by the large wood-burning fireplace and liberated Apollo from his travel bag. The rooms smelled of paint. She opened the French doors that spilled onto a patio facing the Pacific and Point Lobos State Natural Reserve, inviting the sea breeze inside. She looked about her place, furnished with aspen wood, white textiles and blue calcite marble, thinking she'd like to stay beyond the summer.

While Apollo roamed, burning energy, Peyton stood at the railing, digesting the harmony that had been absent from her life. She hadn't been there in four months, but it felt longer. She absorbed the rugged and lush beauty of Point Lobos where, over the years, she'd released many prayers to the stars. The Pacific, inking the landscape teal and gold, restored her spirit. Ice plants spilled over the cliffs, speckling the jade landscape with pink and yellow flowers. To her left, the view was sculpted with white sand beaches and Alpine architecture. To her right, a series of rooftops knifed out, surrounded by lush trees, large succulents, and grasses blowing in the cool breeze. Sailboats dotted the lagoon, winging her to Ashton. If he hadn't bid so high on *The Last Start*, she might never have commanded premium prices for her artwork or bought a house in an art colony by the sea. Reels of her past played in her mind. Before Bryce and Gideon. Before Adler. When her father was still alive and Ashton was front and center. Deep breaths later, alone in a space she loved, tension seeped out of her body, and Apollo joined her, wagging his tail.

"We need to buy you a bed, some toys, and lots of food," she told him. "Let's go to Bruno's Market." She was about to leave when the doorbell rang. On her phone, she could see a delivery driver waiting with a white box wrapped in a blue ribbon.

When she opened the door, the guy said, "It's a special delivery for Ms. Chase. Requires a signature."

Peyton thanked him and accepted the mystery box. There was no card, which told her plenty. Only one person would've had something intended for her delivered so precisely. She cautiously placed her hand over it, as if it were on fire, then unknotted the ribbon. Inside the box was an antique frame with a black-and-white photograph of her on a sailboat. Ashton had snapped it with the Hasselblad. She looked younger and happier than she had in many years. For a moment, she sat in her favorite plushy chair, facing the floor-to-ceiling glass windows that let in the sea, disappearing into the photo and sobbing for loss, for change, for lack of change, and for her helplessness—for a longing she couldn't shake. She calmed down, washed her face and bundled up Apollo. On the way to the market, she phoned Royce.

"How's Carmel?" Royce asked. "I'm sitting on my upper balcony with a blanket on my lap, and it's still summer. You?"

"Driving to the market. It's a gorgeous day, but it'll be nippy later."

The ice cubes in Royce's drink clicked against the glass. "Now, why isn't your husband with you?"

"How'd you know?"

"Your wranglers blab. They saw him pack up enough gear for a year, they say. Of course, this means the neighborhood is already assuming you're separated."

Peyton lowered her window, needing the breeze on her face. "Ever since Scarborough retired and most of his guys along with him, we haven't had a proper crew on the ranch. One more thing we need to overhaul. I really hate gossips."

"What's the man griping about now?"

"Adler is struggling like I am. He needs to regroup and fortify. You know how he does that."

"And how're you regrouping and fortifying? Shouldn't he be holding your hand?"

"He has little left to give, so he's taking time for himself." Peyton slowed down on a turn, still hurt, though she defended him. "Was it you who told Ashton I'm up here?"

"He was curious about developments behind the scenes. Told me he caused you extra trouble."

"Ashton has nothing to feel bad about, and we talked about it, but it's been stressful."

"Then invite him, Peyton."

"That's what he really called you about. I'm protecting my marriage, so I keep away from temptation."

Royce groaned. "We don't always get second chances. Do you see decades more with a man who runs into the forest when you need him most?"

Peyton didn't and had been feeling rejected for a while. Now she felt downright abandoned. She drove on Disneyesque streets with heaping flower boxes, intricate German architecture, vibrant old flora, and the cleanliness of churches. "This past year, Gideon has been a nightmare. We've had many happy years, though."

"Not for quite some time and with no hope of things getting better. I'm only saying be careful about throwing away a chance of living a completely different life with a completely different person."

"Who says I want a completely different life?"

"Lordy, you do, darling, with every tear, with every ounce of sadness and disappointment. At your age, I was merry, with days full of fun." Peyton could hear Royce plunking down her glass. "Look, I never talked through my hat to you, and I won't now."

"You don't wear hats, Royce."

"Then I'll talk through my wig. You're miserable. Something has to change. If that change is someone other than Adler, so be it. Life is short and you're no spring chicken."

"You never liked him."

"Adler kept your life small and confined. Harlow went outside her marriage when she needed to and, frankly, it saved it. And you should've been with Ashton all along. You know this, right?"

"Next time I speak to my husband, I'll tell him I'm saving my marriage by rolling in the sheets with Ashton."

"Darling, only two things make the world go round: desire and fear. Enough running on fear! Maybe you should run on desire instead, at least for a while. I'm old, but my memory is intact. I never regretted the kisses I took—only the ones I didn't."

How she'd loved kissing her husband for hours. "I took vows."

"Take new ones."

She arrived at Bruno's Market, feeling it was about time she reaped the years of seeding and fertilizing. But could she be with anyone other than Adler?

Royce asked, "Remember my advice to you about marriage when you were in your twenties?"

Peyton chuckled and cut the engine. "You told me to hurry and get married, so I could be divorced and happy while I was still young."

"I'm ancient now, so listen. You'll never age if you marry the right person. You'll also find two saggy butts are better than one. And Adler is always climbing mountains, so his butt is never going to sag."

Peyton laughed. "I know you only tell me things as you see them, and I love you for it, but Adler's butt will always be perfect for me."

"I'll have another Old Fashioned now. You have one too… a la French. If only while you're in Carmel."

Under the sun's splintering rays, Peyton and Apollo walked along Carmel Beach, a fifteen-minute promenade from her house. A fissure of orange and yellow grew ever wider, splitting the cerulean sky at the seam. The water was cold but healing for her fractured spirit. Apollo played tag with the waves and nipped at them, while she picked up seashells, hoping for a sand dollar to add to her collection. She'd slept only a few hours but felt rejuvenated. Carmel was her inspirational haven. How nostalgic she was for a time when she lived by herself, for herself. As her feet froze in the clear waters of the Pacific, she was warmed by the idea of living alone again and wondered if she wouldn't in the end. The scent of baking bread wafted down from Ocean Avenue, interrupting her ruminations. She called Apollo over. "What do you say we get bagels, then light a fire and work?"

The dog moved his ears forward and bounced more than walked on their way to Carmel Bakery.

She ordered a strong brew to go with her baked goods and thought of Scarborough, who loved coffee strong enough a horseshoe could float in it. She missed him, missed her father, the dead who were no longer able to guide her. The irony was that being alone, she felt less lonely. Not what she'd expected. She drifted from thought to thought until her phone ringing made her realize she was almost home.

"Adler?"

"I didn't wake you, did I?"

"On my way back from beach and bagels."

"That's the spirit. I don't like how we parted ways. We should've spent that last night together. I'm sorry we didn't."

She could feel the tightening in his chest. "What is it?"

"I'm going up soon, waiting for this rainstorm to pass. As you know, I won't have reception up there, only the satellite phone. But that's for emergencies. I wanted to hear your voice. Are you all right?"

"In some ways." She fell silent, and so did he. After a few steps, she said, "I get the sense you have something else to tell me."

"I know I said I needed time alone, but I stopped in L.A. to confront Gideon. It didn't go well at first, but I made him a deal. He agreed to go camping with me in return for a new car. I also promised that if this experience fails him, we'd never trek that way again."

Peyton stopped walking. "When Gideon is cornered, it brings out the worst in him."

"Well, I made an impromptu decision. I had to bribe him, but he's here. He needs better values. The kind of values a man learns when his back is to the dirt and his eyes to the stars."

Peyton lifted her face to the heavens. "He has school and an enviable job."

"This is more important."

She couldn't keep the anger out of her voice. "Gideon won't keep you from centering yourself, but I would've?"

"Please, don't say that. I have to try one last time. A last-ditch effort at making a decent man of him."

"Last ditch?" she asked, sure it wouldn't be. "You said you didn't want to turn into Ahab."

He exhaled. "It's the last try."

"Did you cost him his job? He's brilliant enough to make up schoolwork, but what about his position? It's superb for someone with no experience."

"He can get another job. I'll use my connections at the naval base in San Diego."

She suspected he'd sabotaged the job to reclaim his place and destroy what had come through Ashton. She could picture him clenching his jaw and pinching the ridge of his nose. "Where will you camp?"

"Colorado border. Want to talk to him?"

Peyton mulled it over but didn't think she could improve anything. "No, that's okay, but make sure he takes good care of his father." She sensed an added layer of vulnerability in him. "Is everything else all right?"

"We were never the couple who said I love you all the time. But you know I love you, right? I know it's ironic to say, given my stint in the woods, but it's truer than ever."

"If you were here with me, you wouldn't need to explain."

"I'll make it up to you."

She wasn't sure he could. "If Gideon acts up, release him from his promise. He's not made for the wild like you."

"Did you hear what I said? I love you, sweet Pey."

"I love you, too, and so very much." She tapped her forehead. "I just don't get how we're not together, living it up."

"I think of you all the time. I know I made a mess of things, but I'm counting on your strength. Gideon acts tough, but he's scared, easy to wound, slow to mend. I'm not asking you to do more for him. I'm asking for one more shot to do all *I* can. Please, support me in this."

She braced against a Monterey cypress tree, shaking her head. Defiant thoughts sparked in her mind, but no words would come out. She hadn't had the chance to tell him about Mrs. Velasco or her commission. The things that lent meaning to their partnership were evanescing, and she feared the sinew of their bond was fraying.

"When we get back to the ranch, I'll *show* you. Please understand."

"When you return… *come back*, and not just for a spell," she said, though it felt pointless. "Gideon won't grow from this, but *you* can."

"I will, sweet Pey, and he can. Since Lightning died, I feel as if my chances died with him. I'm hopeful, and to forgive myself like you asked me to, I have to believe in my heart I've done all I can. You know what Scarborough would say."

"Make tracks, keep your saddle oiled, and your gun greased, right?" It was advice she, too, needed.

"How'll you spend your time in Carmel?"

She told him what was practical and least taxing. "I have a unique commission. It'll keep me busy."

"Send me pics. I'd like to see what you're conceiving."

She wasn't sure whether he was interested or investigative. "I'll send you some photos to give you an idea, but it'll be incomplete." She hung up and prayed things could be put to right again.

Peyton was scheduled for a live demonstration at Geraint's second gallery on San Carlos Street. She parked on the corner and strolled past boutiques, restaurants, and galleries shaded by coast live oaks and magenta bougainvilleas the height of rooftops. The smell of the sea was strong, but the aroma of grilled meat from a local grill was stronger.

Dressed in a short pinup yellow and black polka-dotted dress with a sweetheart neckline and stiletto heels, she walked into Geraint's gallery with Apollo, now twice as big.

Geraint came from behind his desk, thin enough to have defined eye sockets and a bulbous Adam's apple. Since her last visit with him in Los Angeles, he'd gotten a second facelift that pulled his eyebrows too close to his hair plugs. "Lassie, I'm chuffed. You always know how to seduce," he said in his Welsh accent. He was past retirement age, styled like a young rockstar in designer jeans. He gave her a kiss on each cheek and pats on the shoulders. "My Botox is wearing off. What do you think? Tell me the truth."

"Stop playing with your face. Your eyes are almost vertical. And that Joker mouth of yours hasn't relaxed back to normal."

He shrieked and flicked his wrist, adorned with several gold bracelets. "Slash me down, why don't you?"

"You said to be honest."

"In California, darling, honest means lie and tell me what I want to hear. You know nothing? Besides, we don't all live in dry desert air, mummified for eternity."

Peyton asked the question she'd been saving until she saw him in person. "Why didn't you tell me Ashton bought so much of my work?"

He blinked rapidly, then bowed from the waist. "I am but a servant at the feet of the king. Are you kidding?"

She stabbed a manicured finger at him. "You should've told me."

"He pays more than you. My allegiance is to the coffer, deary."

The more she thought of Ashton's collection, the more it felt as if he hoarded her best works away from the public eye. Was it love or ownership? In his eyes, he had lost her to a lesser man, lost a battle he should've won. Was it his way of compensating?

"Have you been working on that study for Mrs. Velasco?"

"It's all I think about. I've already sketched several ideas. My appointment to tour her house is tomorrow. I'm hoping Atalaya will become my muse." She crossed her fingers for good luck. "Mrs. Velasco may be tiny, but she's colossal. I've got to impress her."

"And impress me! Don't forget, I'm your creative consigliere."

Peyton laughed. "Is that why I pay you a commission on everything *I* design and create?"

He pretended to be deaf, raising his eyebrows even more. "Are you ready?" he asked, peeking through the window. Many people already assembled outside the gallery. "We set it all up like usual. You only have to charm them out of their fortunes. The entire front row is repeat clients. Go dazzle."

Over the years, she'd developed an entertaining way to showcase her skills, and whenever she did her live demonstrations, sales at the gallery shot up. She stepped outside with Apollo, who received more accolades than she did. Most of the spectators stood in the shade, enjoying the perfect weather, and applauded as she mounted the gazebo.

She inclined her head in acknowledgment. "Thank you for coming," she said into the microphone. "For those of you who are unfamiliar with my demonstrations, I'll be painting upside down, and you'll get a chance to guess the subject. Today, I'll work on two canvases. The first one is a narrow subject. The second is a portrait of one of you. Should the subject be first to guess it's their face I'm painting, they'll get to purchase the painting at a discount."

They clapped as Geraint stood poised at the controls, ready to play classical music to match her rhythm.

"This is the fun part now. I'll paint fast, keeping up with the music. The composition won't be perfect or smooth, and I'll use acrylics for quick drying, but it'll be clear and professional. I'll be finished before the music ends, and you'll have to guess before then. That's the game." Peyton clutched a bouquet of brushes in her left hand and gave Geraint the nod to start the "William Tell Overture." Though she painted with speed, she occasionally cast her eyes on the crowd, soliciting their guesses. "Remember, I'm painting upside down, so you have to use your imaginations."

"An alien," one person hollered.

"No, an incense burner," someone else said.

Apollo yipped as if he were guessing, too, making the crowd laugh.

Peyton reversed the completed work. "How about now? Anyone?"

"A nose!" shouted a little girl with auburn pigtails and freckles.

Peyton pointed to her and laughed. "That's right, sweetie." She signed it and gifted it to the girl. "Because you're little and clever."

Geraint gawked at her as if she'd given away his platinum American Express credit card.

Peyton stuck her tongue out at him. "I'll also paint the portrait upside down." She scanned the crowd's faces and chose one belonging to an older woman with deep wrinkles and haunted eyes—the poster child of a tourist on a budget. She memorized her features to avoid glancing at her too much. "This one I'll do to Johan Strauss's 'Radetzky Marsch.' It'll help if you clap along."

Geraint said, "To guess, gesture and shout."

The crowd did as bid, clapping to the enlivening music, as Peyton raced her brush across the canvas. Because she painted upside down, she built the canvas from the bottom up. Guesses arose, but they were all wrong.

To help the lady recognize her portrait before others did, Peyton winked at her. Someone declared it was of an older face.

That's when the lady called it right. "It's my face. Mine!"

Peyton inverted the canvas and finished it to the *pasadoble* "España Cañí" as the crowd continued to clap in rhythm.

Geraint pressed closer to her. "Give this one away for free, and I'll kill you."

"Ashton has already paid for it from the ultra-premiums you've been charging him, no doubt," she whispered. "I should kill *you*."

Geraint gave an ahem and an I-don't-approve face.

The lady, whose portrait Peyton had created, stepped forward. "You're so talented! No one has ever painted me before. How much is it?" She wore no makeup, sported a gray bob, and was dressed in worn jeans and sneakers.

Peyton said, "It's also a gift. Sorry, it's not refined or meticulous like my typical work, but it's your likeness, and I'll finish and sign it. Come back in an hour. It'll be dry and packaged."

"I'm really so touched," the lady replied. "Thank you."

It felt good to make someone else spark. She hadn't sparked in a long time—except in Ashton's company.

As the crowd dispersed, some entered the gallery, bringing out the best in Geraint. "Time to do my magic, deary, but you're coming to my party on Saturday next. You're not ditching me like last time. I live one block over, for God's sake."

She didn't tell him she'd skipped his party because Adler hadn't wanted to socialize. "All right." She plunked a kiss on his cheek and prepared to go home to Mrs. Velasco's commission. "From now on, tell me when Ashton buys anything."

"You know I won't. But your Ashton will be thrilled to tell you himself, I'm sure."

"He's not *my* Ashton."

Geraint, who never steered her wrong, said, "I think you've lied to yourself for enough years, don't you?"

twenty-one

For her visit to Atalaya, Peyton wore a one-shouldered black catsuit and gold stiletto sandals. The director, a man with droopy jowls and a double chin, met her outside. She had seen pictures of this architectural wonder, but they didn't do it justice. Atalaya was splendid, smelling of cedar and sea breeze, mingled with the redolence of nightshade and Jeffrey pine.

The man extended sausage fingers covered in gold and diamond rings that cut into them. "Ms. Chase, welcome to Lookout Tower, or Atalaya, as the architect preferred to call it."

"It's spectacular, and I've yet to see the inside. Thank you, Mr. Basha, for meeting me here today."

"You're to have unfettered access as often as you like. Let's begin the tour."

Peyton trailed him, listening to details he shared about the house, mesmerized by the views that included manicured gardens, exquisite marble and bronze sculptures, and classic artworks. The interior wood was rare, from koa to cocobolo rosewood, polished to perfection. Peyton ran her palm over the door frames and walls, registering the heft of her commission. She'd have to match the high standards of the house and was more anxious than eager, but appreciated the responsibility. "Is this fireplace Belgian black marble? I've only seen it used sparingly in French châteaux."

"Great eye. No wonder you're an artist. It's been resourced because of its scarcity."

Peyton was pleased that Atalaya would receive an endowment, allowing a foundation to offer tours to the general public. She wondered if Pioneer Ranch wouldn't one day share the same fate to ensure its survival. She thought of Honovi and Ricky when she said, "Sometimes the adopted are the most precious."

"It's more like Atalaya is adopting the foundation." He laughed, jiggling his double chin. "Let's return to the foyer where your painting is meant to go." He gestured toward a massive wall. "It should be at least half this space. Can you do that?"

"I can do anything," Peyton replied, though she found the scale daunting. "Send me the measurements of this wall and the room, and I'll take it from there."

"Good idea." His phone rang, and he excused himself.

She wandered and took photographs. If she were to honor this house, she'd have to mine the parts of herself she'd rather not excavate. Was that why fate had sent her this commission? Peyton faced the Pacific and acknowledged a haunting truth. To grow bigger wings, she'd have to stand on the edge of the cliff once again and dive.

The earth spun, the moon waxed, and life reset once more. Peyton was restoring more than a painting and frothing more than a study. She hadn't planned on this period of self-care but accepted it was life's plan for her. She took her meals facing an ever-changing montage of ocean and sky, awakened at no prescribed time to warbles and breakers, and fell asleep to twitching logs aglow with hypnotic shapes. It was a restful time of work and creative vigor.

Though the morning had promised a warm day for a swim, the afternoon brought a chill. From her studio overlooking the Pacific, she could spot whales breach the water and raise their flukes. She lit her gas fireplace, while Apollo napped in his bed, then spread out her tubes and tools, took a sip of her cappuccino, and prepared to work. First, she honored her lifelong ritual of quoting Leonardo da Vinci. "'While I thought that I was learning how to live, I have been learning how to die.'" Hours hemorrhaged until a sore neck and back made her aware of the time. "Hungry, Apollo? It's definitely dinnertime."

He stretched and led the way to the kitchen. Peyton lathered grapefruit soap from her elbows down, mindful of the soothing scent and warm water. She'd started chicken, rice, and peas in the slow cooker for Apollo—a meal he scarfed down while wagging his tail. For herself, she chose a filet of wild salmon and sautéed spinach, and was washing her dishes when she heard a car pull into the driveway. She opened an app on her phone and beamed at the sight of Bryce retrieving a bag from the trunk while cradling Myriad.

Peyton ran to the door and swung it open. "I'm so happy you're home."

Bryce came inside and put down her pup.

Peyton hugged and rocked her, then turned her attention to the fox and retriever who were greeting each other. "I wasn't expecting you till tomorrow. I would've made a bigger meal and had the coffee percolating, but now…"

"That's exactly why I didn't tell you. Don't fuss. I can take care of myself."

"I was going to continue working on a study and a Renaissance treasure I'm restoring, but now you're here, I won't."

Bryce followed her mother to the studio and rested her eyes on the Fede Galizia. "This looks expensive. How old is it?"

"The year is 1605, and the price some half a million."

"Sick!"

"But that's not what I'm psyched about. Let me show you what I've been working on." Peyton went to another easel and stood poised, ready to explain the canvas she was preparing for Mrs. Velasco as the final study. She'd created several versions in chalk and was now transferring the study to oils. "The bridge portion of the composition is the trickiest. Drum rolls, please." Peyton pointed to the substantial painting, which was one-fourth the size of the finished work.

Bryce thrust her neck forward, then tilted her head, took a few steps back, and squatted. "I see that it's the Bixby Bridge at first, but the longer I stare at it, the more I realize that five figures, disguised as columns, are holding it up. Am I right?"

She kissed her daughter. "Yes, you clever, clever girl. And who are they?"

Bryce widened her eyes and opened her mouth. "No way… it's us!"

"Yes!" Peyton bounced in place. "The Bixby Creek is an open-spandrel arch bridge, with the bulk of the weight resting on colossal vertical buttresses. They're critical, but there'd be no bridge without the other supporting pillars."

Bryce covered her cheeks with her hands. "Oh my God… That's Honovi and I, and the other three are William, Ricky, and Gideon."

"Bingo! Honovi is the tallest and thickest buttress in the middle, followed by you, my honey, near the southern spandrel, then my other boys."

"It's incredible how you chose so few characteristics to distinguish us, yet it works. Honovi would be so proud!" Bryce clapped. "Are you going to sell it?"

Peyton cuddled her daughter sideways. "It's already sold. It's a commission for a house I must show you before you leave. The lady who owns it has approved the concept. Atalaya is a magical place. I ordered a custom canvas for it. It'll be the largest I ever painted, so big the framers will have to stretch it here."

"So are we your bridge, Mom?"

"It's often about you, my children. You're my priceless treasures who bridge the divide of my life."

Bryce teared up and hugged her mother. "It's the most moving artwork I've ever seen."

Peyton thought her daughter hadn't seen enough art, but pecked kisses on her face. "I titled it *First Sons and Last Daughters.* They hold up the structure of my life. Even your father is a first son, and I'm a last daughter, like you."

Bryce gave curious eyes and bit her lower lip. "Is Ashton a first son also?"

"He is, in fact. But why are you always asking me about Ashton?"

Bryce sighed. "Because we have less and less to say to Dad."

Peyton twined her fingers. "Would you hate me if your dad and I spent some time apart? I know Gideon would."

"Hate you? Never. Besides, it's none of our business, and Dad was the one who decided weeks without you would be fine. This is your life. I'm the youngest and I consider myself an adult who doesn't need to be coddled anymore. I'd hate to see you and Dad separate, but it's possible the way things keep spiraling down."

"Thank you, honey. You might be the only one to feel that way." She grabbed her phone. "I'll text him pictures of the study right now and show him the bridge in particular, since he asked." She sent Adler several photos and gestured for Bryce to sit in a chair facing the large picture window while she cleaned her brushes, knives, and sponges. "What might you enjoy for your birthday?"

Bryce shrugged, sadder as time passed. "Nothing."

Peyton extinguished the lamp and the gas fireplace. "I thought school might distract you." She could see the pondering in her daughter's eyes. "But you're still in a funk."

"If I can hike Point Lobos, swim in the Pacific, and make grilled fish tacos with my mom, I'll be dandy."

"I made a reservation at Anton & Michel for your birthday."

Bryce shook her head. "I don't feel like celebrating anything."

"But it's your eighteenth birthday, and there's no party, not even Dad. We should do something."

"Dad sent me an early gift, as if that would make up for it." She got off her chair, kissed her mother's forehead, and fondled the puppies who were fighting over a stuffed toy. "It'll make me feel worse. Let's skip it."

"I'm keeping the reservation, anyway."

"Do you feel as good as you look?" Bryce's elegant smile enhanced her striking features. "I was worried you'd be all sad and shriveled up, but you're the opposite, all peppy."

"You know, honey, I love you all deeply, but it feels good to live for myself and mind only my own needs. I have my sad and angry moments, but work is a blessing. And you? You haven't talked about William at all."

Bryce rubbed her chin. "I think about him nonstop, while he cavorts with his girlfriend. I spoke to Kelcy, though. He misses us, but he sounded good."

Peyton speared to the kitchen. "Did you speak to Dad?"

"Just once. He called to tell me he'd be off the radar and asked me to keep an eye on you." She grabbed two cups as her mother added water to the coffeemaker. "Have you spoken to Gideon?"

Peyton loathed what she had to share. "No, but he's with Dad. Your father felt the need to try one more time with your brother. Did he tell you?"

Bryce's face morphed into an exclamation point. "But this is Gideon's last semester and Dad wanted to Feng Shui himself or something. I'm confused."

Peyton filled the mugs and added sugar and cream. "Want to know why I'm more relaxed? Because I'm not dwelling on such thoughts. Your dad is doing what he must. We should all do the same." She held out a mug, but Bryce didn't take it.

"Dad rewards Gideon at my expense for being a conniving, evil jerk? He should be with us, not Gideon!" She stormed to her room, as Myriad meowed more than yipped and followed her.

Peyton's crushed spirit tired her, but a call from Gideon made her heart sink. "Something wrong? You never call."

"Something is wrong with *you*!" he screamed. "Dad showed me the pics you sent. I'm a secondary pillar in your painting when Honovi is the main one? I'm your real son, not him. Your first son!"

She had to hold the phone away from her ear, Gideon shouted so much. "Are you wasting precious satellite minutes to yell at me?"

"You're always reducing me when I'm your only son."

"So you didn't see you're one of the essential pillars of my life? You think that though you're two-thirds Honovi's age, you should have a greater place?"

"You say you love me, but you don't. You act like my feelings and opinions matter, but they don't! Even Bryce has a more prominent place."

As a child, Peyton had struggled for her mother's approval. It was ironic that she was struggling in the same way with her son. But no more. She had graduated and replied with her truth. "I know what I am and who I am. If you can't see that, it's on you. I'm done trying to convince you of my love and devotion. Done!"

"I fucking hate you! You're the worst mother on earth!"

"But I love you, Sorensen, and I always will."

He took his time, and she could tell she'd caught him off guard. "Liar," he said. "You mean you love Mikey."

Peyton was also finished chasing after Adler's approval. But she thought she'd never finish weeping.

After two days of hiking, swimming, and watching whales breach as gray herons glided low over the horizon, Bryce was restored enough to agree to a dinner out on her birthday. Her mother applied her makeup for her and insisted she wear a sexy green asymmetric strapless dress to complement her rich red hair. She'd never looked so grown up.

"I find myself wishing you and Dad could work things out."

"Sometimes we can't give a person what they're asking for at the time they ask for it." Peyton cupped her hand. "I fell in love with your father's independence, strength, honesty, and love of nature. I created a life with those qualities, and they gave me you. Some of it might be biting me in the butt now, but *c'est la vie.*"

"I'm sorry I was judgmental, but I don't get what Dad is doing."

"We're fragmented and seem to have lost the synergy, but we can recover it. Your father has always been devoted to us."

"Why're you priming me so much? I'm turning eighteen, not prom queen."

"You're going out to dinner, but without me."

"What?"

Peyton checked the time and grinned, waiting for the doorbell to ring. And it did. "Answer it, will you?" she said, then slunk away.

"William?" Bryce said. "I don't believe it!"

"See you at Thanksgiving?" he asked. "You ignore me and ignore me, and then send me a 'see-you-at-Thanksgiving' message?" He followed her into the house.

"I wasn't ignoring you."

"What do you call it, then?"

"Self-preservation… Why're you gawking like that?"

"My God, you're stunning!" he said. "Didn't you miss me?"

Peyton balled her hands to her heart and widened her eyes.

"You needed to know life without me, William. *Really* experience it. I could tell you were confused about me, but I was never confused about you."

Peyton smiled, proud of her daughter's transparency.

"I was in a nowhere place I hated," Bryce said. "I moved myself to a nowhere place I hated less."

His voice was tender. "Are you happy I'm here?"

"When wasn't I thrilled to see you?"

Silence dominated. Peyton wanted to scuttle closer, but she didn't want to get caught eavesdropping.

"Where's your ring?" Bryce asked. "Why aren't you wearing it?"

"I prefer to wear the bracelet you gave me. I arranged to see you on your birthday because I can't sleep, can't work, can't focus on anything but you."

"What are you saying exactly?" Her voice quivered.

"Why do you love me as you do? No one smiles at the sight of me like you do. No one knows my subtle ways or how to make me laugh like you do."

"Because you're William. I'll always love you, no matter what."

Peyton recalled having said similar words to Adler long ago. She still meant them.

"But why?"

"William is riding fast into the wind, talking into the late hours, and falling asleep at the foot of my bed. William is showing up just when I need him most. Without you, I enjoy nothing, because, somehow, you're everything."

"But I've hurt you, and I can't forgive myself."

"Not intentionally."

"I knew you saw me differently. Honovi and Ricky were always brothers to you, but not me. Then you kept blossoming, getting braver, prettier, smarter, and sweeter. But I was older, too afraid of hurting you and hurting your parents. I feared losing you for it. I told myself I'd hurt you less and risk losing you least by keeping things as they were. But I hurt you more than ever, and you're what I want above anything or anyone."

"And?"

Peyton could picture the way Bryce's face would've been lighting up.

"No one measures up to you, and I doubt anyone ever could."

The muffled sounds that followed told Peyton they were kissing. She pressed her palms together and brought them to her lips.

"You're everything I think about," William said. "I didn't realize how much until I couldn't get hold of you. I'm really sorry."

"How sorry?"

"Sorry enough to give you the best night of your life."

Bryce raised her voice. "You can come out now, Mom."

Peyton scooted their way, grinning. "Blame William. He insisted on keeping it a surprise."

He was clean-shaven, wearing jeans and a buttoned-down white shirt.

Peyton hugged them both, though she worried they were still too young. "And one more thing." She removed the platinum and sapphire bracelet from her pocket and handed it to William. "He also asked for this."

Bryce held out her arm for him, tears filling her eyes, and laughed as he fastened it on her wrist.

"Oh… don't ruin your makeup," Peyton said. "Go out and have fun. I won't wait up."

Her instinct was to call Adler and give him the news, but she remembered he was out of reach. Feeling he had discarded her, she floundered to her bed and dove into the picture Ashton had taken on his boat. How she wished he were with her! She picked up her phone to call him, then thought of everything she'd be inviting, and put it down.

twenty-two

Peyton was standing in the foyer with William, waiting for Bryce to finish packing.

He swallowed and slipped his hands in the pockets of his shorts. "I want to apologize for any pain I've caused you and Adler. I don't blame you if you hate me now."

"Hate you?" Peyton brushed her fingers on his cheek. "Honey, you and Bryce are babies for such an epic love affair, but no matter what happens next, we love you. We don't fault you. You're *our* William."

"You came to my tennis matches, my graduations, all my important milestones. I'm lucky. We told Grandpa. He's ecstatic." He kissed Peyton on the cheek the way he used to as a boy. "Thank you for being okay with me moving in with Bryce. I'll fly back and forth as need be. I won't distract her from her studies, and I'll look after her, I promise."

"I'm sure." She sighed with satisfaction, tilting her head, studying him. "What's this thing you can't get yourself to ask me?"

"Did you ask Adler to leave?"

"Never. What gave you that idea?"

William colored and stretched his lower lip sideways. "You're here, he's not. He packed a lot but hated every moment. It felt off."

She took a deep breath. "How did Gideon look to you?"

William's chocolate eyes searched for a polite answer.

"Other than smug. Seriously, how did he seem?"

"Angry, brooding, stayed in the Jeep until Adler made him help. When I said hi, he gave me the finger."

"Normal then?"

"Pretty much, yeah."

After a week of diligent work, Peyton allowed herself a night out. She was ambling home from Geraint's party, wearing a backless silver dress, her blonde hair cascading in waves. She stepped onto the front patio and was startled to see Ashton stretched on her bench, watching her. "Oh my God, you scared me half to death!"

"You're a vision, I swear." He took three steps and pulled her into his arms, his warm hands on her bare back. "Were you out on a date?"

Peyton sizzled, wishing he'd move his hands lower and keep them there all night. "What are you doing here?"

"I'm walking into your house, since that's what the song says I should've done."

"Ah… 'Leather and Lace.'" His timing was perfect. Ashton ran a multi-billion-dollar company, yet found the time to show up when she needed him.

"I must give you something to remember me by," he said.

"You're unforgettable, didn't you know?" She stared at his handsome face, clear and soft in the moonlight.

He fused his hands to her nude shoulders and tried to kiss her, but she stepped back.

Confident to the marrow, he picked up his overnight bag and a bottle of Chateau d'Yquem. "Invite me in." His eyes said he could smell her trepidation. "You know me. I'm always the gentleman."

"Of course. I never doubt that."

"Then don't make me ask twice."

A chill ran down her spine, and it was frighteningly welcome. She unlocked her front door with a hand scan and removed her shoes as the pups yipped.

"Is that Apollo?"

"And Myriad, my daughter's fox. Bryce left her here for company. I confined them in the laundry room at the end of the hallway. It's roomy but cozy, and not a kennel." Peyton called out, assuring them they'd be released soon. "Take the first bedroom upstairs on the left. I'll get glasses ready."

"A guestroom? At *your* house?"

"No complaining," Peyton said, as he climbed the stairs.

The pups scampered, happy to be let out into the garden fenced with a frameless glass railing.

A part of her rationalized Ashton's presence as mere friendship, while another part chastised it as reckless and potentially incendiary—or the best move she'd ever made.

Ashton came downstairs, ready to open the dessert wine he'd brought. "You always wanted me to show up on your porch. Here I am." He guessed in which drawer the wine opener was kept and reached for it. "You're such a creature of habit. You still keep your gadgets in the middle drawer closest to the sink. How's the back garden?"

Peyton rummaged in the fridge for strawberries. "Fertile."

"I noticed," he said, grinning in his unique way—part angel, part shark. "The garden, I mean. Fertile, sure."

"Stop it." She handed him the glasses.

"You did a great job with this house. Geraint said it had only one previous owner, who lived in it for seventy years. Soothing colors and textures are everywhere. Your new windows and doors, including the front door, don't detract from the history of the house, yet it all says Carmel and beach to me."

They ambled back to the living room. It was a warm night. Ashton opened the French doors, letting in surf, sea breeze, and generous moonlight. She waited for him to choose his spot and grinned as he searched around him.

"The photograph is in my room," she said, marching her polished nails on her wineglass.

"Show me."

She smirked from a place of love, the familiarity exclusive of a long intimacy. "Don't be naughty."

He sat facing the fireplace. "You always read me well and know what I contemplate or fear. You get my soul and understand my motives and visions." He patted the sofa beside him, but she sat opposite him. "So many times over the years, I considered calling you. Did you never think of visiting me?"

Peyton lit the three pillar candles on her coffee table, then tucked her feet under her. "You were always a danger zone. I didn't think I could get away with visiting you. Besides, wasn't your little black book full?"

"Sex is easy to find. Love is a different story. You loved me for who I am, not what I have. That's rare." He put down his glass and rested his elbows on his knees. "Wouldn't it be wonderful to see me every day?"

She longed to touch him. "Of course, but we're more than our loins, even more than our hearts." She pictured him naked on top of her and blew out the candles. "But I want to show you something." She led the way to her studio and turned on the full-spectrum lamp, illuminating *First Sons and Last Daughters*. "It's my biggest commission yet, for Atalaya, a house you'll adore, knowing your love of architecture. The finished work will be eight by twelve feet. What do you see in my painting?"

"That's a huge size. It means your client trusts you implicitly." Ashton took two steps back and jutted his neck. "Are those condors or people?"

"They look like wings at first, don't they? But they're Koda and Layli with their long hair and lofty spirits."

"The bridge is of your children. Wow! Where're you?"

She didn't hint, stood back and waited for him to figure it out.

"Oh… you're the coastal gorge from which they spring. Of course! Now, where am I?"

Though she laughed, she knew he was serious. "Everyone I love, and Mrs. Velasco is in this painting. Look harder."

He moved a few paces right, then back. "Did you disguise me in the clouds? I could swear there's a polo rider in them."

"It's how I always see you… fierce, scoring, and riding high."

"And where's Adler?" he asked in a glum tone.

"How can you miss him? He's the most prominent figure of all."

Adler was in the most appropriate place for him—in the mountain, towering over the bridge, canyon, and beach.

"My parents are the ocean. Scarborough is the hill in the center. And if you alter your vision, where the road turns and the mountain slopes, you should see Margot and Lexi huddled together. The shore is horses and dogs. The buttes are Kelcy and Royce sitting with drinks. And if you step back about ten feet and take in the entire scene, you'll see Mrs. Velasco's wise face."

"This is a different style for you. I'm in love."

Peyton stared at Adler's portrait, artfully concealed within the contours of the mountain. She'd depicted him with one bent knee, every bit of hunter in him on alert. Protective. Sharp. Intense. Exquisite pain washed over her. She wondered whether she'd be with Ashton now if she hadn't been furious with her husband. "I'm at a pivotal point in my life again. It's pure coincidence, but so is my art."

"There are no coincidences. You're at a new stage." Ashton yanked her to his body and kissed her in a way that implied much more.

She pressed a hand to his chest. "Let's cool it." She returned to the living room and collected the glasses, drowning in guilt.

"You're running away," he said, following her to the kitchen.

"I may be absconding, but it's to abide by who I am and to what you deserve."

"Make me a promise." He waited until she relaxed her posture. "Tomorrow, we get to have a full day together. A complete day of you not fearing me. Please."

"I don't fear you."

"No? Then trust me completely, like you once did."

"I trust you. It's me I don't trust around you."

Satisfaction spread across his face. He leaned against the kitchen counter, watching her wash the glasses, dry the counter and sink.

"What's that smile, exactly?"

"Did your fairy godmother let you keep the dress past midnight?"

She tried to slap his arm, but he shifted away, laughing. "Watch it. Cinderella runs away, you know."

"Not this time." He moved her hair out of the way and kissed her long neck.

She closed her eyes for a moment, gleaning intimate memories, allowing herself to dissolve into what may come.

He kissed her again, making her feel she could forget her other life. "Must I stay in a guestroom?"

"No, you can check into a hotel."

He chuckled, took her hand and kissed it. "I'll never forget this image of you in a cocktail dress polishing a marble counter and looking up at me. I'd like to see that painting one day."

"Gotta let in the pups and wipe their paws," she said to cork the moment, then opened the backdoor for her furballs. "It's called independence."

"It's called my darling." He borrowed an expression from the apex of their history, meaningful to them both: "The original. My one and only."

Peyton skipped her habitual dawn walk. She'd had trouble falling asleep, thinking of Ashton sleeping within earshot, and wishing Adler was in bed beside her. By the time the prying sun breached her room, she was dressed for an outing with Ashton. The pups were still snoozing, twined in each other, when she started downstairs, dreaming of coffee.

When she reached the bottom of the stairs, Ashton walked in with two cappuccinos. "At your service, gorgeous," he said, handing her one.

"I didn't hear you get up and leave. Did you sleep okay? I just washed the linens, and the mattress and pillows are new."

"Great bed. Though it was hard sleeping in your *fertile* house."

She pinched his arm. "I should never have used that word with you. Want to sit outside?"

"Let's just go. I have somewhere I want to take you." He saw the quandary in her eyes. "Yes, bring your precious Apollo and Myriad, but they're going in their carriers. My leather seats insist."

"Well, I always put them in carriers for their safety, but I won't bring them. My neighbor fell in love with them. She said she'd look after them any time. I'll call her. Where're we going?"

"It's a surprise."

Peyton was prickling with excitement as they rolled past Notleys Landing, heading south on the Pacific Coast Highway through raw country. Ashton shared his vision of the future, confided his major concerns, and told funny stories. She listened, filling her lungs with the scents of Russian blue and evening primrose. By the time they arrived at Big Sur, the conversation had shifted to shared memories.

"I forgot all the twists and turns on this road," she said as he sped up, enjoying the sharp curves and inclines through redwoods, pastures, the churning Pacific, and untamed wilderness. "Are we driving past Big Sur?"

"So impatient." He raced the engine, adding to the thrill of the ride. "You'll like it."

When he turned left on an unmarked road, Peyton's curiosity piqued. "Are we going to a farm?"

He laughed and gripped her knee. "I'm giving you what you need."

They came to a golden gate typical of Chinese architecture—multi-leveled, with sharp edges and upturned eaves. He scanned a code from his phone and it opened.

"What's this place?" She could see a triple-tiered Buddhist temple. "I've never heard of it."

"No one has. It's a private sanctuary of deep meditation and rejuvenation for advanced monks."

She admired the architecture of the massive pagoda. The driveway was long and well-manicured, bordered by huge succulents and orange pincushion plants. Ashton parked beneath a golden dome with a colossal gong.

"How do you know about this monastery?"

"I may be a significant benefactor." He leaned over and kissed her on the mouth. "We have an appointment with Bhante Tenzin. I thought you might enjoy a one-on-one with a venerated senior monk."

"What do you mean?"

He pointed to a junior monk coming their way, dressed in an orange *kāṣāya* and a yellow sash. "Here comes our guide."

"I thought you didn't believe in hocus-pocus."

"This is different. Bhante Tenzin has a sophisticated brain. He's an expert on happiness."

"I'm Bhante Tenzin's personal assistant," said the monk. "Welcome."

Ashton greeted him with a bowed head and palms pasted together. "Thank you for meeting us promptly."

The young monk had almond eyes and a sincere, warm smile. "Bhante Tenzin likes precision. Please, follow me." Walking and talking, he gave his instructions in a Chinese accent. "When you enter the jeweled hall, please say nothing. Just sit on the cushions opposite Bhante Tenzin and open your hearts. The more sincere you are, the more likely it is he'll speak to you. Though I must warn you, he doesn't speak to everyone. In fact, I'd say your chances are fifty-fifty." The monk moved at a brisk pace. "Please, don't speak, don't ask questions. Bhante Tenzin tells you what you need to know, not what you wish to know. When he's done, he'll ring a brass bell. Don't linger once he does. He can only give so much energy. That's why he sees only a handful of people a year. Any questions?"

They walked past a Zen sand garden to a courtyard bordered with imposing statues of the Buddha. A smaller temple was nestled within it. The young monk instructed them to remove their shoes and enter. "Bhante Tenzin awaits you." He placed a finger over his lips. "Remember, no speaking, and open up your hearts."

Peyton walked into the dim space where Bhante Tenzin sat in a lotus position on a gold cushion, dressed in the same kāṣāya and sash his assistant wore. Pure compassion shone on his face. His head was shaven, and he had a sleeve of tattoos on one arm and a jagged scar on the other. He was spot lit from above, immersed in a cloud of incense. His eyes remained closed as they sat opposite him. She knelt on a silk cushion and folded her legs beneath her, bent her head, and gave her heart permission to relinquish its fears and dreams with sincerity and humility.

Time stretched as she surrendered and allowed him into her heart.

Bhante Tenzin spoke in a French accent, his eyes shut. "You're the lady of the horse. You carry others in this life, but you're tired of the run, tired of the chase. I feel a layered meaning here for you, but it's up to you to decipher it."

Glued to his every word, Peyton's temperature shot up.

"Your spirit is a library of questions. I find it necessary to tell you the evildoer stirs dust against the wind. His evil rebounds on itself. I also see the pure. That too is a circle that folds onto itself."

She felt the monk peer into her soul, but she wasn't afraid.

He raised a straight palm. "Every child is the little Buddha who helps his parents to grow up."

She resisted tears, but they overtook her.

"Your love is abundant and deep. Others may question it. You mustn't. At its best, it's unjust. At its worst, it robs your soul."

She knew he spoke of her son and cried harder.

Bhante Tenzin raised his other hand. "Love is the gift that makes us whole. Accept it with the same generosity you give it." He opened his blue eyes and stared at her with empathy. "Accept him."

She wondered if he still spoke of her son.

"You already know happiness is a journey, not a destination. But you live too much in the future. Live only in the now. Pain will visit you again. If you allow it to enrich you, it won't turn to suffering." The monk gestured for her to approach.

She rose and scurried, then knelt closer, as he removed a white *khata* from his shoulders, blessed the scarf, and placed it around her neck. "I give this gift because of your self-respect and overflowing compassion. But you must also have compassion for yourself. Wear this khata for strength and healing."

She returned to her cushion, stroking the silky sheer khata. Overtaken by emotion, she bowed from the waist and placed both hands over her heart.

Bhante Tenzin closed his eyes and inclined his head toward Ashton. "You feel you're alone on your path. We're always alone on our paths. It's no different for you than it is for me or for her. But we can thrive better in unison." The monk placed his upturned hands on his lap. "You sat under your tree the day you stopped confusing a deferred investment with a loss. Your soul took a turn, and your life will follow. Though you lack patience, it still rules. You are your thoughts. Whichever thought you believe in is the one you'll come to know. In the cyclical nature of death and rebirth, we move in pods, like whales." He fell quiet and squinted. "I say this to both of you. Karma has always brought you together, but it's up to you to close your circles." He turned toward Peyton, and said, "A pod includes more than two."

Ashton looked at her with bright eyes and smiled with pure love.

Bhante Tenzin rang his bell and closed his eyes.

Peyton bowed and stood up, considering who else might be in her pod. But she knew.

In the hallway, the assistant whispered, "Bhante Tenzin must have liked your inner light."

"Why do you think that? All I did was weep."

"He took a long time with you and gave you his khata. It's rare. He only does that with mature souls. You can probably read people well."

She held out her trembling hands. "I'm so moved, I can't stop shaking."

"Bhante Tenzin's presence is potent. People can feel faint afterwards." He gestured to glasses of juice on a brass tray.

Ashton cuddled her and kissed her forehead. "Sit down and take deep breaths."

"She'll be as right as rain in two minutes," said the young monk as he handed her a glass of juice.

Ashton tied the laces of his leather shoes, while Peyton took a mirror from her purse and fixed her face.

As they walked back to the car, she asked him, "Have you visited Bhante Tenzin before?"

"Yes, and he was right then too." He ran his hand over her back. "What do you think of his advice?"

"I guess what's important is how I interpret it. He said pain will visit me in the future. It felt like he meant something bigger than usual."

"I mean it, Peyton. You never have to carry your cross alone. I'm here, my darling."

She needed him—at least she needed his attention—more than ever.

The look he gave her was dense with emotion, though he snickered. "I pay their bills, but they give *you* a khata?"

She laughed and leaned into his sturdy embrace before he opened the passenger car door. "Thank you. Every time I see you, you lighten and brighten my soul."

"We work because it's reciprocal." He opened the passenger door for her. "Remember the time we got caught in torrential rains and got off the road at the first place we could find?"

"You mean the Alila Ventana?"

"Yeah, where we spent a great night. We hadn't even heard of it, but it was phenomenal."

"Ooh, that chocolate mousse." She saw his disappointment. "And what followed, which was even better."

The road wound between the Pacific and ribboning mountains.

"I kept returning to that night in my head, so I made a reservation. They're preparing a private, haute cuisine menu. A chef's choice, nine-course meal, with the perfect wine pairing."

"Come again? Chefs like that are meticulous. They need ample time to prepare."

"That's exactly what money is for."

"How did you know I'd come out with you today? You made plans ahead of time. How were you sure?"

He slowed down and glanced at her. "When I saw you in Sedona, it was you and Honovi. In Texas, it was you and Bryce. In Lake Tahoe, it was you and Scarborough. Carmel, it's you and me. I've noticed you don't get many texts or phone calls from your husband. You call him a problem solver, but he's part of the biggest problem you have. From the outside in, yours is an unhappy marriage, Peyton." He laughed. "Where's this awesome husband of yours? Why is such a priceless, bright, beautiful, and talented woman alone?"

"Are you preying on my vulnerability?"

"I think you sacrifice and tolerate too much, give more than your share, and take less than you deserve. Am I wrong in trying to tip the balance for you?"

The truth slashed. Being understood, seen—exposed—was too much to bear. She looked away and bit her tongue.

He pulled off the road. Windsurfers dominated the air on the beach below. "Not what I wanted. Please, don't cry." He cut the engine and coaxed her into looking at him. "You put on a brave face, but I know you too well, and I admit I've been studying your life closely. There are major tears and rips in it. You can have better. You *deserve* better."

Peyton took tissues from her purse and dried her face. "Don't you have tears and rips?"

"Of course, I do. They're because you're not in my life. We belong together… We should've been together all these years."

She crossed her arms over her tummy and looked down.

He lifted her chin and turned her face toward him. "Such beautiful features should never be tucked away, yet your life gives you reason to hide. I want to change that." He unstrapped his seatbelt, leaned over, and kissed her for a long time. Her head told her to stop. Her heart said to take more than her share.

She wasn't sure she'd made a mistake, but she knew she'd sinned, and though Father Gabriel would surely absolve her, she had to be sure she could absolve herself. "I'm starving," she said, buying time to decide.

Alila Ventana Big Sur comprises vast property with farm-to-table dining and a clothing-optional pool, set in a dense redwood forest overlooking an unspoiled coastline. The resort received them with champagne and savory and sweet amuse-bouche.

They were shown to a table with views of endless ocean and sky, close to a firepit that flamed on top of a stone pony wall. A quartet played "*Mariage d'Amour*," while blue swallowtails hovered over zinnias. The romantic setting and elevated cuisine made Peyton feel valued, young, and optimistic.

As they finished their meal with chocolate mousse and port, Ashton said, "Let's get a room."

"Okay, let's really discuss this. You're paying me the most flattering, generous attention I could dream of, but what will it be like when my kids end up hating you?"

"Look, I don't have it all figured out, but there are no children to raise. Bryce likes me, and Gideon more so."

"They're not my only children, and they might feel differently if they view you as wrecking their home. And I love my ranch, love the people on it, love—"

"—the ranch you can keep and your friends and family you can see, at my houses or yours, but don't say you love your husband."

"But I do, and very much!"

"You just have the habit of him. You always belonged with me and your kids are adults. Why can't you get out?" He gave her eyes she couldn't escape. "And answer me this… How often do you sleep together?"

It wasn't often enough, and half the time, it wasn't what it used to be. But there was love in their touch, and a merging of souls, not just bodies. If Bhante Tenzin gave her his khata, it was because of her integrity. "You're oversimplifying my life. You and Royce never understood my choice in Adler. We grieve each other these days, but I can't hurt him this way, and I love him deeply. He's always been in my blood."

Ashton looked down and drummed fingers on the table. "You chose him because he wasn't married, wasn't resistant to the idea of children, but that's irrelevant today. I've seen you look at him, and it's not how you look at me. Am I wrong?"

"You've only seen us under duress." Too much pain sat between her and Adler in the present. There was pain with Ashton, too, but that was in the past. "I do think of life with you. But he and I share a long history and many trials. Most of it quite beautiful." Adler had been her partner and witness. And her most vital years had been with him.

"More downs than ups, at least in the last several years." He sipped port. "When you made your choice twenty years ago, you told me how some people melt us down, yet others reforge us. Do you recall?"

Peyton nodded, her memory intact. "I told you how good you were at melting me down, but not at building me up."

A glint in his cinnamon eyes reminded her how perspicacious he could be. "And now, Peyton? Which one of us melts you down and which one reforges you?" He clasped fingers with her. "I really need an answer."

"You're right. You do both in the best sense." Her marriage wasn't happy at the moment, but it had substance and resilience.

"Come back to me and never leave."

Ashton was reaching his limit. He was as sick of waiting for her as she'd been of waiting for Adler. But Honovi had urged her to be cautious. And she was nowhere near processing Adler out of her system. She feared she never would. "Take me home."

On the drive back, Peyton contemplated the changing landscape of her life. It was as if the sharp peaks of her mountains were breaking off into an avalanche of rocks, pulverizing parts of her.

When they pulled up to her house, she stepped onto the patio facing the Pacific, weary of her precarious footing. Ashton pressed his body to hers. He leaned down and kissed her neck, then her mouth. "You belong with me."

"Let's assume we can live happily ever after, jetting all over the world."

"Uh-huh…"

"It can't start this way, Ashton." She studied his reaction, a poker face she'd seen many times. "My kids will blame you. My friends will feel they have to take sides, and Adler will be profoundly hurt. I'll be plagued with guilt, and that's just the beginning."

"And I thought I was irresistible."

"You're a juggernaut. Are you kidding?"

"You understand what I'm asking, right?"

She chuckled at the irony. "You want from me what I wanted from you long ago. You want me to get a divorce and move to your house in Malibu."

"*Our* house—the one we shared during the happiest days of my life." He kissed her again. "I'm saying let's get married as soon as our divorces are settled."

The backyards below her house were dimly illuminated. On the beach, piping plovers dipped their beaks into the sand, still foraging, and someone played a sweet guitar. But none of it calmed her nerves. The longer she stared at him, the more she missed her husband. She and Adler had only just become empty nesters. She had to give that chapter of their lives a chance. "I know you've been patient, and perhaps we do have a future together, but I'm not where you are. My marriage needs a lot of work, but I'm not ready to end it."

He clasped her face. "You're asking for nothing, and I'd rather you asked for everything."

For years, her life had been rolling back and getting stuck. She'd been pining for a relationship without accusations and contempt, but Ashton was moving too fast, and she didn't think she could quit Adler overnight. "You want to make up for lost time, but I feel silly discussing marriage when I'm already married."

"Then we won't discuss it. We'll just do it." His playful eyes turned melancholy. "You want me to leave, don't you?"

"You must… Sorry." She listened to the waves, formulating her next thought. "I want too much, and some of it can't coexist. Of course I want to sail to Hawaii with you… to a different future. But I'd have to walk away from my life to do it, and I'm not ready for that just yet. It's best if I come to you because you're my choice, not because I crossed a line of no return."

Ashton sighed in frustration, tugged her harder. "He'll accuse you of cheating, anyway. Why do you care?"

Hard moments with Adler assaulted her: neglect, distance, and unjust accusations. But for the majority of her marriage, she'd had understanding, support, love, and a soulful connection with him. "Because I'm Peyton Chase. And this is what a Chase does, especially when it comes to the people she loves."

"It's part of what I love about you, but it's kicking my ass now."

"Principles matter only when they work against us. Adler and I disagree on too much." She cupped his face. "If he and I don't make it, I don't want anyone to accuse you of being the reason. Adler and I own those reasons."

He looked perturbed. "I think you're kicking a dead horse." He brought his index finger to his thumb. "Fine, you want to be kind, so be it. It's not like you can help it, but I hope you no longer require his forgiveness." He kissed her, but there was irritation in it. "We can have thirty, forty years together, my darling, maybe longer. And it doesn't matter how busy I am. I'll stop everything for you. Whatever you need, I'm here. Can we stay in touch, at least?"

"Before a house can be occupied, it has to be cleared out, right? I won't ghost you or play with you, but I need time to figure things out at home."

After he grabbed his bag, she walked him to his car, watched as he reversed out of her driveway and faded away. He wasn't gone two minutes before she missed him.

<h1 style="text-align:center">twenty-three</h1>

Carmel had been filled with tourists, bustling restaurants and galleries, and pristine beaches and sonorous breakers. Tranquil Abiquiú felt muted in comparison. Peyton often welcomed the stillness, but not now. What had been peaceful felt oppressive. She walked her property, visited the horses, and worked in her garden, but nothing eased her spirit when her thoughts were stapled to Adler and Gideon camping in the woods.

To burn through her apprehension, she swam laps in the pool. Soon Gideon would confront her again, and she had to re-establish parameters with Adler. She sliced through the water, burning frustration and rage, until the shadow of someone standing on the edge caught her attention.

"Who're you trying to murder?" Layli asked, her hands on her hips.

"I looked for you everywhere before leaving you that message." Peyton climbed out of the pool, dried her face on a beach towel, and kissed Layli on the cheek.

"You're back early." Layli brimmed with vitality. She never colored her hair, wore minimal makeup, but she was vibrant and vigorous. "I'm happy you're here. I have news."

Peyton sat on a chaise, ringing her hair, and sang more than said, "Does it have anything to do with BearClaw?"

"You're brilliant!" Layli stretched out on a chaise beside Peyton's and laced her hands behind her neck. "While you were gone, I went to Utah to fetch him. Against his wishes, I might add. He wasn't doing well, drained, but he let me drag him back here. Then I lay beside him, and one thing led to another."

"This is a big deal!" Peyton grinned, squeezing her friend's hand. "And he's here then?"

"We just got back from hunting." Layli clapped, smiling from her core. "Got to use my bow. I have pheasants and grouse to pluck and roast." She sat up, studying Peyton with a cocked head and dancing eyes. "You look different. What happened to you? You're tan, extra fit, lively with a newfound energy, but worried."

"You're the brilliant one." Peyton wrapped the towel around her head and straightened up. "I got a lot done in a place I love."

"Flower Child, are you hiding something?"

"A lot happened, and it'll change my future."

"Let me guess… Ashton Grant."

"It may not be accurate to say my life is full of have-tos, but it feels that way."

"That's because you're having to exercise exceptional willpower. It heightens your sense of deprivation." Layli leaned forward and lowered her voice. "What happened with Mr. Exquisite?"

"Everything and nothing. He came to see me. What you're thinking didn't happen, but something bigger did." Peyton exhaled and dropped her features. "Being with Ashton confirmed how much I don't want a life with anger and antagonism. I'm resetting expectations with Adler when he gets back. If we're to survive, we'll have to mind each other's feelings way more."

Layli scooted to the edge of her chaise and laced her fingers over a knee. "You know as well as I do, the reasons we choose someone differ from the reasons that keep us with them. Why are you with Adler today, and why is he with you?"

Peyton pronated her bare feet until her big toes touched. "There's always been love, a true partnership, and then…"

"And then Matanto sent you Gideon." Layli tapped Peyton's thigh. "During the first ten years, you and Adler played and laughed all the time. Then slowly but surely, tears prevailed over laughter. No marriage can survive that. So, do everything in your power to outline what he must do going forward."

"And what I must do for him." Peyton's phone buzzed with Honovi's ringtone. "Good or bad news?" she asked her son.

"Dad isn't with you, right?" Honovi asked.

"No, why?"

"I had a vision of him in the woods, facedown. That dark, unclear vision was for him. I didn't get that till now. I only knew it would affect you and me."

Peyton darted up. "I don't understand."

"Mom, go find Dad. Now!"

"What about Gideon?"

"I never get much on him," Honovi replied. "It's like there's no reception with Gideon."

Her heart raced, and her temperature boiled. "But where is your father, exactly?"

"Oh my God, you don't know?"

Sprinting toward them, panting, obviously hurting, BearClaw said, "Adler is in trouble, I feel it! Where is he?"

Peyton looked at BearClaw with a quivering chin and put her son on speakerphone. "He's on the Colorado border, but the woods there are humongous."

Honovi said, "I see a coyote den."

BearClaw looked drained with pale lips and a sheen of sweat on his forehead, but he was still the best tracker in the Southwest. "I need Finn and lots of water."

Layli said, "The pickup has parachute rope, gallons of water, and a bunch of other supplies, even an emergency kit. We'll take that."

"We? No! You'll slow me down."

Peyton yelled, "We're coming with you and that's that! I'll change and call Sheriff Dunn. He'll know who to mobilize."

"Sheriff Dunn?" Layli asked. "He hates spending resources on rescues."

"When it comes to stupid, unprepared tourists, but we're locals. Besides, he'll hate losing my donations more. Time to pay up."

Honovi said, "Call me when you have news, and if I have anything else, I'll let you know."

"Is he alive?"

"I don't know, Mom. In my vision, Dad wasn't moving, but I feel if you hurry… Just run. Go!"

Peyton climbed into the backseat of the pickup and clung to Finn, praying for her husband to be safe, assessing what could've gone wrong. Adler was skilled and seasoned. He knew the ins and outs of those woods. Why was he lying prone in the dirt?

Layli rode shotgun while BearClaw broke the speed limit. He plucked a cigarette from his pocket and lit it with a red pocket lighter. "Peyton, you all right?" He eyed her through the rearview mirror.

"Did you have a vision too?"

"Not a vision, just a warning in my heart. Got something for Finn to sniff?"

"Yes, a jacket Adler wears lots." Peyton sat on her hands. "Will you find him?"

"I always sensed I'd go first. Here I am, still taking up space." He coughed and sweated more than usual, turned up the air-conditioning and blew smoke out the window. "He alone up there?"

Peyton's worst fears preyed on her. "He has Gideon with him."

Layli watched as BearClaw lit another cigarette, not daring to lecture him on his chain smoking as she often did. "Then perhaps he's safer than we think."

Peyton couldn't get herself to contradict Layli out loud, but she feared the opposite. "Oh God, why didn't I fight him on his stupid trip? Nothing good has come out of it."

"Nah…" BearClaw scratched at the three scars on his face. "No one could ever talk that man out of what's in his heart."

Layli clasped the handle above the passenger window, bracing against the fast turns. "How're you gonna find him?"

"I know his favorite spots. Two of 'em have coyote dens nearby. Hopefully, enough tracks remain to lead me to the right one or Finn will." He flung the lit butt out the window. "I'll find him no matter what."

Peyton futilely called Gideon, pleading with God to keep them both safe. Adler must be gravely injured. If she hadn't been sure how much she still loved him, she knew now. "Honovi said Adler is lying motionless. How long can he do that?" She shivered. "I've pictured many things going wrong, but never this." If she could, she'd sacrifice some of her own years to save him and her marriage. She had only wished for freedom from angst, neglect, and blame. Not freedom from him.

"No point in thinking that," Layli said. "Gideon would've run down by now and called for help."

"Then why can't I reach him? I must've called him two dozen times, and wouldn't he have called me by now of his own volition?"

BearClaw said, "I'll find Adler for you, or die trying."

"I feel sick to my stomach," Peyton said. "We have flares in this truck, right?"

"Heck yeah," Layli said. "Scarborough's orders from long ago."

At the mention of Scarborough, Peyton tucked her face in her hands and called on her ancestors and all the saints for help.

After what felt like days, they reached a dirt lot where Adler was most likely to have parked his Jeep, but it was empty.

"Where the fuck is his truck?" BearClaw shouted, banging on the steering wheel.

Peyton heaved with anxiety. "But this is where he parks, right?"

BearClaw stepped out, took a deep breath, and raised his face to the heavens, appealing to something greater than himself. "The Great Spirit says to go up." He shuffled to the cargo bed and grabbed rope, a rifle, and a bottle of water, which he strapped to his shoulder. He let Finn out of the back and gave him Adler's jacket to sniff. "Run, boy. Find Adler!"

Peyton and Layli jumped out of the truck, awaiting instructions.

"You step where I step. I can't have either of you getting hurt, you hear?"

Peyton dialed emergency services while she still had reception, informing them of their whereabouts. She grabbed more supplies and ran after him, keeping up with his startlingly spry pace as his adrenaline kicked up. The higher they climbed, the more they shouted Adler's and Gideon's names, moving as if pulled by a divine force, leaping over rocks, pushing uphill across boulders.

After an hour, BearClaw stopped and raised his hand. "That's a camp up there. God, let it be his."

They hustled faster until they reached a camp someone with Adler's skills might've built. Not a simple tent, but a log cabin with a stone fireplace and a cooking station. Towels and familiar camouflage clothing were draped over branches. Adler's trademark bear cache was nearby—a raised platform for protecting food stores from animals. Peyton scoured through a duffle bag she recognized as his and found more of his clothes and one of his favorite knives. She shouted his name louder. Finn barked, peeking over a ledge, wagging his tail, and rising on his hind legs.

BearClaw got on all fours and slinked to the edge. "I found him. Send up a flare!" he shouted. "Mustang? Adler, can you hear me?"

Peyton aimed high and shot a flare. "What do you see?" She dove and belly crawled until half her torso hung over the ledge. Face down, motionless, Adler gave no sign of life. "Blake? Honey?" she called out, sobbing.

Then she saw what sat near him and shrieked. "Sweet Mother of God, there are coyotes beside him. I mean, seven or more!"

BearClaw laughed, surprising her. "They're guarding him. That lucky bastard. He would've shared meat with them. He loves to feed everyone."

Layli said, "If the coyotes haven't touched him, it's a good sign."

Peyton bargained with God, Adler's words reverberating in her mind. When she'd saved Gideon from being dragged to death by Bryce's horse, Adler looked her in the eye and swore on his life he wouldn't let Gideon hurt anyone or himself. She now feared God was excising his due.

BearClaw tied the rope to a tree and rappelled down the rocks, his eyes on the docile coyotes, who retreated a hair. "Still alive!" he yelled up. "He has a pulse!"

Peyton ran to a wide bald spot near the camp and sent up another flare. "A medevac helicopter can land here," she said, thanking God and her friends, grateful for the coyotes and Finn, who kept trying to lick her face now she bent over. Where's Gideon? She thought of Adler's missing Jeep, and her heart thundered. She searched for the satellite phone, suspecting it would still be there. When she found it on site, she wondered why her son hadn't used it. She paced, heat blazing through her, and phoned Gideon with the satellite phone. This time, she left him a different message. "Just go home, Gideon. Do nothing and speak to no one. Listen to me this one time. Go home and keep mum."

twenty-four

Peyton was sitting in a chair beside Adler's hospital bed with her face in her hands. She bulleted up at the sound of his voice calling her name. "Thank you, Mother of God. Blake, baby, you're conscious!" She grabbed his hand, kissed it repeatedly, and pressed closer, careful not to lean on him. "Are you in pain?"

"You smell good," he mumbled.

Relief washed over her. "I smell of chlorine and dirt."

"I love it." He tried to smile, but there was a tear at the corner of his mouth. "How long have I been out?" he asked, feeling his face.

"Hours since we found you, but you were already out." She wanted to hug him, but was afraid she'd hurt him. "What happened up there?"

He felt the bandage around his head and realized his other arm was broken. "My face feels numb."

"It's swollen. Can you even see out of your left eye?"

He tested the limits of his sore body and tried to rise. "Is Gideon all right?"

"I don't know. I haven't been able to reach him." She picked up her phone and double checked. There was still no reply. "What happened?" She could tell he wasn't ready to talk just yet. "Sheriff Dunn ordered a missing person APB on Gideon. There's no way you just fell, Blake."

"How did you know to come for me?"

"Honovi and BearClaw." She pressed his good hand to her cheek. "They saved your life."

A nurse came in, heavyset, pretty, with sable hair and a sweet smile. "I'm Maria. I let the doctor know you're awake. How're you feeling?"

Peyton stepped back, giving her space.

"Your vitals are remarkably fine. Painkillers wearing off already?"

A knock on the door interrupted them. Sheriff Dunn stepped in, holding his hat to his chest. "Finally found you, folks. I had the wrong hospital at first."

The nurse said, "The doctor will want to examine the patient soon. Can it wait?"

"Not really." His expression made Adler sit up, despite the pain. "I've real bad news, I'm afraid. You might want to sit down, ma'am."

Peyton squeezed her husband's hand. "Gideon?"

"He must've gotten flustered on his way to getting you help, sir. He flipped his truck, then suffered a head-on collision with a six-wheeler. The paramedics said he would've died on impact." He smoothed his white horseshoe mustache. "He wouldn't have suffered much, if it be any consolation."

Peyton felt numb, her body heavy and hot, her stomach churned. She was sure she'd throw up.

Adler asked, "Where?"

"Past Esquibel Canyon, northbound. Very sorry, folks. Can I get you anything? Do anything for you?"

Her son crashed north of the camp, despite the closest emergency services being south of it. Her good upbringing kicked in, though the rest of her was disoriented. "Thank you for promptly sending help to us. Without it, Adler might not have survived."

"Just doing our jobs, ma'am." He fumbled with his hat. "We're writing this one up as an accident. My condolences."

Peyton couldn't stop nodding, aware yet foggy.

Adler asked, "Sheriff Dunn, was anybody else hurt?"

"No, sir." He pressed his hat to his head and tipped it. "Will stay in touch on the particulars, and sorry to also report your Jeep is totaled."

Adler flicked his hand and looked away.

The doctor on call showed up scowling. "Your blood pressure is rising, Mr. Adler. We can't have that."

The sheriff took his cue and left. Peyton felt faint and collapsed in a chair.

"When can I leave?"

The doctor shone a flashlight into Adler's pupils. "Leave? Your MRI came back negative, but let's verify there's no internal bleeding. You were very lucky, Mr. Adler. The medics said you fell on a thicket of ferns that broke your fall. Do you remember what happened?"

He cuffed an ear, glassy-eyed.

"Is it true coyotes just watched the whole time? They frightened the medics. They couldn't stop talking about it."

The nurse said, "Not bizarre. The coyotes are shadowy figures, but revered. They can bring harm, but also healing. In the Story of Creation, the coyote—"

"—Maria!" the doctor said. "Now that Mr. Adler is awake, follow the usual protocols for trauma patients… in silence." He looked at Adler with a softened gaze. "We'll have you out of here before the weekend. You're resilient. I wish all my patients were so strong. Need anything else?"

"Water." Adler turned to his wife, shell-shocked, breathing hard. "And Father Gabriel."

Peyton waited until they were alone. "What happened, Blake?" she asked, closing the door. "You have injuries on both sides of your face. A fall alone doesn't cause that."

"Gideon is dead," he said, and sobbed, making his monitors light up. "My boy is dead."

Peyton's tears wouldn't come. Couldn't come. "He struck you and ran, didn't he?" She helped him sip water through a straw and handed him tissues. "He didn't call me… didn't call any of us."

"He must've panicked. How else would he have made such a terrible, fatal mistake?" He tried to get up, but his left leg was bandaged, uncooperative. "He would've called eventually. I know it."

She didn't believe him, but she didn't want to hurt him more. "I must call Bryce. We need her home."

Swaddled in black, Peyton was sitting on a teak bench in the upstairs gallery surrounded by some of her original works. She'd interred her son that morning.

Her sister, Lexi, found her. She was carrying cocktails and handed one to Peyton, then ran a hand through her short red hair and huffed. "I can't believe we outlived Gideon. I've often felt Harlow's curse looms over us. With this disaster, I feel it more."

Peyton didn't believe in curses, but she believed in unwise and unconscionable actions. "When he was an infant, he needed to be carried constantly. He'd wail the minute I'd put him down. As a toddler, I couldn't use the bathroom or stir a pot without him glued to me. In adulthood, he was no different, really." All his life, her son had needed her to feel his weight. In death, he was lighter and heavier all at once.

Lexi drained her cocktail and widened her blue eyes. "Mom will look after him. Don't worry."

"Dad will too." She hadn't eaten in days but had a bitter taste in her mouth. "Thank you for coming today. It's good having you."

Father Gabriel softly knocked and entered. "Adler said you'd be up here."

Lexi nodded and excused herself. "I'll see you at the repast."

Peyton said, "We really need you extra today, Father. Thank you for coming."

He made the sign of the cross and joined her on the bench. "I can't imagine your grief, my child."

Peyton fixed her eyes on the floor. "I feel terribly guilty, Father."

"Why would God's beloved child feel guilty?" The friar pulled his purple stole from an inner pocket and garlanded his neck with it. "Perhaps you can unburden in confession."

"God forgive me, I feel relief. I told no one else, but I buried my son and I feel a reprieve. Not just grief or loss, but freedom from the pending doom." She went to the window overlooking the rose garden, whose blooms were dull and withered. "What kind of mother feels release at her son's death?"

"Grief takes many forms. Perhaps it's not my place to say this, but I know you'll forgive me for it." The Franciscan monk smoothed his purple stole and gave her sorrowful eyes. "Along the way, Gideon scarred a part of you. He tried all of us, may he rest in peace… 'For the wages of sin is death, but the gift of God is eternal life in Christ Jesus our Lord.'" He joined her at the window. "You're sure Gideon's death wasn't suicide?"

"He'd have to have had a conscience to do that. I highly doubt my narcissistic son killed himself intentionally." She crossed herself. "I'm livid with him, and for so much, but I also love him. I longed for happy times with him, but they never came."

He kissed the wooden cross he wore around his neck. "Listen, Peyton, it's one thing not to lament the passing of someone who injured you repeatedly and was most likely going to continue his assault for many years to come, but it's another to continue to resent him. God forgives all, as should you."

She leaned her shoulder against the wall, eyeing the storm gathering on the horizon. "My son died thinking I'm a bad mother." She'd once struggled to forgive her mother by understanding her bipolar disorder. She couldn't comprehend how circumstances with Gideon had deteriorated to this degree. "Did Adler tell you what happened, Father? He told me nothing. He might have confessed to you, if only to get it off his chest."

"He didn't. Adler just wanted assurance God Almighty would receive Gideon in his embrace."

Peyton wound the silk khata around her neck. She'd been wearing it for days. "They say it comes in threes. This is funeral number two this year."

"No need for such morbid thoughts, and since when are you superstitious?"

For the first time in days, her tears threatened to prick through. "What if I caused it? A part of me wanted Gideon gone. A part of me wanted him neutralized so he couldn't hurt us any longer. What if God or the devil killed him at my behest?"

Father Gabriel placed his palms on her upper arms. "No! God doesn't work that way. Gideon drove his father's Jeep so fast he lost control. Neither you nor Adler are responsible for his disastrous actions." He blessed her and mumbled a prayer. "You must forgive Gideon and forgive yourself."

And forgive Adler, but can she? Peyton remembered that her father had been unable to grieve her mother and thrashed with an anger that deteriorated him bit by bit. "What if I never grieve my son?"

"You can't control how you feel, but you can control your actions. I've known you for decades." Father Gabriel pointed to her heart. "You're pure, in here. God sees all. He knows you paid your dues. Let go, my child. In his infinite wisdom, God took Gideon for a reason, and in my heart, I know it has to do with giving Bryce a real chance."

She hadn't considered that and worried Bryce might feel false guilt.

Father Gabriel reached for his rosary beads. "Gideon took a toll on you and Adler. You were always my loaves and fishes. I was there when you met and when you married. I've witnessed your evolution as a couple, and I have to say Gideon, may God have mercy on his soul, wasn't always a blessing, especially the older he got."

She knew in death, Gideon wouldn't be a blessing either. He'd vowed that he'd win in the end. He sure did when he mutilated her marriage, not just his soul.

"May the merciful Lord have pity on thee and forgive thee thy faults; in virtue of my priestly power, by the authority and command of God expressed in these words, whatsoever you shall bind on earth shall be bound in heaven, I absolve thee from thy sins. I absolve thee from thy thoughts, from thy words, from thy deeds, in the name of the Father, and of the Son, and of the Holy Ghost, and I restore thee to the Sacrament of the Holy Church, Amen."

"Amen." Peyton bent her head and confessed an excruciating truth. "I figured out what Gideon was supposed to teach me in life. But I have no idea what he should be teaching me in death."

"You will." He tapped her forearm. "I'm glad you're keeping today's funeral small and private. It's easier."

Peyton nodded, reflecting on how big and celebratory her father's funeral and Scarborough's had been. "I need to speak to Adler alone, before the repast."

"He was in the study. Perhaps he's still there."

Dressed in black pants and shirt, bruised and swollen, Adler was on the sofa flipping through an album and tracing baby pictures with the tips of his fingers. "We shouldn't have stopped printing photos," he said. "I know we were the only ones who still did, but I like real albums."

"I brought you special brownies." Peyton deposited a plate at his elbow. "They're lightly spiked, so they'll just take the edge off."

He ignored them and continued caressing Gideon's face in the photographs.

"I know you need to feel your pain. Just one is okay."

"I want my wits about me."

"You didn't shave." He'd kept the beard he'd grown in the woods. It reminded her of his distance and absences. She sat beside him and stroked his hand. "I need to know what happened. Please, tell me."

His chin shuddered and his nose turned red.

"You owe me the truth. He was my son too."

Adler closed the album. "Gideon hated that trip, but I never for a single moment thought he meant me harm." He jostled for a clearer look at his wife. "That morning, I confronted him again about why he thought he could get between us. His look stunned me. He slashed eyes at me, a look of disdain, malice, and triumph."

How many times had Gideon looked at her that way? When she'd tell Adler, he'd insist she exaggerated. She rubbed his hand, but was more impatient than she let on.

"He said… he said…"

"It's okay, you can tell me."

"He said, 'Oh, Dad, I succeeded in that long ago.'" Adler buried his head in the back of the sofa and sobbed. "I'm so ashamed."

"You have nothing to be ashamed of."

"Of course I do."

She'd never seen him so distraught before. "What did Gideon do then?"

"I said I might never get over how jubilant he was, causing misery and discord to those who loved him best." He caught his breath and looked at her. "I walked over to the ledge in despair. The alpha coyote locked eyes with me. That's when I knew. It was like she was speaking to me. I'd left her and her pack enough carcasses to earn her friendship." He sobbed, but soon steadied his breathing. "I turned around and there he was swinging a log at me."

Peyton finished for him. "That's when you fell, and he ran off."

"My guess is he thought he killed me. He panicked and ran away. He would've called for help if he thought I had survived the fall. But it was from such a height, he must've presumed me dead."

Peyton didn't believe Gideon would've tried to save his father. Not if it meant incriminating himself. Anger quaked in her chest. She felt compassion for Adler, but her rage was greater. "Gideon had dangerous impulses none of us could control or cure. Yet you kept going after him." Bhante

Tenzin's words played in her head. When he'd mentioned an evildoer, he'd meant Gideon.

Adler shook his head. "I have many regrets… so many."

Four words played in her head—too little, too late. "Gideon was bound to hurt us whenever we brought him into our midst. That always divided my thinking from yours."

He flung his good arm in the air and shouted, "What was the alternative? He was my son!"

Peyton didn't raise her voice, but spoke firmly. "You should've listened to me when I told you he was not you. He wasn't even like you, but you kept forcing him on us and pushing us away." She knew she pained him and stopped. "Sorry, I shouldn't have said that. You always loved and protected us, except when it came to him. I know it's because you never saw how dangerous he really was. But I don't know how to live with that."

Bryce peeked in from around the corner. "The food is on the table. Everyone is asking for you."

Her father gestured for her to sit with them. "I've been thinking about you in this big mess, honey. I hope you're not feeling responsible for anything."

She sat between them and fastened her knees together. "I feel weird… can't describe it."

Peyton gave her a sad smile. "It's okay not to tear your hair out, weep or wail."

She eyed her father. "How can I help you?"

"You can be happy."

Peyton wanted to tell him he'd contributed little to his daughter's happiness, but she knew how much he loved her.

He used a cane to stand up. "Will it be annoying if I drop in on you at Berkeley way before Thanksgiving?"

Now he wants to go to California. Now he's thinking of someone other than Gideon.

Bryce invited him to lean on her, though her mother knew she had her own ire to overcome. "I thought maybe you'd stay in Carmel for a while, Dad. If you do, I can see you both often."

"We'll see," he replied, which made Peyton and Bryce exchange a discouraged look.

Tansy came in holding a dishtowel. "You're needed on the phone, Ms. Chase."

"Who is it?" Adler asked.

Tansy stood with her legs far apart, fiddling with the dishtowel. "I didn't get a name."

From her body language, Peyton knew who it was. "I'll take it in here. Thank you, Tansy, and sorry we're too much today."

"Layli has an extra person helping. We're doing okay. Just sorry for your loss."

After Bryce led her father out, Peyton sat behind Sorensen's executive desk and picked up the receiver. "You never call the house."

"My favorite voice ever," Ashton said. "How're you coming along now the burial is over? Can you handle the repast?"

"That's the easy part." Peyton sat back, rocking. "I got your enormous flower arrangement and food basket. Too much, Ashton."

"Nothing is ever too much for you."

"I realize you're being your generous self, but splashy gestures like this hurt Adler." It was Ashton's way of etching his mark. "I don't want that."

"I was thinking of you, not of him, but okay," he replied. "I wish I could be with you."

"I also got your gift certificate to Glen Ivy Hot Springs."

"You need to de-stress."

"It's for seven days of treatment after treatment, Ashton."

"You need a lot of de-stressing." He chuckled when she did. "It's silly to ask you how you are, but I'm asking."

"The last time I saw my son was at 71Above. I spoke to him on the phone once after that. The last thing he said was how much he hated me and what a liar I am. He accused me of not loving him." She opened a drawer and picked up the watch and ring she'd given Gideon. The Sheriff's office had returned them to her. The watch was broken, and the ring was stained, but she weighed them in her palm and heart. The inscription on the watch said: "*Fear not the end, Sorensen. Fear only never getting started.*" It was as if she'd had a premonition. Reunited with his belongings, she mourned two men named Sorensen.

"You have nothing to feel guilty about, my darling. If Gideon gave you credit for anything, it was your honesty. He knew you loved him."

She wrapped one arm around her torso, recalling how she'd cradled him when he was little and kissed his fingers one by one. "Maybe, but he died knowing how disappointed I was in him. Not what I wanted at all." For the first time since learning of her son's death, Peyton broke down. She slipped to the floor, thinking how God had broken Gideon's arm after all. Only God had broken and mended much more. "My son is dead. Dear Lord, he's gone forever!"

Ashton listened to her cry. "You only ever told the truth with hope and kindness. But Gideon didn't want love. He wanted possessions, not people."

She took a deep breath, hoisted herself off the Persian rug, and eased back into the desk chair.

"Did you have any conversations about the future?"

She understood his real question. Gideon's death had changed everything, and it was to his advantage. "We hardly talk."

"Why on earth are you staying with someone who isn't even talking to you?"

Ashton had never had to tussle with serious challenges. He hadn't raised a family or lost a child. He'd never understand, and she was the most fatigued she'd been in memory. "Why do you even want me? I'm more broken than ever, and I may never mend."

"Then I'll reforge you with that much more care… Just come home to me."

For repast, the family gathered in the dining room, where Layli had lit beeswax candles.

In honor of her son, Peyton went around extinguishing them. "Gideon hated beeswax candles," she mumbled, wondering if she hadn't accommodated him enough. It might've been the magic brownies, but Peyton was grateful for the light energy in the room.

Kelcy started the conversation with a story about Gideon while heaping his plate with carne adovada and mashed potatoes. "One early morning, when he was about ten, I found him piling stones on my porch. I told him to clear them off, maybe do something useful with them."

Adler knew the story and was already smiling.

"Then I forgot about it until I opened my front door again to leave the casita and found the rascal had bricked me in."

Everyone at the table laughed.

Honovi helped himself to calabacitas and passed the basket of horno bread. "My favorite was when Bryce was brought home as a newborn. Gideon asked me when the hospital would be picking her up."

Ricky said, "Remember when he made wine by adding yeast to grape juice, only he added nutritional yeast instead?"

William laughed, shaking his head. "It was disgusting, but he insisted he was starting the trend for savory wine."

Royce said, "He poked me in the eye once to turn me into an authentic pirate."

"Gideon hardly ever cried," Peyton said. "When he came home from school one day sniffling, I was alarmed. I asked him why he was so upset. He said it wasn't fair he had a penis, but his sister had China."

Royce said, "Oh… He had China envy!"

She watched her loved ones laugh, eat, and enjoy themselves. It saddened her how much nicer it was with Gideon gone.

Layli spooned chicharrones and blue corn on BearClaw's plate. He drank more than ate. "One year, Gideon was maybe six," she said. "He gave me a list of 'Best Places to Hide Christmas Presents' for his mother, who was too good at keeping him from finding them."

Koda took a bottle of wine from the server and went about the table refilling glasses. "Hey, Father Gabriel, remember when Gideon was seven years old and was preparing for his First Communion with a young priest?"

"Father Thompson," the friar said. "He was fresh out of seminary, but he was no match for Gideon."

"Tell the rest, Father," Koda said, topping the friar's glass.

"Father Thompson asked if anyone knew who had named the animals. When no one replied, he declared, 'It was Adam, as is written in the Good Book.' Well, Gideon called him names, insulting him because everyone knew Carl Linnaeus named organisms. I had to look that one up myself. Father Thompson was mad and sent him to me. I asked Gideon to humor me and keep things literal with the young priest."

Ricky finished the story. "Gideon then said, 'I am keeping it literal. I called him literally a nitwit.'"

Partly in admiration and partly chagrin, Peyton shook her head. "Gideon was always clever."

"Too clever for his own good," Adler said. "Gideon would've loved being the center of attention like this."

"He liked you best, Margot," Peyton said. "I'm glad you're with us today."

"Auntie, I knew Gideon and I would be good friends when he made me a picture of himself with a naughty angel on his shoulder. I asked him if there shouldn't also be a good angel. He said he never listened to the good one, so he died of loneliness."

Koda said, "You have a good angel on yours, Margot. I've seen it."

She pointed a playful finger at him. "But I bet you never heard it."

"To Gideon," Lexi said, raising her glass, "who once told me he couldn't act his age because he'd never been that old before."

Peyton simpered. "I toast to you, who always guide and support us. We appreciate you more than you know. My son was never easy, but he sure wasn't dull."

BearClaw lit a cigarette, the only person allowed to smoke in the house. "You don't look so hot, old man."

"Just fatigued." Adler grabbed his cane and pressed himself up. "I'll have a lie down and leave you to enjoy dessert. I haven't been able to sleep much lately, but I feel I can now."

Peyton wasn't surprised her husband didn't speak of the nightmares he had every time he closed his eyes. "We're really grateful for all of you," she said, getting up to help him, but he told her he wanted time alone.

Coffee, cake, liquor, and pie were served, and Tansy brought Honovi his yerba maté.

"Mom, can you tell us what really happened?" Bryce asked once the staff had withdrawn.

Peyton scanned the loving faces at the table. "I trust you won't allow the truth to leak outside our circle." She sipped coffee. "As I'm sure you've all suspected, Adler didn't just trip and fall. He's heartbroken on many levels. He's still with us thanks to Honovi and BearClaw."

BearClaw guzzled a shot of bourbon. "Never seen such docile coyotes when a man lay vulnerable like that."

Honovi said, "The Great Spirit decided more needs to be learned."

Peyton questioned what Gideon's purpose in her life had been. If he'd been the little Buddha raising her, what had she learned? He'd taught her to seek no one's approval, that self-validation was enough. But was that all?

William ran a hand over Bryce's neck. "We're flying back to Berkeley tomorrow. Is that okay?"

"Life goes on, honey." Peyton looked around the table. "You made today as easy as it could be. Thank you for the stories, for focusing on what was positive, especially for Adler's sake. We're moved and touched. Funerals should be celebratory. You made this one just that."

"Will Dad be all right?"

BearClaw answered, "Your father, Bryce, has always known life is a journey walked in stretches of darkness, not just in light. He's Mustang, tough as nails. He'll heal up all right."

Life and death are one as the wind and air are one. Peyton was sure she'd always keep Gideon snug in her heart and grieve him forever.

Honovi reached for the apple pie. "Mom, Gideon might become a breeze that cools the burn instead of a wind that whips the fire."

"I hope so." She knew her son would be closer to her in death than he'd been in life.

Late that night, Peyton sat at her kitchen table alone, watching the lightning storm and listening to the thunder. Her mind scuttled from one intrusive thought to another, keeping her awake. The clock knelled midnight, yet she sat in the dark, sober, hypnotized by the show of lightning on the vast horizon until Bryce barged in on her.

"How're you?" Peyton asked. "You seem okay, but I'm making sure."

She sighed. "It feels unnaturally fine. My brother died, but all I can think of is Dad is safe, and now I can look forward to family get-togethers. Sorry, Mom. Am I disappointing you?"

Peyton splayed her arms for her daughter. "We're all conflicted in the same way."

"Not Dad, I don't think."

"Believe me, honey, he's conflicted worst of all, but he just wants to keep everything Gideon in a positive place."

"I saw the massive basket Ashton sent."

"Hard to miss."

Bryce placed her hands on her lower back. "Dad saw it."

"What are you trying to say?"

"What'll happen now?"

"When a couple loses a child, it's rough, but when the relationship is already strained, it's even worse."

Her tears trickled. "A divorce?"

"I love your father, but I don't know how to live with someone who's always angry with me, reproving, and resentful. In time, as his grief deepens, he'll blame me more. That's not the future I want. Then again, I don't want a divorce or a life without the other version of him."

"Soulmates stay together, don't they? It's what he always called you—his soulmate." The sky exploded with shards of lightning, making Bryce jump. "It's magnificent tonight, wow."

"Lightning is what I used to think of your dad. Electrifying. Impactful. Impressive."

Bryce leaned forward as if sharing a secret. "Lightning is what Gideon pretended to be."

"Wanted to be," her mother said. "But he was like lightning bugs to your father's lightning." She tucked her daughter's hair behind her ears. "*You're* true lightning. You just haven't had a reason to spark big yet, but you will."

"Thank you, but Dad doesn't think that, and don't tell me otherwise. I know what I experienced." She embraced her mother, lingering in her arms. "I hope you're not feeling guilty. Gideon was always on a destructive bend."

"Too many feelings congest my heart, but time is a friend." Peyton kissed her and stroked her forehead. "I'll have pancakes for you before you leave tomorrow. Your favorite."

"You're my favorite."

Peyton sent her flying kisses. "You redeem me." Alone again, she sat still, joyous memories of baby Gideon leapfrogging in her mind. The sky thundered, and a sound made her spin around. "Adler, why're you out of bed?"

"Same reason you are," he said dryly.

Peyton went to the fridge and filled a tall glass with water. "To heal, you need to sleep and it's late."

Lightning lit him up like a candelabra. "Do you prefer to sleep alone? Is that why you've been staying up?"

"Is that how you feel?" She handed him the glass of water.

He didn't take it. "Do you blame me?"

Goosebumps prickled her skin. "Twice I asked you to stay and leave Gideon to blow off steam. The first time you insisted on fetching him, he and I both could've been killed. The second time, he attempted to kill you, then killed himself." She pictured his corpse with its injuries and wounds. "I wanted him happy but unable to maim us. I didn't want him dead, leaving you broken, body and soul."

He raised his voice. "You pushed him away, kept isolating him! It fell on me to show him he was still in this family!"

Peyton knew he blamed her, that he was resentful and unforgiving, but she hadn't realized he thought she hadn't done her best. "So, we blame each other. Fine!"

Adler angled his body sideways, bracing against the doorframe. "I'll sleep in a guestroom. When I can drive, I'm going up to Chama."

"A separation?" she asked, disdain replacing love.

"I don't know."

She feared a divorce was more likely than ever. "After our first night together, those many years ago, you promised you'd give me what I wanted. You even assured me all I had to do was ask. Why did that stop?"

The rancor in his voice was thick and thorny. "Because what you wanted from me was bigger than your need of me."

"Not true," she said, crying. "I thought maybe you'd learned to take me at my word. But somewhere along the line, you reverted to your distrustful self. And hard as I try, I can't figure out why."

"And how did you contribute to that?"

She wasn't perfect, but she believed she'd poured her heart and soul into their marriage. "We should've never reached this place. I withheld nothing and loved you with every bit of me. In the end, it cost me almost everything."

"This is not the end," his voice lingered before fading away.

twenty-five

The couple who once shared lungs, breathed deepest together, now found each other stifling. Gideon's death had sent boulders crushing Peyton's chest. Where intimacy once thrived, avoidance and estrangement flourished. The slithering weeks left only venom. Peyton set a deadline for herself. When Adler no longer needed his cane, she'd demand they go to Carmel-by-the-sea.

On a frosty morning, she was missing beachy California, listening to the radio as she used to with her father. She was cooking oatmeal with cinnamon, nutmeg, and maple syrup and brewing cowboy coffee. She loved Adler with her marrow and feared leaving a twenty-year marriage, but she couldn't forget Royce's words: "Fear and desire make the world go round." Which did she want to fuel her future?

Koda entered the kitchen, sniffing. "What smells sweet and aromatic?" He placed a large rectangular package by her chair. "This came for you. Required a signature."

Peyton ladled oatmeal into two bowls, topped them with cream, and handed Koda one with a spoon, then opened the package. She found Harlow's *Retrouvailles* painting with a letter from a lawyer and a handwritten note signed by Mrs. Velasco and had to read both twice. She rested the painting on her lap. Her mother had painted it before she was born. It was in Harlow's less mature style, but it was moving. Peyton summoned memories of Harlow painting at the ranch and was grateful that her mother hadn't stopped speaking to her through her paintings and hoped she'd never stop.

"What's that?" Koda asked.

"According to the lawyer's letter, Mrs. Velasco passed recently, soon after Gideon. She bequeathed Mom's painting to me. It's strange. I only met her in person once, but I poured all my love and truth into that commission. I think she knew."

"You obviously left an impression." He finished his oatmeal and gave her a gummy smile. "Your mother's paintings aren't cheap."

"This painting is worth much more than its price. I'm blown away, humbled to no end. When I finally get to exhibit it, I'm going to frame Mrs. Velasco's note and hang it alongside it."

"Does the letter explain why she left it to you?"

Peyton read the note aloud. "'We spend a lifetime bridging past and future with days full of sorrow and duty. The wise learn that a bridge can be wide enough to house us, but long enough to keep us moving. Retrouvailles, Ms. Chase. Waste no more time—retrouvailles.'"

"Is that French?"

"Yes, it means finding yourself again or rediscovering a long-lost love. She knew my mother and had a grandson who was a version of Gideon. I suspect she wanted to make a point."

"Geez, that makes death number three this year." Koda took a bottle of mineral water from the fridge. "What's she trying to tell you?"

She propped the painting on the table. Ashton was the only person who ever sent her love letters. "I believe she's telling me the same thing a revered Buddhist monk said to me recently." She shot up, propelled by an epiphany. "I know how to complete my bridge!"

"Ah, the one in your painting."

Peyton had more than one bridge to finish, but kept that to herself.

"You don't feel at fault regarding Gideon, do you? You shouldn't."

She disappeared into her mother's painting. It depicted a woman bathed in morning sunlight at a table with a stack of old love letters, intending to read them all over again. "I was his mother. I loved him with every atom, but I couldn't save him."

"My people say children aren't ours. They're lent to us by the Great Spirit. What's that word again, retrouvailles? In the Christian tradition, Gideon is now reunited with the creator."

"You sound like Father Gabriel."

"When are you returning to California? I can join you and drop in on Margot."

"Good. I'd rather not travel alone. But tell me, are you seeing each other more often now?"

"Seems like it, the older we get. We should've always been together. How stupid that we weren't."

"It takes two." She brought the painting to the study, wondering if Adler had given up on her. Out the glass doors, the expanse of mountains was dyed purple and honeycomb, bearded with aspens that glittered like gold coins.

Ashton phoned, unspooling her from her trance. "I have a proposal for you. Just hear me out."

Peyton was sitting cross-legged on the leather sofa, her heart racing.

"It's been two months, Peyton. Things have only gotten worse, and you'd rather be here in California, closer to Bryce."

"Are you asking me to come to you?"

"I'm still in Dubai, but I'll be in L.A. on Friday. I set it up so you can access the alarms and the front gate in Malibu. Tell me you'll be home before me. I instructed the staff to give you unbridled control."

She was nowhere near ready, but she needed a reprieve. "I don't know if I can handle it."

"*The Last Start* awaits you, and I'm sure you can handle feeling better for a change. I can arrange for a private plane to pick you up in Santa Fe. Take time off, make up for lost time."

Peyton didn't want to be lonely anymore. "If I do that, Ashton, I'll be changing everything."

"It's what you need. Come home to me in Malibu. Then we'll head to Carmel, so you can get back to work on your painting. After that, we'll sail to Hawaii. How is that a bad plan?"

Bryce, William, and Margot were in California. So was her art world. Shouldn't she be there as well?

Peyton went to her airy laundry room, where she kept her luggage, but she couldn't get herself to pack a bag. Abiquiú was home, not Malibu, but it was time to insist that they go to Carmel for the rest of the year. On her way out, she noticed the empty space on the shelf, where Adler always stored his luggage. Her thoughts rumbled as she ran up the stairs to the bedroom.

His bags were packed and piled by the door. He stood there like he'd never set foot in their room again. He needed a haircut, and his beard was long and untidy, but it didn't compensate for his sunken cheeks. Since the fall, he'd hemorrhaged weight, but he no longer needed his cane.

"Are you going to Chama?"

"Aren't you going to California?" He hid none of his anger when he said, "It's damn ironic. You told me to come back to us after my stint in the woods. To really come back." He waited until she nodded. "But what did you do? You went to California and never came back yourself!"

There was some truth in his words. Her feelings for Ashton had strengthened, but she hadn't defaulted on their marriage. "You used to be interested in solutions. I don't know when you grew more interested in blame, especially when you can tag it to me. I don't want to be angry or sad forever. And I know in my heart, you'll punish me always, like you are now. It's not what I want. I haven't packed my bags, but you have."

Adler screamed, balling his fist. "He took my son and you let him! I'll never forgive you, Peyton. Not ever!" He banged the wall. "He took you, too, that greedy son-of-a-bitch!"

"Did Ashton take me from you, or are you throwing me away? I begged you to stay, to give me hope. You didn't. Wouldn't! And you're doing it again now!" She'd believed they'd last a lifetime, but even lifetimes expire. "You know… I can claim Gideon stole you from me, and you let him. And for the record, I'm standing in our home with *you*, not with anyone else."

The look he gave her was disdainful. "You decided before all this. I took a deep look at the study you sent me. Spent a long time deciphering the photos up in those woods. *First Sons and Last Daughters* is your new self-portrait. You left me and Gideon a while back."

It was unfair. She'd painted Gideon as one of her pillars and Adler as her mountain—the tallest summit in her most prominent creation. Why did he refuse to stay with her, to release the children and embrace their marriage? "You left me first when you knew I needed you more than ever, yet you used it against me. To *punish* me! Maybe you thought you were reminding me of your place, but what you did was strip me of mine. Did you think it wouldn't break our bond?"

"All I ever did was love you and fight to keep this family together!" He looked older. His shoulders slumped, his eyes saying he'd lost everything. "I'll return to the place where I was before you, and you to where you were before me. The circle is now broken."

Bhante Tenzin's voice resonated in her heart. He'd told her what she did with her circle was up to her. Peyton wasn't sure if her circle was broken now or mended.

Peyton waited for Ashton at the house in Malibu where they'd spent their first and last nights together. She'd asked him to give the staff time off. Why had she rejected Ashton's terms those many years ago? She'd simply obeyed her authentic self. What would that same authentic self do today? She hadn't been willing to accept less than she deserved then, and she wouldn't now.

She fiddled with her wedding ring but couldn't remove it. The house was filled with her favorite tropical flowers, a fridge replete with nutritious foods, and in the bedroom, she found the same black-and-white photograph Ashton had taken of her the day they sailed on Lake Tahoe. He'd had it enlarged and framed, hung beside a photo of them taken long ago.

Grief shadowed her and would continue to for a long time.

Always.

But Kelcy had been right when he said: "It either is, or it isn't." Wasting time was for fools. She had reminisced over *The Last Start* painting through photographs but hadn't reunited with it till now. Harlow had begun it, but Peyton had finished it two decades later. *The Last Start* had saved her many times before and it rescued her again. The painting had hastened her mother's death. Now it hastened Peyton's rediscovery—her retrouvailles.

The Last Start depicted a dead Hopi woman about to begin her journey in the afterlife. The longer she stared at it, the more she thought of her mother's and son's untimely deaths. They had both been prone to dark behaviors. Both had hurt her yet made her brave and decisive. Her sadness didn't leave her, but it receded a little, unfurling the way for a rejuvenating start. To process the massive, irrevocable step she was about to take, she phoned Royce.

"Are you all unpacked?"

"I didn't bring much, but I ate an avocado and pomegranate salad on the terrace and watched beachcombers and surfers. Ashton has updated everything, yet it feels so familiar."

"If you're there for the holidays, I'm coming. Make room."

Peyton chuckled. "I have no idea how to handle the holidays, but I'd love to have you. The kids will want to see their father. My guess is he'll insist on remaining in Chama, so they'll have to go to him… unless he returns to the ranch. I came to be with Ashton, but I'm not sure it's the right thing to do. I'm so confused."

"If Adler cares so much, why is he in Chama? You lost a son as well. And I wouldn't be surprised if he camps there through the entire holiday season. Besides, you're where you belong. Don't question it. It's okay if you don't spend the holidays with everyone this year."

"Just because I'm moving forward with Ashton doesn't mean I don't care about Adler. I love him, you know. I just can't be happy with him anymore."

"Did he bring up a divorce at all?"

"Are you kidding? He's a staunch Catholic, doesn't even call this a separation. He says it's resetting, but I know better. Why can't things be opportune?"

"Because life is short. Believe me, it hurls the older we get. You're with the right man, in the right place and time. Go with him to Hawaii and you'll be in paradise, especially if you take me with you."

She stepped onto the terrace, drawn by the moon reflecting on the ocean, and filled her lungs with the scent of gardenias. "When my father died, I felt him around me, as if he hadn't left. He was just out, all around." She found it hard to articulate what intensified her grief. "I don't feel Gideon. I would even speak aloud to Dad, pretending he could still hear me, but I don't believe Gideon can. Why not?"

"I don't know if souls linger, but maybe those who don't listen in life don't listen in the afterlife, either. Accept and let go."

Hadn't she already learned that she could only find a foothold by surrendering? "I spent so many years doing and managing and trying. Maybe it's because I'm devastated and getting older, but I want to just be. No more doing, for a while at least."

"Doing is easier, but being is what growth and healing require. Take it from this old woman. Sadness has a cure, and it's rated R."

Peyton asked, "Rest?"

"What are you a hundred? Rum and red-hot sex!"

"Thank you, I needed that," she said, giggling.

Peyton had awakened to the sound of seagulls. Now she was waiting for Ashton in the foyer in jeans and a white T-shirt. Surf rolled, the redolence of hot sand and wild tea roses infused the dining room, and the smell of paella drifted in from the kitchen—saffron, white wine, and paprika. One of Ashton's favorite dishes. She was in the home of a man she'd never quite removed from her heart, surrounded by her own artwork and her mother's. Her circle was also an ouroboros—a serpent with its tail in its mouth, continually devouring itself and being reborn from itself.

One way or another, she'd complete her circle, if only with paint.

Ashton drove up in a Porsche 918 Spyder and hustled up the glossy granite steps. "You make me feel young and invincible." He picked her up and kissed her as though he hadn't seen her in years.

She ran fingers through his dark hair. "It's damp."

"I took a shower at the airport club. Wanted to be spick and span for you." He pulled her upstairs to the bedroom.

Peyton had a gift for him, and he recognized it the moment he stepped into the bedroom that faced the pristine white sand beach.

"You brought the two portraits you made of me?" She'd once promised she'd never sell them. "You really came back, my darling."

"About that… I came here with good intentions, but I'm not ready."

"Not ready, how?"

She sandwiched his hand in hers. "You're miles ahead of me. Adler and I are separated, and it looks like we're headed toward a divorce, but I still need to deal with so much. I won't be the best version of myself with you until I can mend. Do you understand?"

"I'm happy with this version." He pressed her hand, frowning. "Wouldn't you mend best with me?"

"It doesn't work like that. If we're meant to be, we'll be. I'm not saying I don't want to see you, but I'm not moving in with you, and we're not getting involved until I know where my marriage is going. I need more time."

He took a step back. "You want him back, don't you?"

Adler had brought out her purest self. He was the father of her children and the guardian of her most precious memories. "We're probably over, but I haven't truly accepted that yet, and I'm still grieving so much."

"Did you bring me these two portraits because you're free to be with me or because you're freeing yourself of me?"

She didn't know. "For obvious reasons, I never hung them anywhere. They deserve to see the light."

"How much time do you need?"

"I don't know."

"Okay, but can we still see each other as companions at least?"

Ashton could dab her wounds if she'd let him. But the stitching and cauterizing were hers alone. "One day at a time."

As happy as Peyton was to be in Carmel, she didn't go out, except to swim and walk the fox and retriever on the beach. She had a commission to complete, into which she poured her grief and relief. Now that Gideon was gone, she agonized over completing her study. But she dared herself and changed the design, repainting Gideon as a translucent figure. All his life, her grip on him had been tenuous. Adler had been right. This was her new self-portrait, and it included the son who was lost to her.

Not because he'd died. Because she had been dead to him.

Over and over, she repeated her mantra, Leonardo's words: "'While I thought that I was learning how to live, I have been learning how to die.'"

It would take a year to complete the massive painting, but the study would be ready soon. Before she could finish it, Peyton did what she hadn't since *The Last Start*. She pricked her pinky finger, squeezed blood into a dab of paint, and marked *First Sons and Last Daughters*—another circle she saw to completion.

At sunset, she was facing Point Lobos State Natural Reserve, painting Monterey cypress trees against a blazing sky when the doorbell rang. It was a package from Adler who hadn't sent her anything in years. The box was addressed in small, tight cursive, but the feelings it stirred were enormous. A pair of Toggi equestrian gloves surprised her. When they'd first met, she'd dropped her gloves, and he'd returned them, forming a lasting bond that spanned decades. He didn't write letters, wasn't coy with playful gifts or romantic surprises. His handwritten note shook her.

Peyton,

You're not just my wife, but the one person I see without needing to look.

I'm not the man you married, just some washed-up version, but I want to be that man again. It's been a while since I've given you new reasons to feel me right, and the best new reasons are the old ones. I don't know that I can forgive myself—never mind you—but I don't just blame you. I also blame myself, and I'm livid and hurting, but I still love you and would've never left our home if I hadn't thought you'd left it first. You may have broken me, but first you'd made me whole and deeply happy. For that alone, I should be able to forgive you. But I need to gather my fragments. I've been shattered into a million pieces—some of which you and Gideon took with you.

Yours, now and always...
Blake

Peyton flopped on a kitchen chair and wailed, unsure what the true message was. She knew Adler wouldn't make it easy, but she didn't figure he'd reach out in this way. Having him angry was easier. She'd love parts of him always. At minimum, she'd love their happy memories. She re-read his letter. Questions she'd been pondering for weeks resurfaced. Could they still make it? Could they truly forgive each other? Did they still have enough reasons to fight for each other?

Harlow's *Retrouvailles* painting hung on the opposite wall. Peyton was like the figure in the portrait, re-reading love letters, but hers weren't on paper.

She paced with compressed lungs. What was she supposed to learn from Gideon in death?

She'd already learned that control is an illusion, and that each moment is a gift. She'd also learned that death never erases love. But one last lesson remained. She wrapped her arms around her body and rocked until she heard the answer in her heart.

Grief and joy can coexist.

If grief is like roots bogged in dank, dense earth, joy is the treetops swaying in the wind. And she had become a tall tree.

Peyton was expecting her children for their first weekend at Carmel-by-the-sea since Gideon's funeral. It would be an adjustment for everyone. She was in the kitchen marinating fish for the grill and preparing pico de gallo.

When Bryce and William pulled into the driveway, the pups danced to the front door. Peyton drank a glass of water, slowing her breathing, concealing the extent of her ongoing agony.

Bryce and William brought a box of goodies from Fournée Bakery.

"You need to put some weight back on, Mom, so I brought you Paris-brest."

"I made key lime pie for you, William."

"Let me guess," he said, "and grilled fish tacos for Bryce."

"Oh yeah, and chicken potpie for Honovi and Ricky. But where are my boys? I thought they'd beat you here." She heard car doors slam shut and hustled to meet her sons.

Ricky scurried with tears in his eyes. "Dad should be here. It feels wrong."

Peyton pulled him into her embrace and kissed his face.

Honovi, carrying a bouquet of brushes, hugged her tight. "I've been using Kolinsky sable brushes. I don't know why I waited so long to try them. Love them so much, I brought you some."

"I can't wait to paint side-by-side with my priceless."

Bryce hugged her brothers, a cocktail of sadness and relief. "Dad will always endure in our lives. We love him very much."

"We'll always be family," William said. "Adler too."

Peyton tried to uplift the mood. "Come see the painting I created of all of you, my darlings."

Honovi walked into Peyton's studio first and studied her surrealism meet realism canvas. "Blood and paint," he said with a knowing grin. "That's us."

She took the measure of a son she loved with her breath. "Dearheart, in some fantastic twist of fate, you always had my DNA."

"That's why you're my mom."

Ricky said, "I think I'm thinner than this, Mom."

"No, you're not," William said, shoving him.

Peyton took a step back, watching her family engrossed in a discussion of the work. They were classic, like a vintage fair, as bright as the color wheel. She absorbed the first sons and last daughters of her life. They were her true wealth—her unbreakable and everlasting circle. Yet, the absence of Adler and Gideon left an undeniable fragility, like a rope so frayed, its fibers were wearing off. She hadn't escaped pain or sadness, but her heart was brimming with love and gratitude.

Bryce pointed to her mother's study. "Did you finish your bridge?"

Peyton thought that her daughter would one day extend that bridge and perhaps a granddaughter after that. "It'll never be really finished. And that's the only bridge worth building."

The doorbell rang. Everyone Peyton was expecting was there, but she went to the door. When she opened it, she burst into tears. "Blake?"

He was clean-shaven with a fresh haircut, holding a big bag. "My mountain, your coast," he said. "But in Carmel, mountains meet coasts, don't they?"

They had much to work out, and she was sure he hadn't forgiven her yet. "They do… and not just here."

A Note from the Author

Dear reader,

Thank you for joining me on this literary journey. I hope you enjoyed the adventure and found the story captivating. Your feedback is essential to me as an author, and I'd be incredibly grateful if you could take a moment to leave a meaningful review on Amazon. Your review will not only help other readers discover this book, but it'll also inspire me to continue crafting more enthralling stories for you. Thank you for your support!

The Three Layers of a Moment

THE PIONEER RANCH SAGA

Book Three

A Sample

Chapter One
Abiquiú, New Mexico

Under the thirty-foot ceiling of the great room, Bryce gazed at Kelcy with tenderness and concern, feeling the weight of his illness. She was holding Kelcy's frail, leathery hand as he lay on the sofa, washed in golden light that streamed through a wall of glass. "I brought you whiskey and carrot cake."

He attempted to chuckle but managed only a wheeze. "Doll, you're always spoiling this old Texan. A man should go out satisfied, and I'm quite pleased with you and William."

She concealed deep distress behind a perennial smile and stroked his clammy forehead. He was slipping away, but she clung to his hand. "I called everyone like you asked."

He'd marked a century, but like always, Kelcy didn't dwell on the gloaming of his life, only on its glitter. "The bells toll for me, but I still have something to say. Tell me again, what have I taught you all your life?"

She was a veterinarian and the mother of two, but she wanted to placate the man who'd buttressed her childhood. "Get up, look up, show up, and never give up."

"I taught you that when you were a showjumper, but I meant it as a lesson in life. Since William is my grandson, it may be selfish of me to ask, but you need to do that with him more than ever."

She fastened her gaze to a point in the distance as if she were sharing a secret with the universe. "I'm afraid for us."

He nodded. "I knew I wouldn't live forever, but I aimed to leave what I could behind. I'm not speaking of my estate, but of love, of a family that builds great things together."

"I love William with everything I am."

His eyes watered. "I'll take a sip of that whiskey now, hon."

Bryce patted his eyes dry, helped him raise his head, and brought the whiskey glass to his lips.

"And William loves you in that same way, but something is wrong. I've seen it for a while. You try to hide it, but I didn't make it to a hundred by being blind and deaf."

"We're not doing so hot, I won't lie to you, but we made it this far."

It was an effort for him to raise his hand and touch her flaming red locks. "You look the angel you are."

"In this light, even fallen angels glow."

"Which is why I look so beautiful right now, I'm sure."

She snickered and kissed his barbed cheek. "One of thousands of lessons you taught me is that life must be deep, if not long. You leave ripples in your wake. Few people can say that—and we live in the desert."

"You and William are one, as the river and sea are one."

She smiled through drizzling tears. "I do what I can."

"It may be unfair to put it on you, but you're the river without which the sea runs dry. I'll go easier if you tell me you know that you and William are gifts to each other." He licked his lips, growing more pale. "William always came to you, even when you were little, Bryce. You'll have to wait him out. Can you do that, doll?"

She didn't know what she could and couldn't do anymore. Life had gotten frayed, and with it, her tolerance. "I don't mind scaling mountains, but usually I can see the summit. Now I'm in a fog."

"Listen here… People die twice—first to themselves, then to the world. Seems to me the sooner a person dies to themselves, the later they die to the world. You're thirty-eight years old, darlin'. It's time you found out that true strength is in surrender. Your mama can tell you a lot about that." He asked for another sip of whiskey, and she helped. "What if, for once," he asked, "you didn't organize or prepare anything, and just let life fall where it may, hmm? What's the worst that could happen?"

"I'm yet to find out." She shrugged, petrified of letting go. A face from deep within her memory forced its way to the forefront. It had been two decades since her brother died, but Gideon remained a solid presence, an opaque, weighty burden—akin to sin—a curse she couldn't shake.

"You're gonna find out and more. I have a ton of faith in you." Kelcy gestured to his grandson's portrait hanging on the wall near the substantial Kiva fireplace, one of several Bryce's mother, Peyton, had painted of him. "He needs you more than ever. He wrestles with himself… with his values, even. Give him time."

Kelcy gasped, which made Bryce wish her mother would arrive.

"Remember these words when he makes you angry enough to want to deck him one."

She dug her nails into her palm; her habit when petrified. "There hasn't been a moment in my life when I didn't love William."

"You're too smart, but it's not love that keeps a marriage going."

She knew exactly what did. "I'm very much committed to William. Don't you worry." She feared Kelcy was alluding to William's commitment, not hers.

He gave her wizened blue eyes. "Marriage lasts only when you change alongside it."

She heard her mother running toward them with the children. "In the great room, Mom!" she shouted.

Her children rushed in ahead of their grandmother and skidded to a stop at their great-grandfather's side.

"Are you really dying, Great Papa?" Kelcy Charles William Loving the Fourth was ten years old.

"Yes, and there's nothing to be afraid of, big guy. My number's up, that's all." Little Kelcy was in William's spitting image. Same straight brown hair, big chocolate eyes, and a smile that melted stone. "You have your father's courage and your mother's stamina. You'll go far in this life."

"How about me?" asked a seven-year-old girl with chestnut waves and intelligent green eyes. "Do I go far, Great Papa?"

"To the moon and back if you choose to, Sedona. You have your father's passion and your mother's swiftness, not to mention your great papa's wit. There's nothing you can't do."

"And she has her grandmother's grit," Peyton said, kneeling beside Kelcy, on a Native rug with diamonds, crosses, and bands patterns. She was old enough to groan when she bent down, but still vibrant and fashionable, her blonde hair cut in a trendy style.

Bryce eyed her mother proudly. Long gone were the days when Peyton begged a departing loved one to stay. She was in her winter years now, and modeled what she taught. She'd told her daughter that the best gift to give the departing was the knowledge she stood strong on her own.

She'd known Kelcy for over forty years. "A part of me will die with you, Kelcy," Peyton said, "and a part of you will remain alive within me. Together, we're the circle of life." She unholstered a fat cigar and placed it in his hand. "In case the line at the Pearly Gates is long and you need to keep busy, dear old friend."

He gave her his puckish smile. "Little lady, you made room for me for decades now. I'm not afraid. What's that Leonardo quote of yours?"

In the words of Da Vinci, Peyton said, "'While I thought that I was learning how to live, I have been learning how to die.'"

"I love you all very much," Kelcy said. "Now where in God's name is

William? He's missing out on all my last-minute manipulations."

For a moment, laughter replaced tears, and hope overtook desolation.

"Here, Grandpa." Fit as a colt, William penetrated the vast space with long, confident strides.

Peyton moved to a chair near the sofa on which Kelcy stretched, making room for him.

William pressed his cheek to his grandfather's chest, as he used to when he was knee-high.

"If you're checking my ticker," Kelcy cracked, "I'm still alive."

At forty-five, William was even more handsome than he'd been at twenty. He swept a constantly errant lock of hair from his chocolate eyes. "You'll be out in the open with all there is, more alive than ever." He'd spent hours discussing life after Kelcy with his grandfather, the man he loved and admired most.

Now he lay dying, Kelcy touched his grandson's square jaw. "What a pile of crap."

"It's what you said, Grandpa!"

"Well, I take it back."

Peyton laughed and clapped. "Ten out of ten for Kelcy Loving, better known as loving Kelcy."

"Kids, there's carrot cake in the kitchen," Kelcy said. "Go get some with Grandma."

Peyton lifted off her seat and kissed him. "We wouldn't be able to mosey on down the road had it not been for our own Teddy Roosevelt." Her tears were streaming, and she kissed him again. "You make us proud, grateful, and incredibly loved."

"You changed my life and you sure as heck changed William's. Now, you'll be the one to point out who's being stupid and who's being too smart. Take it from this Teddy, whisper, but carry a big stick. William needs it."

She laughed, squeezing William's shoulder. "Sleep sweet, old friend."

"You go on now, little lady."

Peyton told the kids to hug their great-papa one last time, then ushered them out.

"You two try to hide it," Kelcy said, "but you've been different this last stretch. I can't leave this world with you being stupid and too smart all at once. And I know I'm being indulgent, but promise me you'll continue to put each other first. Not little Kelcy and Sedona. Not the ranch. But each other."

William rubbed his wife's back and pulled his straight brows together. "We will, Grandpa."

Kelcy pointed to his glass of whiskey. "You can bury me in a barrel of that stuff or cremate me, but don't let them stick me in the columbarium down in Texas. Keep me close to you. Spread my ashes on this ranch."

"Whatever you want, Grandpa."

"And Bryce, I left my Cobra Mustang sports car to you because you need to step on it a bit more. Risk has an upside, hon."

Has she been risk averse? She didn't believe so, but she found it difficult to recall the last time she'd rolled the dice. "We'll cherish your every word. Go with love, dear Kelcy."

He'd been given permission to vacate his throne; his smile faded. He shut his eyes as his breath grew shallow. A last whisper of air escaped his lips, fading into silence. His jaw slackened and surrendered.

Bryce and William embraced each other and sobbed. William mopped his tears on the heels of his palms. "Things will never be the same," he said.

She stood up, more than one kind of grief clashing in her chest. "Things haven't been the same, period."

Unlock Perks and Giveaways

Elevate your experience with Samar Reine's newsletter—your VIP pass to insider info, discounts, and giveaways. Join to learn about limited-time offers your wallet will love. Sign up at https://samarreine.com/

Acknowledgments

No one accomplishes a feat like publishing a book alone. I've been incredibly fortunate to have had the support of a remarkable team of professionals whose expertise and insights have made all the difference.

In alphabetical order, I would like to extend my sincerest thanks to Danielle Acee for her exceptional work in proofreading and formatting.

Tim Barber, your book design skills have given my words a visually captivating presence.

Joie Davidow, your editorial prowess and keen eye are nothing short of superb.

Yash Sharma, your social media graphics and book trailer designs connect my literary works to the digital world with thoughtful beauty.

Hayley Webster, your gifted editing and deep understanding have brought my manuscripts to new heights. It's rare to have such depth of intellect, clarity of vision, and a soulful touch. You're the ultimate gift!

We may be spread across the globe, but your collective efforts have propelled me to a place of extraordinary accomplishment. I am immensely grateful for your invaluable contributions to this project. Your dedication, talents, and astute feedback have transformed my manuscript into a true work of art.

Thank you for sharing your expertise and for being an integral part of this incredible journey. I am truly honored to have collaborated with such an exceptional team of professionals.

9 798989 884110 62